THE TIME OF TERROR

THE TIME OF TERROR

a novel

McBooks Press, Inc.
www.mcbooks.com
Ithaca, New York

Published by McBooks Press 2010
First published in Great Britain by Headline Publishing Group, a Hachette
UK company, 2008
Copyright © 2008 by Seth Hunter
This McBooks Press edition of the work has been revised from the original
U.K. edition by the author's request.

Cover image by Peter Zaharov.
Cover design by Stephen Mulcahey.
Interior design by Panda Musgrove.

Visit the McBooks Press website at www.mcbooks.com.

Printed in the United States of America
9 8 7 6 5 4 3 2 1

If there must be trouble, let it be in my day,
that my child may have peace.

—Thomas Paine

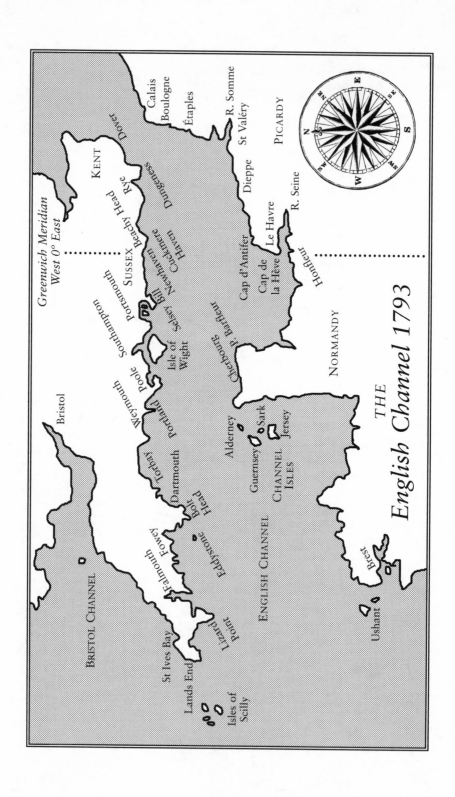

THE *English Channel 1793*

Greenwich Meridian
West 0° East

KENT

Dover

Calais
Boulogne
Étaples
R. Somme
St Valéry

PICARDY

SUSSEX
Rye
Beachy Head
Dungeness

Dieppe

R. Seine

Cap d'Antifer
Le Havre
Cap de
la Hève

Honfleur

NORMANDY

Southampton
Portsmouth
Newhaven
Selsey Bill
Cuckmere
Haven

Isle of
Wight

Cherbourg
P. Barfleur

Weymouth
Poole
Portland

Dartmouth
Torbay

Bolt
Head

Alderney

Guernsey
Sark
Jersey

CHANNEL
ISLES

Bristol

BRISTOL CHANNEL

Falmouth
Fowey

St Ives Bay
Lizard
Point
Lands End

Eddystone

Isles of
Scilly

ENGLISH CHANNEL

Brest

Ushant

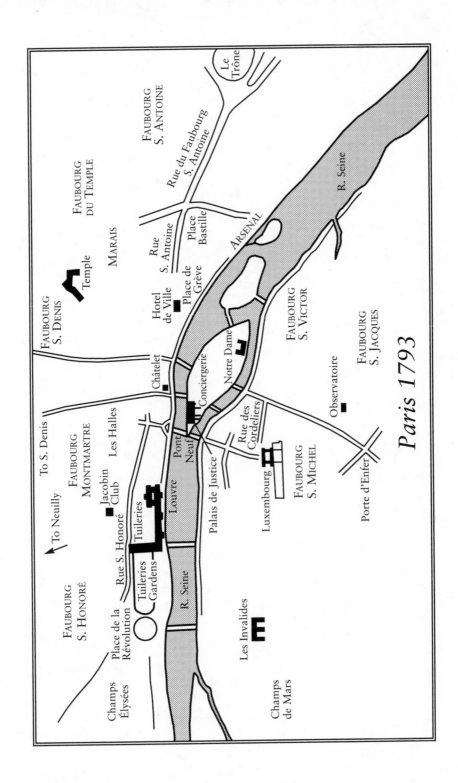

Paris 1793

Le Trône

FAUBOURG S. ANTOINE

Rue du Faubourg S. Antoine

FAUBOURG DU TEMPLE

ARSENAL

R. Seine

Place Bastille

Rue S. Antoine

MARAIS

Temple

Place de Grève

FAUBOURG S. DENIS

Hotel de Ville

FAUBOURG S. VICTOR

FAUBOURG S. JACQUES

FAUBOURG S. DENIS

Châtelet

Conciergerie

Notre Dame

Observatoire

To S. Denis

Les Halles

FAUBOURG MONTMARTRE

Pont Neuf

Rue des Cordeliers

To Neuilly

Jacobin Club

Palais de Justice

Luxembourg

FAUBOURG S. MICHEL

Porte d'Enfer

FAUBOURG S. HONORÉ

Rue S. Honoré

Tuileries

Louvre

R. Seine

Place de la Révolution

Tuileries Gardens

Les Invalides

Champs Élysées

R. Seine

Champs de Mars

I—GERMINAL

the Time of the Seed

PROLOGUE

a Death in Paris, January 1793

IT WAS A TIME WHEN YOU could not leave home and know that you would return alive and in one piece. You might die in an act of random violence, butchered by the fanatics on the streets, or by the dubious legal process favoured by the authorities which was slower but every bit as bloody. It was pointless to stay in because they knew where you lived and if they didn't the neighbours would tell them. Your best friend could be an informer, your landlord a patriot who would report you for lack of revolutionary zeal, especially if you were behind with the rent. The city was in a state of siege, the prisons full, the shops empty. It was a daily struggle to obtain enough food and fuel to stay alive. Medicines cost a fortune on the black market and were probably fake. You had better not be ill or pregnant or old.

Or a king.

She watched from her window as his carriage went by taking him to his trial at the Palais de Justice. A hired carriage and a shabby one at that with a clapped-out old nag and the drummers walking ahead beating the step. The streets were otherwise quite empty—people had been told not to stand and stare—and most of the windows were shuttered.

They found him guilty of course; there was never any question of that. And then they killed him. She did not go to watch though many did; they said the crowd was unusually solemn and that he died with quiet dignity.

She snorted at that. You wouldn't catch me dying with quiet dignity, she said. I'd be screaming and shouting all the way. Make it hard for the bastards. Let them know what they're doing to you, the swine.

The horror of it.

She imagined what it must be like to mount those steps with your hands tied and your neck bared and your legs turning to jelly and that Thing waiting for you at the top. The *guillotine*. Or the Humane and Scientific Execution Machine as the Revolutionists called it, without apparent irony.

That night, as she sat reading she saw eyes staring at her through the window, hands pressed on the glass, wet with blood. It might have been her imagination—she had terrible dreams lately—but it could well have been real with what was happening in the streets.

"I wish I had kept the cat with me," she wrote. "I want to see something alive; death in so many frightful shapes has taken hold of my fancy . . . For the first time in my life I cannot put out the candle."

Her friends thought it would mean war with England. They were Americans living in Paris, writers like herself, and they found the prospect both alarming and exciting. She pooh-poohed the idea.

"What, to avenge the death of a French king? I think not," she said.

But privately she was not so sure. Men could always find reasons to go to war.

It was the night of January 21st, 1793 . . .

CHAPTER I

the Black Lugger

ABLACK NIGHT AND COLD, EVEN FOR the first month of the year with a chill wind whipping across the Channel from France. A night to be indoors by a good fire with a mug of hot punch, not gadding about off the Sussex Downs in support of the Revenue service fighting a futile war against the smugglers. Nathaniel Peake, master and commander of the brig sloop *Nereus*, bent his bum against the nearest of her sixteen guns with his coat collar turned up and his chin thrust deep into his muffler and cast an anxious eye at the familiar hump of Seaford Head off the larboard bow. Even on such a dirty night, with a scrap of a moon dodging in and out of ragged clouds, he could make out the line of surf at its foot. He had the sailor's healthy respect for a lee shore and in his mind's eye he saw the rocks where in times past he had clambered with his shrimp net when the tide was out.

"We must hug the coast and take them by surprise," he had been instructed by the Revenue Collector, Mr. Swales, who had joined them at Shoreham: a stout burlesque of the breed with an opinion of his own competence that Nathan was inclined from sheer prejudice to doubt.

It was a coast Nathan knew well. Beyond the headland was Cuck-mere Haven where he had first set foot in salt water, bawling not in fear—as he was later told—but for his nanny to loose her hold upon him so that he might venture farther. Here, too, he had sailed his first boat and set a course for America till a slack wind and a stern tutor recalled him to his responsibilities. And one summer's night when the household thought him safe in bed he had crouched at the top of the cliff and watched the smugglers landing contraband: the fleet of small boats in the haven and the long line of ponies and tub-men straggling along the Cuckmere with their illicit booty.

They'd be there tonight if the information laid before the Collector was correct; some of the same men in all probability for it was only ten years since Nathan's last sighting of them. He imagined sweeping them with grape or shot and shook his head at the absurdity of the notion. Yet not so impossible before the night was out.

He crossed to the weather side of the little space he liked to think of as his quarterdeck—though the *Nereus* was flush-decked like all the vessels of her class—and gazed across the sea towards the black bank of cloud that masked the proper enemy to the south. France and England had been at war for much of the century and would be again before it was out, if you could believe what you read in the newspapers. Yet there had been peace for ten years, the whole time Nathan had been in the Navy, with precious few enemies to fight save some unfortunate aborigines in the South Seas and importunate pirates in the Caribbean . . . and of course the smugglers.

There was a flash of lightning from the clear sky to the east and a thin crack that was a far cry from thunder. A moment's pause and then a veritable barrage. Nathan came off the rail and arched his brow at Mr. Collector Swales as if to enquire if this was all part of his plan, knowing full well that it was not. The gentleman relieved himself of an oath and stamped his feet upon the deck, possibly under the impression he was travelling post and could thereby induce a faster turn of speed. Nathan met the questioning eye of his first lieutenant, Mr. Jordan, and instructed him to beat to quarters though he was not impatient for battle with men with whom he was at least half in sympathy and had probably known since childhood, smuggling being a way of life on the Sussex coast. To his certain knowledge many of his own father's labourers were employed in the trade, earning more in a few hours carrying tubs of contraband brandy and tobacco than they could earn in a week on the farm.

Nathan made his way forward through the rush of men and took up a new mooring at the foremast shrouds so that he might see what was afoot the moment they cleared Hope Point.

Not far now and closing fast. Their consort, the little Customs cutter *Badger*, was already turning, almost jibing as she rounded the point. Then she veered abruptly to windward so that she lay broadside to the shore with her own guns run out: four little 4-pounders that would scarce scare a bum-boat but might play the very devil on that open stretch of shore. Nathan could see it clear in his mind's eye: the steep bank of shingle and the wide flat marshland beyond and the cliffs of the Seven Sisters sweeping down to Beachy Head . . .

Then they were round the point, the moon suddenly clear of the scudding clouds and the white cliffs making a perfect reflector for the spectacle on shore. As great a shambles as Nathan could have predicted though it surprised him that the mistake was so elementary.

The dragoons had come down on the wrong side of the river.

Either that or the lookout—the spots-man—had signalled the incoming boats to switch the landing. Whatever the cause, the troopers were stranded on the west bank of the Cuckmere and the smugglers were on the east. Even in the dark Nathan could see them fleeing along the shore towards the gentle slope of Haven Brow: above a hundred of them and half as many ponies with the dragoons riding their horses into the river and blazing away with their carbines with not a hope in hell of hitting anything. And a fleet of small boats fleeing along the foot of the cliffs towards Beachy Head . . .

And there, a mile or so farther to the east but silhouetted against the white backdrop of the Sisters, was the black lugger . . .

"The *Fortune*," cried the Collector, fairly dancing in his agitation and pointing. "There is our prize, sir."

The *Fortune* had been the main topic of his discourse since leaving

Shoreham: a big, fast lugger with ten 6-pounders and a crew of more than a hundred which made her more than a match for any of the Revenue cutters on the station and was the main reason for a naval presence. She had been fitted out in Newhaven ostensibly as a privateer during the American War but was now known to be wholly engaged in smuggling (as in all probability she was then): her normal practice being to run the contraband over from one of the French Channel ports and transfer it to the tub-boats off the Sussex coast.

In which occupation she had clearly been disturbed and was now fleeing out to sea with all the sail she could carry—and the little Customs cutter snapping at her heels. No chance of catching her of course, much less of engaging her as an equal, but if the lugger lost a single spar it would be enough for the *Nereus* to come up and make an end of it. Unhappily, her skipper was of the same opinion and as the *Badger* closed on him he came even farther into the wind and fired a rippling broadside on the roll with a greater approximation to thunder than anything Nathan had heard thus far.

He had been staring straight at her and was momentarily blinded by the sudden eruption but when he could see again it was to observe the *Badger* taken aback with her topmast down and a shamble of headsails and rigging on her foredeck. Nathan had already brought the brig as close to the wind as she could sail but he had to fall off to avoid a collision and he came up on the cutter's lee and called out did she need assistance. The skipper replied with a string of oaths indicating that Nathan would be better occupied with catching his assailant but a glance in the lugger's direction suggested the contrary. Nathan had entertained some faint hope of crossing her stern and raking her from a distance but it was clear now that he would be lucky to come within a mile of her and thereafter their courses would be steadily diverging.

He heard the Revenue man asking why they did not give chase and left it to the junior midshipman to explain in his superior way that the lugger, being rigged fore and aft could sail at least a point closer to the wind, do you see? While the brig, being square-rigged would have to beat to windward and tack. A futile course of action unless the wind changed or the lugger was taken aback. Nathan would be better employed rounding up the tub-boats still creeping along the foot of the cliffs in the hope that no one had noticed them. Yet he despised the notion of hauling in a few poor fishermen while the real culprit sailed safely back to France. Better to tack in the lugger's wake, vain though it was, and hope the Revenue officer would not propose an alternative strategy until it was too late.

He was about to give the order when he caught the eye of one of his junior officers. It was something of a speculative look, hedged with caution, and it caused Nathan to delay the manoeuvre for a moment or two while he considered what it might mean.

Martin Tully was a Guernsey man who had joined the *Nereus* a month or two before Nathan. In his briefing the first lieutenant had explained that Tully, like every second man in the Channel Isles, was a former smuggler: the mate of a *chasse marée* taken off the Isle of Wight and her crew given the option of volunteering for the King's Navy or facing the full fury of the law. He had been rated able seaman but swiftly raised to master's mate by the previous commander of the *Nereus*. Nathan had formed no more than a sketchy assessment of Tully's abilities but he found him agreeable enough and certainly competent, quietly spoken with the manners of a gentleman and none of the airs. He seemed wary of putting himself forward lest he be laid aback. Hardly surprising in view of his previous career as a smuggler. As to his social background, Nathan had overheard the two midshipmen whispering that he was the by-blow of a Guernsey seigneur, which might have been a myth he had perpetrated to win their respect for they were both the sons of gentlemen, of course, and deplorable snobs who would honour the bastard of a noble far more than the legitimate spawn of a tradesman or less. Yet he did not seem given to invention and there was something in his face and bearing that would have inclined them to respect, Nathan thought, whatever his breeding. Nathan had resolved to know him better but the opportunity had slid by—like so much else on his present commission.

Now he joined Tully at the rail and after returning his salutation and contemplating the horizon for a minute or two he begged him for his opinion of the distant chase.

"Well, sir," said he, "for the moment I believe he is content to put as much space between us as is possible in as short a time—and so he will sail as close to the wind as he may."

"And then?" Nathan prompted.

"And then I believe he will make for the Somme."

"The Somme?" Nathan knew it from the charts of course, though he had never been there: a wide estuary about halfway between Dieppe and Boulogne. But why the Somme? Dieppe, surely, was far more likely.

Tully seemed to be considering the question, though it was hard to tell. His face lacked expression. There might be more knowledge locked in there than he deemed prudent to release.

"She is the *Fortune*, I believe, of Newhaven?" he ventured.

"She is."

Tully nodded. "Her captain is a man called Williams—or was when I last heard of him which were no more than a few months since. A Sussex man by birth and a privateer in the past, but he has a woman in St. Valéry and spends more time there than in any English port though his crew are mostly English and American."

St. Valéry. Again Nathan consulted his memory of the charts and located it on the south bank of the Somme very close to the mouth. A smaller port than Dieppe or Le Havre, used mainly by fishing boats.

"He will set his course for there, I think," said Tully, "as soon as he believes we have abandoned the chase."

He spoke without any sense of conceit or consequence but in such a manner that Nathan was inclined to believe he knew exactly what he was about. The question was whether he wished to aid or hinder the chase.

Nathan joined the first lieutenant who had been following their conversation from the weather rail, his face marked with suspicion or disapproval or both.

"Mr. Jordan, I believe we will set a course for the Somme," Nathan informed him with a cheerfulness that masked his own doubts, "and see what *Fortune* it may bring us."

CHAPTER 2

the Somme

THE FRENCH COAST LAY OFF THE starboard bow under the same black cloud as before but *Fortune* was playing hide and seek. Twice the *Nereus* had sighted her—or something suspiciously like her—but each time she had vanished into the witches' brew of mist and rain to the west. Now they were halfway through the forenoon, hove-to off the French coast almost in the mouth of the Somme. A filthy morning battered with rainsqualls, sea and sky poured into the same grim pot and stirred about till there was no telling them apart.

The wind had dropped considerably through the night but it still blew from the southwest with sufficient force to hold the *Nereus* against the flood with her yards braced by. And as long as the wind stayed there Nathan was confident he could come down on his quarry if she tried to slip past him into the Somme.

If the Somme was where she was headed.

The longer the day advanced the more he began to doubt. And it was a doubt shared by the majority of his officers if he did not mistake the looks passed between them. They did not trust him. He was new to command and still on trial so far as they were concerned. Their natural loyalty was to Jordan, the first lieutenant who had been passed over for promotion. And they had even less trust in a former smuggler who might be sending them on a wild goose chase to save an old acquaintance from the gallows.

Nathan joined Tully at the rail, staring into the murk to the west.

"So what manner of man is this Williams," he inquired, "the skipper of the *Fortune?*"

Tully made a face. "I only met him once," he said, "though I knew him by repute. A vain man, a braggart, and greedy. He's a good enough seaman, I believe, but I did not like him."

So was this why he was ready to betray him? Or was it a more noble cause: the oath he had taken to serve the King, perhaps? There was no way of asking such a question, not for Nathan at least, and besides, he was committed now. And his officers would judge him for it. Happily, Collector Swales had gone below to sleep off the effects of a large hip flask that had comforted him through the hours of darkness while Nathan spent the night on deck, worrying.

He wondered what made him so concerned: to lose sleep over a smuggler? Nothing to do with honour, for where was the honour in such a mission? It might earn a commendation from his superiors but would do little for his self-esteem. It was more a matter of his own competence. Of judging himself fit for command.

Doubts of this nature had begun to assail him from the moment he had stepped aboard the *Nereus;* perhaps earlier, during the long months ashore on half pay. He had been ten years in the Navy and it seemed a little late to be considering that he had chosen the wrong career and yet he was increasingly of the opinion that this was the case.

He had been happy enough for the first few years—as a midshipman on the West Indies station and then a lieutenant on a survey vessel in the South Seas—but he had been fortunate to escape many of the restrictions and the formalities that were the norm in the King's service. When the *Hermes* was paid off in '91 he had spent almost eighteen months ashore, mostly in London, and discovered there were more ways of spending one's life than on the deck of a ship of war and companions for whom the Navy was not the be all and end all of life.

Then he had been offered the command of the *Nereus*. It was a surprise appointment and he suspected his father's influence in the matter. Nathan's father, Sir Michael Peake, had fought in three wars against the French and retired with the rank of rear admiral but he still had friends in high places and was always willing to use them to his son's advantage. Nathan had briefly considered turning the offer down—effectively ending his career—but it would have broken his father's heart. Besides, what else could he do? He painted a little. He wrote verse. He was interested in astronomy. He was learning to play the flute. The accomplishments of the average gentleman of leisure with aspirations to learning. He was afraid that if he permitted himself the time to focus on any one of these endeavours he might discover himself to be totally without talent.

Yet he could not help but reflect that there had been something of the coward in his acceptance of the commission. And his restlessness would not be abated. He felt a persistent sense of restriction that he could not quite identify or define—though the physical restrictions were obvious on a vessel barely a hundred feet long and thirty in the beam, crammed with over a hundred officers and men.

But it was not that. The simple truth was that he loved the sea but not the service. And, of course, it did not help that he was employed in nothing more heroic than the hunting down of a smuggler of fine wines and full proof brandy in the service of His Majesty's Customs.

Yet another squall to the west. Nathan stood and eased his cramped limbs over to the weather rail and gazed out at the distant rain. It seemed to be flowing up rather than down, as if the clouds were replenishing themselves from the ocean. He would have liked to try and capture the image on canvas but he could imagine what his officers would have made of that, let alone Collector Swales, should he ever emerge from his slumbers.

Sirs, I beg to report that the master and commander of the King's sloop Nereus, *forsaking the chase and sailing above ten hours to the coast of France, proceeded to set up easel*

*and canvas upon the deck and indulge himself in painting
the view . . .*

*After which he treated us to an improvised arrangement
upon the flute. The smuggler, meantime, made good his
escape.*

It would at least end the dilemma over his naval career.

A shout from the maintop, an arm flung out to sea, two, perhaps
three points on their quarter. Nathan could see nothing from the
deck. Just those dirty strands of rain twixt sea and sky. There could
be anything out there or nothing but the direction was right. He
swung himself up into the shrouds and joined the lookout in the top.

"Damned if I can see her now, sir," the fellow muttered, chastened,
shaking his head, avoiding his captain's eye. "But I did I swear it. A
black lugsail to nor'-nor'-west and then she vanished, by God, as if
by sorcery."

Nathan caught the implication. He'd seen it in the faces of the crew
on deck. They were beginning to think of her as a ghost ship, with
her black sails and hull. A nautical legend, manned by skeletons. He
stood up with his arm through the foretop shrouds and stared out at
the drifting cobwebs of rain. Nothing. Then . . .

"Yes," he said. It was almost a growl in his throat. He felt the seaman gazing at him in wonder and felt the same boyish satisfaction he
had as a midshipman when he'd played the same game. He took out
his glass, slid it open and clapped it to his eye. It took him a moment
to fix her and in that time he heard the shout of exultation from the
lookout as he spied her again. Then Nathan had her framed in the
lens, heading straight for them with the wind a little abaft her beam
and those great lugsails heeling her hard to leeward. Keep right on,
my beauty, he silently urged her. She could lead them a merry dance
on a bowline but if she kept going large the *Nereus* had her measure.
The problem was her skipper knew it as well as he. He could come
round in an instant and vanish in the murk.

But *would* he? He could not possibly know the *Nereus* by sight, not from that one brief glimpse of her off the Cuckmere in the dark. And why would he think to find her off the Somme? He would know her for a ship of war but *Nereus* flew no ensign. He would take her for a Frenchman, surely, standing off the coast, or waiting for high tide to enter St. Valéry as he himself intended.

Nathan slid down to the deck and favoured Mr. Tully with an appreciative nod before he let the first lieutenant know—but he stayed him from calling the watch below. If the lugger did hold to her present course they'd be watching his every move through the glass and he wanted nothing to alarm them, not until she was beyond redemption.

"And Mr. Harris," he turned to the marine subaltern standing with the elder of the two midshipmen by the rail, "would you oblige me by keeping your men below for the time being."

Nathan wanted no redcoats on deck to give the game away.

"And perhaps you would be good enough to give my compliments to Mr. Swales," he said to the midshipman—Ericson, "and tell him I would be obliged if he would step on deck."

Fortune came on apace. They could see her now from the deck without a glass and the figure at her head: a bare-breasted goddess with flowing hair, white as marble; and those distinctive lugsails, not quite black but a very dark crimson, the colour of dried blood. She could not go through him so which way would she bear? Best it were to larboard so he could force her out to sea. But she'd not run past him—not on either side, not if he ran out his guns. One broadside would finish her: if he had the nerve to fire it.

He crossed to the weather side and raised his glass to study the nearer of the two batteries that guarded the entrance to the Somme. No apparent sign of life apart from the large tricolour at the flagstaff. Six gun ports. Forty-two-pounders by report. Britain and France were not at war—as he kept reminding himself—but if he was to fire upon another vessel so close to the French coast what would they do?

Swales was at his side, bleary-eyed and puffy-faced.

Nathan handed him the glass.

He applied himself to it for a moment. Then, begrudgingly, "How in God's name . . . ?"

"What can I do?" Nathan asked him. "What jurisdiction do we have?"

"Jurisdiction?" For a moment Nathan thought he would have to explain the term. Swales gazed through his naked eye at the vessel bearing down on them. A furred tongue flicked over dry lips.

"Well . . ." he began, "we have every right to board her."

"And what would we find?"

The man appeared to deflate, knowing as well as Nathan that she was no longer carrying contraband and was well outside English waters.

"Would you swear she is the same vessel we saw off the Cuckmere," Nathan pressed him, "that fired into the *Badger*?"

Swales blew himself up again. "That I would," he replied. "No doubt in my mind. And you?"

Nathan nodded. But this was scarcely the point. Would a jury convict on such evidence—and a Sussex jury at that?

She was coming up a little into the wind. She meant to pass between the *Nereus* and the shore. Then he saw her sails shiver for a moment and fall aback. A moment later the slap of his own sails against the mast announced that they had lost the wind. The bow began to swing at once into the mouth of the Somme.

Nathan considered his options. The *Nereus* carried sweeps but it would be hard work against the flood. Better to drop anchor in the mouth of the river until the wind picked up. Almost certainly the *Fortune* would do the same, for she would not wish to enter the Somme until the tide was up and Nathan could send his boats to board her.

A loud boom from the direction of the shore and he jerked his head to catch the puff of smoke from the battery on Pointe du Hourdel. A moment . . . and then the tall splash about a cable's length off the larboard bow. The officers exchanged glances. Nathan swore quietly, more in exasperation than alarm. A warning shot, he thought, to tell him they did not want him in their river. Serious enough but . . .

But it wasn't. It was a ranging shot. Moments later the fort vanished in a cloud of black smoke shot with orange as the rest of the battery opened up. The sea rose up off the larboard bow in several enormous waterspouts. One shot skipped twice and sank a few yards from their stern.

"Man the sweeps," Nathan commanded the first lieutenant. His voice sounded calm enough but his heart was pounding. In ten years of service it was the first time he had been under fire, at least from cannon—and these were no little pop-guns such as the *Fortune* carried or even the *Nereus*. They were 42-pounders, bigger than any of the long guns carried on a first-rate. A single hit and the *Nereus* would know she was in a battle. But what really upset Nathan was that they were not at war.

"Let them see the ensign," he instructed the first. Then, as Jordan gave the order to hoist it from the flagstaff, "No. Between the yards." He had no wish to see it hanging limply from the stern so the French could claim they had not seen it. Let them know they were firing upon a King's ship and think on what it meant.

They had the sweeps out now and the bow was coming slowly round but Nathan was alarmed at how far they had drifted into the mouth of the Somme. They were already within the jaws of the two headlands and still moving.

Another salvo—but from the other battery on Pointe à Guile.

This time Nathan heard the whine of the falling shot and the sea erupted all along their starboard side, close enough to soak the deck in spray.

They must have seen the ensign, even in the poor light. They had fired on the flag: an act of war. Nathan's indignation surpassed his concern and even as the gravity of the occasion impressed itself upon him, a strange logic persuaded him that they would go no further than that; that having thrown down the gauntlet they would let the *Nereus* crawl away with her tail between her legs. It surprised him when they fired again—and again. Both batteries with scarcely a space between them.

It was astonishing that the sloop was not hit. The water boiled around her and several shots passed through the rigging with the noise of a great wind through a forest but without bringing down a single spar. Nathan still had the sails rigged in hope of an offshore breeze but they hung sullenly from the yards, sodden with rain, while the crew toiled gamely at the sweeps. For all their efforts they were barely making headway against the flood and Nathan had the two watches ease off in turn so the brig slewed and shot about like some ungainly water boatman in a bid to spoil the gunners' aim. But the gunners could not make such practice for long without a hit. One shot skipped up off the water and struck the hull amidships just above the waterline with a sound like someone beating upon a big bass drum; another parted the backstay with a great twang; and the orchestra was augmented by an enormous clang and a thud up forward that had Nathan puzzled until he realised it had struck the bower anchor and shattered, one half flying high in the air and dropping on the deck, the other going God knows where. The crew were tiring. Nathan and most of his officers had joined them at the sweeps but as far as he could judge through eyes near blinded by sweat and spray they were barely holding their own against the flood.

When he felt the wind on his cheek he thought it was another near miss. Then he saw the sails fill. They missed the next stroke as the brig lurched and Nathan went sprawling on the deck in a tangle of arms and legs, officers and crew all cheering and laughing, dignity and discipline gone by the board. When Nathan scrambled to his feet and reached the helm they were scudding under a fair breeze. He looked astern as both batteries fired together and the space the sloop had so recently vacated rose in fury like some multi-headed sea monster robbed of its prey. The next salvo fell astern by half a cable's length and the one after that was a waste of powder. Then another squall scrubbed away the shore, forts and all.

Nathan looked for the *Fortune* but she had vanished into the rain and he was not displeased to see the last of her. He set a course for Shoreham so he might see the last of the Revenue officer, too, and asked Mr. Jordan for a damage report. There was the backstay, of course, spliced already, and some timbers slightly sprung amidships by the spent shot, which the carpenter said he could attend to. But the surprise for Nathan was the damage from the shot that had struck his best bower anchor. The anchor was sound enough but—the lieutenant informed him, lowering his voice for the shame of it—part of the shot had flown forward and smashed the heads.

Nathan went forward to see for himself, more in wonder than alarm—he had his own more civilised arrangements in his cabin. It was the crew who would suffer by it. Then he saw that the figure-head, old Nereus himself, the old man of the sea, had lost a large chunk of his beard.

"They have added insult to injury," he complained to the carpenter who he knew took a special pride in the figure, which he somewhat resembled.

The boatswain's mate brought him the half cannonball that had landed on deck, neatly sheared where it had struck the anchor, and Nathan had it put in a canvas bag with some notion that it might be kept for posterity: the first shot in a new war. For the French had fired on a King's ship and he was confident their lordships would not suffer the wrong to go unavenged.

CHAPTER 3

Chez Kitty

NATHAN SAT IN THE CROWDED WAITING room of the Admiralty with his cannonball at his feet and small lump of lead in his heart. When the commodore had commanded him to make report to their lordships in person and to take his trophy with him by way of evidence, Nathan had entertained some notion of celebrity, even advancement. The war of '39 had commenced with a not dissimilar incident when the skipper of an English merchant vessel, about his lawful business, had suffered the loss of an ear in an encounter with the Spanish garda costa off Cuba. The severed organ having been displayed in Parliament and the House being in temper, a state of hostilities had ensued which became popularly known as the War of Jenkins Ear. Though unbloodied and with all his organs intact, Nathan was of the opinion that firing upon a King's ship must constitute a greater offence to the dignity of the realm than the physical injury to a merchant seaman and that it was not impossible, given the current mood of Parliament and the humour of the press, that Peake's Ball, or even Peake's Heads, might achieve a similar notoriety.

He had been instructed to report to the Second Secretary but understood this official to be a mere conduit to the First Lord himself. However, on his arrival he had discovered the establishment to be in a state of turmoil and tumult, his visit having coincided with more dramatic news from the continent.

The King of France had been killed—murdered, in the view of the London press—and the regicides had declared war upon England; or England had declared war on the regicides, no one seemed to know the precise sequence of events. But war it was and the fleet had been ordered to sea and every half-pay officer in England had converged upon the Admiralty in the hope of securing a position.

After waiting more than three hours for his appointment Nathan had an increased perception of the vanity of human endeavour. After another half hour he gave up and went home, taking his cannonball with him—home in this instance being his mother's house in St. James's, where he was at least assured of a welcome and his cannonball a place of prominence among the family memorabilia.

His mother was not there—an eventuality he might have anticipated—but her steward, Phipps, assured Nathan that she would be back shortly. He proposed a dish of cold meats, which Nathan took in the kitchen, and a hot bath, which he took in his room. He was comfortably immersed in the latter and contemplating whether to call for more hot water when his mother burst in with her usual lack of ceremony and hailed him from the open door while several maids blushed and giggled in the background.

"My darling boy," she exclaimed, in tones of surprised delight, "I had persuaded myself you were sacrificed already on the altar of false patriotism."

"No, Mother," he assured her. "I did my best but they are looking for virgins. I will try again later when they are not so particular."

She shook her head at him dutifully but with no loss to her composure or the arrangement of her curls. His mother was not easily shocked.

"So why are you in London," she inquired as she entered the room, considerately shutting the door behind her, "and not striding the main brace or splicing the quarterdeck or whatever it is you do when you are at sea? My God, what is that?"

She had stubbed her toe on his canvas bag.

"A cannonball," he told her.

She observed it with caution. "And what is it doing here?"

"I brought it back from France," he informed her, "to show the Admiralty."

"Why, Nat, have they none of their own? And what were you doing in France?"

"Oh, making a fool of myself as usual," he sighed. "I suppose you have heard we are at war."

She settled herself in an armchair by the fire, after first turning it round to observe his ablutions.

"Well, I do not expect you to agree with me, of course," she began, "but it is a very sad day for England when she elects to make common cause with the Prussian and Austrian tyrants in the suppression of liberty and equality."

Fraternity was clearly accorded a lower status in his mother's notion of Utopia.

Lady Catherine Ann Peake—known to her friends as Kitty—had been born in New York of an American father and a French mother, which made her wholly cannibal in the view of civilised society and went some way to explaining the more bizarre aspects of her nature. She and Nathan's father had lived apart for some years—since he retired from the service, in fact, and expressed the intention of farming sheep in Sussex. She was a woman of forty-three, which was not the first information she would have disclosed to an inquisition even when shown the instruments of torture, and was generally regarded by her admirers as being in her prime. Her critics, who enjoyed a substantial majority, were less complimentary but even they were inclined to find more fault with her opinions than her appearance which they conceded to be striking. But then, as they invariably added, the same had been said of Messalina. Her admirers were rather more disposed to compare her to Cleopatra whom "age could not wither nor custom stale of her infinite variety"—as Kitty was fond of repeating—and though Nathan winced at such comparisons, he could appreciate why his mother might attract similar extremes of emotion.

While her enemies castigated her as a scheming hussy, her friends extolled the virtues of a generous spirit, a flawless complexion and a superior intellect, though the latter was understood to be a mixed blessing in a woman. By such means and the assistance of a modest fortune, Lady Catherine had succeeded in placing herself in a position of some eminence among a particular segment of society. Her salon in St. James's—just across the park from the King's London residence—attracted the most vociferous of his critics. As these had at one time included the Prince of Wales and the leader of His Majesty's Opposition, this had not necessarily detracted from her standing in fashionable society. The perceived iniquities of the French Revolution, however, had caused many a faint-hearted liberal to recoil in horror from the taint of progressive politics, with the result that Chez Kitty had become the refuge of only the most hardened radicals and revolutionaries, though in Nathan's view most of them were "all talk."

It was dangerous talk, however, and he was not best pleased when his mother informed him that she was entertaining some guests that evening whom he was sure to find "interesting."

"If by interesting you mean expressive of opinions that are almost certainly treasonable," Nathan began but was interrupted by an expression of disdain and a brief exposition on the nature of treason.

"Besides, how can it be treason if they are French?" she concluded plausibly.

Nathan scrutinised her for signs of levity. There were none.

"French?" he repeated incredulously, though he supposed she might mean some of those émigrés forced to flee the oppression in Paris. This hope was promptly dashed.

"I have decided to give a small party for some of my friends in the French Embassy," she confided, "before they are obliged to quit the country."

"Mother, they have just declared war on us."

"Nonsense. You must not believe everything you read in the press, my dear. The British declared war on *them*. It will be instructive to hear their views on the subject."

Nathan groaned and placed the flannel over his face. Since adolescence he had always refused to take sides in his parents' conflicts but if he stayed with either one for much above an hour he was very much inclined to see the other's point of view.

"So," his mother continued, "do not lie there like a great white whale—I observe that you are putting on weight, by the by—but see if you can struggle into some of your old clothes and prepare yourself for an occasion. But not naval uniform. It would not be appropriate."

"I fear I may not be good company," Nathan protested, removing the flannel. "I have had a bad day at the Admiralty."

"Nonsense," she said again. "Besides, you do not have to say anything; only listen and you may learn something to your advantage. But how wonderful it is to see you, my darling, and still in one piece."

She planted a kiss upon his forehead, gave his cheek a pinch as if he were a two-year-old and left him to attempt drowning.

He was moved, however, by a certain curiosity that not only compelled him to prolong his life on this occasion but obliged him to present himself at the appointed hour to greet his mother's guests. They turned out to be the usual gang of freethinkers, republicans and revolutionaries—and only two Frenchmen among them: one a minor official from the Embassy who had been sent to present the Minister's apologies. He and his staff were entirely occupied in preparations for departure, he explained, and regretted they would be unable to take a proper leave of their friends in London. The other was more interesting, being a diplomat from Paris lately arrived in England as head of what he called a "peace mission." This had been rendered superfluous by the declaration of war and he had expressed himself horrified at the execution of King Louis and had petitioned to stay in England. He now awaited the verdict of the authorities.

Nathan suspected from various signs that his mother had formed an attachment to this gentleman whom she described in an aside as "one of the most brilliant minds in Europe." His mother was not infrequently attracted to brilliant minds though her preference in this instance surprised Nathan a little, not on account of the gentleman's comparative youth, which had proved no impediment to her in the past, but rather on account of his looks, which were not pretty. He had a long, thin face, a sickly, almost cadaverous complexion and a pronounced limp, the overall effect being rather more sinister than sad. Nathan would not have been surprised to discover that he had been a police informer before the Revolution or possibly a highwayman forced into early retirement when a coach ran over his foot. In fact he said he had been a bishop and when he observed Nathan's astonishment he laughed and said his own mother had been so outraged by the appointment she had written a letter of protest to the Pope. His name was Talleyrand, which held no especial significance for Nathan at the time though later he was to reflect that it might have caused a small shiver of apprehension at least.

"And your mission?" he stammered in confusion. "It was on behalf of the Church?"

This caused further amusement. Talleyrand, it appeared, had been excommunicated and his peace mission was on behalf of Georges Danton.

Danton was a more familiar name to Nathan. Indeed, he was notorious throughout Europe as the instigator of the attack on the royal palace of the Tuileries and was widely blamed for the massacres that had followed. Since then he had become the most powerful man in Paris, successfully rousing the population to resist the foreign armies then closing in on the capital. Nathan ventured to suggest that his popular image was not widely associated with the search for peace.

"This is true," conceded the diplomat, adopting a more serious aspect. "But Danton, he does not wish for the war with England. In fact, he does not wish for the war with anyone. But he is no more the force he is in the past. It is *Les Enragés*—the angry ones, the fanatics, who make now the policy."

Lady Catherine was concerned for the safety of several of her friends in Paris: among them the writer Mary Wollstonecraft whose *Vindication of the Rights of Woman* was among her required reading—she had presented Nathan with a copy when he had gone back to sea. Mary, it appeared, had travelled to France to write a series of reports for the radical press in England, arriving just before war was declared.

"Poor Mary has scarcely a friend in Paris," Lady Catherine lamented, "and for all her intellect has not the slightest idea of how to look after herself."

Others demurred. Mary was quite capable of looking after herself, they argued, and if she ran into any difficulties there was always Thomas Paine.

Nathan winced a little for mention of Thomas Paine invariably set his mother off on one of her favourite stories—as it did on this occasion. When Nathan was seven, she avowed, he had overheard her extolling the merits of this worthy, who was then stirring up her American countrymen against King George. She had referred to him as the "Great Revolutionist," and Nathan had quite naturally confused him with a gentleman he had seen at a travelling fair who revolved on a giant Catherine Wheel while another gentleman threw knives at him.

There was the usual laughter at Nathan's expense and he smiled dutifully though privately considering that he had not been far wrong.

Nathan's mother was a great admirer of Mr. Paine and claimed to have read both volumes of *The Rights of Man*—"all the way to the end"—unlike so many of her acquaintance who were unable to progress beyond the first few pages but kept the books lying around "for show." Paine had been a regular visitor to the house while Nathan was living there as a half-pay lieutenant and they had enjoyed a number of animated discussions on a great many subjects without coming to any substantial agreement on a single one of them. But Nathan preferred him to many of his mother's friends. "Mad Tom," as he was dubbed in the popular press, had led an adventurous life as a seaman on a privateer called the *Terrible* under the unlikely command of a Captain Death and then as a customs officer in Sussex before taking himself off to America to fan the flames of rebellion and fight the British Army, for which iniquity he was held in the utmost loathing by all who considered themselves loyal subjects of King George. Yet at the end of the war he had returned to England with no apparent regard for his safety or his countrymen's finer feelings and devoted himself to writing the book that would persuade them to follow the example of their American cousins and throw off the shackles of tyranny. *The Rights of Man* had proved an enormous literary success but prompted His Majesty's Government to issue a warrant for the author's arrest on a charge of seditious libel, obliging him to flee to France and assist in throwing off the shackles of tyranny there instead. He had promptly been made an honorary French citizen and elected to the new National Assembly. He had even been asked to help write a new constitution. According to Talleyrand, however, he had excited the wrath of the Jacobin Club by refusing to vote for the execution of the King and was now in some danger of losing his liberty, if not his life.

"For those who are not for them are said to be against them," claimed the diplomat. He had the usual problem in getting tongue and teeth to agree upon the English "th" which detracted a little from the profundity of his remarks: *for zose 'oo are not for zem are said to be against zem.* "They regard such ones as suspect, which is not a very happy place to be since the Revolution."

"No more was it in the days of the tyrants," growled one of the company, a Scottish shoemaker called Hardy who had founded his own Jacobin Club at a pub in the Strand under the guise of a Corresponding Society. "And if you think we are free to express our opinion in England, you are very much mistaken, mon-sewer. Indeed, now that war is declared, you will see more repression, I believe, than you ever did in France."

There was a murmur of agreement from the company.

"For now is a perfect opportunity for the government to crack down on dissent at home," opined a brewer called Whitbread, who was one of the wealthier men present and thereby obliged to express some of the more extreme opinions, "and curb some of our most cherished freedoms."

He claimed to have evidence that the Home Secretary Henry Dundas was funding newspapers like the *Sun* and the *True Briton* to campaign against reform and turn the people against honest reformers such as himself.

"They whip up the mob against us," he complained, "so it is not safe for us to walk the streets."

"Aye, it's as well some people don't have to," growled Hardy, who was thought to have a chip on his shoulder, "and have fine carriages to go about in."

But either Whitbread didn't hear him or had trouble with his accent, for he continued regardless: "Wherever I go I am followed by government agents. They attempt to recruit my servants to spy against me and bribe my workers to withhold their labour." He had even discovered a plan to water his beer, he revealed to general consternation, and thereby ruin his reputation.

He had succeeded in putting a dampener on the proceedings and Lady Catherine was forced to signal Philip to pour more champagne.

"I had a suspicion I was followed here," confessed an Irish anarchist called Blood, looking over his shoulder and dropping his voice lest he had been followed indoors.

"I have no doubt you were," Whitbread assured him complacently, "though it would be quite unnecessary as they have a hackney carriage parked outside for their informants to observe the comings and goings in reasonable comfort. I have told Kitty to write to the Home Secretary and suggest she keep a visitors book and hand it over to them every forenoon to save the expense."

This drew some unconvincing laughter and a few nervous glances towards the windows which were draped against the dark and whatever government agents might be tempted to press their noses against them. Later, when supper was served, Nathan could not resist going over to take a look. Sure enough, there was the cab parked down the road, with a clear view of the front door and whoever entered or left by it.

"I fear you are now suspect, my friend," commented a familiar, foreign voice at his elbow. "The British officer who meet with the enemies of the King in the very heart of Saint James. The associate of the revolutionists and the traitors and the French spies . . ."

To say nothing, Nathan reflected, of having Cleopatra for a mother.

"When the Lord of the Admiralty hear of it," continued Talleyrand with his sardonic smirk, "he make of you the example, I think."

CHAPTER 4

the Banker's plot

J OHN PITT, SECOND EARL OF CHATHAM and First Lord of the
Admiralty, was, at that precise moment, dipping his long nose into
a glass of port wine at his brother William's residence in Downing
Street, just a short walk across St. James's Park. Indeed, had Nathan
glanced out of the back windows of his mother's house and not the
front, he might have observed the lights burning in the upstairs room
where they held their conference.

Chatham, though the elder of the two, had long deferred to his
brother's genius, besides having a natural respect for his status as the
King's chief minister, and yet there were times when he wished they
were back in the nursery and he could give him a good kicking.

This was one of them.

The earl had spent the hours since early morning in meetings with
his colleagues at the Admiralty. They had appointed admirals to the
command of fleets; they had dispatched squadrons, ships and officers
to the far corners of the world; they had attended to one thousand
and one items they considered vital to the defence of the realm. It
was not exceptional to be diverted from such duties by a summons
from Downing Street but it would have been encouraging to find his
brother in conference with the great officers of state. Instead of which
Chatham had discovered him sharing a bottle of port wine with a

seedy little man called Bicknell Coney who looked like someone you sent to collect the rents but was introduced as a director of the Bank of England. And his brother should know, Chatham reflected sourly, given the time he spent there counting the nation's money and wishing it were his own.

The banker, though small of stature, had a lofty sense of his own importance and for ten minutes or more he had subjected the First Lord of the Admiralty to a condescending lecture on matters that were of little or no interest to him. Chatham strongly suspected that his brother had put him up to it, doubtless after explaining that despite his vital role in the nation's affairs, the First Lord had no head for figures and would profit by a greater appreciation of the merits of a sound economy as compared to, say, an extra few ships of the line.

Now the fellow took out his pocket book, removed a large bank note and placed it reverently upon the table. It was to the value of ten pounds.

"This was printed during your father's tenure at the Treasury," he informed them, as if their father had been a piddling little bank clerk and not the First Lord of the Treasury and the greatest statesman of the age. "A temporary measure when specie was in short supply."

He reached into his pocket book again.

"And this," he said, displaying it to them like a conjuror who was about to make it disappear, "is a French *assignat* to the value of ten livres. There is however a considerable difference, and not only in design."

He tapped the English note with a stubby forefinger.

"If you were to take this to the Bank of England in Threadneedle Street, you would be able to exchange it for ten pounds of silver. Not that you would need to of course," he smiled indulgently, "as the note itself is good for that amount and considerably lighter on the pocket, ha, ha."

The smirk was replaced with a frown as he indicated its neighbour.

"The value of this fellow, however, is not based upon silver or gold or any other precious metal. It is based upon land. Land owned by the state. Or I should say *stolen* by the state from its previous owners—the aristocracy and the Church."

The banker went on to apprise them of the fact that the Church of Rome had, over the past fifteen hundred years, acquired between one-fourth and one-third of the total land and property of the French nation, worth approximately two thousand million livres or fifty million English pounds.

"I need hardly remind Your Lordship that the annual budget of the King's Navy amounts to a little over three million," he said smugly. "So you will appreciate that we are speaking of a substantial sum of money, a very substantial sum indeed. However," he picked up the French bank note and waved it in Chatham's face, "if you were to present this note for payment would you get your piece of land to the value of ten livres? No, sir, you would not. Indeed you would more likely get your head cut off."

Chatham restrained a strong impulse to damn him for his impudence.

"No, the value of this piece of paper depends entirely upon the presumption that people trust it to be worth exactly what it says it is worth. If that trust should ever be lost it becomes worth less than the paper it is printed upon."

He screwed up the note in his fist and tossed it back upon the table.

"Which is why I believe we are here," he concluded, looking very pleased with himself.

A silence. Lasting a little longer than it should. Chatham, who had entirely forgotten why they were here—if he ever knew in the first place—regarded his brother expectantly.

Pitt was undoubtedly cleverer than he, always had been, though he was always in debt. How could you be First Lord of the Treasury with all that money at your disposal and still be in debt? It was quite beyond Chatham.

His brother picked up the crumpled bank note and began to straighten it out as if it would be a pity to let it go to waste. His eyelids were heavy from lack of sleep or drink or both. He had always been a tippler and he had been hitting the bottle with a vengeance of late.

"Is it one of theirs or one of ours?" he inquired.

"That's the Frenchie," Chatham informed him, shaking his head a little. "The fellow's just told you."

The banker was smirking again.

"One of the first batch from Haughton Mill," he declared as if he had just done something very clever. "Only an expert could tell them apart."

Pitt put it back on the table.

"And so now you want a ship," he said.

"Ah," exhaled Chatham as the fog cleared a little. "A ship." His department, ships. Very good. Except that everybody seemed to want one and there were nothing like enough to go round.

"Yes, my lord," said the banker, fixing him with his fanatic glare. "A ship and a crew that may pass for American. And a captain. One whose discretion may be relied upon and who speaks at least a little French. And while I would not say he should be *expendable*, he should not be of such seniority or influence that his *apprehension*, as it were, would be an embarrassment to us."

CHAPTER 5

an *Unusual Commission*

THE TOWN OF RYE, HIGH AND dry on its little island above Romney Marsh, basked in the warmth of the sun: as warm, indeed, as a mid-summer's day though April not yet out. Nathan leaned against the parapet of the battery, high above the town, and closed his eyes for a moment, hatless, his long hair untied, luxuriating in the warmth of the sun on his face and the red glow that flooded his eyelids. He was, as near as damn it, happy.

There were a number of reasons for this rare condition. Primarily, a simple pleasure in being alone after several weeks at sea with never a moment, even in the precious sanctuary of his cabin, when he was not aware of the noxious presence of 108 human bodies crammed into 110 feet of hull.

He could see the brig riding at anchor in Rye Bay a little off the mouth of the Rother with a small fleet of bum-boats around her and her sails hung out to dry. He could just make out the small cradle under her beak where the carpenter or one of his mates was finally repairing the damage to the figurehead. The war had started badly for *Nereus*, and prematurely, but the next three months had seen an improvement in her fortunes and in Nathan's. Though HM Customs continued to petition them for support and the smuggling fraternity continued to put profit above patriotism, the war had given the

Nereus more useful employment. Nathan had sailed her across the Channel on a number of occasions to look into the various harbours, rivers and inlets between Dunkirk and Dieppe, taking note of the defences, harassing the coastal shipping, landing the odd spy and generally making a nuisance of himself. In short, fulfilling the purpose for which the sloop had been designed.

She had even taken her first prize, the *Bonne Jeanne*, off Étaples: an eighty-ton hooker with a cargo of cider, salt pork and ship's biscuit. There she was, out at the mouth of the river, a little closer to shore than the *Nereus*, among a score of other coastal traders moored under the guns of Winchelsea Castle. No Spanish treasure ship but a welcome boost to the crew's morale for all that; and to Nathan's meagre fortune, for he had only a small allowance from his father and would accept nothing from his mother on the grounds that she who paid the piper would invariably call the tune. So the several hundred pounds of prize money he anticipated was not to be sniffed at.

There were other, less material factors that contributed to his good humour. The sun, the cloudless sky, the apple trees dense with blossom: blossom so heavy on the bough that for all its fragile impermanence he felt he could reach out and feel the weight of it in his cupped hands like a bunch of grapes or—such was the current state of his imaginings—a woman's breasts.

He allowed himself to fantasize about the woman he had met the previous day . . . Not met, precisely, but seen: a vision of loveliness comparable to the blossom itself, emerging from the Mermaid Inn in the company of an older woman who might have been her mother. She had given him a look—the vision, not the mother—that Nathan considered encouraging. A mixture of curiosity and regard, he thought—for he had dwelt on it subsequently and at length—and he had high hopes of meeting her again and of knowing her better.

He was on his way to the Mermaid now for a conference with the commodore of the Dover squadron and several of his captains whose ships and sloops lay moored in the bay. The narrow streets of the town were filled with their crews, sent ashore on various missions, a jaunty, jostling sometimes boisterous assembly of blue jackets and sailcloth trousers, tarpaulin hats and tarred pigtails (and all the stripes and embroidery that the service would allow) so that Nathan's previous impressions of Rye as a smuggler's port occupied by hostile forces and glowering faces was entirely altered.

The town clock chimed the half-hour and he resumed his climb—he had only paused so as not to arrive in a sweat—fanning his face with his folded hat and looking forward to a jug of ale with only a little less enthusiasm than the possibility of running into the Vision of Loveliness once more.

He was approaching the inn, in the shade of the houses across the street, when he saw her. Emerging from the dim interior just as she had the previous day and almost as if she had been waiting for Nathan to appear. But she was not alone—and her companion was not her mother. It was the master's mate of the *Nereus*, the former Guernsey smuggler, Mr. Tully.

Nathan stepped back into the shadows, the better to observe them as they came down the steps of the Mermaid. Tully guided her gently by the hand and then tucked it in the crook of his arm as the pair set off jauntily down the street. They were chattering away, so engrossed in each other's company—and there was such a confusion of carts and carriages and what-have-you in the forecourt of the inn—that they did not notice Nathan standing under the overhang of the building opposite. Tully looked happier than Nathan had ever seen him and the young woman if anything more gorgeous than yesterday, her features animated now where they had then been thoughtful. A few strands of blonde curls strayed artfully from under a pert little bonnet, she had delicate feet in white stockings with pink bobbles on them—Nathan had observed them as she tripped down the steps—and her bosom was . . . Nathan rejected the blossom analogy as entirely inadequate but could think of nothing comparable for the moment. She had a kind of *glow* about her.

He watched them walk down the steep hill and realised that he was smiling to himself rather foolishly; they looked so charming together, the beautiful young woman and the handsome naval officer. Lucky devil, he thought. He was as much pleased for Tully as envious of him. His respect for the master's mate increased. He shook his head to remove the foolish grin and the dreams of yesterday and stepped across the road into the inn.

Commodore Harris was seated at a table in the saloon with an officer Nathan had not encountered before, a captain of marines.

"Ah, Peake, there you are," the commodore greeted him. "This is Captain Marsh. He has been sent by the Admiralty especially to find you and bring you to London. Indeed your carriage awaits you."

"What, now?" Nathan recoiled theatrically, half thinking it was a joke. But no one was smiling.

"If that is not inconvenient," the captain responded with a polite but uncompromising bow.

"I will have to send word to my sloop," Nathan heard himself say as he collected his scattered thoughts. His mother, he was thinking. The report of his presence at her little soiree had finally reached their lordships and he was called to account for consorting with the enemy.

"That will be arranged," the commodore assured him firmly.

"And when shall I expect to return?"

"That is for their lordships to determine. I leave you in the safe hands of Captain Marsh."

Nathan wondered if he was already under arrest.

His gloom deepened with every mile they advanced along the London Road and the weather adjusted to his mood. By the time they reached Maidstone the sky had clouded over and the first drops of rain were spattering against the carriage window. They travelled in silence, a circumstance suspicious in itself, as if Nathan's escort could think of no topic safe enough to discuss with so tainted a companion. The reflections that had so pleased Nathan earlier now returned to torment him as grim parodies of their previous incarnation. His passion for the young woman now appeared foolish fantasy, the jolly tars a pack of rowdy thugs in garish finery, no better than smugglers—in fact considerably worse for at least the smugglers displayed their malice openly. The *Nereus* was a mere brig, one of the smallest sloops in the service, the prize she had taken a piddling little hooker. And besides, now he came to think on it, he had no business taking the vessel in the first place, for it was little better than piracy. He blushed now to think of the self-righteous satisfaction he had felt as he watched the crew scramble into their launch when he might so easily have taken them prisoner for the head money. He remembered the way the skipper, probably the owner, had stood up in the stern and shaken his fist at them with the tears pouring down his face. The *Bonne Jeanne* had doubtless been as beautiful to him as the *Nereus* had to Nathan; more so, for she was his living and he faced an impoverished future without her, a broken old man on the beach . . . The more Nathan thought about it, the more it seemed that his present predicament was a judgement upon him. What business did he have to be making war on civilian mariners, French or otherwise?

Nathan was not a great admirer of Dr. Johnson whose observations he frequently regarded as trite. As a writer of verse who often struggled to find the right word he had cause to resent such remarks as, "A man may write at any time if he will set himself doggedly to it," but he was inclined to agree with the good doctor's assertion that "patriotism was the last refuge of the scoundrel." Nathan had always felt uncomfortable raising his glass with his fellow officers and drinking to "the next war and promotion for us all," as if the mere fact of holding the King's commission justified any atrocity they may take it into their heads to commit. He had sworn loyalty to King George and was not disposed to break his oath; he would do whatever the King or the King's ministers required of him. On the other hand he had no particular regard for either the King or his ministers. He was neither Whig nor Tory and inclined to wish a plague on both their houses. He had felt some admiration for Billy Pitt when he had become chief minister, approving his youth and his zeal for reform, but it had swiftly faded and he shared the contempt of his fellow officers when Pitt appointed his own brother—a soldier—as First Lord of the Admiralty.

And now they were at war with Revolutionary France.

Nathan had been nineteen when the Paris mob stormed the Bastille and began the Revolution. He could not remember what he had thought about it at the time—he had been in the Pacific and when they eventually heard the news, it had appeared so distant he could not regard it as important much less earth-shattering, but he had spent some months in America later that year with his cousins in New York and everyone he met had been most persuasive in its support. It was much the same in England. And not just among poets like Wordsworth but politicians too—even Pitt had spoken cautiously in its favour. Then the Revolution turned ugly and the mood in England turned against it. Nathan's mother and her friends said the situation in France was nothing like as bad as the press reported and the government wanted people to believe. They exaggerated the violence in order to persuade their own people to keep things as they were and not be forever clamouring for change or progress or higher wages. The Tories wished to provoke a war to crush the newfound freedoms in France and stop them spreading to England . . .

Nathan was not normally inclined to agree with his mother's politics. Only a short time ago he had been only too happy to be involved in a war against Revolutionary France and to profit by it. But now . . . Now he felt that if their lordships were to utter one word against his mother, or condemn her for the friends she kept, he would hurl his commission in their faces.

He glanced at the marine officer, dozing in the far corner of the carriage. One word from you, he thought, one sneer of those fastidious lips and I'll split them against your teeth. But the officer remained comatose, his head nodding in rhythm to the jolting of the coach, and after a while Nathan's own eyes began to droop and his chin to fall on his chest and he did not wake until they were on the outskirts of London.

"Peake," said the First Lord of the Admiralty, bringing his nose up from his papers like a fractious rodent disturbed in its hunt for scraps. He blinked at Nathan from across his desk as if he was trying to remember who the devil he was and what he was doing here.

It was dark outside and raining still. Dark inside, too, for the most part, it being late evening and the Admiralty apparently deserted, save for the hall porter who had let them in and the cleaning lady they encountered on the stair. And of course the First Lord scratching at the papers on his desk. (Though it was entirely possible, Nathan considered, that the same officers still waited behind the closed door of the waiting room in hopes of a commission or command while the cleaning lady came in from time to time to flap at them with her feather duster.)

He had not met Chatham before. Nor had he expected to meet him now. An interview with the First Lord was rare, even for a post captain; it only happened, Nathan had been led to believe, if you were up for a particularly important command or an important mission, neither of which appeared likely in his case. He suspected that a serious complaint had been made against him and that out of respect for his father Chatham had decided to meet him face to face before passing sentence.

The door closed behind him and Nathan realised that they had been left alone. He began to think he was not considered dangerous. He looked about him and tried to relax. There was a haze in the air from the small fire in the grate and the seven or eight candles, two of which were smoking furiously. Portraits of the First Lord's predecessors peered down from the walls through a veil of smoke and varnish. Most of them were admirals, one or two civilians, but none of them, as far as Nathan was aware, had been a soldier—as Chatham had, before his brother made him head of the King's Navy. A flurry of rain spattered on the window and the frame shook a little.

"Peake," Chatham repeated, thoughtfully. His eyes darted down to his papers again and he ferreted among them for a moment until he unearthed a letter. He frowned as he waved Nathan to a chair. "Admiral Gardner speaks highly of you," he said in a tone of surprise.

Nathan contrived an expression of polite interest but his blood quickened. Admiral Gardner was a lord of the Admiralty, an inferior one to Chatham, but a serving officer and a former shipmate of Nathan's father.

"He tells me you speak French like a native."

"I would not say that, my lord," Nathan objected cautiously.

A look. Not pleasant. The features jaundiced in the candlelight. Chatham had the wary eyes of a man who knew he was not greatly liked or respected and that most of his colleagues considered he would not have risen above the rank of major if his father had not been the greatest man of the age and his brother the King's chief minister.

"What *would* you say? Can you speak it or not?"

"I can make myself understood, my lord. I sometimes have difficulty understanding—if they speak too fast."

Why were they talking about his French? Was he to have a job as interpreter?

"And your mother is American?"

Ah. Here it was.

"She was born in New York, my lord, when it was an English colony."

But perhaps it was a mistake to remind Chatham of its current status. The loss of the American colonies still caused apoplexy at certain levels of society and was widely blamed for driving the King mad. One did not mention "the former colonies" in his presence for fear of another seizure and perhaps it was the same with Chatham whose father, too, had succumbed to an affliction of the brain in his later years.

"And she has lived in London for many years," he continued lamely.

"Yes. So I have heard."

Not good. Not good at all. Nathan felt the blood rush to his face as he prepared his defence, or a swift, savage attack before he was sunk.

"And your father, is he well?"

"Very well thank you, my lord."

"He farms, I believe, in Sussex."

"He does, my lord. It gives him an interest. After the sea."

Nathan felt on surer ground here but Chatham's nose was in his papers again.

"And you have been having some adventures with smugglers on the south coast."

As if they were a game devised for the amusement of junior officers.

"We have been called upon to act in support of the Revenue officers on occasion, my lord."

"Quite so. And on one such you were fired upon by the French—before hostilities were declared."

Clearly the report had found its way to the First Lord's desk, if not the cannonball.

"Yes, my lord. We were swept in by the tide but managed to beat out again."

"You are well acquainted with the French coast at that point?"

"I have learned to know it better since, my lord." He smiled to indicate he meant this humorously but the rheumy eyes regarded him coldly across the beak of a nose.

"I have it in my mind to send you back there."

"To the Somme, my lord?"

"To Le Havre."

Nathan's face doubtless reflected his incomprehension.

"To be blunt," said Chatham, "we would like you to land a certain cargo."

A short silence broken only by the rain on the window and the guttering candles.

"A cargo, my lord?"

"To a certain party in Le Havre."

Nathan nodded slowly as if this made perfect sense, to take a King's ship into a French port at time of war and land a cargo.

"In *Nereus?*"

Chatham regarded him thoughtfully as if some doubt had arisen in his mind.

"I do not believe that is to be contemplated," he said, "unless you wish to give the French a second chance to maul you. No, you will assume command of an American vessel presently berthed at Bristol and sail it to Le Havre under an American flag where you will deliver its cargo to an American gentleman currently in residence there."

"An American vessel," Nathan repeated with a nod that implied understanding though this in fact was still far from being the case. The British blockade applied to American ships as to any other. Any vessel attempting to run that blockade was liable to be seized by a British cruiser—whatever flag she was flying.

"Quite." The First Lord was consulting his papers again. "The *Speedwell* of Salem. Two-hundred-ton barque. Taken by a British cruiser off La Rochelle and fetched into Bristol as a prize. She is now owned by the Admiralty but she has been issued with papers in the name of the gentleman in Le Havre. In a few days it is our intent that she will resume her voyage with a new cargo and a new captain."

He looked up and met Nathan's eye.

"It is an unusual commission," he conceded. "Should you decline it you may return to *Nereus* without blemish to character or career. You will forget this conversation. It will not have occurred. I know I may rely upon your absolute discretion in this." His frown warned of the consequences should this reliance prove to be misplaced. "However, if you accept, you will be doing your sovereign and your country a considerable service—and that will *not* be forgotten."

Nathan bowed his head politely but he felt his heart pounding with something very like exultation. Clearly the prospect of advancement was of far more importance to him than he had been prepared to acknowledge. But his mind seethed with questions.

"And the *Nereus*, my lord?"

"Will be under temporary command until your return."

"And my officers?" The frown had returned but Nathan persisted. "I beg you, allow me at least one, my lord. If only to keep a proper watch."

"You may take one officer," Chatham conceded, "and a servant. But you must understand that the slightest indiscretion would not only jeopardise your mission but almost certainly cost you your life."

Presumably he meant at the hands of the French though this was not something one could be sure of.

"And when would I . . . ?"

"You would travel to Bristol tonight with Captain Marsh. You may send to your servant for whatever you require from the *Nereus.*" A slight pause. "I take it from these questions that you accept the commission."

Nathan inclined his head in a polite bow. "Of course, my lord."

But he could not prevent his face from relaxing into a wide grin. "Thank you, my lord. You will not regret it."

Chatham arched his brow in indignant surprise. "I sincerely hope I will not," he said, and stuck his long nose back into his papers.

Nathan was halfway down the stairs when it occurred to him that transferring his command from a 16-gun sloop of war to an American blockade runner might not, outside the confines of Bedlam, be regarded as a promotion. And that sailing the vessel into Le Havre at a time of war—for all the service it might do King George—might well end in his own bloody execution.

CHAPTER 6

the Secret Cargo

HE WAS AWAKE IN AN INSTANT, out of a deep sleep, staring into the dark, wondering where he was and why.

For weeks now he had slept in a dockside tavern. He was familiar with all its smells and sounds: the creaking stairs and the banging shutters, the puttering snores of the landlord and his lady and the more carnal sounds of his fellow guests. He was inured to the crooning of cats and the hectoring of whores; even the raving drunks seldom woke him.

This was not the tavern.

For a moment he imagined he was back on *Nereus* . . . But it was too quiet. On *Nereus* at any time of day or night there would be half a hundred men on deck and as many below. If you did not hear them you would smell them, that packed mass of humanity, and if you did not smell them you could sense them in other ways, like a great breathing animal in the dark.

But of course this was not the *Nereus*. This was the *Speedwell* of Salem. He pronounced it in his head, deliberately, to assure himself he was not dreaming or deluded.

The *Speedwell* of Salem.

It had an ominous ring, as if she had been waiting for him all these years, a raddled corpse rising from the sea—or his own past.

His mother had told him the story of her great-grandmother Sarah Good who had been hanged as a witch in Salem. One of nineteen falsely accused by children who had known no better and wrongly convicted by magistrates who should have. But Nathan had been a child himself when he heard the story and the old witch, innocent or guilty, had come to him in his dreams night after night and scared the wits out of him. He would see her flying across the moon on her broomstick or twisting on the gallows with her face black and her tongue hanging and her eyes staring. And he would wake as he had now, staring into the dark with the fear of death upon him.

He had even been to Salem once. His American cousins had taken him there—to the bustling seaport and to the quiet village of the same name that was properly called Danvers or Old Salem. They had shown him the courtroom and the place where the gallows had stood. And the graves.

Nathan shook his head clear of the memory. He should have no fear of it now and yet ... The *Speedwell* of Salem. Such a portentous ring and the figure at her bow very like a witch, flying on her broomstick ...

He drew the smell of her into his lungs. The usual smell of any vessel long at sea, of hemp and tar and timber and bilge water; and a sweet stench of corruption that could be dead rat or the meat for tomorrow's dinner, a hint of lye ...

But no brimstone.

And no tobacco, either.

Their cargo had arrived two days ago, weeks after Chatham had said it would, by river barge from Gloucester, escorted by Captain Marsh and four of his men. Tobacco. Best Virginia. In five hundred wooden chests.

Nathan wondered.

Was it normal to ship tobacco in chests, padlocked and bound with rope? Was it not usual to ship tobacco in hessian bales? Tully said that it was sometimes packed in crates to avoid becoming too damp or too dry, adding with a straight face that smugglers always packed

it in crates or half kegs to make it easy to carry. They had hauled the
chests up by the yardarm tackles, out of the barges and into the hold,
with Captain Marsh counting them in like a tally clerk and insisting
Nathan sign for them personally. Nathan had shrugged and signed,
wondering if he was signing his own death warrant, for he had no
doubt that it was contraband and he was now a smuggler, according
to the law. The gamekeeper turned poacher. But on whose behalf?

If you are apprehended, the First Lord had assured him, we will be
obliged to disown you.

No surprise there.

He had long suspected he was born to hang, like his unfortunate
ancestor, the witch of Salem.

He could not sleep.

He swung out of his cot, pulled on his clothes, and went up on deck.

It was a cool night for midsummer. Midsummer's Eve. He gazed
down the length of the deck. One hundred and twenty feet from
stern to stem. About the same size as the *Nereus* and built for
speed. But lacking the status of a King's ship—and the complement.
Nathan's command had been reduced from 105 officers and crew to
just 18. And a disreputable crew at that, little better than smugglers
if he was any judge of character.

A dark figure detached itself from the starboard rail and approached him, touching his cap. Tully. The one officer Nathan had
been permitted and he had chosen Tully. Why? His smuggling background or something else? An element of reliance, a sense of their
both being outsiders?

"Where is the watch?" Nathan asked him, his voice a little sharper
than he intended.

"There are two men forward," Tully replied, looking a little embarrassed. "An anchor watch, only."

Nathan looked forward and saw the huddled shapes below the
belfry in the bow, almost certainly asleep. Some things would have
to change when they were at sea—but not until. Half her crew had
done a runner or been pressed into the Royal Navy before Nathan

had joined her and he did not want to lose the rest. Tully had gone scavenging along the Bristol waterfront and brought him six more hands, all American. They were reliable, he said, as near as he could judge. And so they should be, on the pay they were getting and the promise of a bonus when their cargo was safely delivered.

Nathan walked to the rail. Still no wind. He looked up through the rigging. No stars. A hint of rain or mist in the air. He felt it tingling on his face and the backs of his hands and knew it for what it was: not rain or mist but dew. The rail was soaked with it.

He gazed out over the crowded anchorage. Upwards of a hundred vessels waiting for a wind to take them down the Bristol Channel and out into the open sea, their lights glinting on the oily water. The tide was on the ebb. Where it moved through the lights it seemed to be rushing like a mill race. An illusion. The ship's gig barely bobbed at the side, knocking gently on the hull, the water chuckling under her bow.

A faint movement in the air, scarcely a breeze and yet . . . He turned his head and felt it on his cheek, saw it move the rigging. The American flag, the Stars and Stripes, at their stern stirred and flapped. A breeze—and from the northeast. If it held it would take them out into the Bristol Channel and away.

One of their neighbours was moving. Nathan heard the commands across the water as she got underway, saw the lights at masthead and stern drifting slowly across the surface, the outline of her sails against the harbour lights. Lugsails. He remembered the lugger *Fortune* that had started it all. Or so it seemed to him now. For it was that incident at the mouth of the Somme that had surely brought him to the attentions of their lordships. And now here he was a smuggler himself, taking five hundred chests of Best Virginia to a mysterious American in Le Havre and a bundle of dispatches in a sealed oilskin bag marked for the attention of the American Minister in Paris.

Why?

Nathan knew the American Minister in Paris. Or at least knew of him. His name was Morris. Gouverneur Morris. A French Huguenot

name. The family had fled France at the time of Louis XIV like
many French Protestants, like his own mother's in fact. They owned
land on the Harlem River but their real business was banking.
Most of them had stayed loyal to King George during the war but
not Gouverneur who had been a secretary to General Washington.
Nathan had met his brother once in New York. He, too, had backed
the rebellion. It was said the family had backed both sides so that,
whoever won, they should not lose by it.

It was entirely possible, of course, that there was nothing in the bag,
or nothing important; that it was meant to provide cover, a form of
diplomatic protection so no one would go rooting among the chests.

So what was in the chests?

He crossed the deck to the small inspection hatch leading down into
the hold and pulled aside the tarpaulin. Tully was there at once with a
light and a wooden mallet to knock away the clamps. Nathan thanked
him but took the lantern and climbed down the ladder alone.

It was a tight fit. They had left about two feet of space at the end
of the hold, jammed with baulks of timber to stop the cargo from
shifting. Nathan had barely enough room to lift the light. The chests
rose above his head, each about the size of a tea chest: four feet high
and two feet wide and two feet deep. He chose three at random and
rapped on the sides. They all sounded the same and told him nothing
except that they weren't empty. He put his nose to them; he even put
his ear to them. He took out his pocket knife and inserted the blade
between two lathes of wood and tried to slide it along. He could just
about move it but there was something there, an obstruction, something not quite solid but solid enough. He pulled it out and smelled
it. Tobacco. Might even be Best Virginia; he was no smoker.

Should he be relieved?

But why were they shipping tobacco at time of war to an American
shipping agent in Le Havre? Was it intended for the American
Minister in Paris? A bribe for services rendered? Or a means of bribing others?

And what services?

It was quite possible that Morris had been left as chargé d'affaires by the British. But if so it was a secret arrangement. Certainly not something Nathan had read about in the newspapers.

He could speculate all night and every night and still not get to the bottom of it. And nor was he meant to.

He climbed the ladder to the deck. The breeze had freshened. Another vessel was moving out of the anchorage. Nathan looked up at the sky to the east. Another hour and it would be dawn.

"Rouse the crew," he told Tully. "I believe we will make sail."

CHAPTER 7

the Chase

THE *SPEEDWELL* OF SALEM CLOSE-HAULED IN the chops of the Channel, ten miles off the Lizard; a fine summer's day with the wind holding steady from the northeast and Nathan fifty feet above the deck with one arm hooked through the shrouds and the glass to his eye. What he could see was not at all to his liking.

A ship of war—a brig very like the *Nereus*, was running before them at a distance of about three miles and on a course that would bring them up with her, Nathan reckoned, within the hour. He steadied the glass as best he could and searched for clues to her identity. She was flying the ensign from her stern but she was still too far off to see her pennant. He could see her gun ports though—eight of them ranged along her starboard side. To all appearances she was a King's ship but an instinct bred from ten years at sea and in a trade that had honed the art of deceit to perfection persuaded Nathan that she was making game of His Majesty's commission.

There were grounds for this suspicion.

He would have expected her to come running down on them the moment they were sighted. Even if they had seen her flag the Navy was greedy for crew and had no respect for neutrals, especially not Americans; they'd have taken at least half his topmen on the spurious grounds that they had been born subject to King George and were liable for impressment.

And then there was the set of her sails. She was close-hauled like the *Speedwell* but sailing a little *too* close and her sails kept feathering, slowing her down. If this was sheer carelessness it was not what he would expect of a Navy crew, and if it was not, then they were deliberately spilling the wind to let the *Speedwell* catch up with them. But why? They had the weather gage; it would be easy enough for them to come round and they could be down on him in no time ... Unless they were afraid he would run and did not wish to put themselves to the trouble of a chase.

He chewed his bottom lip while he considered his options. If she *was* a King's ship and planned to board him, he had papers to prove he was Southampton bound with dispatches for the American Minister in London and if they tried to press his crew he could show them his Admiralty protection. A King's ship did not worry him. What worried him was that she might be a privateer—and a French one at that.

The region was infested with the breed, many of them little better than pirates, licensed by letter of marque to sweep the seas of enemy shipping. Nathan had papers to show the French, too, if the need arose; papers that stated he was bound for Le Havre and carrying dispatches for the American Minister in Paris. But privateer captains were infamously poor readers. They'd take what prize they could, whatever papers her captain had in his possession, and leave it to the whims of fate and the courts to determine whether or not he was trading with the enemy. Nathan would not risk being seized by a Frenchman and sailed into the nearest French port to take his chances with a corrupt magistracy.

He fixed his glass on her again. They had closed noticeably since the last time he looked. He could see the guns bowsed up against the gun ports: 6-pounders, the same as *Nereus*, and a pair in the bows that he could not see properly but looked as if they might be of a greater calibre. He focused on the small cluster of figures at the stern.

Unlike Nathan in his reefer jacket and Breton fisherman's knit, they looked like men who held the King's commission. He could see their bicorn hats and their blue coats, entirely in keeping with what you might expect of officers in His Britannic Majesty's Navy except . . .

And then he knew. And was sliding down the weather backstay to the deck before his mind had put the thought into words. No King's ship of that size would be without her contingent of marines— *Nereus* had seventeen—yet he could not see a single red coat on deck.

Tully was waiting for him at the helm with an inquiring eye.

"If she is a King's ship," said Nathan, "then I am the Bishop of Rome."

The captain's pretensions to the papacy had been exposed too often for Tully to speak in support of them now. Nathan glanced up at the sails and the barque's blue pennant streaming out to the southwest. If they were to run that must be the course they took for they had no hope of slipping past her, not without exposing themselves to her broadside.

"Bring her round to sou'-sou'-west," he instructed the helmsman, adding for Tully's benefit, "We'll run for Ushant and see how far he will chase us."

Tully let out his first great bellow of "Hands to the braces" and Nathan left him to it while he crossed to the weather side with his glass. If she was French and the *Speedwell* ran for France it was possible she would let them go and wait for the next ship bound for England. But as soon as Nathan steadied the glass that little hope was dashed. Her deck and shrouds were swarming with men and within a minute they were bringing her round. Nathan took his eye from the glass and watched his own crew anxiously as they manned the braces. Tully had them well drilled but they were so few compared to the crew of a ship of war. His only hope was to keep the wind on his quarter and keep manoeuvres down to the minimum. The yards finally came round and he felt her instant response. If the wind held they might have the legs of her.

His head was full of calculations . . . The tide on the ebb, four hours before it began to turn . . . He looked back across the stern

rail towards their pursuer. By God, she was close; there was hardly
a mile in it. He could see details with his naked eye he had barely
seen through the glass before—among them the two black ports
for her bow chasers. She would hardly run them out at this range,
though, unless they were bigger guns than he thought.

Tully was at his side. Was that the hint of a smile?

"Cook says dinner is ready," he said.

Dinner? He only just stopped himself from repeating it in his incredulity. He glanced up at the sun which was where it should be at
noon on a summer's day and then once more at the brig which was
closer than he would have liked but no longer gaining. Dinner. Why
not? It would reassure the crew. They might even think he knew what
he was about.

They sent the starboard watch off first. Nathan could not bear to
leave the deck even for an instant and if he would not go, nor would
Tully. He regretted this and not only for Tully's sake. He was quite
hungry though he was accustomed to dine an hour later than the
men on *Nereus*.

And right on cue here was his steward, Gabriel, with a tray followed by a small boy carrying a stand to put it on—and a chair. And
a dish under a cover.

"What have we here?" Nathan inquired, as Gabriel set the dish on
the tray and lifted the cover.

What he had was a large chop from the pig they had killed yesterday, rather overdone by the look of it, with a mush of peas on a tin
plate and a jug of ale to wash it down, which it looked like it needed.
The cook was a man called Small—possibly a nickname—and he did
not aspire to greatness. Nathan suggested to Gabriel that he might be
good enough to bring Mr. Tully his dinner, too, and though the mate
demurred it was done. He saw smiles from the watch still on deck
which was better than scowls and murmurings.

Inevitably the crew called his steward the Angel Gabriel though
had they known what Nathan knew about him they might have
considered it blasphemous—or ironic. He had been among the jail

sweepings taken aboard his father's old *Ajax* in the American War
and had been trained up as a steward from God knows what whim:
perhaps because he had the aspirations of a gentleman—he claimed
to have been a highwayman—but more likely because he was useless
at anything else aboard ship. He was certainly a novelty to the crew
of the *Speedwell*. They were clearly not used to captains with their
own personal servants. But as far as they were concerned, Nathan
was their new owner, an American by the name of Turner, born and
raised in New York but based in London, the better to make a fortune from the war. He had told them when they were well out into
the Bristol Channel that they were bound for Le Havre and would
draw a year's pay upon arrival—but any who wished would be put
ashore at St. Ives. Thankfully, there had been no takers, for they
would have been difficult to replace. They were blockade runners
when they left Boston—possibly smugglers too in the West Indies
trade, Tully said—so it was business as usual for them.

"Your health, Mr. Tully," said Nathan, raising his jug. He was beginning to enjoy himself though he had to keep a tight hold on the tray
and he could not prevent sneaking a glance every minute or so back
at the brig. He saw the boy was doing it too, perhaps more often.
Francis Coyle, cabin boy. Twelve years old, though he looked younger,
taken on in Boston for his first voyage. Why, in God's name—at a
time of war when they must have known the risks they were taking? But Tully said he was a by-blow of the mate, who had since ab-
sconded or been pressed into the Navy. The crew all had stories of
why they were here and where they had come from and most of them
would be lies; it was best not to ask, said Tully.

"Have you eaten yourself?" Nathan asked the boy.

"Yes, sir. Thank you, sir."

Nathan doubted it but did not pursue the inquiry. He had been
much the same age when he first went to sea and always hungry but
he had not seen action then. Nor since, unless you counted the incident off the Somme.

He half turned to look back towards the brig—and by God she

had run out her bow chasers . . . He leapt up and took another look through his glass. They were 6-pounders—a long shot at this range, an impossible shot, he told himself. He swept her decks with the glass and saw that they had hauled in her false colours and broken out the tricolour at her stern, not that he needed the glass to see that. It billowed out to leeward as big as a sail: the new flag of republican France, America's friend and protector, though the French ports were filled with American merchantmen taken as prizes. He was still looking at her when she fired—the two guns in the same second, two spumes of flame through the smoke and an instant later the double report carried across the water. Nathan observed the twin spouts falling close together, a cable's length astern. He put down his chop, wiped his fingers fastidiously on his napkin, and pulled out his watch to consult the time. He saw the boy looking up at him, he rather hoped in admiration but it was no pose. He wanted to know how long it took them to load.

The hands were tumbling up from below, either having finished their dinner or having no appetite for it.

"Send down the larboard watch for their dinner." Nathan saw the look in Tully's eye and shared his doubts but now he had issued the order he did not care to rescind it. He crossed to the stern rail to observe the brig. Was she gaining? Perhaps a little. He measured the angle of the braces. Perhaps if they clewed up the mainsail on the weather side and veered a point or so off the wind . . .

"I am going to see what I can do with the stern chaser," he told Tully.

The *Speedwell* carried a broadside of six 4-pounders—pop-guns that any ship of war would have despised—but she had a sting in her tail: a long 6-pounder that Nathan had bought himself and had fitted in Bristol, moving the ship's wheel forward a few feet to allow for the recoil. It was one of the new Blomefield pattern made by Samuel Walker and Company, with a loop at the top of the button for the breech rope which made it much easier to fire at an angle. Nathan had indulged in several hours' target practice during the long haul down the Bristol Channel and picked five men for a gun crew.

Though they would never compete with the crew of the *Nereus* when it came to speed he was satisfied they were competent to load and fire her. Now they came aft to his summons, tying their handkerchiefs round their ears and grinning at their shipmates whose encouragement sounded to Nathan disturbingly close to jeers.

He already had his hand on the breech, gazing out across the stern towards their pursuer and estimating the distance. One 6-pounder against two was much shorter odds than their respective broadsides and they might not fancy the duel. Not with the seas full of British warships that might snap them up if they suffered even a minor wound to their rigging.

He caught the eye of Solomon Pratt, the man he had designated gunner. Nathan strongly suspected he was a deserter from the British Navy and long practised at his trade. Even in the short time they had sailed together a certain rivalry had emerged between them as far as the gun was concerned and to Nathan's secret regret, it had become known to the crew as Pratt's Prick.

"Cast loose your gun," he ordered, ignoring the insolent way the gunner was shaking his head and pursing his lips at the range.

A squealing of iron trucks as they rolled the gun back from the port and held it on the side tackles.

"Open the port."

The powder boy, a man of at least forty called Joseph Gurney, brought up the cartridge, and the rammer took the tompion from the muzzle and rammed the cloth bag hard down into the bore.

The gunner fished for it with his priming wire through the vent.

"Home," he cried.

"Shot your gun," ordered Nathan.

The rammer rammed down a 6-pound ball and the wad on top of it.

"Run out your gun."

They heaved on the side tackles and ran the carriage hard up against the rail.

"Maximum elevation," Nathan instructed Pratt, moving aside as the rammer heaved up the breech with his handspike and the gunner hammered in the wedge to bring the muzzle up ten or eleven degrees, which was all the port would allow.

"Prime."

The gunner thrust the priming iron down the touch hole to pierce the cloth bag and then poured fine powder from his powder horn into the quill. He did this with a certain air of disdain, for Nathan had recently acquired flintlocks for the guns and Pratt, a conservative to his soul, was firmly attached to the slow match and the tub, which he considered more reliable, even if it frequently blew out.

You can always light her again, he had informed Nathan, whereas if your flint don't work . . .

You replace it with another, Nathan had instructed him firmly. He was glad enough to have a Navy man for a gunner but he would take no instruction from a deserter.

"Point your gun," he said now.

They heaved and grunted until the gunner was happy or as close to it as he ever would be at this range. He nodded to Nathan and stood to one side of the carriage, crouching down to stare fixedly out of the port with his hand on the lanyard.

Nathan felt the deck under his feet. He felt the bows rise and then begin to fall; he felt the sea rising towards the stern and the stern with it . . .

"Fire!"

The gunner jerked the lanyard and the flint came down with a flash and on the instant the charge exploded.

A thin jet of fire leapt from the touch hole and a much greater blast of flame and smoke from the muzzle; the carriage leapt back eight feet and Nathan and the gunner almost cracked heads as they leapt in to watch the fall of the shot through the port.

A brief white plume about a cable's length short of the bows. A pause. And then a smaller splash, and another as the ball skipped across the choppy sea and sank, almost in line with the bowsprit and a few yards to windward.

A moment later the bow chasers replied—with a few seconds now between each—both balls still falling well short of the *Speedwell's* stern and far to starboard. Nathan dragged out his watch. Almost four minutes since the first shot. Not good. Encouragingly bad, in fact. But then they might have been waiting for the range to close.

Out of the corner of his eye he saw young Coyle standing over by the rail, watching eagerly. What was he to do with him? He could order him below, of course, but he would be hurt and humiliated. A demon voice proposed that hurt and humiliation were the lot of small boys and reminded him of his own sufferings in that regard but demons, like gunners, should know their place.

"You, boy, up to the top with you," he said, "and watch the fall of the shot. Sharp now, for we are counting on your report."

He turned back to the gun, ready swabbed and loaded, and ran her out for the next shot.

"Prime..."

And so it went on, the slow running battle in the chops of the Channel to the fiendish music of the wind and the gun—the squealing of the iron truck wheels and the whining of the breeching, the creaking complaints of the ropes and every few minutes a loud bang ... And the crew toiling in silence save for Nathan and the gunner and the boy in the maintop marking the fall of the shot.

"A half cable short . . . A few feet to leeward."

And then, dancing with delight, "A hit! A hit!" Capering like a lunatic so that Nathan feared he would jump straight down the lubber's hole and come crashing onto the deck and all for a small ragged gap in the brig's fore course that would not slow her in the least.

Then a shot from the brig skipped up from the waves and struck a great splinter off the rail a few feet from where Nathan was standing and it shook him for a moment, the force of it and the thought of what it would do to flesh and bone, and he had to force himself to put it out of his mind and concentrate on the slow, methodical firing of the gun.

They hit her again: another small hole in her canvas and still she came on, closer now, as if they were joined by a long line and it was slowly being hauled in. Twenty minutes Nathan reckoned, a half hour at most, and she would veer into the wind and give them her broadside. He looked to the sun but it seemed suspended in the sky, a lingering, indifferent spectator to their deadly sport.

Barely a thousand yards between them now and the next shot came in with a howling and a shrieking that had Nathan looking to the boy in the top for they were firing chain to cut up the rigging. A prayer half formed in his head but what fair-minded god would heed a prayer for the boy and not for the Frenchmen they were trying to kill.

"I will lay the next shot myself," he told the gunner, stepping up to the breech. The last two shots had gone high and wide and he had them draw out the quoin an inch or so to bring down the muzzle by two degrees. He checked the flint in the lock—for it would have given Solomon great pleasure to see it misfire—and sprinkled the fine priming powder from the horn, took hold of the lanyard, waited for the bows to rise and fall, felt for the sea rushing under the hull, sensed the exact moment when it would lift the stern and then . . .

It was wonderful how the jerking of a thin cord should make such a riot of sound and fury, such a rumpus of iron and fire and smoke, and three hundredweight of gun carriage hurtling past within an inch of his foot to be brought up with a great screeching of tackle . . .

"A hit, a hit!" The boy was dancing again. "Oh, sir, you hit the gun, you hit the gun!"

Nathan leapt to the ratlines and clapped the telescope to his eye. As the smoke cleared and the hair blew from his face he saw the mayhem in her bows. The shot had struck the muzzle of the starboard bow chaser and thrown it back off its carriage, smashing through the port and doubtless making a terrible slaughter of her crew.

"She's coming round," the boy cried, but Nathan had already seen the flash of white along her side and the guns run out and he gave a great shout of, "Down! Get down!" an instant before she raked them. A banshee howling and screaming of chain, a splintering tearing of wood and canvas like a high wind in a forest and he knew it was all over for the boy but when he looked up he was still there, gazing about him with a shocked and indignant air and the rigging in ruins all about him.

Nathan yelled a stream of orders that had half the crew swarming aloft to save what was left of the mainsail which was flapping wildly to leeward and the maintop yard, hanging by a thread. He looked back at the brig, expecting her to resume the chase but astonishingly she was completing the turn, showing him her stern as she came up into the wind. Running, for God's sake. The broadside had been her parting shot, a vengeful kick of the heels before she bolted—from one lucky shot that had unshipped a single gun. He could not believe her captain could be so shy.

And nor was he.

"Sail ho! Two points off the starboard bow," came the frantic cry from the foretop. And Nathan jerked his head round and felt his heart leap to his throat as he saw the massive ship bearing down on them with her great spread of canvas and the long double row of guns thrust out from the ports along her black and yellow hull.

CHAPTER 8

the Billy Ruffian

THE BELLEROPHON, 74, WAS ONE OF the fastest ships in the British fleet, named after the hero of Greek mythology who tamed the winged horse Pegasus and attempted to ride him to Heaven only to be thwarted by the great god Zeus who sent a gadfly to sting the beast and unseat the rider. But it was a different story that sprang to Nathan's mind as he presented himself in the captain's cabin with the sealed envelope prepared for him at the Admiralty for just such an occasion.

The unlucky hero had suffered another calamity when sent to the King of Lycia with a sealed letter falsely accusing him of sleeping with the King's daughter. In later years a Letter of Bellerophon had become a euphemism for a document that was prejudicial to the bearer and while Nathan did not imagine the First Lord of the Admiralty had written anything quite so malicious he did wonder why he had not been permitted to read it before it was placed in the envelope and fixed with the distinctive black seal.

He saw how the captain's eyes flickered briefly over the words written on the single sheet of parchment, flashed sharply across his desk to Nathan, and then applied themselves to more sustained study. Then he folded the document and carefully replaced it in the envelope.

"Weel, weel, weel," he said, regarding Nathan with a speculative frown. Bellerophon being a difficult word in the English tongue, or at least that spoken by the majority of her crew, she was known by them—and to a significant proportion of the fleet—as the *Billy Ruffian* but the name might be equally applied to her captain, Nathan considered: a genial bruiser in his fifties with a large freckled face and large freckled hands and quite possibly a large freckled head beneath the powdered curls of his unfashionably large wig. Thomas Pasley was a Scot—quite probably he had never been mistaken for anything less—a Lowland Scot with the rash, roguish air of a certain style of Highland gentleman. Nathan knew him by repute but they had not previously met, a circumstance that must be counted fortunate if Nathan was to maintain his character as a New York merchant and captain by the name of Turner.

"I am required and requested to give you every assistance in going about your business, lawful or otherwise," declared the captain, with an arch look, "a duty which I believe I have to some extent fulfilled in seeing off yonder Frenchman who I doubt was as eager to be of service."

Nathan agreed he had been under the same impression and expressed his appreciation, once more, for the *Bellerophon's* timely arrival.

"Aye," growled his champion, "that's as may be. Doubtless you would also appreciate some assistance in mending the mess he has made of your rigging."

He dismissed Nathan's protests to the contrary and summoned a servant to convey his instruction to the first lieutenant and to bring a bottle of brandy on his return.

"For I believe the gentleman has time to take a glass with me?" Raising his sandy eyebrows at Nathan in a manner that brooked no dissent.

The glass was succeeded by another, and then another, in the course of which Captain Pasley became more genial and revealed an unexpected warmth for Nathan's supposed countrymen.

"A great people," he declared, "and a great nation in the making, though 'tis a pity it were so painful a birth."

Pasley had fought in the American War but with deep regret, he assured Nathan, at the rift that had led first to the rebellion and then to the loss of the American colonies, both of which might have been prevented, "Had the parcel of toadies about the King had as much sense between them as a soused herring."

The captain, Nathan gathered, was a dyed-in-the-wool Whig and while he had not gone so far as those of his persuasion who had rejoiced in the American victories over the King's Army he could obtain no satisfaction in suppressing the liberties of those he considered his fellow countrymen.

And so they raised their glasses in successive toasts to President George and King George. "God bless his addled wits," added the captain in an aside that would doubtless be considered disrespectful if not treasonable in some quarters. The *Bellerophon* had been detached from blockade duty with the fleet off Brest to serve as guard ship to the royal family during their present visit to Weymouth, he disclosed, the King having developed a fondness for sea bathing and his ministers being fearful that the French, hearing of this whimsy, might send a raiding party to carry him off.

"Doubtless towing his bathing machine behind them," the captain concluded with a smirk.

They agreed that the Ministry's folly was the *Speedwell's* good fortune and drank to that. Then to the port of Salem, which Pasley had visited once during the French and Indian War and been welcomed heartily.

The captain had by now become quite hearty himself and when Nathan apologised for the delay he had occasioned, Pasley observed that he might repent of it by offering up half a dozen of his topmen as volunteers in the King's service, for he had no doubt that the buggers were deserters in the first place.

He laughed jovially at Nathan's confusion and apologised himself for the "joke."

Aye, thought Nathan, as he joined in the laughter, and how much of a joke would it have been had he not carried the Admiralty's protection?

"We will be off Weymouth sooner than any French raiding party, I dare say," Pasley declared, "and His Majesty may take his bathe with an easy mind, if that is not impertinent in me. You were running for Ushant, I take it?"

"Only to keep the wind on my quarter," Nathan confided. "I did not expect to sail so far."

"No." The captain appeared thoughtful. "You are acquainted with the English Channel?"

"Not as well as I would wish," Nathan replied cautiously, in his character as Captain Turner of New York or Salem or wherever it was he was supposed to hail from; he had begun to forget.

"Well, 'tis wider than you might think. Thirty-five leagues from Ushant to Scilly," he informed Nathan with a twinkle in his eye that should have warned him what was coming next. "D'ye ken the verse?"

To Nathan's frank alarm he let out a long groan which proved the prelude to song: "Ohhhhhhhh . . ."

> We'll rant and we'll roar like true British sailors,
> We'll rant and we'll roar across the salt seas . . .

—banging his feet in what he supposed to be the rhythm—

> Until we strike soundings in the channel of old England,
> From Ushant to Scilly is thirty-five leagues.

A tentative knock on the door brought timely relief. The repairs to Nathan's vessel were completed, reported the captain's servant, with a wary look at them both, and he was free to resume his voyage.

"Do you take care of yourself, now," said the captain in a low voice as he saw Nathan into the gig, "and do not be consorting with the enemy any more than you can help."

Nathan's return to the *Speedwell* was greeted with grins and cheers from the crew, many of whom had doubtless anticipated their prompt transfer into the service of King George.

"Silence there," roared Tully but even he struggled to keep a straight face as he inquired of Nathan what course they should set.

"Whatever will take us directly to Le Havre," Nathan instructed him, forming his words with care, "and let us trust there will be no more diversions."

In the privacy of his cabin he took out the letter that Pasley had returned to him. The black Admiralty seal had clearly been broken and resealed by the captain of the *Bellerophon* with a blob of red wax. After a moment's hesitation Nathan slid his dirk under it and lifted it away from the envelope.

The letter was, as he had anticipated, embossed with the familiar fouled anchor of the Admiralty and bore the signature of the First Lord. But the content was surprising. It instructed "whomsoever it concerns" that "the bearer of this letter, Captain Nathan Peake, is an American national proceeding with dispatches to the American Minister in Paris" and that "the said Captain Peake is to be permitted to continue his voyage without let or hindrance and to be given such assistance as may be required."

On the surface there was little to trouble "the bearer of this letter" but Nathan could not help but brood a little over the use of his real name and the description of him as "an American national." Why not the agreed nom-de-guerre of Turner? Possibly the First Lord feared he might be accosted by an officer who knew him, but in that case why state that he was an American? If the letter was meant only for the eyes of a British officer why not state that Nathan, too, was British?

It was not inconceivable that Nathan's parentage made him over-sensitive on this subject but he could not help but feel that the First Lord wished him to be known as an American, and not only to the French.

But why?

Could it be that if anything went wrong with his mission—if he was, for instance, revealed to be carrying contraband—then he could be exposed as an American acting in American interests, or even his own?

He shook his head. He could not fathom it, not with his wits befuddled by Pasley's cognac, and he doubted if it would be much clearer to him if he were sober. But one thing was certain: he had become the puppet of politicians and whatever knavery they were up to, he very much doubted if it would be to his advantage. He put the letter back in the envelope, resealed it as best he could, and replaced it in the secret compartment of his chest.

When he rejoined Tully on the deck, the *Bellerophon* was hull down to the north and the coast of France a dark smudge off their starboard bow.

CHAPTER 9

Street Theatre

I T IS CURIOUS," REMARKED GILBERT IMLAY, when they emerged from the theatre, "that despite the war and the food shortages and the death carts and the prisons and the fact that one might be strung up for wearing clean linen or the wrong kind of shoes, Paris does not lack entertainment of a more conventional nature." He cast a glance back over his shoulder. "A pity it is so mundane. I confess I have seen better acting at the waxworks."

"We bow to your insight, my dear," murmured his wife in her deceptively mild manner, "doubtless gained from the time you spend there, watching that little Swiss girl making wax heads from real ones."

Sara Seton smiled to herself as she arranged the threadbare shawl around her shoulders. She had not known the Imlays long but she found their relationship far more intriguing than anything she had observed at the theatre, particularly the recent performance which had been every bit as bad as Imlay had proposed. And yet the theatre was enjoying something of a renaissance in Paris—as if there was not enough drama on the streets. Sara frequently felt she was part of some vast audience swept along from one performance to the next. Except that you could never be sure if you were in the audience or on the stage. And everyone a player, ready to speak his lines as if a lifetime had been spent in the rehearsing of them, with a little clerk scribbling away in a corner, taking it all down for posterity. Or your trial.

"Come along, my dears." Imlay offered each of the women an arm. "Let us be on our way." He raised his voice for the benefit of any police informers that might be lurking in the vicinity. "I am looking forward to my bowl of gruel and a morsel of bread and if we have any wine in the house we will raise our chipped mugs to Citizen Robespierre and the Committee of Public Safety. *Vive la République*."

"Fool," said Mary but she took his arm as happily as a young bride and Sara took the other and they hobbled off together in their wooden clogs down the Rue des Sans Culottes, as it had been recently renamed, though most Parisians continued to call it by its original name, the Rue Gratte Cul—the Street of Arse Scratchers.

They were almost home when they heard the drum.

It was a familiar sound in Paris but it was wise not to ignore it; it might be the last sound you ever heard. They could hear the shouts now, not clearly but enough to know what they were selling, the new street criers of Paris. Death was a word that carried.

"*La mort aux riches. La mort aux prêtres. La mort aux aristocrates*."

Sara stumbled on a cobble, cursing her clogs, not quite running, not yet frightened, more *apprehensive*, as if anxious to avoid an embarrassing encounter. There was an opening to the right, leading to a little court behind a tall iron gate. Imlay tried it but it was locked. He rattled vainly at the bars. On the other side was a pleasant cobbled yard with a tree and a well and a line of washing . . .

"I suppose I might lift you both," he considered, but with a doubtful glance at Mary that might, in other circumstances, have been taken amiss. Then they looked back and saw the mob surging up the street: a tumult of rags and banners and flambeaus, red bonnets and ruddy faces in the light of the torches and the little drummer leading the way, rat-a-tat-tat. Imlay started shouting and waving his hat, urging Sara and Mary to do the same. "*Vive la Nation. Vive la République. La mort aux aristocrates* . . ." It was better not to be specific; you never knew who was in and who was out. And then the mob was upon them and the mood, thank God, was friendly, or at least not overtly hostile. Those were grins, yes, and not snarls? They were calling them Citizens anyway, and Sara was glad for once of her drab costume: brown skirt, black shawl, the grubby tricolour in her hat. She put her hand up to make sure it was there. She was swept along again and someone had an arm round her waist and was twirling her around in some kind of a dance: a man with one eye and a battered beaver hat and a meat cleaver in his hand. She took him by the wrist to make sure she knew where it was and he grinned in her face. A blast of—God, *what?*—through rotted teeth.

She could see Mary in the crowd as they danced, not too far away, trying to reach her and then they were in her own street and Imlay was at her side, catching her by the arm, swinging her away with an ingratiating smile at the man with the meat cleaver. Then he said, "*Merde,*" and she looked up and saw they'd got someone. A man of middling years with no hat and his wig awry, dark clothes, spectacles at an angle on his nose—he looked like a clerk in a law office or a minor official. Sara thought of a mole, burrowing away at a filing cabinet in the dim light of an office, minding his own business or his employers' . . . Harmless. No apparent reason why he had attracted the attention of the mob. But then the mob was moved by hidden currents. Surges. Moods you could never fathom until it was too late and they'd pulled you down. Perhaps it was the wig—the wig was bad. And was it powdered? Fatal. He was mouthing protests, his head twisting this way and that in a bid to engage one of his tormentors, to lock on to a face, to evoke a shared humanity. She heard the cry, "*À la lanterne*"—taken up, turned into a bay, a howl. There was a street lamp on the wall above their heads and they threw a rope over the bracket and strung him up in a flash, his little legs working furiously just a few inches above the ground and his fingers clawing at the noose. Sara stepped forward impulsively but Imlay hauled her back and shook his head, glaring: was she mad? And when she looked again someone had gutted him with one quick, clean stroke of a butcher's knife so his insides slid out like a bunch of sausages on to the cobbles.

Sara was sick on the cobbles. Then she pushed her way back through the crowd, wiping her mouth with the back of her hand, hoping no one would take exception to such delicacy of feeling. She knew what would happen next. After the evisceration there would be the beheading and then they would drag the corpse after them through the streets, displaying it in those districts where they considered it would prove most edifying, sometimes leaving parts on a window ledge or in a doorway to make the point more strongly. But it was impossible to move against the tide of bodies and they were carrying her along with them down the street, dancing and singing and with the head of their victim bobbing on a pike before them.

Then they stopped and set up that terrible baying again, "*À la lanterne, à la lanterne,*" and she saw they had someone else.

He was taller, more upright than the other but he had a rope round his neck and they were pulling him along like a wild beast. A young man, personable but with a weathered complexion and long, dark hair untied and hanging loosely around his face—he could have been a gypsy, she thought, or a seafarer—though respectably dressed in a dark blue jacket and trousers and a linen shirt with a clean white stock. As he came closer she saw he had a cut on his bottom lip and blood in his hair. She looked round for Imlay, wishing he could stop it. He usually carried a pistol in his coat, though it would take more than a pistol to stop a mob like this.

They had thrown the rope up over the lamp and were trying to haul him up but he had hold of it and was—my God, *he was climbing it.* Swarming up it hand over hand and kicking out at the crowd below and crying out to them in English, though not the English they had taught her at convent school.

And then Mary was there, shouting at them in the excellent but by no means native French of an English governess and Sara struggled towards her, thinking it was all over for them now, and all for an English spy they'd kill anyway, but Imlay was already at Mary's side, berating the crowd in that cool, authoritative manner of his.

"Can you not see that he is an American?"

It seemed to have some effect. They formed a circle around their victim and stared up at him as if at some exotic beast in the zoo. He dropped to the ground and tugged the rope from his neck. His expression, one might say, *attentive*.

Everyone was talking now, expostulating, explaining, and Sara gathered that his crime was that he was not wearing the tricolour. But now that they had discovered he was *Américaine* some at least were inclined to be indulgent. And while the matter hung in the balance the man stood up and put his hand in his pocket and produced not a knife as she half expected and feared—for that would have been fatal—but a tin whistle.

He put it to his bloody lips and began to play, tapping out the rhythm with his boot. The tune was familiar to Sara though she could not place it at first until someone started singing the words—in English. And she saw with a shock that it was Imlay.

> *Yankee Doodle went to town*
> *A-riding on a pony,*
> *Stuck a feather in his hat*
> *And called it Macaroni . . .*

He started on the next verse but faltered over the words and the piper ceased his piping and sang them in a confident tenor, waving the whistle as if it was a baton:

> *Yankee Doodle keep it up*
> *Yankee Doodle dandy*
> *Mind the music and the step*
> *And with the girls be handy*

And Sara swore he caught her eye and winked. Then he put the whistle to his lips again and did a jig, and there was something so wild, so mad, so *infectious* about it, he had them all joining in, dancing and singing along with him in a crude approximation of the words.

A sorcerer, she thought, a magician. And then the crowd was moving again, their shadows dancing on the walls and their corpse bouncing along behind them like a lucky rabbit's foot on a piece of string and they were left standing there looking at each other like guests at a party whom no one has thought to introduce.

"I believe I owe you my life," said the man. It seemed to embarrass him a little.

"Never go out without the tricolour in your hat," said Imlay primly. "It is a sentence of death."

"I protest," said the man. "I did have a tricolour in my hat. But it must have fallen off. And now I have lost my hat."

Sara saw it lying by the side of the street and ran to pick it up. She felt like a schoolgirl as she presented it to him.

"Thank you." He appeared to notice her for the first time. She was conscious of her drab appearance and the vomit on her shoes but he did not look down at them. "My name is Turner," he said, looking from her to Imlay. "Nathaniel Turner, from New York."

Sara detected a guarded look about Imlay's countenance but he introduced himself and his two companions . . . "My wife, Mary, and our friend Madame Seton."

"Imlay?" the man repeated. "But you are the very man I have come to Paris to see. I was waiting for you on the step." He half turned towards the house behind him—Sara's house. She saw the bag lying at the bottom of the steps, very like the kind that seamen carried over their shoulder. "The maid said you would be returning shortly. Thank God you did."

"Wretched woman," said Imlay, glaring at Sara as if it was her fault, "to leave you standing on the street."

"Do you not think it better that we do not stand here now?" said Mary coolly. "Especially since it is become a slaughter yard."

The man suddenly seemed to notice the pool of blood and guts on the cobbles and the flies already gathering in a cloud above them. He looked a little shocked.

"Welcome to Paris, Mr. Turner," said Sara to cover his confusion and her own. "Were you planning to stay long?"

CHAPTER 10

the Hyena in Petticoats

"IT WAS NOT THE WELCOME I had anticipated," Nathan confided as he sank into the soft cushions of the sofa in what he took to be the Imlay's drawing room, "but I am very glad to have found you at last, even with a rope around my neck."

"Good, good," nodded Imlay, though Nathan detected an underlying suspicion in the look he gave him. "Unless, that is, I owe you money, ha ha."

His wife shot him a glance that made Nathan wonder if this was not an entirely implausible supposition.

"Not at all," Nathan hastened to assure them both, attempting a smile whose effect was rather ruined by the jab of pain from his cut lip. "In fact I have something for you. Only I have left it in Le Havre."

This elicited an even sharper glance from Imlay.

"You have come from Le Havre?"

"Directly. Except that it is not called Le Havre, apparently, but Port Marat in honour of a gentleman who was unfortunate enough to be stabbed to death in his bath in the cause of Revolution—or so I was informed—and the street names have been changed which made it difficult to find the address I was given and when I did it was only to learn that you had departed for Paris with no immediate prospect of return so . . ." He took a quick breath. "As I had instructions to deliver my cargo into your hands *and no other* and dispatches marked for the *urgent attention* of the American Minister in Paris, and as I was led to believe the journey would take no longer than a day in the diligence, I determined to set out for the capital. Though it has taken me three days rather than the one, the route being more bog than road and most of the horses at the relays taken for the war."

He paused again, aware of how he was babbling. He was not feeling at all himself and indeed a part of him was hanging from a lamppost or being towed at the heels of the inconsiderate mob. He was aware that the Imlays were staring at him in silence.

They were a handsome couple, older than Nathan by about ten years—the man possibly more though there was a youthful air about him. He was tall and thin and distinguished-looking in the American way—which was to say there was more than a little of the frontier about him for all his grooming; a man more used to being outdoors than in. Nathan sensed a kind of constrained energy or restlessness there. Gilbert Imlay, American shipping agent in Le Havre. And what else besides? Nathan wondered. As for the wife, she was strangely familiar though surely it was not possible that they had met. He scanned his memory but it was as scattered as his speech.

Imlay found his voice first.

"My cargo?"

"I beg your pardon?"

"You said 'my cargo'?"

"Ah, yes. Forgive me. Tobacco. Five hundred chests. In the *Speedwell* barque. Of Salem."

Imlay's eyes shot across to his wife and then back to Nathan.

"Tobacco?" he repeated, as if it were a species of wild animal not previously seen in Europe.

"Tobacco, sir," Nathan affirmed. "Best Virginia."

Further discussion of the mysterious cargo was prevented by the entry of the other woman carrying a basin of water and followed by the maid with towels. Nathan protested that she must not put herself to the trouble but she said something in French he did not catch and applied herself to the matted blood above his right ear while the maid spread a towel to catch the drips.

"What did they hit you with?" demanded the lady, in perfectly good English, dabbing gently at the wound with some liquid out of a bottle—possibly alcohol; certainly it stung like it.

"I am afraid I was not looking too closely at the time," Nathan confessed, "but it felt like a club."

His memory of the encounter was confused; the mob had been on him so quickly. One moment he had been sitting on the step watching them advance up the street as if it was a parade and then they were all around him, snarling like wolves and waving butchers' knives and steel hooks in his face. They seemed to have something against his hat.

"My hat," he had said, "what about my hat?" And his hand went up to it and he realised he was no longer wearing the tricolour. Then they started pulling him down the street and shouting something else he did not understand.

"À la lanterne, à la lanterne!"

Then he saw the street lamp and the man hanging from it and knew. He winced at the memory.

"I am sorry if it stings a little but it is not as bad as it might have been," said his pretty surgeon. More than pretty: her face was strong but not in the least masculine, her lips full, her complexion flawless. What was her name? He had forgotten already. "Press this towel to it until the bleeding has stopped. And perhaps you might like to use this."

She handed him a damp flannel and he wiped it over his face with one hand while holding the towel to his head with the other. He felt absurdly like a child tended by his mother after taking a tumble. In fact she rather reminded him of his mother though she was a good few years younger. He could smell the freshness of lavender about her and something else more elusive, less innocent.

The flannel when he took it away was stained with blood, presumably from the wound on his head. He must have looked a sight. He squinted down at his collar and thought there was blood there too. He hoped there was none on the sofa. He reached for another towel from the maid but her mistress took it and dried his face herself. He blushed for shame but with pleasure too. He caught her eye as she removed the towel and the pleasure increased. But she left without a backward glance, taking her basin and her towels and her maid with her.

There was an exchange of glances between husband and wife and after a moment—and a small but forceful jerk of Imlay's head—the wife stood up and followed the two other women out of the room, closing the door a little forcefully behind her.

"This . . . cargo?" Imlay prompted Nathan. "If you feel well enough to . . ."

"Oh, I am quite well, thank you," Nathan assured him. "Yes. Tobacco. Were you not expecting it?"

"I was expecting it some months ago," declared Imlay with an odd look. "In fact I had given it up for lost." He appraised Nathan thoughtfully. "I assume it does not come by way of Salem."

"Not directly," Nathan prevaricated. He did not know how much he was at liberty to disclose.

"And it is now in Le Havre?"

"Aboard the *Speedwell*, sir, awaiting your instruction."

Imlay nodded. "If you are feeling up to it," he said, "we will set off first thing in the morning and I will make arrangements for its storage. But of course . . ." He indicated the towel which Nathan still had clamped to the back of his head.

Nathan removed it with some delicacy so as not to set the wound off bleeding again.

"Oh, I am perfectly up to it," he said. "In fact, from my point of view, the sooner it is disposed of the better."

"Quite so." Imlay's tone made it clear he saw no need to discuss the matter further. He paused a moment. "You said you came with dispatches for the American Minister . . ."

"I did." Nathan was prepared to be as terse about these as Imlay had been about the cargo, though in fact had they met in Le Havre he would have been perfectly willing to hand them over for the agent to deliver.

"So you have met Mr. Gouverneur Morris?"

There was something in the way he uttered the name that indicated a measure of, if not disapproval, then a certain reserve.

"I have. In fact he told me I might find you here."

You will probably find him at number 188 Rue Condé, Morris had said. *He tends to stay there when in Paris.*

Probably. Tends. The suggestion of a curl about the lip. And nothing about a wife.

A brief knock and she was at the door again, looking only a little less displeased than when she had left.

"Sara says that Mr. Turner must stay the night," she said, looking at Imlay and not at Nathan. Her tone was neutral. "And dinner will be served in a few minutes."

Nathan opened his mouth to protest but no words came, though his mouth stayed open rather longer than was polite. He had just remembered why Imlay's wife seemed familiar to him. He *had* met her before—at his mother's once when he was on half pay. Only her name had not been Imlay. It was Wollstonecraft. Mary Wollstonecraft, the author of *A Vindication of the Rights of Woman.* The woman Horace Walpole had called a hyena in petticoats.

"So what does America make of the present situation in France, Mr. Turner?" inquired Mary Wollstonecraft or Imlay or whatever name she was presently trading under.

There was a note of irony in her voice and in the look she gave him across the dinner table but Nathan supposed it to be with reference to America rather than himself. There had been no indication that she remembered him from their one brief encounter; it had been at one of his mother's soirees about two years ago when her book had just been published and she was for a time the most famous—or notorious—woman in London.

"There is some concern about the violence," Nathan replied

cautiously, though it was a safe enough assumption. He found himself in some awe of the woman—as he had been when last they had met. He had not read more than a few pages of her book—it ran to more than three hundred which was a little too much for him to digest at one sitting—but he understood from the title and such criticisms as he had read or heard spoken of that its singular proposition was that women should be treated as the equals of men. Nathan had no particular difficulty with this. He had always considered his mother to be the equal of his father in most things and his superior in the rest, except possibly the command of a ship of war which she had not yet attempted. And farming sheep. But conventional society had refuted the suggestion of female equality as outrageous—and its proponent as a monster. *I am the first of a new genus,* she had proclaimed; and as far as society was concerned the first would be the last.

She did not look like a monster. In fact she looked quite attractive: though a little on the large side and with a slight droop to one eyelid that made you think she was winking at you, but there was a fine, bold, be-damned-to-you look about her that he rather approved.

"Ah the violence," she said now. "Yes, well, we are all concerned about the violence, Mr. Turner."

Though she had instructed him to call her by her first name she continued to address him as "Mr. Turner," with what he took to be a slightly mocking formality, as if he was not quite mature enough to be deserving of the title. He found that he did not care to meet her level gaze and looked instead at the dish that had been set before him by the maid—some sort of stew, mostly vegetable but with some bits of meat in it and dumplings with herbs. It tasted good though his lip called for careful navigation. He feared it might have swollen.

"I had thought the violence exaggerated before I came to Paris," Mary continued, addressing the room in general. "After all, London is not immune from riot. And as for the executions, I cannot approve them of course but I dare say there are as many hanged or transported for the stealing of a sheep at any county assizes in England. But there is an ugly mood on the streets and I cannot help but suppose that it is encouraged by those in power—or seeking it."

There was no immediate response to this. Imlay was consuming his stew as if it was the first meal he had been permitted in days and the other woman, Sara, was trying to catch the eye of the maid and making motions as of pouring something from a bottle. She had changed her nondescript dress and shawl for a silken gown, remarking that she might have to wear rags in the street but in the privacy of her own home she could wear whatever she liked; an assertion that Nathan for one was not inclined to dispute for though it was a restrained mauve in colour it had a neckline that showed her bosom to its best advantage. Unless of course she wore nothing at all. With his senses now more or less restored, he found her perfectly seductive. She was older than he, possibly by four or five years, but this only added to her attraction. She had dressed her hair high and added some colour to cheeks and lips but she used very little powder. He could barely take his eyes off her.

"Who exactly *is* in power?" he inquired politely when the silence had stretched a little longer than was comfortable.

"No one is in power," said Imlay, without looking up from his dinner. "That is the problem. There is a vacuum."

He filled his own with a slurp.

"Nonsense," said Mary. "Everyone knows who is in power, even if he pretends not to be."

"The Incorruptible," Imlay murmured mysteriously over his stew.

"Robespierre," Sara informed Nathan kindly.

Imlay shook his head. "Robespierre has no official position . . ."

"Except that he is the voice of The Committee," put in his wife.

"The Committee of Public Safety," Sara added for the benefit of her student, "which is nominated by the National Assembly to oversee every aspect of government."

"He owes his power to the mob," Imlay asserted, "and the mob is notoriously fickle."

"The mob is the real power in Paris," Sara explained. "And there are those like Robespierre who aspire to control it."

"Or Danton," put in Imlay.

"If only he would stop drinking and chasing women," added his wife.

"Oh, he has stopped chasing women," Sara corrected her mildly.

"Even you, my dear?" Imlay interrupted with a naughty schoolboy grin. There was much of the naughty schoolboy in him, Nathan reflected, despite his height and his distinguished appearance. One who would forever be playing tricks on his fellows—and his masters—and thinking he could charm away the consequences.

"Even me, sir, since he has taken a new young wife. But I fear our friend is bemused by our conversation."

This was true. Nathan knew of both Robespierre and Danton—much lampooned as demagogues in the English press—but he was reeling under a broadside of information. Clearly their hostess moved in interesting circles. Like his mother? The thought came unbidden and was a disturbing one.

"The situation in Paris is such that no authority can exist without the support of the mob," Sara declared, "but it is like riding a whirlwind, or rather a monstrous beast, and if you fall . . ." She opened her mouth and clashed her teeth together in a biting motion. Nathan found himself wondering what it would be like to have her biting on him. He was nodding intelligently as if he were following the debate but in truth he found himself rather more interested in the situation of his hostess than that of the French Republic.

This appeared to be *her* home and not the Imlays' as he had first supposed, though he gathered that Gilbert Imlay occasionally stayed here while in Paris, despite the fact that Mary appeared to live in a small village on the outskirts. So was there something between Imlay and Sara? Nathan could detect no frisson between them while Mary seemed to look upon her husband with genuine fondness.

And what of Sara's husband? Thus far there had been no reference to such an item though Mary had mentioned a child—a boy called Alex—who was asleep somewhere in the house.

Nathan was wondering how to raise the subject when it came about naturally in the course of the conversation. They had been discussing the war—which they agreed was the excuse for all manner of repression—when Mary asked her, in a lowered voice and with a glance to ensure that no servants or government agents were in the room, if she had heard lately from Turenne.

Nathan took this for a place until it became clear that it was, in fact, the missing husband, who had fled France to avoid imprisonment or worse and was now with the French court in exile in Koblenz. Nathan gathered that his wife had remained in Paris partly from preference but also to safeguard their property and the interests of her young son, for which purpose she had reverted to her maiden name of Seton.

"My father was a Scottish soldier and adventurer," she informed Nathan, with a hint of pride. "That is his picture above the fireplace and that is the family seat you can see in the background."

Nathan twisted round in his chair to observe the likeness of a fierce, bearded gentleman with both hands clenched round the hilt of one of those murderous weapons he believed the Scots called a claymore. The "seat" to which she had referred must be the ancient castle over his right shoulder.

"He fought for Prince Charles Stuart at the Battle of Culloden," she told Nathan, "and was forced into exile."

"Then you are Scottish?"

"Half Scottish. My mother was French and I was born in Provence."

"So we are all exiles," remarked Mary, "in our different ways." There was a brittle tone to her voice which suggested to Nathan that she was not prepared to tolerate a private tête-à-tête. "Though I expect you will be returning to your native land very shortly, Mr. Turner."

"As soon as I have delivered my cargo," he confirmed, with a glance at Imlay who gave him a look that conveyed an element of warning.

"And where is it you live in America?"

"My family are from New York," Nathan told her, "but I have been many years at sea."

"Ah New York. I could not quite place the accent."

"You are looking tired, Captain," observed Imlay, a little sharply. "I believe you would welcome your bed tonight."

This was true. Nathan felt as if he could barely keep his eyes open.

"But of course, how inconsiderate of us," declared their hostess with concern. "And hardly surprising after what you have been through . . ."

Nathan wondered if it was his recent ordeal that had made him so weary or the fact that he had spent the last two nights on the road. But he had moments when he still felt the rope round his neck and thin air beneath his kicking feet.

"Well your room is ready for you, sir, and you should not stay up on our account."

"Indeed, and we should be leaving shortly, my dear," said Imlay to Mary, "for I will need to organise our journey to Le Havre."

It was the first time Nathan had realised that neither of the Imlays planned to spend the night here. He would be alone with the lady of the house—apart from her servants, and the sleeping child.

"Is it necessary for you to leave tomorrow?" she inquired of Imlay. "Surely Mr. Turner needs time to recover from his ordeal."

"I will hire a chaise," Imlay declared, "and Mr. Turner can sleep all the way to the coast."

"Then we had better get you to bed," said Sara, looking at Nathan in a way that for all his tiredness stirred certain of his facilities into a high state of alert.

"Sleep well," said Imlay as they parted at the door. "I will be here first thing in the morning."

"Safe journey," said Mary, adding in a voice so low as to be a whisper, "and give my regards to your mother when next you are in London."

CHAPTER II

a Man of Many Parts

NATHAN SPENT THE NIGHT BEFORE THE journey to Le Havre compiling a detailed inventory of his character as a New York shipowner. Should Imlay voice his wife's concern that he was in fact the son of one of her closest London friends and an officer in His Britannic Majesty's Navy, he was prepared to suggest that she might have mistook him for another and, in extremis, to question the reliability of her eyesight, not to mention the possibility of madness in the family.

He need not have bothered. Imlay betrayed not the slightest interest in Nathan's nationality, family background, politics or religion. He was far too interested in talking about himself.

"I have been called a man of many parts," he informed Nathan in reply to his polite inquiry as their coach proceeded westward through the Bois de Boulogne. "And indeed I have been soldier, adventurer, explorer, backwoodsman, author and now, it appears, merchant and shipping agent. A gypsy once told my mother I would have seven lives and by my own reckoning I have used up five of them. But I would like to be remembered as a man of letters."

He had begun his adventures as an officer in Washington's army "fighting the British," he said (with a roguish grin that suggested he was not entirely ignorant of Nathan's true character). After which he had joined with other veterans in exploring and surveying the frontier territory of Kentucky. He had blazed a trail across mountains and through forests, shot rapids, travelled on a flatboat down the great Ohio, fought redskins, mapped an entire new territory, purchased eighteen thousand acres on the Licking River and found time to write a book about it all. "*A Topographical Description of the Western Territory of North America*," he pronounced grandly but with a dismissive wave as if it was altogether too imposing a title for so modest a work. But then belied the gesture by informing Nathan that it had been published by Debret in London with a view to encouraging emigration.

"A vast country with vast potential," he informed his companion as if he were a potential investor. "All it requires is people and we will possess a new empire of the west."

Nathan raised the delicate matter of those living there already.

"Why, it is a wilderness," Imlay replied in surprise, "with scarce a living soul west of the Ohio saving a few French trappers and backwoodsmen—and the savages, of course."

It was the savages he had in mind, Nathan admitted, having heard his mother's views on the subject, though she was more inclined to blame the English for giving away their title than her own countrymen for seizing it.

"A noble race," Imlay intoned. "I have spent some time amongst them and speak a few words of the Cherokee."

He assumed an appropriate pose and uttered a series of grunts for Nathan's edification.

"Which is to say in English: 'Would you care for a pipe of tobacco?' But they are nomads for the most part who have no more understanding of the value of land than we do of the composition of the moon. Unless you are one of those who subscribe to the notion that it is made of cheese. No, as I have written, they must be taught the very rudiments of agriculture and civilised life to have any chance of survival."

"And yet they seem to have managed quite well for some thousands of years," Nathan ventured a direct quote from his mother with whom he had, in fact, been arguing at the time.

"Ah well, that is progress, you know," replied Imlay obscurely.

"But will they not resist?"

"There have been instances . . . but for those of an adventurous disposition this does but add to the drama of the enterprise. Indeed, this is partly the subject of my second book, *The Emigrants*, which was published earlier this year in London. You may purchase a copy on your return . . ." Another sly dig? "It is a novel. An adventure story with a love interest. Some of the passages, I dare say, will shock the more prudish reader. It contains scenes of violence and depravity. Rape and nudity. A modest woman, her clothes torn from her body staggering into the street, dazed and bruised, clutching her scanty rags to her naked bosom . . . And the assailant, her own husband! I have spared no blushes."

"Indeed. And has Mrs. Imlay read it?"

"She has, and I believe approves its candour and lack of cant. It has a serious theme comparing the freedom of the New World with the hypocrisies of the Old. It favours equality between the sexes and has some harsh words to say about the institution of marriage as it is practised in Europe."

"And yet it has not deterred you from entering into such a union . . ."

Imlay gave him a sharp look. "Mary is an exceptional woman . . ."

Nathan bowed in acknowledgement of this fact.

"Her circumstance, too, is exceptional. As an Englishwoman living in Paris, her situation was delicate to say the least. I felt it incumbent upon me to offer the protection of my name, as an American citizen."

This was not the same as saying they were married. Nathan pondered this in silence but could think of no diplomatic way to pose the question.

"And Madame Seton," he ventured after a while. "Is her situation also delicate?"

"More than that. It is extremely dangerous. If her true identity were to be revealed . . ." Imlay dropped his voice, although it was quite impossible to be overheard. "Her husband is Raymond de la Tour d'Auvergne, Count of Turenne."

He observed Nathan's expression carefully but discovering no more than polite interest, added, "They are one of the most esteemed families of France. Descendants of the great Turenne who led the French armies at the time of Louis XIV and was widely regarded as the most accomplished military mind of the age."

"And has the present count inherited his genius?"

"Alas no, he is more of a courtier. Currently attached to the émigré court in Koblenz."

"His wife is unable to join him there?"

"It would be difficult. Besides," with a leery grin, "I do not suppose either party is anxious for a reunion."

Nathan raised a mildly inquiring brow.

"I may tell you, in confidence, that the marriage might be held as an example of all that is vile in the institution, as I have described it in my novel."

"The brutal husband, the modest wife?"

"As to that I would not know but the count is a collector of rare and beautiful objects in which category we must place the delectable Sara. As the daughter of an impoverished Scottish soldier she was effectively purchased by the gentleman to add to his collection. To tantalise his acquaintances with his possession of such an object of desire."

"And yet he was not loath to part from her."

"The Count's own desire was not perhaps as strong as his appreciation of beauty. Sara was eighteen when they married, the count some thirty years her senior. He is now quite an elderly gentleman and I do not believe they were ever close." He noted Nathan's expression. "I said it was vile, did I not?"

"You also said she was in some danger if her true identity were known."

"At the very least she would be imprisoned and the boy cast into an orphanage."

"Then she is in hiding?"

"On the contrary, she is very much exposed to the public gaze."

He smiled at Nathan's confusion.

"She attends the studio of Jean-Baptiste Regnault in the Rue Honoré as a pupil . . . and also, it is rumoured, as a model. Thus paying for her lessons. Regnault has painted her *en déshabillé* on a number of occasions and also, I believe, quite nude."

He slapped Nathan's thigh and laughed aloud.

"You blush, sir. I do believe you are smitten. Oh, there are many young men who attend Regnault's classes who would die for her. It is said she poses for them too if she requires a little extra food for the pot."

Nathan wondered if Imlay had allowed his writer's imagination to get the better of him but it was not an image easily dismissed from his own and he was silent for a time.

"Are we to spend the night on the road?" he inquired at length. It was growing dark and the coachman had stopped to light the lamps.

"No, but we should press on until we reach Rouen," replied Imlay, "so that I may arrange for your cargo."

Nathan was confused. "My cargo? But the cargo is at Le Havre."

"Yes," replied Imlay tolerantly, "but the cargo you are to take back is in Rouen."

"What cargo is this?" Nathan demanded, with a frown. He felt he was being put upon. "I received no instruction to embark a cargo in France."

"Only some wine and spirits. And a quantity of silver plate I have managed to purchase from a confiscated estate. It is all quite legal and aboveboard, I assure you, and I am sorry if you were not informed of it. It was most remiss of . . . those that sent you. I assure you it is expected."

"Expected by whom?"

"According to my instructions, you are to deliver it to a Mr. Williams of Newhaven. A short crossing from Le Havre, as you are doubtless aware."

The name Williams of Newhaven sounded familiar to Nathan though it was a moment before he had placed it.

"This Mr. Williams, would he be the owner of a lugger called the *Fortune?*"

"I believe that is the name of one of his vessels. He was engaged in the cross-Channel trade for some years until the war but now he is in the service of government, like yourself."

"Which government?"

"Why the British government, of course." Imlay made a quaint arch of the brow. "Do not look so shocked, my friend, it is one of the perquisites of government service. And my lord Chatham is perfectly acquainted with it, I promise you. You will exchange your cargo for another like any respectable man of business. And if certain other gentlemen profit by the transaction, why then, as we say in France, *c'est la guerre.*"

He clapped Nathan once more upon the thigh and laughed aloud at his discomfort, or his own wit, or both.

CHAPTER 12

Fog in the Channel

THE SPEEDWELL EASED HER WAY THROUGH the patchy fog muffling the mouth of the Seine as the last dregs of light leaked from the westward sky: perfect conditions for a blockade runner slipping port; all it lacked was a wind. It had been with them from Le Havre, the merest zephyr from the southeast but enough to bring them smoothly down river with the current and the ebbing tide. Then, minutes after dropping the pilot in the Petite-Rade, it failed them completely and left the barque drifting in the shipping channel in a flat calm a little over a mile to the south of Cap de la Hève.

Nathan gazed reflectively upon the damp sails, hanging like limp rags on a line of washing.

"I think it will pick up a little," said Tully at his back. "There should be something of an offshore breeze at this time of the year."

Nathan nodded as if this confirmed his own conviction though in truth he was convinced of no such thing and he did not know how Tully could be. They were still moving, drifting through the ghostly banks of fog on the ebb and with just enough speed to give them steerage-way, the entire crew up on deck or in the tops, looking out for other vessels in the haze, and every minute the silence broken by the piercing whistle of young Francis Coyle in the bow. The pilot had washed his hands of them, consigned them to oblivion with a curse. Any reasonable man, he had informed Nathan, would lie up in the roads and wait for daylight and a fair wind, knowing full well that blockade runners had a different notion of reasonableness and that in any case it did not jingle in the pocket like coin. Nathan, besides, had other motives. He felt like a smuggler. He probably *was* a smuggler. The *Speedwell's* hold was stuffed with Imlay's contraband—there was no other name for it—and as far as he was concerned, the sooner he discharged it the better, even to the notorious Mr. Williams of Newhaven.

There had been a surprising lack of interference from the French authorities. Bribes had doubtless been paid and as Imlay had pointed out, the port depended on trade for its existence, even trade with the enemy. Even so he had been nervous. There had been a change of regime in the port. A *représentative-en-mission* had been sent from Paris with orders to crack down on such dealings. The mayor and several leading merchants had been arrested. It would blow over, Imlay assured Nathan, but the sooner they left the better.

Before they parted he had handed Nathan a sealed envelope, instructing him in his most irritating, conspiratorial manner to ensure that it was placed into the hands of "he who sent you." It was now fastened inside Nathan's jacket. He would very much like to have opened it but even if he could have brought himself to contemplate such a flagrant breach of trust, he dared not tamper with the seal.

He leaned back on the rail and listened to the gentle gurgle of water past the hull and other sounds, overloud in the muffled stillness. Creaks and groans from rope and timber. The squabble of invisible gulls in the murk ahead. And from the waist a low-voiced discourse in an accent that had become familiar to him on the voyage out and was oddly comforting now though he could not place the speakers.

He knew the crew little better than when they had set sail from Bristol, although it must be supposed that Tully did after their stay in Le Havre. Promisingly, none had skipped ship though they had been freely allowed ashore. Tully had warned them to be discreet and as

far as Nathan could tell they had been, for all the cheap wine poured
down their throats. It was significant, at any rate, that none had been
taken up by the authorities though several had been teased for information. They were smugglers, Tully said simply when Nathan expressed his guarded surprise: they knew to keep their mouths shut.
And Tully was a smuggler too, Nathan reminded himself, and the
only man aboard beside his servant, Gabriel, who knew he was not
an American.

He caught the eye of the second mate—Keeble. Jonathan Keeble
from Marblehead. Most of the crew were from Marblehead or one
of the other small ports to the north of Boston. He noticed Nathan
watching him and gave him an easy nod and a wink. Nathan was
stunned. He nodded uneasily back but he felt as if he had been embarrassed in public.

He was still not used to the informal ways of a merchantman—
and an American merchantman at that. Tully was so much better
at it: able to joke with a man one minute and bawl him out the next
with a string of colourful abuse. This made Nathan uneasy, too, for
they were officially a Navy ship—His Britannic Majesty's hired vessel *Speedwell*—and subject to naval discipline. And yet a kind of
discipline prevailed that was as impressive in its way as it was mysterious. Everyone seemed to know what they had to do without too
much agitation from Tully or Keeble—even their obscenities did not
sound agitated—and the two men appeared to get on well enough.
They had all behaved well during the confrontation with the privateer. Possibly there were other ways of working as a team than the
iron discipline enforced by the Navy. But then these were not pressed
men, nor driven to the sea by a brutal, impoverished life ashore. And
they were earning three times the rate of an able seaman in the Royal
Navy with the promise of a bonus on completion of the voyage.
Could you depend on men who worked for profit and each other as
readily as those who served their country and feared its just retribu-
tion if they failed? Nathan's natural instincts inclined him to think
you could—but he had been in the service since he was thirteen and

was accustomed to the formal, ordered life of a ship of war backed by the lash and the rope. On *Nereus* he was surrounded by an invisible wall of privilege and authority. *I say to this one, go and he goes; and to another, come and he comes* ... No one dared question a single command, no matter how absurd or dangerous, on pain of death.

So which did he prefer? He pondered this now as he leaned back, seemingly as relaxed as any, upon the rail. Probably, for all the uncertainty, he was more at ease as a privateer or a blockade runner than he was as the captain of a King's ship. Certainly he felt that the crew of the *Speedwell* accepted him as their commander far more readily than the crew of the *Nereus*, though his authority in the latter case was buttressed by all the majesty of his position, a phalanx of commissioned and warrant officers and a squad of armed marines. Perhaps this was his own perception of himself as the son of an admiral promoted beyond his abilities, resented by his first lieutenant and not entirely trusted by his crew. But why should it be any different now? He had arrived from nowhere, assumed command, taken them off on a wild gambit across the Channel, left them to stew in Le Havre, and now he was guiding them through mist and darkness to they knew not where. Yet they had seen him outrun and outgun a French privateer and apparently outwit a British ship of the line, and they had sailed in and out of French waters with impunity. Nathan sensed that they considered him "gifted": blessed with mysterious powers, or at least uncommon good fortune. But this might have been wishful thinking on his part. Besides, he told himself, he must not count his chickens ...

"Ship ahead! Two points off the starboard bow."

"Port your helm!" Nathan, running to the starboard rail, saw the dark shape looming out of the mist. Heard more shouts, in French, but could not immediately take them in. He watched the distance narrow—Tully had half the crew lined along the rail to fend her off—but they were travelling so very, very slowly, barely sufficient to give them steerage-way and there was a good half-cable's length between them as the bow came ponderously round. Nathan had seen the long row of gun ports in that first swift glimpse but they meant nothing—most merchantmen had gun ports painted on their sides even if they did not carry guns—but he saw now she was a true ship of war: a frigate of 28 guns or more and her sides filled with men. He could make out the officers now on the quarterdeck and his mind registered what they had been shouting at him across the water. He jumped up in the shrouds and leaning far out over the side he called back in a deliberately clumsy French: "*Barque Américaine* Speedwell. *Depart à New York.*"

The gap was closing and he could see that the Frenchman was moored at stem and stern—but with spring cables so she could bring her broadside to bear. And by God they were running them out already. He could see the glow of slow matches on the quarterdeck.

"*Ne tirez pas, messieurs—Citoyens—nous sommes Américaines.*"

He braced himself for the command to drop anchor and bring the ship's papers for inspection; they might even send a boarding party to search the vessel and if they suspected him of trading with the enemy he would be back in Havre-Marat facing an interview with the man from Paris. The two vessels were almost level now and he could make out her name in gold lettering across the stern: *La Vestale*. Then came a voice in heavily accented English warning him that there was an English cruiser in the bay and he would be advised to wait for a wind.

"But then I will miss the tide," Nathan objected.

Then a mischievous thought crossed his mind. He raised his voice for they were almost past. "Can you not escort us out into the bay?"

The response, when it came, was from another voice and in French.

"*Mes regrets, Citoyen, mais le capitain il est au port avec la plupart du peuple. Vous êtes seuls.*"

His final *bon chance* came from behind the falling curtain of mist. Nathan found his heart was pounding and there was sweat on his brow. He saw Keeble and several other of the crew grinning at him and managed a genuine grin back.

La Vestale. He turned to look back to where she lay in the stagnant haze. When he was with the Dover squadron, in the service of

His Majesty's Customs and hoping for better days, he had made an inventory of every ship in the French fleet above the rate of frigate. *La Vestale, La Vestale* . . . He delved in the neatly labelled catalogues of his mind—the comprehensive lists of guns, winds, dogs, horses, wild birds, stars, planets and other articles of greater or lesser import, filed there since early boyhood, and found her in a matter of seconds among warships, French, frigates . . . *La Vestale*, 32-gun frigate of the *Magicienne* class, built in the '80s . . . Twenty-six 12-pounders and six 6-pounders on her quarterdeck, with a crew of about 250 officers and men. A complacent crew at that for there were no boarding nets rigged and if his French confidant could be believed, her captain ashore with many of the crew. How many? Nathan wondered. *La plupart*, he had said. Did that mean most of them or a small number? Then a ragged gap appeared in the mist and he saw her again and another vessel off her starboard quarter—a two-decker of 74 guns or more—and beyond this grim guardian the blurred outlines of the fort on the headland. No wonder they were complacent.

He felt a breath of wind on his cheek—the offshore wind that had torn a hole in the mist—and looked up to see the topsails twitching away from the mast, flapping back and then filling. Then the courses, with more reluctance, shaking themselves free of the clinging damp. But the wind was firm on his cheek now and the pennant at the mizzen above his head pointing to the east. No, not quite. He glanced at the compass. East-southeast. It could hardly be better. Already he could feel the barque responding, moving with a new purpose towards the open sea and almost at once they met the first hint of a swell. He considered his course by the light of the binnacle and instructed the helmsman to bring her round to nor'-nor'-west.

"Nor'-nor'-west?" By God, the man was questioning him and he almost laughed. Buchan, was it? Ned Buchan? Jed Buchan? Another Marblehead man. He caught Nathan's eye and shrugged as if it was all one to him: "Nor'-nor'-west it is, then."

They would know now they were not heading back down the Channel, not back to America, not even to Bristol. And so would any

Frenchman who saw them. But there was no chance of that from the shore and precious little at sea. As for the British cruiser . . .

A cry from the lookout as the fog lifted and there she was: half a mile off their larboard bow, a wraith among wraiths; ten seconds more and she would vanish again but it was five seconds too long and the watch too sharp. He saw her start to wear as the mist closed round her and when he saw her again she was bearing down on him on the starboard tack with her guns run out. Instantly the flash and bang of her starboard chaser and the shot skipping across his bows.

"*Merde!*" he swore aloud in the French that had become second nature to him now. Having little choice in the matter he gave the orders to bring her up into the wind and counterbrace the yards. The men obeyed him glumly but he saw some expectation in the covert glances they gave him, waiting to see what rabbit he would pull out of the hat. But all he had was the First Lord's letter in the locked box in his cabin. An awkward sod of a British captain might insist that as he could no longer claim to be delivering dispatches to the American Minister in Paris the least he could do was spare a few of his best topmen to serve King George. And, come to think of it, what *was* he carrying on his return to His Majesty's former colonies . . . ?

Then he looked back at the cruiser, clear now of the lingering shreds of mist, and saw with a shock of recognition that she was the *Nereus*.

"I had orders to look out for you these past five days," said Richard Jordan, "and escort you back to England."

He made it sound like an accusation—and a threat.

They were in Nathan's old day cabin on the *Nereus*—he supposed it must be Jordan's now—while the man who must be Jordan's steward made them coffee.

"I am grateful to you," Nathan told him with a small bow, "and to whoever gave you the order, for I knew nothing of it." It puzzled him still. "I cannot tell you how glad I was to see the old brig charging through the mist."

"Well, it appears your mission has some priority," Jordan acknowledged stiffly. He seemed to have grown a little older and greyer since Nathan saw him last. The weight of command? But he was still a lieutenant; he had no commander's epaulette on his left shoulder, which might add to his discontent.

Nathan recalled what the First Lord had said to him in his office in Whitehall: the *Nereus* will be under temporary command *until your return*. Well, now he was back and might justifiably resume his command. But it would have to be handled with some delicacy. There was an ambiguity here—particularly as Jordan had instructions to escort him back to England—and he did not want to create a problem. Choosing his words with care, Nathan began to explain the plan that had formed in his mind the moment he saw the *Nereus* bearing down on him in the misty shoals of the Baie de Seine.

Jordan did not take it well.

"I have no orders," he began.

"You have *my* orders," Nathan reminded him pointedly. Then, in a more conciliatory tone, "Oh come, sir, we are at war. We must take every opportunity to strike at the enemy—and we will never get a better chance."

Jordan shook his head. "It is too much of a risk."

"They watched us sailing past them in the mist," Nathan pressed him with rising impatience. "The American barque *Speedwell*. Barely an hour since. And now she is running back. From the same British cruiser they warned us about. What are they going to do—fire on us?"

"They might," Jordan argued, still shaking his head.

Nathan fell back on his authority. "It is entirely my responsibility. If you wish, I will give you the order in writing."

"I do not like to insist," Jordan said, "but if it goes wrong and you are no longer . . ." He spread his arms, not wishing to complete the sentence.

"Fetch me pen and paper," said Nathan, tight-lipped. "I will do it straight way."

He was far more accommodating to the crew of the *Speedwell*.

"Lads, this is well beyond the call of duty," he told them as they gathered on the deck with the two vessels lurching side by side in the swell like two drunks in the Strand and the Nereids swarming across the rail behind them. "Any man who wishes it may step aboard the brig without disgrace, or loss of pay, and may rejoin us on our return."

Some shuffling, an exchange of glances. Most of them seemed to look towards Keeble or the ex-Navy gunner Solomon Pratt. The silence felt uncomfortable. Nathan knew they would be reluctant to step aboard the *Nereus* for fear of being detained permanently.

"Needless to say you will have a share in the rewards."

Nothing. Not so much as a grin. But no one moved towards the brig.

"Then you are with us?"

"Aye, I reckon we're with you, eh, lads?" Keeble looked around at them and there were nods and something that was more growl than cheer but just as heartening. Nathan swallowed hard.

"Good," he said and, in the emotion of the moment, "Then you will form part of my division in the bow."

The other two divisions he gave to Canning, second lieutenant of the *Nereus*, and Tully, each with their own specific objective. Everything depended on taking the *Vestale* by surprise—and keeping the Nereids out of sight until they were close enough to board.

There was still plenty of mist in the mouth of the Seine, more than there was out in the bay, but it was patchier than before and swirling a little in the faint breeze off the shore, like wraiths dancing a reel. Nathan leaned out over the rail, straining his eyes to discern a hint of masts and rigging in the shifting phantom shapes. They were running under reefed courses and headsails only and as close to the wind as she could sail but the tide was on the flood and the barque was moving faster than he would have wished. If he had calculated right they would cross the frigate's bow at a distance of about a cable's length. But if he did not see her in the next half minute he would have to come about and he was dangerously close to shore.

He would have to wear. He opened his mouth to give the order and then the dancing wraiths moved apart and he saw her. Close. Christ, so close. And they had seen him. Shouts. The sound of running feet. And worse, far worse: the squeak and grind of them running out the guns. He leapt to the larbourd shroud, clinging with one arm and leaning out over the water.

"*Speedwell* barque," he called, and then in his clumsy French with a sense of panic in his voice that was not entirely feigned: "*L'Americaine. Nous sommes Americaines. Souvenez . . .*"

They had to believe him. They would not fire into an American. Not when they had seen her barely an hour since. The words of Lieutenant Jordan returned to taunt him.

They might.

"*Nous avons retrouvé votre Anglais, mes amis,*" he shouted, forgetting to stumble over the words. "*Mais nous l'avons perdu dans la brume.*"

She was swinging at the cables and he saw the long row of guns, the glow of the slow matches at the tubs. A broadside of 168 pounds. He wondered that he could call this to mind as he clung to the shrouds, staring at Death.

A voice in English.

"Come about and bring her into the roads."

Thank Christ.

He heard Tully repeat the order, inwardly exulting, watched the bowsprit coming round, turning with painful slowness into the wind. Did they have enough way to complete the manoeuvre? The sails feathered and for one awful moment he thought they were taken aback. Then they filled on the opposite tack and the crew were hauling on the braces to bring the yards round, bringing them on a course that would take them past the frigate's stern and into the roads under the guns of the two-decker and the fort on the headland. Nathan ran to the opposite rail and watched the gap narrow. Closer, closer . . . He could see the pale faces watching him in the light of the stern lantern, smell the smoke of the slow matches at the tubs. He glanced to right and left. The Angel Gabriel was at his side, back to his wicked ways

with a pistol in each hand and a cutlass at his belt, Keeble behind
him with a pistol and a tomahawk—a weapon favoured by many of
the Speedwells; then the grumbling gunner, Solomon Pratt, with a
boarding axe muttering to himself in an undertone—it might be a
prayer; the cook Small with his cleaver . . . Then a string of orders
from Tully at the con, the courses coming up and the helmsman
spinning the wheel and the bows coming round, farther, farther.
Frantic shouts from the frigate as they saw her heading straight for
their stern instead of passing beyond it. And then the *Speedwell*'s long
bowsprit pierced their mizzenmast shrouds like a lance and there was
a terrible grinding and splintering as they struck. With a great yell
Nathan led his Americans over the bow. He ran straight up the bowsprit through the torn rigging, dropped down on to the quarterdeck
on all fours, pistolled the gunner as he was bringing his match to the
sternmost 6-pounder and struck out with his cutlass to right and left.
One of his own men jumping down from the bowsprit crashed into
him and sent him sprawling. He struggled to his feet, saw Gabriel
livid in the light of the stern lantern, his face a demon mask of blood-
lust and rage, firing both pistols.

"Take the wheel, take the wheel," Nathan yelled at Keeble. A
French officer came running at him with his sword. Nathan turned
it with his own and slashed back across the man's chest; saw the almost comic expression of dismay and the thin red line appearing at
his white waistcoat before he fell away. Ran to the companionway as
a marine popped up with fixed bayonet, knocked the bayonet aside
with his sword and kicked him back down again, turned and saw
the marines from the *Nereus* pouring up from their concealment below decks.

The two vessels were locked together at the *Speedwell*'s bow and the
Vestale's stern, swaying like two great stags with locked antlers. And
the tide was pushing the barque's stern round laying her alongside the
frigate. Nathan looked up and saw the ghostly shapes of Tully's topmen through the mist, running along the yards to lash the two vessels together. And now the Nereids were pouring up from the hold,

yelling like demons and flinging grapnels across the diminishing gap.

The frigate's gun crews, frozen like so many tableaux, finally sprang into life. But the Nereids were already swarming over the rail, driving them back from the big guns. Nathan saw Lieutenant Canning among them, a small almost doll-like man, lashing about him with his sword. Two of his men had run straight for the bows and were hacking at the cable with axes. And then the main course came down with a rush blocking Nathan's view and he saw Tully up there with his division, lowering the topsails, and the frigate began to move from her moorings, dragging the *Speedwell* with her, still locked by the head. He peered through the murk to starboard but there was no sign of the 74. They must have heard the noise of battle though, through the mist. No time to be lost. The Speedwells held the quarterdeck now and Keeble was at the helm but the waist was still filled with struggling figures and there were more of the *Vestale's* crew pouring up from below, marines among them with fixed bayonets. How many were there? How many had the captain taken ashore? Not many by the look of that hoard streaming through the open hatches.

Nathan helped drag one of the 6-pounders to the top of the quarterdeck steps, glancing to his right to make sure they were doing the same on the starboard side. His own marines were lined up along the quarterdeck rail with their muskets at the ready. He lifted the whistle from its lanyard round his neck and gave one long blast and the Nereids in the waist began to fall back, slowly at first and then breaking away and running towards the quarterdeck as instructed. Some of the Vestales went with them but were cut down when Canning's men turned with the bulkhead at their backs. The rest stood in a confused mass with most of their officers dead on the quarterdeck and the frigate now clearly under way heading out to sea. Then came the crashing volley from Nathan's marines on the quarterdeck: and another. Terrible slaughter among the packed mass of men in the waist. When the smoke cleared they looked up to see the two quarterdeck cannons pointing down at them, the gunners poised with their slow matches waiting for Nathan's order to fire. He leapt up on the rail and roared at the Vestales to throw down their arms. No response. Too late, he realised his mistake. He had shouted the command in English. He opened his mouth to shout again and one of them shot him.

A confused void in time. He seemed to be sitting on the quarter-deck but he did not know how he had got there. There was a hole in his thigh with smoke coming out of it. He put his hand over it and felt blood but no pain. There was a pounding in his ears. He looked up and saw Gabriel kneeling at his side. Keeble too, and now Tully, his face full of concern. What was Tully doing there? He should be in the rigging.

"Are we under way?" His voice was harsh.

"Yes." Tully carefully lifted Nathan's hand from his leg and peered at the wound. "We are round the cape."

Nathan felt a sudden stab of pain. "Jesus Christ!"

"We will have to get him below," he heard Gabriel say.

"No!" Nathan did not want to go below. Below was the screaming horror of the cockpit and the surgeon with his saws. "Not until we are out to sea," he added desperately.

"We *are* at sea, sir. We are out in the bay."

The distant thunder of cannon.

"The 74," he began as he tried to raise himself.

But Tully was shaking his head. "She is still at her mooring," he said. "They are firing from the battery on Cap de la Hève and we will soon be out of range."

"We have to get him to the surgeon," Gabriel said again.

"No," Nathan groaned. He did not want to go to the surgeon. The surgeon was a butcher and a drunk.

But there were hands round his shoulders lifting him up. He reached out and grabbed Tully fiercely by the arm.

"Don't let them take my leg," he said.

But he saw the look on Tully's face and knew that they would.

CHAPTER 13

Gone to Ground

HALF THE COUNTY BENEATH NATHAN'S BEDROOM window: the veiled ladies all in black and the pink huntsmen, the hearty squires and the sporting parsons, the fat farmers on their fat mares and the restless hounds . . . And Nathan in his chair looking down and thinking of the painting it would make if only they would stay still long enough for him to make a half-decent sketch. With the steam rising from the farting horses and the mist rising from the fields and the winter sun just showing above the Long Man of Wilmington . . .

He watched his father sitting high and handsome on his big grey Billy, greeting his guests as they gathered at Windover House for the first time that season, and the stirrup cup passing round. Gallantly doffing his hat to the ladies, a word here, a word there, as composed and commanding a presence as he had been on his own quarter-deck; you would never know he was a shy man at heart. Nathan was proud of his father, who might have retired gracefully after a lifetime in the service but at the age of fifty-five had begun a new career as a gentleman farmer and made a surprising success of it, joining his more progressive neighbours in improving the breed of Southdown sheep so that already they were become the wonder of the age. But he was a stickler for tradition too, a solid Tory in good standing with the county establishment. He looked up, caught Nathan's eye and mouthed some instruction or query. Nathan frowned and tilted his head until it was repeated, accompanied by an unmistakeable gesture. *Come down.* Nathan pulled a face but ever loath to disappoint his father he hauled himself up from his chair and took up his cane and limped to the door.

The ragged cheer as he emerged. Applause and some amiable ribbing and Gabriel fussing over him as if he was an invalid.

"Shall I fetch you your coat, now, before you catch a chill?"

"No, sir, you may not but you may bring me the stirrup cup while it's passing."

And now here was my Lord Egremont, one of his father's band of improvers. "I am sorry to see you lamed, Nathaniel, but by God it was boldly done and we are all proud of you, my boy, eh Admiral?"

"I thank you, my lord, but it was little enough and I hope I am not lamed by it, just a trifle inconvenienced."

He caught his father's eye again, who knew how close he had come to losing the leg. Tully had threatened the surgeon with violence if he as much as looked to the saw and got him to St. Thomas's in London where they had dug the bullet out and set the bone with splints. But it had been touch and go for weeks after.

"Little enough, my arse. Not by the account I read."

The news of Nathan's exploits had been carried widely in the press but while giving him full credit for the victory, the papers had been strangely remiss in entirely omitting the part played by the *Speedwell.* The official report was that the *Nereus* had acted alone, boarding a 32-gun frigate in the mist and carrying her off under the guns of Cap de la Hève.

"Well, I'm glad to see you on your feet again, sir, and trust you'll soon be at the Frenchies again, even if you must leave Charley to the rest of us."

The hunt, being generally of the Tory persuasion, had taken to calling the fox Charley after Charles James Fox, leader of the Whigs, which presumably added to their pleasure at seeing it chased halfway

across the county and torn apart by hounds at the end of it, an outcome denied them in Parliament.

"Well, I'm sorry not to be riding with you today, my lord . . ."

Lying through his teeth for he was no great shakes as a huntsman,
but then he caught the eye of my lord's eldest daughter, Fanny, with
whom he had enjoyed a tussle in the past while riding to hounds—
she had let him pop out her tits on the last occasion in Windover
Wood and her present expression promised more. He was briefly
tempted but the doctor had warned against violent exercise and the
splints had only been off a week.

So with a prolonged blast on the horn they were off and away in a
clatter of hooves and a final clearing of equine bowels, leaving Nathan
and the servants alone on the steaming terrace. He stood for a while
looking out over the lake with its sheen of ice and broken rushes, one
lonely heron stalking the shallows, lamenting its own lack of sport.
Then, reluctant to retire indoors and listen to the clocks, he walked
round to the farm where those of his father's labourers not engaged
with the hunt were scraping up a season's dung and loading it into
carts for spreading on the fields, which was one of the few occupa-
tions left to them at this time of the year. With three big sheepfolds,
stabling for fifty horses and sheds for a dozen Sussex ox and a score
of cows, they had plenty to keep them busy and Nathan watched
from the lea of the barn as they shovelled and scraped, thinking how
he had known most of them since he was eight years old and wondering how many had been in Cuckmere Haven on his last visit . . .
The huntsman's horn sounded across the frosted fields and he lifted
his head to observe the distant riders spreading themselves across the
lower slopes of the Long Man and the hounds foraging at the edge
of Wilton Copse. England. Many of Nathan's colleagues would have
said this was what they were fighting for—but was he?

"Ben't gon t'jine hunt today, young maister?" Old Abraham
Eldridge, senior shepherd, in his smock and gaiters and the curious
fringe of whiskers endemic to the breed. Nathan had observed him
leaning on his crook and delivering a few sardonic words of advice to

the labourers, having little better to do since Guy Fawkes when he had put the rams in.

They embarked on a familiar ritual that had engaged them, off and on, since Nathan was a boy.

"No, Dad, I ben't. I be agoin' to watch thee instruct thy underlins in the rudiments o' shovellin' shit, it bein' more of an entertainment than chasin' varmints half the day."

"Oh aye, an' if we wus all of that same opinion where'd us be?"

"Why, same place as us be now, Dad, I reckon."

"And where be thy father's lambs come spring time but in bellies o' they same bloody varmints thou wouldna chase in winter, eh?"

"Well, as to that, Abr'm, I's a weakness for mutton mesel' but've niver bin chased t' Jevington and back for't."

"Aye but thou's bin chased t'Alfriston an' I 'member right an' had thy hide tanned somewhen for scrumpin' o' parson's apples when thou wert a boy." This with a hearty chuckle at the memory of it, taking off his tall hat to wipe his brow as if he'd done an honest day's work and not been leaning on his crook all morning watching others.

"Chased I may a bin, Dad, but never caught an' I recall. Though *informed upon* by them that ben't so nimble."

"Aye well, thou ben't so nimble thysel' now, boy, since Frenchies nobbled 'ee. Reckon ah could give 'ee half mile start an' still beat 'ee t' Market Inn, old as I be." Another cackle at this rejoinder and a wink at several of his associates who had gathered round to witness the debate.

"Reckon thou'd beat any man in county to any inn they cared to name, Dad, if they wus payin' an' not 'ee."

But further intercourse of this nature was prevented by the arrival of young John from the house with a letter that had arrived for Nathan by special delivery. He recognised the black seal with the fouled anchor and tore at the envelope in his haste to know the content.

"Not bad news, Nathaniel?" The old man's face creased with concern, ever wary of the death and disease that might be carried by post.

"Not bad news, Abraham," Nathan replied in the King's English after scanning the brief note above the Second Secretary's signature, "but I must have the chaise if there are horses for it." And to the messenger, "Do you run to Gabriel, boy, and beg him to have my best uniform ready and an overnight bag for I am summoned to the Admiralty and must leave directly."

Frost on the fields the short day long and darkness falling before they topped Shooter's Hill. Nathan huddled in his navy cloak with his chin sunk deep into a muffler and his boots resting on a pan of coals. It was a foul day for travelling but he trusted it would be worth the inconvenience; the First Lord would scarcely require his presence at Whitehall to order him back to *Nereus* when a messenger would have sufficed. He knew his father and others anticipated he would be made post for his victory in the Baie de Seine—or what little they knew of it—with some plum beside and yet he was assailed by doubt. It was four months now since he had taken the *Vestale* and there had been no word from the Admiralty, no official commendation, not even an inquiry after his health. Just that erroneous account in the Gazette. He could not help thinking that this silence was significant: that he had given some offence. Perhaps his father had been making too much noise among his old friends in the service and it had ruffled their lordships' feathers. And it was true that he had taken a risk with his command . . .

Perhaps the *Speedwell* and her precious cargo was more important to some people than the capture of a 32-gun frigate.

They pulled into the George at Croydon to change horses and he hurried indoors to warm himself at the fire while Gabriel fetched a hot toddy from the bar. It was raining when they left and by the time they reached Southwark it had turned to sleet.

A dirty, London sleet whipped up Whitehall by a wind from the northeast, the horses skidding in the slush and the cabbies hunched like gargoyles streaming water. Nathan showed his pass to the frozen sentry only to be greeted by the head porter in the lobby with the news that his lordship had gone to attend his brother at Downing

Street and he was to meet him there.

"In Downing Street?"

"Aye, number ten," said the porter in case he did not know where the King's chief minister lived.

Nathan lingered in the porch watching the sleet in the light of the dancing street lamps. He had sent Gabriel off in the coach to his mother's so as not to keep the horses standing in the cold and wet and left his stick behind so as not to seem a cripple.

"Shall I send for a cab, sir?" asked the porter with the hint of a sneer, for it was no more than a short walk down Whitehall and Nathan was no admiral.

"Thank you I'll manage," said Nathan and exaggerated his limp as he lurched into the sleet.

The porter at number ten was no more amiable, scowling at Nathan's dripping hat and the pool he was making on the hall floor.

"I will see if his lordship is still here," he said in a voice that indicated it was as likely as sunshine. He showed Nathan into a miserable little waiting room with a threadbare rug and a beggarly fire that crouched in the grate as if it was afraid of being noticed and raising questions in Parliament. Nathan's soaring expectations—a captaincy, a knighthood, an audience with the King—had now plummeted but he had scarcely stopped dripping when the fellow was back with an obsequious face and the news that his lordship would see him directly. Relieved of cloak and hat Nathan followed him up the stairs and along a landing to a rather more elegant chamber and a far more impressive conflagration with two like-looking gentlemen sitting on either side of it in easy chairs like matching ornaments.

"Ah, Peake, come in, come in," said the First Lord, rising. "I do not think you have met my brother."

William Pitt, the King's chief minister, not quite the gangling, pop-eyed, chinless wonder the caricaturists made of him but just about recognisable from their designs, bobbing briefly up and down as Nathan made his bow and gesturing for him to take the third seat at the fire.

Nathan nervously sat, wondering what in God's name he was doing in such company while his racing mind chased fantasies.

"I trust the leg is on the mend," began Chatham with a general nod at his nether regions.

"Yes, I thank you, my lord, much better than it was."

"I am glad to hear it for I cannot condemn your enterprise, or your bravery, though it might easily have jeopardised the more vital work you were about."

"With respect, my lord, I fail to see how the delivery of a cargo of tobacco . . ."

"There is much you fail to see, Commander, but you must trust in the judgement of those who are able to view the whole picture." A glance at his brother who declined to comment, merely fixing Nathan with a glare. Again, not as pop-eyed as his caricatures but no less disconcerting for that. Nathan felt like a schoolboy brought before the headmaster, though head prefect might have been more apposite for even in his thirties and wearied by ten years in office, Pitt still looked as if he needed to fill out his suits.

"Yes, my lord," Nathan replied stiffly.

"Well, it does not seem to have done as much damage as it might. We were able to suppress the details of the affair and provided you have been discreet, the *Speedwell*'s part in the affair remains undetected, at least by our friends over the water."

So this was what grieved them. But why? Unless . . .

He was not long in doubt.

"We want you to go back," Chatham confirmed his growing suspicion, "with another consignment."

"Of tobacco?" Nathan made no attempt to hide his disgust.

"If that is agreeable to you?" Coldly, looking down his long nose.

"I will do my duty, my lord."

"Very good. And there is another thing . . ." Another glance in the direction of his brother and this time Pitt responded.

"I believe you were in Paris, sir?" he said, leaning forward a little.

"Yes, sir. My contact being removed there and having dispatches to deliver to the American minister, I thought—"

"Quite. You acted with commendable resource. And what did you make of Mr. Imlay?"

"What did I make of him?" Nathan repeated with a frown.

"You travelled with him to Le Havre, according to your report. It must have given you time to form a judgement."

"Well, sir, I confess I thought him a little brash—and with a very good opinion of himself."

"But his insight—into French affairs?"

Nathan could only think of what he had said about the affairs of the Countess of Turenne, which could not possibly interest the present company.

"I believe he is as well informed as any," he temporised.

"Better, I would hope. We have read his report." He flapped a languid hand at the papers on the table beside him: the report that Nathan had brought back from France presumably. "He is most interesting on the prospects of the peace party in Paris."

"The peace party?"

"Danton's party."

Danton. Nathan remembered the name arising during the conversation around Sara's table. But all he knew of Danton was that he had stirred the mob into an attack on the royal palace, was generally regarded as being responsible for the September massacres and had rallied the people of Paris against the foreign invaders. Not the actions of a man of peace.

"I had not thought, sir, that there was a great movement for peace," he ventured cautiously, "either in France or England."

"Yes, well, I will be frank with you, sir, the war is not going as well as we might have hoped. You will have read in the newspapers of several recent setbacks . . ." Indeed Nathan had. The news from every front was bleak. "The emergence of a peace party in Paris would be of some interest to us."

Nathan inclined his head without comment. Indeed, he was more than a little bewildered at the direction the conversation was taking.

Had they confused him with a diplomat of the same name? Pitt's next sally was even more confusing.

"I believe you are acquainted with Mr. Thomas Paine."

The Great Revolutionist. A need for caution here.

"I have met him, sir, at . . ." But better not mention his mother in this company. "In London. Before he left for France. But . . ."

"We want you to talk to him."

Nathan was startled. "To Thomas Paine?"

He looked to the First Lord in some confusion but Chatham was studying the weave of the carpet with great interest.

"Yes. We want you to sound him out on certain matters. To see if he would be willing to act the broker, as it were."

"But . . ." Nathan's mind was racing again and going nowhere. "Where should I find him, sir?"

Pitt arched his brow. "Why in Paris, sir, where else?"

II—VENTÔSE

the Time of the Wind

CHAPTER 14

Mad Tom

A FOUL DECEMBER CROSSING WITH A CHILL north wind whipping the Channel into white rage and scouring their faces with sleet. But at least it drove the British cruisers off station in the Baie de Seine for fear of running upon a lee-shore, and the French welcomed the *Speedwell* into Le Havre like a bird of good omen, bringing news of the outside world and another load of Best Virginia. No one, it seemed, had linked the barque with the capture of the *Vestale* four months since and the Jacobin representative had been recalled to Paris, leaving more amenable men in charge. Imlay was not there—gone to Paris according to his steward, who assured Nathan he would take good care of the cargo and arranged a chaise for his own journey to the capital.

So Nathan entered Paris on what would have been Christmas Eve, if Christmas had not been abolished. The fourth of Nivôse by the revolutionary calendar: the month of snows, though in fact it was raining and the guillotine under a tarpaulin shroud like some grim icon of Death with his scythe shielded against the rust.

Nathan leaned back in his seat, withdrawing a little into the collars of his cape as the coach proceeded along the Rue Saint Honoré. Or rather the Rue Honoré as it was now, saints having gone the way of Christmas. There was little life on the streets but the Philadelphia

Hotel was ablaze with light and when he climbed stiffly down from the coach he heard sounds of revelry from within. Clearly the residents were in the mood to be festive, or possibly it was like this every night, Nathan reflected as he tugged upon the bell pull for the third time and hoped someone would hear it above the raucous bellowing of "God Rest You Merry, Gentlemen"—in English—that echoed around the Passage des Petit Pères.

Eventually came the porter with a lantern and stared lugubriously at him through the bars.

"It is the Americans," he said wearily. "We have asked them to keep the noise down but they are in spirits, so to speak."

Nathan explained that he had not come to complain but to see one of the guests, a Citizen Paine. "I believe he is staying with you at present," he persisted when the porter showed a blank countenance.

"And if he is," said the fellow, "and I were to inquire for him, who would I say is asking?"

"Captain Turner," said Nathan. "Of New York."

The man sighed heavily and searched among his keys.

"You had better come and wait inside," he said, "while I find out if he is here."

Nathan followed him across the small courtyard into the lobby where he could better appreciate the subtleties of the verse—and the fiddle and drum that accompanied it. He began to tap out the rhythm with the fingers of one hand on the desk and was thus engaged when a voice behind him inquired: "Captain Turner?" and he turned to find the familiar features observing him from the doorway.

He had last seen Thomas Paine two years ago—at his mother's of course, where he met all the King's enemies—and he had changed very little: the same funny-sad shambles of a man with his quizzical smile and his beak of a nose and the eyes of a rheumy old eagle. It was apparent that he recognized Nathan almost at once, though he had the wit not to denounce him.

"Captain Turner," he murmured, taking Nathan by the arm and escorting him to a sofa on the far side of the lobby beyond the hearing of the porter. "You have a twin in London, sir, though the name is different."

"I beg you will not take offence," Nathan replied in the same low tones. "It is a necessary subterfuge in the circumstances."

. Paine shrugged. "Subterfuge in Paris. One might as well take offence at whores in the Haymarket. But you take a considerable risk, my boy. Are you still in the British Navy or has your mother finally persuaded you to desert and join the Revolution?"

"I am still in the service," Nathan admitted. "In fact . . ." He paused a moment before committing himself but if he could not trust the man he might as well have stayed at home. "I am sent by Mr. Pitt to offer you passage to England, if you wish it, and all charges against you dropped."

Paine stepped back a pace with an expression of exaggerated surprise: the Mad Tom of popular perception with his fanatical stare and his big red nose reeking of rum and revolution. Indeed there was more than a hint of spirits about him now—but it *was* Christmas.

"All charges against me dropped," he murmured drily. "And in return?"

"I beg your pardon?"

"Well, I do not expect it is for nothing. Billy Pitt gives nothing for nothing."

"To be frank," Nathan dropped his voice even lower, "Mr. Pitt hopes that you may use your influence with certain parties to bring about negotiations that may lead to peace."

Paine stared at him a moment longer. Then he sank down on the sofa. "By God, boy, and he has sent you to tell me this?"

Nathan sat down beside him. It did, on reflection, seem something of a long shot.

"What makes him think I have any influence with the current bunch of fanatics in the Tuileries?" demanded Paine. "My attempts to influence them in the matter of the late King lost what little credit I ever had with them. I doubt I could plead my own case, let alone Billy Pitt's."

"Well, the current French administration may have to change for the better." Not a good choice of words . . . "That is, to reflect a more reasonable point of view."

"Ah, now we have it. Does Mr. Pitt have anyone in mind?"

"Monsieur Danton was mentioned."

Paine loosed a bray of violent laughter. "So Georges Danton is now become 'reasonable.' Well, I might yet be received at the court of St. James."

"Mr. Pitt did not go as far as to suggest that possibility, but there are funds at my disposal . . ."

"You offer me a bribe, sir?" Paine clamped his hand on Nathan's knee, his brow fierce. Then he smiled. "Pitt were wise to save his gold for Danton. What am I to offer him?"

"Whatever resources he requires," replied Nathan, "within reason."

"Quite so. He being a reasonable man. Well. How very interesting. But Danton is a French patriot. What can we offer France? The return of Canada is, I suppose, out of the question."

"It did not arise in the course of our conversation," Nathan admitted.

"No. I did not suppose it."

"Mr. Pitt believes a suspension of hostilities is as much in the interests of France as it is of Britain."

"He does, does he? And would he want us to restore the monarchy?"

"It is not specified as a precondition for talks, though the release of the young King from the Temple would be appreciated."

Paine made a courteous if mocking bow.

"And a constitutional monarchy has always been favoured in Britain," Nathan continued smoothly—he was become quite the diplomat, "as it is by Monsieur Danton if I am not mistook."

A door opened within the hotel and they heard voices raised in song.

I saw three ships come sailing in,
On Christmas Day, on Christmas Day,
I saw three ships come sailing in,
On Christmas Day in the morning.

Paine regarded Nathan thoughtfully. "Billy Pitt knows how to pick his couriers, I'll say that for him. There are few men in England I would have trusted, even so far as we have gone. How is your mother, pray? Still as beautiful as ever?"

"She was in good health the last time I saw her," Nathan assured him a little coolly. He was always cool when a man spoke of his mother in a certain way, though as far as he was aware Paine had not been one of her paramours.

"She knows of your mission?"

"No. I regret I was not at liberty to tell her."

"It would probably amuse her greatly, if she were not so worried about you coming back to her in one piece. It will certainly amuse Danton."

"Then you will speak to him?"

"I wonder. Paine the Peacemaker. It is an interesting possibility. And certainly Danton would stop the Terror. Let me think on it." He glanced down at Nathan's bag. "You are staying the night?"

"If there is a room."

"Oh I am sure there is a room. We are a dwindling band of brothers, I fear. You are lucky to find me here. I am no longer a permanent resident. I live a quiet life these days in Saint Denis but I came into town for the revelry. You must join us for dinner."

"That might not be wise," Nathan suggested. "I do not want to be questioned too closely on my character as an American."

"My dear boy, you could wear a ring through your nose and speak Hottentot and they would take you for an American tonight, they are so much in drink. However, as you wish. We will meet at breakfast." A frown crossed his brow. "Perhaps not breakfast. Dinner might be more 'reasonable' as it is Christmas, do you not think?"

He drew back a little the better to form a view of Nathan's features.

"Well, well, who would have thought it when first we met, eh? And you thought me a fairground entertainer, I recall."

He clapped Nathan on the knee once more. "Tomorrow," he said, "and we will talk more soberly."

The bell tolled its way into Nathan's consciousness. At first he thought it was a church bell for in his dreams there had been a church. A church and a gallows and a cart full of women stripped to their shifts as for a hanging.

And then he woke up and realised it was the bell at the gate. And he was in a room at White's Philadelphia Hotel. He was up at once and running to the window. A gleam of bayonets in the *lanterne* above the gate and tall black shakos . . .

Nathan pulled on his clothes, grabbed his sword and hanger and rushed out of the room. Other guests, in various stages of undress, were already in the corridor, gazing at each other uncertainly and there was a little huddle at the top of the stairs, gazing down. Nathan joined them in time to see the soldiers clattering up, the porter at their head. Soldiers or gendarmes, he could not tell: they wore blue uniforms with white slashes down the front. And two officers in dark capes with large bicorn hats decorated with plumes of red, white and blue.

"Which is Tom Paine's room?" Nathan demanded of the men at the top of the stairs.

"Room twelve, I think," one of them offered, "on the floor below."

He ran down the stairs but the invaders were already banging on doors.

"What is going on?" Nathan demanded, in the hope of diverting them for he knew instinctively who they had come for. He had drawn his sword from its hanger and the guards turned on him, levelling their muskets but getting in each other's way in the narrow space and then one of the officers pushed his way through with his hand on the hilt of his own sword. His gaze swept across Nathan and to the Americans gathered on the stairs.

"I am Commissioner Gillet of the Bureau of General Security," he announced, in a voice that carried. "And I have a warrant for the arrest of Thomas Paine. Any man who interferes with that commission will also be arrested."

"What is the charge?" Tom Paine stood in the doorway in his nightcap, with the same quizzical smile he had worn when he had seen Nathan earlier that night in the lobby but considerably paler about the gills.

The officer turned his head and stared at him for a moment.

"You are Citizen Paine?"

"I am."

"Then you will get dressed, if you will, and come with us. We can discuss the charge on the way to the Luxembourg."

He turned again to confront Nathan who had not moved or put up his sword. He stepped up close to him so they were almost eye to eye. A long, lupine face that might have been thought handsome had it not been for the arrogance and the cruelty in it; the face of a man who has been given more power than is good for him—or for anyone he encountered.

"Now stand aside, boy, before I take your little sword off you and give you a thrashing with it."

There was a moment when Nathan might have taken him by the throat but it passed. He stood aside as they marched Paine away down the stairs.

CHAPTER 15

Christmas in Paris

S ARA SETON HAD GROWN UP IN the conventional wisdom that
Death was essentially a silent presence: the thief who comes in
the night. You awoke to find him standing at the foot of your
bed, crooking a bony finger. He crept like a miasma into the room
where your mother lay ill and stole her breath away. He lingered
discreetly in the graveyard where you buried her like one of the pale
statues on the tombstones. But Death seemed to have grown noisier
of late. He came rampaging through the streets at the head of a mob
banging upon a drum and yelling, *Mort aux aristocrates.* He rattled
and creaked over the cobbles in the Rue Honoré with a cartload of
victims for the Machine on the Place de la Révolution. Or he came
banging on your door in the early hours of the morning escorted by
a squad of gendarmes with a warrant for your arrest, signed by the
proper authorities.

The one thing Death did not do in Paris in Year II of the Revolution was surprise you.

So when Sara was awoken by a determined knocking upon the door
early on Christmas morning her first thought was that it was Death
come for her at last, and the second the rather uncharitable hope that
he had got the address wrong and come for one of the neighbours.

She sprang from her bed and ran to the window but it was just one man and he did not look like a policeman. Then he stepped back a pace and looked up and she saw that it was Nathan.

She grabbed her robe and ran out on to the landing. Alex was standing at the open door of his bedroom looking anxious. He said nothing but there was a world of questions in his eyes.

"It is good," she told him. "It is the American. The friend of Mary's that I told you of. Go back to bed before you catch cold."

"Hélène!" she shouted. "The door."

But then she remembered. She had sent the maid off to her family for Noël. And the cook had gone to stay with her sister. She and Alex were alone in the house. She inspected herself in the mirror on the landing and lifted her hands to her hair to tie it back in a ribbon but then she thought better of it and let it fall back to her shoulders. She made a lion's roar to stretch the skin round her mouth and gnawed at her lips to put more colour into them. Then she ran down the stairs to the door. She had to struggle with the bolts and she was quite breathless when she finally opened it but it was only partly to do with her exertions.

"Madame, I am sorry, I . . ."

He tugged off his hat and stared at her like a delivery boy who has come to the wrong address.

"I am desolate to disturb you at such an hour."

His hair was longer than she remembered it and his face thinner; but he was still a mere child.

"I was hoping to find Imlay," he said.

"Imlay is not here," she told him.

"Oh."

They stared at each other in silence for a moment.

"Oh come in, come in," she said, standing back from the door. "Out of the cold."

"I should try and find him," he said but he stepped into the hall.

"I have sent all the servants away for Noël," she told him, as if she had a whole household of them and not just two women and a part-time gardener. "Whatever the authorities have to say about it, it is still the festive season, at least for some families."

But not hers. She had not wanted to draw attention to herself. She had not even been to Mass.

"Come down into the kitchen," she said. "It is warmer there and you can talk to me while I make some coffee."

She had banked the fire up for the night and happily there was still a small glow among the embers. She began to rake fiercely at them.

"Let me do that," he said, as if embarrassed for her.

"Just pass me a log from the basket," she told him. She had raked enough fires in her time. "Have you had breakfast?"

"No. But please do not trouble yourself . . ."

"It is no trouble. Sit."

She pointed at the table. Why did he make her feel like such an old dame—and why did she act like one? And what was she going to give him for breakfast? Gruel? They had some bread somewhere; a bit stale but she could toast it—and perhaps some cheese. Toasted cheese. The juices stirred at the thought of it and her stomach rumbled. She started grinding coffee beans to hide the noise. Her precious hoard.

She glanced sideways at him while she worked the grinder. He was resting his chin in his hands, gazing into space and looking worried. Not at all as she remembered him. She had made several sketches of him after they last met but she saw now that she had not got him quite right. She had made him too . . . Like something out of a fairy tale with high cheekbones and a wide mouth: a Puck or an Ariel, playing on his tin whistle. But he was not so fantastical. Beautiful, like a woman almost, but his features were stronger and his eyes more slanted; she had made them too big and round.

She had not thought to see him again. She still could not believe it was him and that he was sitting here in her kitchen. She caught his eye and felt herself blush.

"So you are back in Paris," she said to cover her confusion.

"I arrived last night from Le Havre. They said Imlay was in Paris and we have some business to attend to."

"He is probably with Mary in Neuilly."

"Neuilly?"

"A little village just outside the *barrière*. She rents a house there. You probably came through it on the way in from Le Havre."

"*Maman?*"

Alex stood at the door. Still in his nightdress.

"Little one, I said you were to stay in bed. Come over to the stove, then, to keep warm. This is my son Alex," she introduced them. "Monsieur Turner. Monsieur is a friend of Monsieur and Madame Imlay."

She really must learn to say Citoyen and Citoyenne but it seemed so ridiculous. Pretentious even. Everyone was forever pretending to be something they were not. But she did not want Alex saying the wrong thing in public and being denounced to the authorities. She had heard of children being taken away for little more than that and their parents thrown in prison.

"Alex, will you set the table for us?" she asked him. "We are having breakfast in the kitchen."

As if they were accustomed to dine in state with footmen to serve them.

She watched him as he set out the dishes, wondering what their visitor would make of him. He was a pretty child; people said he had her looks and not his father's. He looked so thin though. He caught her eye and she smiled. At least he had good manners. He was growing up in a very different world from his father—but that was not so very bad a thing. She filled the kettle and set it on the hob.

"Is it very urgent that you see Imlay?"

He nodded. "One of his friends has been arrested. Well, he is Mary's friend, really. They came for him at the hotel this morning."

She shook her head reprovingly, though it was not the most surprising event in Paris.

"What is his name?"

"Thomas Paine."

"Oh, but I know Mr. Paine!" Her hand flew to her cheek. "And they have arrested him? Oh, but how shocking. And he is a representative of the people. What are we come to? Assassins! Do you know where they have taken him?"

He frowned. "I thought they said Luxembourg, but I may have misheard . . ."

"No, you heard right. The Luxembourg. It is a prison—where they take most of the foreigners. All the English are there. Is that why they arrested him—even though he is American—because they say he is English?"

He looked puzzled. "I have no idea. They would not state the charge. Is it far from here, the prison?"

"Not far. It is the old palace of the Medici. Half the neighbourhood is in there."

She glanced towards the window as if they could see it from here and blinked in surprise.

"My goodness," she said, "it is snowing."

They made their way to the window, all three, and peered up at the snowflakes drifting down from the grey and purple sky. Great beautiful snowflakes. They were already sticking on the rooftops opposite, transforming the city into something different, something almost magical instead of the cruel, dangerous place it had become. Sara looked down at Alex and saw the wonder in his eyes and she knelt down to his level and put her arm round him and raised her face again to the window and the falling snow. But her eyes met Nathan's looking down at her and there was an expression in them that caused her some agitation. Too many feelings, they were upon her in a rush, like the mob, and as impossible to separate or control.

"Merry Christmas," he said and he grinned down at her and she saw him then as she had seen him with the mob, with the tin whistle to his lips and his eyes dancing with mischief and a kind of delight in the danger of it all.

"We could be snowed in," he said. "We could be trapped here for days."

She stood up, feeling shaky, disorientated. She did not know what to say but what came out surprised her.

"My husband died. In Germany. A fever of the blood."

He stared at her, the smile fading from his lips and his eyes.

"We only heard a month ago." She gathered her robe at her neck. "We are in mourning, officially."

"I am sorry," he said. His eyes said, what are you telling me?

She put her hand on Alex's head. It steadied her.

"So there is just me and Alex," she said, smiling down at the child.

"And Hélène," he reminded her, looking up at them both with his grave countenance.

"Oh, and Hélène," she confirmed, adding for the benefit of their guest, "our maid, though she has become more like a friend."

"And Marie-Eloise," the boy persisted.

"And Marie-Eloise," Sara confirmed—and to Nathan: "The cook."

"And Figaro."

"The cat." She silently indicated the creature, sleeping in his basket near the stove, or pretending to.

The kettle was boiling.

"Let us have coffee," she said.

They had coffee with toast and cheese, the three of them at the table and the cat wrapping itself around their legs, hoping for a share.

"Our affairs are in a muddle," she told him, a masterly understatement. "The Republic has confiscated my husband's property in the south. I have some land of my father's in Provence but it is poor and so are the tenants and the rents are not paid since the Revolution. I am not against the Revolution. But we are not rich and they make it very difficult for people like ourselves."

She wondered why she was telling him all this. Some compulsion to be open with him. To eschew pretence. You see me as I am, with no make up, thirty-two years old, the mother of a young child, and no money.

They had barely met.

He looked towards the window. The snow seemed to have eased a little.

"I should find Imlay," he said.

CHAPTER 16

a Thief in the Night

IT WAS SNOWING HARD NOW. NATHAN pulled up the collar of his greatcoat and bent his head into the blizzard as he set off in the direction of the river where he might find a cab. The whirling snowflakes mirrored his thoughts. Searching for a nautical analogy, he felt as if he was sailing off a lee shore with an unpredictable wind, no compass and a crew he could not rely upon.

But he did not know Paris as he knew the sea. He did not know its winds and its tides, its moods and shifting currents. He did not know where the rocks were, or where to shelter from the storms. And its storms were formidable, manic, terrifying . . . What he did know, even after so brief an acquaintance, was that Paris itself had become the central character in the drama that was engulfing France. Like the Dionysian chorus in the Bacchae: a frenzied, menacing madness that could and did engulf all the other characters. This was partly a matter of geography: the filthy, narrow streets with their workshops and wine shops and overcrowded tenements and dark courtyards . . . A breeding ground of riot and rebellion. Every neighbourhood, every Faubourg, a labyrinthine fortress with a core of agitators who could muster thousands of insurgents with the ringing of the tocsin.

Suddenly—and appropriately—Nathan realised he was lost. And not just in the metaphysical sense. He was not unduly concerned for although there was no one about from whom he could ask directions he knew he had only to walk downhill and sooner or later he would come to the river. He was trudging on with his head down and his thoughts far away when he became aware of a figure in his path. He looked up and was not entirely amazed to see a pistol aimed at his head.

"Stand," said the man who was holding it. "And give me your purse."

"I beg your pardon," said Nathan, with a frown.

"Make haste," the brigand insisted. "I am a desperate man."

This, Nathan concluded, was probably an accurate representation. His voice was high, verging on the hysterical, and his appearance, too, smacked of desperation, if not despair. He wore an old-fashioned tricorn hat and a scarf pulled over the lower part of his face—which was the accepted apparel for a footpad—but he had neither cape nor greatcoat and his jacket was thin and threadbare. Nor was he sturdy. Indeed he looked as if a sudden increase in the power of the wind would blow him over. He was shaking, either from cold or trepidation or a combination of both.

Nathan observed that the pistol was cocked but he could not tell if it was loaded. It seemed to him that if there was any powder in the pan it must almost certainly be damp. Since the incident with the mob and the *lanterne,* Nathan had taken the precaution of carrying his sword with him but it was hard to get at through his greatcoat and besides it did not seem necessary. He knocked the pistol aside with his left hand and struck out with the right, landing a blow high up on the side of the man's jaw. He staggered back and—with a completeness that rather surprised Nathan—measured his length in the snow.

Nathan stooped to pick up the pistol. The hammer had fallen but it had not exploded. No powder. He put it in his pocket and continued on his way.

After a few yards he stopped and thought for a moment. Then with a sigh he retraced his steps to where the man lay and prodded him with his boot.

"Come, sir," he commanded sternly, "do not lie there prevaricating or you will catch your death."

He did not stir. Nathan bent down and observed him more closely. He appeared to be breathing but if he were left to lie there in the falling snow Nathan's prediction would almost certainly be realised. But what was to be done with him? Nathan supposed he might cover him with his coat but he was not sure he was that much of a Samaritan. Besides, the Samaritan had saved a man who had been left for dead by footpads; whether his charity would have extended to the footpads themselves must remain in doubt.

He looked about him. No one in sight. He could try knocking upon one of the doors of the houses but it did not seem likely they would let him in, much less take a stranger into their care. It was possible he might carry him back to Sara Seton's house but he was still not entirely sure of the way and she might well regard it as an imposition.

With another sigh he stooped again and lifted the man up on to his shoulder. He was not quite as light as he had looked. Staggering a little, Nathan resumed his journey towards the waterfront.

Fortunately it was not far. And there was a tavern—or at least a wine shop—immediately to his right. It was not one he might have chosen in other circumstances but the clientele barely spared him a glance despite the body over his shoulder and by the time he had kicked the door shut behind him they had resumed their discourse, such as it was. Presumably they assumed the man was drunk and were accustomed to such an event. Nathan deposited his burden at an empty table and crossed to the bar.

"Hot punch?" he inquired with no great expectation. Mine host almost laughed in his face. "Brandy then. Two glasses."

He carried the tumblers back to the table and set one down in front of his comatose companion. Either from coincidence or some deep mental stimulus he came immediately to his senses. He stared at Nathan and then rolled his eyes around the room, clearly confused.

Nathan reminded him of the circumstances that had delivered him here.

The villain put his hand to the side of his head and winced.

"You hit me," he recalled.

"I did," agreed Nathan, offering the brandy.

The villain drank and was immediately seized by a fit of coughing that threatened to carry him off entirely.

"That's good," he said, still choking but reaching a trembling hand once more for the tumbler. He paused however as his fingers closed around the glass and glanced suspiciously about the room.

"You did not send for the police?"

"It would surely have been easier for me to leave you in the snow," Nathan pointed out, "and let them find your body in the morning."

The villain appeared to see the logic in this. He attempted to say thank you and was wracked by another fit of violent coughing.

"Well, if you're feeling more yourself," said Nathan, "I'll be on my way."

But the creature was waving at him helplessly, still hacking, but clearly wishful that he should stay.

"I am not a violent man," he managed to impart. "But I am desperate."

"So you informed me upon our first acquaintance."

"I am not a professional brigand." Nathan inclined his head in polite agreement, having seen nothing that might cause him to dispute the claim. "I am an *égoutier*."

This was an unfamiliar word to Nathan but on further inquiry it transpired that his new companion was one of that rare breed of creatures that maintained the Paris sewers. Rarer still since the Revolution, by his account, for the Commune was less punctilious in its payments than the old City Provost appointed by the King. Kings being more offended by smells, perhaps, than commoners.

"And I have a wife and child to support," the fellow concluded miserably.

Nathan nodded, not without sympathy, but wondered where the conversation might be leading.

"What I am saying is—I am sorry." He lowered his head in shame.

"Think nothing of it," said Nathan, kindly, "though you would be well advised not to repeat the attempt on another. You have not the voice for it, nor if I may make so personal an observation, the build."

He rose to leave but the fellow had not quite finished with him.

"I wonder," he began, hesitantly, "if you have my pistol."

"I have," said Nathan, frowning.

"Well, I wonder if I might have it back."

"No you may not, you rogue."

"It was only borrowed," said the fellow, "and if I do not return it there will be a price to pay."

Nathan sighed. He sat down once more, took the pistol from his pocket and slid it across the table. Then, after a moment's hesitation, he took out the folder where he kept his paper money and placed a hundred livre note next to the pistol on the table.

"Get something to eat," he said, "and a coat, if that is enough." He frowned. "*Is* it enough?"

The fellow was staring at the note on the table as though mesmerised. "I do not know what to say," he began.

Nathan rose to his feet but a claw-like hand seized him by the coat sleeve.

"If you are in need of a service, ask for me at the Café de Carthage in the Rue Saint-Antoine."

"Assuredly," Nathan replied politely, though he did not consider the man's undoubted knowledge of the Paris sewers would be of much use to him in his present predicament.

"Ask for Philippe," the man insisted. "The *égoutier*."

CHAPTER 17

City of Death

"E MUST SET OFF FIRST THING in the morning," Imlay
insisted. "Before it snows again."
He appeared more interested in the fate of his cargo
than in that of Thomas Paine. Perhaps this was not a surprise.

Nathan glanced pointedly out of the window. They were in Mary's
house in Neuilly and the garden was deep in snow. He had ridden
out of Paris because the cabs would not venture on the roads outside
the city. It would be a nightmare journey to Le Havre and from the
look of the sky there was more on the way.

"We can go by river," Imlay insisted, "if the roads are too bad."

"Gilbert," Mary complained gently but he shot her a look and
shook his head to quiet her.

"The tobacco is safe enough in the hold of the *Speedwell*," Nathan
attempted to reassure him. "It will keep until the weather improves."

"I am not at all happy with the situation in Le Havre," Imlay fretted.

He paced restlessly about the small room. Mary had lit the candles
though it was not yet dark and there was a cheerful fire. The remains
of dinner were still on the table. Nathan wished he had stayed with
Sara in Paris.

"We can leave from here," Imlay continued as he walked the room:
like a captain, Nathan thought, pacing his quarterdeck or a prisoner

his cell. He pounded his fist into his palm gently as if he was beating out a rhythm.

"There are barges in Neuilly on their way down the Seine. You can stay the night. It is longer than by road but . . ."

Nathan shook his head firmly.

"I have business in Paris," he said. "I cannot leave immediately."

"Business?" Imlay frowned. "What business?"

"Imlay!" Mary protested, shocked. "You are not polite."

Imlay's face, already glowing from the fire and his dinner, grew a shade more crimson.

"I am very sorry, my dear, but this is important."

"My business was with Thomas Paine," said Nathan. He wondered if this was wise. "And I cannot leave him to rot in prison."

"No more can we," said Mary firmly. "You are too concerned with commerce, my dear," she chided Imlay gently.

"It is commerce that pays the bills," he snapped and Nathan saw her flinch as if he had struck her. Imlay flung himself down in a chair.

"What are they doing arresting Paine? He is an American citizen. A friend of Washington." He looked at Nathan as if it was his fault. "Unless it is this 'business' of yours."

The thought had occurred to Nathan but he resented hearing it from Imlay. Was the man drunk? It was entirely possible.

"I had better return to Paris," he said, rising to his feet. He turned apologetically to Mary who looked ready to burst into tears.

"Oh sit down, man, sit down." Imlay flapped a hand at him. "I am sorry if I have vexed you. I am out of sorts. It is this blasted cargo. I cannot let it rot in Le Havre. And if you cannot go with me, then I must go by myself."

"Well, the ship's mate has the bill of lading," Nathan assured him coldly. "He is perfectly capable of loading five hundred chests of tobacco into a few barges."

Imlay looked across at his wife, sitting at the far side of the fireplace. "I am sorry, my dear," he said, though he sounded more exasperated than regretful, "but I fear I must go, just for a few days."

"Then go," she said, her face white. "We will have to manage our affairs without you."

"Do not, I beg of you, do anything foolish while I am away."

"What could I possibly do," she inquired, "tucked away here in Neuilly like a little mouse?"

And Nathan caught a glimpse of the old Mary that had been the terror of London.

He viewed the prison across the frozen gardens, a vast, sprawling Renaissance chateau with a sprinkling of snow on its soaring abundance of turrets and rooftops. It had been built early in the seventeenth century for Marie de Medici, widow of the murdered King Henry IV, and even with its boarded and shuttered windows it retained elements of Renaissance grandeur, though it suggested to Nathan more the castle of an ogre than the palace of a queen. And now it was a prison, though the only physical barrier preventing a closer approach to the walls appeared to be a wrought-iron railing about seven or eight feet high tipped with *fleurs-de-lis*. There were sentry boxes at intervals but no sentries that they could see. Perhaps they were inside keeping warm.

He heard shouts and looked back. Alex had made a snowball and hurled it at his mother and now she was trying to scrape up enough to throw back at him. She appeared very young—and happy. She caught his eye and looked a little sheepish. They were not supposed to look happy with Thomas Paine in the Luxembourg and Mary risking her own safety by visiting him there.

They walked on beside the lake with its frozen fountain and its sepulchral statues. They seemed to be the only human figures in the frozen landscape and Nathan felt exposed to the gaze of hidden watchers high in the palace turrets. The gardens were open to the public but not many people went there these days, Sara had warned him, and it was wise not to stop and stare. Then they entered an avenue of chestnut trees flanking the west wing and saw a small crowd at the far end just outside the railings.

"They are friends or relatives of the prisoners." Sara had dropped her voice, though only the trees could have heard her. "There is a large room—a gallery—on the upper floor with windows overlooking the gardens and the prisoners are allowed to walk there about this time of day."

Nathan wondered how she came to know so much about the interior of the prison and its workings but kept the thought to himself. The crowd was composed mainly of women and children, huddling in the cold like mourners at a funeral. Two guards stared stonily back at them from inside the railings.

"We should not go too close," warned Sara. "There will almost certainly be policemen or informers among them."

"How long will they wait?"

"Oh, hours sometimes. It is quite wretched to see them, the children especially, stretching out their hands to their fathers inside the prison."

They turned off along another path that led back out on to the streets. Most of the snow had gone from here or turned to slush and the light was fading. They waited in a small café in the Rue Medici where they had arranged to meet Mary and drank hot chocolate and ate small honey cakes. Nathan paid. People were starving in the Faubourg Saint Antoine, it was said, but you could still eat and drink well in Paris if you had money. The trick was not to dress as if you did. He wore his greatcoat and his knitted Breton hat with the tricolour pinned firmly to the side.

"Are you a sailor?" asked Alex through a mouthful of cake.

"Yes," said Nathan, after considering a moment and finding no apparent danger in the admission.

"Where is your ship?"

"In Le Havre."

"Did you sail it from America?"

"I did," Nathan lied. He thought he saw Sara look sharply at him. Had Mary told her he was from England? He avoided her eye for the moment.

"I would like to go to America. My father was a soldier in America. He fought against the English. Did you fight against the English?"

"No. I was too young," Nathan told him.

Was he? He tried to work it out. But of course he was. All these lies were unsettling him.

"I would like to fight against the English."

"Alex, please do not speak with your mouth full."

Nathan smiled at her but she did not smile back and her eyes were guarded. Happily the door opened and Mary swept in looking flushed and excited.

"Villains," she said, hurling herself into an empty chair.

"Would they not let you see him?" Sara kept her voice low.

"Oh, I saw him." She shook her head fiercely. "He is in a damp cell, below ground level, with water streaming down the walls and no fire. No fire or even any light, not so much as a candle."

"Keep your voice down," Sara warned her glancing about the café. It was practically empty and the proprietor was watching them from the bar.

"They let you into his cell?"

"No. There is a visiting room. But he told me what it is like."

"How is he?" Nathan asked her.

"How do you think in those conditions? He looks like death. I complained to the governor."

"You saw the governor?"

"Well, his assistant. I said he is an American citizen and a representative of the National Convention and they dare to treat him like a common criminal."

"What did he say?" Sara seemed amazed. Clearly this was a side of Mary she had not seen before.

"He said it was a temporary measure until they received the papers from the Police Bureau. Then they would move him to a proper cell. But he seemed shaken when I said he was a friend of George Washington."

"*Is* he a friend of George Washington?"

"Well, Imlay says so." She shrugged. Nathan gathered that she did not regard this as the firmest of endorsements. "I said he has committed no crime, broken no laws and was imprisoned for one reason only—to prevent him from writing about the crimes against liberty."

Their expressions reflected a degree of concern.

"Well, someone has to tell them."

Nathan could understand why she and his mother had seemed to get on so well.

"They said he was imprisoned under the Law of Suspects. Ha. Are you rich?" she demanded of Nathan, though she might have been addressing the entire café by the volume of her voice. "You must be cheating the state. Suspect!"

The proprietor looked up in alarm.

"Are you poor? You must have sent your money out of the country. Suspect!"

"Mary," hissed Sara in horror. Two people got up and left the café.

"Are you a recluse? You must have something to fear. Suspect! Are you cheerful? You must be celebrating a national defeat. Are you sad? The State of the Nation must depress you. Are you a philosopher, a writer or a poet? Suspect, suspect, suspect."

Nathan offered her the last cake.

"Do you want a hot chocolate?" he asked her.

"No," she said, standing up. "We haven't the time."

"Where are we going now?"

"I know where *I* am going. I am going to see the American Minister. You can come with me if you like. If you have had enough cake."

"So you are back in Paris," the American Minister remarked to Nathan, as if it was a circumstance very much to be regretted.

Gouverneur Morris was a tall, confident man of middling years with handsome if florid features, marred, to Nathan's thinking, by the supercilious contours of his mouth. If it was a smile it was one that reflected the Minister's good opinion of himself rather than anyone else in the world. His most dominant feature, however, was a wooden leg which gave him a certain piratical air, though Imlay said he lost it falling out of his carriage, drunk. It fitted into a kind of basket at the knee with straps attaching it to the thigh and as he leaned back in his armchair it pointed directly at Nathan's groin, rather disconcertingly like a cannon or a swivel gun.

They were in the library of his house in the Rue de la Planche with the curtains drawn and a fire lit. It might have been cosy but their welcome had not been as warm as Nathan might have wished. He and Mary Imlay sat side by side on the sofa while the Minister regarded them haughtily through the pince-nez that he kept on a silk ribbon round his neck.

"I am only lately arrived," Nathan told him, "from New York."

"And for what purpose on this occasion, if I may make so bold?"

"The study of astronomy," replied Nathan. "I am making a study of the works of Tycho Brahe in the Paris Observatoire."

He felt Mary's stare but the Minister regarded him with a new interest.

"Really? So you are a scholar, sir? Have you had anything published?"

"An insignificant little paper on the mathematical relationship between the cube of a planet's distance from the sun and the square of its orbital period."

"Really?" Morris appeared genuinely impressed.

"And an article in the *Harvard Science Review* on Herschel's discovery of the planet Uranus and the mathematical probability of there being another just behind it."

Mary cleared her throat and moved her foot next to his. He suspected that in a moment he would feel some pressure.

"I am heartened that Paris continues to attract the attentions of a scholar and a gentleman," Morris confided, "for all that her most accomplished citizens are led to the guillotine, or butchered by the mob and tossed into holes in the ground like dead dogs. Bailly, the previous mayor, was an astronomer, I recall, with an international reputation, but it did not save him from losing his head."

He sighed and Mary cleared her throat but he had not finished.

"Ah Paris, how she bleeds. Art is gone. The dancers are gone. The *modistes* are gone. Paris is left to the mercy of the provinces for its fashions whence come little bonnets trimmed with yellow flowers." He pulled a face as if a quantity of bile had been stirred. "Only the theatres appear to thrive. I wonder if that is significant, the national temperament being somewhat inclined to drama? And duelling, I believe, is more popular than ever, being no longer confined to the quality. The morning procession of cabs to the Bois de Boulogne resembles that of the tumbrels in the afternoon, I am told, and produces almost as many corpses. Yes, Paris does its best to divert us from more serious pursuits. One goes to one's club to murder a little time. I have seen enough to convince me that a man might be incessantly occupied in this city for forty years and grow old without knowing what in the least he has been about."

"Thomas Paine," Mary said at last, recalling him to the purpose of their visit.

"Paine." The American Minister closed his eyes and gripped the bridge of his nose between finger and thumb as if the source of his discomfort had taken up residence there and could not be dislodged. "I cannot tell you how that man has plagued me since he came to France."

"I am sure it is to be regretted," agreed Mary. "However, he is now incarcerated in the Luxembourg and . . ."

"Do you know why he came here in the first place?"

"I understood," said Mary, "that it was to assist the cause of Revolution."

"In fact it was to build a bridge."

Nathan thought he meant in the metaphysical sense but no, he meant a real bridge.

"He fancies himself as an engineer as well as a philosopher. Building bridges is his forte. Indeed he offered to build one for me once—across the Harlem River, where we maintain a modest estate. He said it would increase the traffic to New York and we might charge a toll. We thanked him politely but declined and I fear he took it amiss. And so he became a Revolutionist."

He addressed Nathan. "You are familiar with his works, sir?"

As if they were the Devil's . . . Nathan had seen both volumes of *The Rights of Man* on the Minister's bookshelves beside the works of Rousseau and Voltaire but they were books that might be found in the library of any gentleman with pretensions to learning.

"I am," he confirmed. Mary made a small noise of disgust.

"'America is to be the hope of mankind,'" Morris quoted satirically. "'A safe haven from which the friends of liberty might pour forth and spew . . .'"

"'*Spread* their campaign for free and equal citizenship around the world,'" Mary completed the quotation accurately in acid tones.

"Indeed." Morris arched his eyebrows at her. "I had forgot you are an educated woman, Mrs. Imlay. I wonder if the French were as well informed when they elected him to the National Convention. I am inclined to doubt it. One of his first speeches—he hardly speaks a word of French but it does not prevent him from making speeches, alas—was to call for the abolition of slavery. This did not go down at all well. In fact I doubt it would have been more coldly received in Virginia. You appear bemused, madam. Yes, you might think the Revolutionists would oppose slavery but without slaves they would have no coffee, sugar or tobacco. Life would be even more insup-portable than it is already. So Paine was not so popular of a sud-den. People began to call him Tom le Fou. 'Tom Fool' or 'Mad Tom' like the English. Tom o' Bedlam. Then he opposed the execution of the King. Another surprise, given his views on monarchy. He would take his crown but not his head. He is not a sanguine man, our Thomas, whatever else might be said about him. He wished to have the King banished to America. With his entire family. He proposed that Congress should purchase a farmhouse for them somewhere near Philadelphia and that I should escort them thither. You smile, madam. Have I said something amusing?"

"Your pardon, sir, it was the image of the King and Queen of France on a farm in America."

"If it were that or the guillotine you might not consider it such a poor choice, madam," he snapped. "Unhappily it was not a choice they were given."

He looked away into the fire and by its glow Nathan saw his eyes were moist. Morris and Marie Antoinette had become close friends, Imlay had said, and perhaps more.

"It is partly because he spoke up for them in the Convention," Mary reminded him, "that Mr. Paine is now in prison. The very least we can do, I would have thought, is to make a strenuous protest on his behalf to the French Foreign Ministry."

Morris regarded her coldly. "The reason Mr. Paine is in prison is that the present rulers of France entertain hopes of American aid in the war against England. They need American grain and American tobacco and," he waved a hand airily, "whatever else is grown in America. They do not wish this notorious troublemaker to poison the Congress against them."

"I would not have thought that it would recommend the present rulers of France to the American people that they have imprisoned its greatest philosopher and a hero of the American Revolution," Mary pointed out.

Morris sighed and rubbed a hand across his face. He did not look at all well, Nathan thought. Imlay said he was a martyr to the gout and was often to be seen with his right foot swathed in bandages, which given the absence of its neighbour seemed especially unfortunate.

"Perhaps a letter to the Foreign Minister," Mary persisted, "reminding him that Thomas Paine is an American citizen and a friend of President Washington."

Morris frowned, shaking his head.

"It would do no good," he said. "No good at all. The Foreign Minister has no influence whatsoever. You might as well appeal to the ticket clerk at the Comédie-Française."

"Then what is your advice, sir?" she demanded coldly.

"My advice, madam, is to wait upon events and trust that the

French authorities will come to recognize Mr. Paine's worth as a philosopher."

"And if they condemn him as an enemy of the people?"

"Then I trust he will find comfort in philosophy."

Nathan emerged from the Palais de Justice with a *permis de passage* extending his leave to remain in Paris until the end of the month. He had used the story he had given Morris: that he was studying the astronomical works of Tycho Brahe in the Paris Observatoire and needed more time for his research. Although this had occurred to him without much thought, it seemed singularly appropriate as a reason to stay in Paris, for Brahe had been the protégé of Marie de Medici, the chatelaine of the Luxembourg.

He stopped for a moment on the river and watched the barges being unloaded on the quays and thought of his own cargo which should now be well on its way to Paris. Imlay had returned by coach two days ago: a much more cheerful man than when he had set out from Neuilly. The *Speedwell*'s cargo had been loaded into a smaller 80-ton vessel and brought up to Rouen whence it would be transferred into barges for the journey into Paris. Tully was now waiting for Nathan to rejoin them in Le Havre.

And yet he lingered in Paris.

He told himself that he had a mission to complete: a mission far more important than the delivery of contraband tobacco to an American shipping agent. Whatever services Imlay was prepared to render to the British government, they could not possibly be more important than the prospect of peace, and while there was still hope of Paine's release, Nathan could not bring himself to admit his mission a failure.

But was this the real reason he stayed in Paris?

The bells of Notre-Dame tolled the hour. At noon he was meeting Sara after her art lesson in the Rue Honoré. He could not get the woman out of his mind. But what did he want from her? Well, one thing was obvious; he could not delude himself about that.

Romance? Yes, certainly there was that, but the sexual element was paramount. She seemed to exude some drug that had intoxicated him. Being close to her was like ... he sought an analogy, and found one in his study of the planets. Magnetism. He was like a planet orbiting the sun, unable to escape its pull, destined to make that eternal trajectory, never coming any closer, never getting away.

Fool. Poor, bloody fool that he was. And the *Speedwell* waiting for him in Le Havre.

He crossed the river and began to walk westward along the front of the Louvre and the Tuileries, walking for no particular reason except that he had an hour to kill and his head was full of questions and doubts. The waterfront was busier here. Gangs of stevedores were working on the barges moored two or three deep along the quays. More people, more activity than he had seen in the course of his dismal journey inland from Le Havre through the drab, dispirited villages with the black-shawled women silent in the doorways and the men gone to the wars. But this was the front-line of the Revolution and these its crack troops mustered at the ring of the tocsin to do bloody execution in the cause of liberty. Certainly they looked as if they might be useful in a fight with those savage hooks they carried to thrust into the bales of cargo and heave them on to their backs. And would as soon thrust into living flesh ...

He had been walking for some minutes along the waterfront and now he came to a bridge, swathed in scaffolding, with barges on the river below, laden with stones from the Bastille, the great prison that had been taken by the mob in '89, at the start of it all. Stones that were now being used to build new and more useful edifices for the Republic. Nathan remembered the excitement of his friends in New York when they first told him of events in Paris that summer, which now seemed so long ago. As if they were seeing the dawning of a new world order. As if the spirit of their own revolution, their own sense of liberty, had spread back across the Atlantic and the Old World had been born again in a new image. Even in England there had been such hope—and not just among his mother's friends.

And now . . .

He looked up as he heard the sound of a drum. He had been walk-ing without noticing much where he was going and now he saw that he was in a large open space, part meadow and part town square, with some great buildings on the far side and a large crowd of people in the middle, gathered around an object that he recognized with a shock as the guillotine.

Or the Humane and Scientific Execution Machine, as the Revolu-tionists called it.

No longer shrouded.

A macabre curiosity compelled him to seek a closer view of the device. It had been designed by the King himself, he had heard, who had amused himself by making locks and other mechanical contrap-tions while his country slid into chaos. But its popular name was de-rived from Dr. Guillotine, the man who had tested it at the School of Medicine in Paris, using corpses, it was said, of criminals who had suffered the traditional forms of execution by hanging or being beaten to death with iron bars. It was supposed to be much more hu-mane than either. The blade fell so fast and cut so cleanly, the severed arteries gushed like a fountain but there was no pain, the good doc-tor reported; it was like someone blowing on the back of your neck.

Nathan shivered and turned away, ashamed to be so ghoulish. He was not in favour of public executions, nor inclined to watch them. But then from the street opposite, parallel with the river, there emerged a grim procession.

First there was the drummer, beating the step, then a file of foot soldiers in blue uniforms with fixed bayonets. Then a troop of horse. And then the carts. Farm carts with high sides that the English called tumbrels and the French *charrettes*.

Nathan stood as though mesmerised. The convoy turned and came across the square and passed within a few yards of where he was standing. Two carts with about five or six prisoners in each. And all of them women.

Women of all ages, though mostly young. Their hands were tied behind them and their clothes torn at the front, as low as the breast. And their hair cut short to expose the neck. Some were crying, the tears coursing down their grimy faces, some were moving their lips as if in prayer, others simply looked dazed.

The sight stirred memories that were buried deep in Nathan's memory—or perhaps not memory, for he had not been alive at the time; more of an instinctive response that combined elements of loathing and horror and fear. Like a family curse. The witches of Salem.

And some of this must have shown in his face for after they had passed he saw a man looking at him with suspicion. A man better dressed than most he had seen in France, with red, white and blue plumes in his hat and thigh-length boots and a sword at his hip.

"Why are they all women?" inquired Nathan. It came out almost without thinking, as if in explanation of his shock, for he thought the man might be an official.

The man continued to stare at him silently.

"What have they done?" Nathan persisted, unwisely perhaps.

"They are whores," said the man. "Or nuns." With a shrug as if there was no distinction.

The carts had reached the scaffold now and the women were being led out of them and stood in two rows with their backs to the machine.

"Are you a foreigner?" said the man, stepping closer, and his hand was on the hilt of his sword.

Nathan shook his head and turned away, pushing through the crowd.

He stopped after a while, when it was clear he was not pursued, and found he was shaking. From fear or anger or something of both. And disgust. He felt as if he was walking through a city of death.

He could not walk away from this. But what could he do?

Danton would stop the Terror.

Nathan recalled the words but not who had said them. Then he remembered: Tom Paine on the night before his arrest. He felt an excitement and an agitation, very like his feelings for Sara. A sense of frustration. He could do something about this if only he knew how.

Could he approach Danton himself?

But what was he to tell him? He was no diplomat. He had no powers vested in him. Danton might denounce him to the authorities as
an English spy.

He would certainly suspect him of being a provocateur.

But should he not take the risk? Or was it all vanity? Vanity and
delusion. Just as he had thought the cannonball fired at him in the
mouth of the Somme would give him enduring fame as the instigator
of war, now he thought to be the instigator of peace.

"Good day, Citizen."

He stopped dead and found himself staring at Sara Seton.

She was regarding him with a quizzical smile and her head tilted
at an inquiring angle.

Of course, he was in the Rue Honoré. It was the route they
took with the death carts from the Conciergerie to the Place de la
Révolution. And it was where the painter Regnault had his studio,
where Sara went for her art lessons.

"What were you thinking?" she said. "You looked as if you were in
another world."

The world of the dead. Did she not see them, did she not hear
them, when they passed below the windows of the studio? Did she
carry on painting her flowers, or whatever it was she painted, while
the death carts rolled through the street below with their hapless
cargo? Did she close her eyes and her mind to them, like the rest
of Paris?

"I have news for you," she said excitedly but glancing over her
shoulder and lowering her voice for fear of being overheard. "From
Mary. The Americans in Paris have made a protest against the arrest
of Thomas Paine. They have been invited to petition the National
Convention and they have asked Imlay to be their spokesman. Mary
is delighted. She is confident that Paine will be promptly released."

CHAPTER 18

the Room of the Machines

NATHAN SAT BETWEEN MARY IMLAY AND Sara Seton in the front row of the public gallery of the National Convention and looked down into the auditorium as it filled up with the representatives of the French Republic. Stoves had been lit to take the edge off the chill and the sense of drama was intensified by the shafts of winter sunlight that lanced through the smoky air from the windows set high in the walls.

It had links with the theatre. It had once been the props room for the royal theatre of the Tuileries: the Salle des Machines where they kept the scenery and the ingenious devices used in masques and other entertainments. Lately it had been redesigned by the artist David as a suitable forum for the voice of the people but Nathan's first and lasting impression was of the Roman circus. This was partly because of the noise: the roar of several hundred voices that echoed around the great chamber; partly the seating which rose steeply from the body of the hall and curved in a wide semi-circle leaving a space in the middle for the tribune where the main drama took place: where reputations were made and lost and where the heroes of the French people fought what had increasingly become a fight to the death; and partly the three great tricolours that hung from ceiling to floor behind the President of the Convention sitting on his throne high above the rabble like the Roman Emperor himself, ready to turn his thumb up or down, to decide who should live and who should die.

The President's was not a permanent office. In keeping with the spirit of the Republic, he was chosen from among the representatives for a period of two weeks and then succeeded by another. Today it was a man called Vadier who was also the chairman of the Committee of General Security—the Police Committee.

"People call him the Grand Inquisitor," whispered Sara as the noise died down to a murmur and the Americans came in.

We who are about to die, salute you.

Unlikely gladiators, they looked for the most part like the respectable men of business they were—brokers, bankers and merchants—the exception being Gilbert Imlay who as usual gave the impression that he would be more comfortable dressed in buckskin riding upon a horse. But he stood with the others, soberly suited with their hats in their hands, at the bar of the Convention—seventeen good men and true—while the representatives of the French people gazed upon them with curiosity or indifference or growled like lions that smelt a Christian.

Vadier leaned forward over his desk, ringing his bell for silence.

"Who speaks for the petition?" he asked, fixing the Americans with a glare over his pince-nez. He was in his late fifties, one of the oldest members of the Convention, a former soldier in the King's Army and a magistrate.

"I do," said Imlay, stepping forward to the long rail that they called the bar of the Convention. He leaned on it as if it was the bar of a tavern and he was waiting for the President to have the courtesy to serve him a drink. Nathan glanced sideways at Mary and saw her staring at him with lips parted and eyes shining, utterly adoring.

Vadier invited him to address the Convention.

Imlay had a good voice. It carried well but without apparent effort. The expatriates had chosen him for his voice and because they said he spoke the best French but Nathan was surprised he had accepted the privilege. It was not without danger. He suspected Mary's hand in it.

"Citizens," Imlay began. "The honour of representing the French people has been extended to the most famous men of other nations. Among them, the member for Pas-de-Calais, Thomas Paine: the apostle of liberty in America, a respected philosopher and a citizen renowned for his virtue . . ."

But already it was going badly. There was hissing from the galleries and a stamping of feet. Imlay looked a little taken aback but he persisted, raising his voice a notch.

"In the name of the friends of liberty, your American allies and your brothers, I beg you to consider our plea for the unconditional release of Thomas Paine. We urge you: do not allow the alliance of despots the pleasure of seeing him in prison. His papers have been examined and reveal only that love of liberty and those principles of public morality that have earned him the hatred of kings and the love of his fellow citizens."

But there was no love here. Many of the delegates were now on their feet howling insults and shaking their fists and the public galleries were a seething mass of hatred and rage. Imlay stepped back among his fellow Americans, smiling a little and shaking his head. Nathan glanced at Mary again. Her face was white.

"It has been orchestrated by the Jacobins," she said.

Nathan looked around him at the howling faces. The sunlight had faded and the tallow candles had been lit and in their smoky yellow light they looked like a pack of snarling dogs. Yes, he thought, it has been orchestrated. This was how it worked.

The President was ringing his bell furiously and at last the noise died down. A man stood up, among the high benches to the left of the tribunal where the leading Jacobins sat, an area known as the Mountain. He began to make his way forward between the rows of delegates and another murmur arose and a single name: Danton.

Nathan watched him as he made his way to the tribune. He moved easily, almost sauntered, with every eye upon him. A colossus in height and girth, with a massive head and neck, like a bull's. There was a story that he once had a fight with a bull when he was a child on his mother's farm in Arcis on the Aube. It was one of the few fights he had ever lost and the experience was engraved on his features. His nose was broken and flattened. A great scar ran down one side of his face, another twisted his lip, lifting one corner in a permanent sneer. An extraordinary face. It surpassed ugliness. There was so much force in it, so much power and vitality. He looked like a stevedore or a blacksmith. In fact, unlikely as it seemed, he was a lawyer by profession and still in his early thirties.

He ascended the tribune, threw back his head and gazed imperiously around the assembly as if someone might challenge his right to be here. It was unthinkable.

"The will of the people is that Terror should be the order of the day," he began. Like Imlay he appeared to be making no effort to raise his voice, there was no strain in his throat, but it carried easily to every corner of the hall. "But Terror, if it is necessary, should be directed against the real enemies of the Republic and against them alone."

There was a murmur of approval from the benches in the middle of the hall where the majority of delegates sat. The Plain. Or less politely, the Marsh where they sank in obscurity under the shadow of the Mountain.

"It is not the will of the people that a man whose only fault is a lack of enthusiasm should be treated as if he were a criminal—and a—traitor. That way leads only to despotism, and the end of liberty."

He turned abruptly from the tribune and was halfway to the benches before the applause began. Some even began to cheer. Nathan looked down at the Americans. Imlay was smiling as if they had won. But could the mood turn as swiftly and decisively as this? Just because Danton had spoken.

It was possible. The Marsh invariably did what the Mountain told them ...

But the Mountain no longer spoke with one voice.

The President was exercising his arm again and Nathan saw that another man had stood up on the benches to the left, not far from where Danton had been sitting. A slight man in a green jacket with white hair.

"Citizen Robespierre," announced the President.

A roar from the galleries. Clapping and cheering and waving of hats as Maximilien Robespierre made his way to the tribune; the idol of the Jacobins and the spiritual leader of the Revolution though he had no office or title. His friends called him the Incorruptible, or the People's Tribune; his enemies the Eunuch or *le chat-tigre*, the tiger-cat.

Robespierre, too, moved slowly but it could never be described as a saunter. His tread was too careful for that, indeed very like a cat's. A cat in high heels. He wore breeches and striped stockings in a style that had been in vogue before the Revolution among aristocrats. Yet he did not look like an aristocrat. He looked more like a tailor who catered for aristocrats. Or a valet, perhaps. There could have been no greater contrast with Danton, though they were both lawyers by profession and much the same age.

He mounted the tribune. It seemed to dwarf him. In fact he looked almost childlike as he blinked at the assembly, his expression pensive, almost perplexed. He pulled down a pair of spectacles that had been hidden in his powdered hair—it was his own hair, Nathan saw now, and not a wig—and adjusted them on his nose, consulting a single page of notes. Then he looked up—and was a different man. The spectacles transformed his features. Green-tinted with thick frames, they gave him a palpable air of menace. It might have been Nathan's imagination but he felt a sudden chill in the air. The chamber was completely hushed.

"People have appealed for indulgence," he began. His voice was unimpressive, thin and reedy. It made you strain to listen—but perhaps that was to his advantage. "The threat, they say, has been exaggerated."

He adjusted his spectacles and gazed around his audience through the green-tinted lenses as if to give himself time to think, or to ensure that everyone was listening.

"France is the champion of freedom. The men of this chamber have been its greatest defenders. But there is a conspiracy to destroy it. Orchestrated by foreign tyrants but supported by the enemy within. Even in this very chamber."

He deliberately did not look up towards Danton and his friends on the highest levels of the Mountain but others did. His authority now was complete. He seemed to have grown in stature as he gazed reprovingly out from the tribune, the green lenses of his glasses like large, gleaming eyes . . .

"If freedom is to be defended, the most extreme measures must be taken against those who would destroy it. We must harden our hearts. We must fight Tyranny with Terror, the cold, pure, virtuous Terror of the state . . ." He glanced now with defiance towards Danton. "There must be no indulgence for the enemies of the people."

He left the tribune to thunderous applause. Especially, Nathan noted, from those on the Plain who had clapped loudest for Danton.

The President rang his bell for order. Then he addressed the Americans standing at the bar of the Convention, with their hats still in their hands . . .

The alliance of France and America was a vital weapon in the war on Tyranny, he began. "But Thomas Paine . . ." He drew his brows together and leaned over his desk, peering down at the Americans over his spectacles like a schoolmaster surveying a class of hopeless dunces. His face was cadaverous, his complexion yellow in the light of the lamps. "Thomas Paine is not an American. Thomas Paine is an Englishman. Born in a country with which we are at war!" The delegates on the floor of the chamber and the spectators in the galleries were now united in their fury and the President's voice could scarcely be heard above their clamour. "An enemy of the people, marching with the enemies of France and Revolution. He will be judged by the tribunes of the people. And if he is found guilty, he will pay the price demanded by the people."

And the howls were like the fury of the mob, baying for blood.

"Well," said Nathan, "I suppose it was worth a try."

He stood with Sara in the gardens of the Tuileries waiting for Mary who had gone off to find Imlay. It was properly dark now and a chill wind moved the lanterns in the trees. There was still a thin layer of snow upon the ground and icy flakes swirled in the wind and stung the face like gravel.

"They are afraid," she said. She was shivering and he wanted to put his arm around her and take her home to bed.

"Of Robespierre?" He seemed such an unlikely man to inspire fear, and yet . . .

She nodded vigorously. "And the mob. Those in the galleries. They are brought here by the Jacobins. Some of them are paid. Paid thugs, that is all they are."

Nathan turned sharply as he heard a sound in the trees. It might have been the sighing of the wind but there was something else, like the hiss of a blade drawn from leather. He saw a figure standing in the shadows and called out.

"Who's there? Imlay—is that you?"

One of the lanterns swung in the trees and in the brief light he saw the features of the officer who had arrested Paine: Commissioner Gillet. Nathan whirled round as he heard the footfalls in the snow, expecting to see gendarmes closing in on him. But they were not gendarmes. He heard the sharp intake of breath from Sara. He stooped swiftly for the knife in his boot—but it was not there. It was not permitted to carry weapons in the Convention or anywhere in the vicinity.

This did not seem to have troubled the men in the trees. He caught the glint of steel as they closed in on him. Five or six of them, armed with knives. No, not knives, hooks. The hooks he had seen the stevedores carrying on the waterfront. He had seen them slashed into a bale of cargo and could imagine what they would do to human flesh. I cannot win this, he thought as he prepared to run at them.

And then the dog was there.

A large dog with glaring eyes and a slobbering jaw. More the size of a colt and sleek with muscles that rippled in the glow of the lanterns. A mastiff.

It snarled.

The men drew back.

A shout from the direction of the palace. The dog fixed them with its eye for a moment as if to impinge them on its memory and emitted a low growl before turning and trotting obediently back up the path.

Whence came a curious procession.

It was led by an urchin carrying a flambeau. Behind him came several of the same species, barefoot even in the cold and dressed more or less in rags. Behind them came a smallish man in a long coat and a tall hat picking his way rather delicately across the lingering clumps of snow on the footpath. And behind him four much larger men carrying staves.

The procession halted. The small man raised his head so the light caught it and Nathan saw that it was Robespierre.

He looked at Nathan with a frown and then at the men with the hooks. They melted back into the shadows. Nathan looked round for Gillet but he was no longer there.

The procession continued, now led by the dog. As Robespierre passed he nodded curtly at Nathan. Nothing was said.

"What," said Nathan when they had gone, "was that?"

"That was Robespierre," said Sara. She sounded short of breath and he saw that her fists were clenched.

"I know that. But who was with him?"

"The animal is his dog, Brount," she said. She drew a deep shuddering breath but when she spoke again her voice was even. "The little ones are the children of the Savoyards who run messages for the Convention, and the men are apprentices who work for Robespierre's landlord, the carpenter Duplay. They always escort him to and from the Convention, in case he is attacked."

"Very wise," said Nathan, "though he could probably get by with just the dog."

"But who were the others?"

He shrugged. "Footpads. Some of your paid thugs. Who knows?" He saw no point in mentioning Gillet. He wondered now if he had imagined him but he did not think so. "We had better move back into the Convention. Or at least wait by the door."

He took her arm and they headed back towards the palace. He felt her trembling slightly but he was impressed at how she had comported herself.

First Paine, he thought, now him. Was it coincidence or did they know why he had come to Paris? Or was it something personal between him and Gillet? Either way, he needed allies.

"Tell me," he said when they had reached the door of the Convention with its armed guards outside and a huddle of delegates in the hallway within. "What did Imlay mean about you and Danton?"

She drew back from him and gave him a look as frosty as the night air.

"You said something about Danton, that he had stopped chasing women, and Imlay said, 'Even you, Sara,' I thought . . .'"

"Well, you thought wrong," she said, turning away.

"I did not mean . . . I only meant that . . . if you knew him . . ."

She turned back but her expression remained cold.

"And if I did?"

He shrugged as if it did not matter. "I wondered if it might be possible to meet him, that is all."

She continued to gaze at him in silence for a moment. Then she shook her head and he saw the sadness in her eyes and the disappointment. "Mary warned me that you were not what you seemed to be," she said in a low voice. "But I suppose in Paris these days, very few people are."

He tried to say something to reassure her but in truth he did not know what it could be. And then he saw Imlay coming towards them through the lobby with Mary on his arm and the moment passed.

Imlay was looking remarkably pleased with himself for someone who had just suffered a defeat.

"I have been talking to Camille," he said. "We are invited to dinner." He beamed at them genially. "The four of us."

"Camille?"

"Camille Desmoulins," supplied Mary. "I thought everyone knew Camille, even in America," she added with a sly glance at Nathan. "He is the man who rallied the mob to march upon the Bastille."

"And the best friend of Citizen Danton," said Sara in the same low murmur as if she were talking to herself. "So you will have your wish, Mr. Turner, after all."

CHAPTER 19

the Bull of Arcis

CAMILLE DESMOULINS WAS IN HIS EARLY thirties but looked younger, with something of the street urchin about him or the gypsy boy. Sallow complexion, high cheekbones, liquid brown eyes. His long hair was tied back with a ribbon but it had either strayed or he had pulled a few strands loose for effect. He had a way of tossing them back from his eyes as he spoke as if they were an irritant but it was more likely a piece of theatre, Nathan thought, who had heard a great deal about Camille Desmoulins from Sara and Imlay, more than he perhaps wanted to know. Everyone knew Camille and everyone called him by his first name: even his enemies. It was as if he had never really grown up. The spoilt brat of the Revolution. Or the mascot. Petted, indulged, never quite taken seriously. Yet he was credited with rousing the mob to storm the Bastille at the very start of the Revolution and he had been involved in most of its twists and turns since.

His apartment was in the Rue de Cordeliers just a few blocks from where Sara lived and quite close to the Luxembourg Palace. It was elegantly furnished with silk-covered armchairs, a velvet chaise longue, an Oriental carpet and tasselled drapes of blue and gold—but it looked lived in. Worked in, even. News-sheets were stacked in a corner, page proofs piled on a sideboard. Camille's wife, Lucille, said it was like a print shop most of the time. People walked in and out all day with copy or news. She had tried to tidy up before they came but it was hopeless. And she shot a dart at Camille as if *he* was.

Lucille was said to be a beauty but she looked tired and nervous. They had a young child called Horace and they had kept him up late so he could say hello. He said hello and they all said, "Hello, Horace" or "Hello, my little one" as the mood took them, and Sara picked him up and kissed him and Lucille took him off to bed. Camille poured champagne and Imlay toasted the *Vieux Cordeliers* which was the name of the newspaper apparently, of which he was editor. Camille pulled a face and said it was as well Lucille was out of the room. She thought it would be the death of him.

"She's terrified that I'll fall out with Max," he told them.

"I thought you had fallen out with Max," said Imlay.

It was a moment before Nathan made the connection with Robespierre. He was confused. He had entertained the notion that Camille was the friend of Danton—not Robespierre—and that this was why they were here. Now it appeared that he was a friend of Robespierre. Could you be friends with them both?

The answer to this, apparently, was yes—if you were Camille.

"Max and I go b-b-back a long way," he said.

"They went to school together," explained Sara who had not entirely abandoned her role as tutor, though she was definitely in a pet about something or other . . . "Robespierre looked after him and stopped him from being bullied and it has been the same ever since. Except when he is being bullied by Danton."

Camille tossed his hair back and looked cross.

"All the same," said Imlay, "he can't have been pleased with what you wrote about him in the last issue."

"I d-d-didn't even m-m-mention him," said Camille. "It was a-b-b-bout the Emperor T-T-Tiberius."

"I think people made the connection," commented Mary drily.

"If people want to m-m-make c-c-connections, that's up to them," declared Camille sulkily.

Imlay had warned Nathan about Camille's stammer on the way over.

"His friends say that's why he writes," he said. "His enemies say he talks like he's constipated and writes like he has diarrhoea but it's the same old crap."

Imlay clearly knew Camille well. Well enough to be invited to supper and to treat him like an irresponsible playmate. Quite why he had invited Nathan was still something of a mystery but it would no doubt be solved before the evening was over.

The one thing Nathan was sure of was that it was not purely a social occasion.

"He's frightened," Camille said over dinner. "He doesn't know which way to turn."

They were still talking about Robespierre.

"*He's* frightened?" repeated Imlay in astonishment. "What about the rest of us?"

"Everything's going wrong for him," Camille explained. "He had this dream, you see. The dream of Rousseau. A Republic of Virtue. A free people devoted to justice, community, self-sacrifice. Gentle, learned, bucolic, working their own land. No more hunger or thirst, no more superstition. But it's not happening. Everywhere he looks he sees greed, ignorance, suffering. The people don't care about freedom. They just want to eat."

"How unimaginative of them," murmured Sara softly. "How maddening for him."

"But that's the root of the problem," Camille continued. "Food. People are starving and he can't do anything about it."

He contemplated the remains of the chicken. A black-market chicken. In the mellow light of the candles he looked like a petulant child who has stayed up too late. They were wax candles, the best, exuding a scent of sandalwood.

"It's the price controls," Imlay argued. "They don't work. The farmers hide everything they grow. They'd rather let it rot than sell at a loss. So there's no bread and the poor starve."

"Don't you think he knows that?" said Camille with a passion that clearly took his stammer by surprise. "But what can he do? If he gets rid of the price controls he'll have riots on the streets. If he doesn't there's no bread—and more riots. He's f-f-f-fucked."

"We're all fucked," said a voice from the door. "What I can't stand is to be fucked by a fucking eunuch."

"Evening, Georges," said Lucille. "I see you've brought your own salt with you. I thought everything was a little bland."

"How did you get in?" said Camille.

"You left the door unlocked. I suppose you might as well. When Vadier sends his thugs for you, they won't have to kick it in."

Danton. The Bull of Arcis. Larger and uglier than he had looked at the tribune even. If he had filled the Convention with his presence, in an average-sized dining room he was devastating. They made a place for him at the table but he was incapable of sitting still. They offered him food but he refused it and then helped himself from Camille's plate. He paced about behind them making the occasional pounce to grab a bottle and refill his glass. And all the time with a stream of invective—against Robespierre, his disciples on the Committee of Public Safety, Vadier . . . Did they hear what Vadier had called him? A fat turbot.

"And he's going to have me gutted, he says. Vadier. That nobody. I'll cut off his head and piss in the skull."

"Yes, Georges," said Lucille. "So you have said. Many times."

"I thought we were going to stop cutting off heads," said Sara quietly. Danton glared at her.

"'He that would make his own liberty secure must guard even his enemy from oppression,'" quoted Mary, "'for if he violates this duty he establishes a precedent that will reach unto himself.' Thomas Paine. Who is still in the Luxembourg, in case you were wondering."

"What ever happened to that fine old tradition of the ladies leaving the gentlemen after dinner?" inquired Danton with deceptive mildness. Then he ran to the window and pulled it open.

"Vadier, do you hear me, you fucking scorpion? I'll cut off your tail and stuff it down your throat."

"For God's sake, Georges, what are you doing?" Camille pulled him back by his coat-tails and slammed the window shut.

"He's got men watching the house," said Danton. "I'm letting them know I'm here."

"They know you're here, Georges," said Lucille. "They can hear you in Marseilles. You don't have to open the window."

Finally they went into the sitting room, which had more space for him to move around in, but he'd had a change of mood by then and slumped sulkily in an armchair with his wine. He told them he was sorry for being a bore but it was because he had been crossed in love. He had loved Lucille from the moment he first saw her, he declared, but she had spurned him for a sop like Camille. No wonder he was crazy.

"You're crazy about your wife," Lucille reminded him. "You were telling us only yesterday. Remember?"

"That was yesterday," he said.

This would be the second wife, Nathan presumed, the first having died a year ago while Danton was in Brussels with the army. His grief was in character. She'd been dead a week when he came back to Paris but he ordered them to dig open the grave so he could cover the corpse with kisses. He had retired from politics and buried himself in the country. A few months later he was back in Paris and married again—to the girl who looked after his children. Louise, a girl of sixteen.

Now he was singing Sara's praises.

"Is she not the wonder of Paris?" he demanded. "Her complexion, her hair, her . . ." He made a shape with his hands but clearly thought better of expressing it in words. "The sultry Mediterranean beauty meets the bold Scottish adventuress, do you not think?" He gazed benignly around the company. "What does our American friend think?" With a dart in Nathan's direction—the first time he had looked at him, or even acknowledged his presence.

Nathan cleared his throat and tried to clear his brain. Danton made him nervous. It was one thing to express a desire to meet him, quite another to confront him in the flesh. He did not know what Imlay had told him. Or how much Imlay himself knew of his mission.

Danton might be pro-English but he was first and foremost a Revolutionist—and a French patriot. The merest suggestion that Nathan was an English agent and he could have him shot. He might even shoot him himself.

"I cannot see much in Madame Seton that I think of as Scottish," Nathan replied with a modest bow in her direction. "But the Mediterranean beauty, assuredly."

"Too beautiful for me," growled Danton. He was too much of a peasant, he said. He needed his women to have something of the peasant in them, too, like Lucille—with a wicked glance in her direction.

Nathan did not think he had seen anyone less like a peasant than Lucille Desmoulins. She was a Parisienne to her fingernails.

"Georges has enough of the peasant for both of us," said Lucille.

"Pity he's no good with b-b-bulls," said Camille.

A roar of laughter from Imlay in which most of the company joined, even Nathan. Only Mary looked puzzled. She had not heard the story of the bull.

"I was sucking milk from a cow's tits," Danton explained, "and the bull took exception. I cannot say I blame it. It must have seemed an unnatural act from the bull's point of view, though it is quite commonplace in the region of the Aube. I had probably seen my sisters doing it—but not in front of the bull."

"And is it true that you went back the next day to renew the fight?" Imlay prompted him.

"Certainly not. I was only three at the time but had more sense than that. More than I have now. No, the next day I was trampled on by a herd of swine." He shook his head. "The country is a dangerous place. Far more dangerous than Paris." And then with scarce a pause and another glance at Nathan from under his brow, "So my friend, what brings you to Paris, apart from our Paris beauties?"

"I have business with Mr. Imlay," said Nathan.

Danton nodded to himself. "Secret business, no doubt."

"Like most business," Imlay smiled, "in these troubled times."

"So you have not come to teach us the meaning of democracy," Danton continued to address Nathan, "like most Americans?"

Whatever else Imlay had told him, he had clearly been discreet about Nathan's nationality.

"I would not be so discourteous," said Nathan, "or so arrogant."

"A pity. We need someone to instruct us. And at least you have leaders who do not appear to be corrupted by power or startled by the concept of opposition to it."

"Give us time," said Nathan. "It is all very new to us."

"It is new to us," observed Danton, "and we are cutting off each other's heads. But how would President Washington instruct us, do you think, if he were here?"

"I cannot speak for President Washington," Nathan responded cautiously.

"Oh, can you not? Why are you here then? Why are we listening to you?"

"Do not be impolite, Georges," said Lucille sharply. "Any more than you can help."

"I believe Captain Turner is speaking for most Americans who are anxious for peace," Imlay answered for him. "Peace and the freedom of trade."

"Ah. Peace."

Now we are come to it, thought Nathan. Bravo, Imlay.

But Danton was still glaring at him.

"So tell me, Monsieur American, why are we at war? No—let me make it easier for you—why are France and England at war?"

Mary seemed about to tell him but he continued with scarcely a pause. "You do not know. No one knows. But I will tell you. France declared war on England because they thought England was about to declare war on France. And France can never bear to let England be first with anything."

It seemed to Nathan that this was as good an explanation as any.

"But there is no great issue between us," Danton continued. "Not at present. There is no reason why we should not make peace tomorrow. Neither of us would have to give anything up, or make any concession whatsoever, except to leave each other in peace."

"So why does it not happen?" Imlay prompted him.

"I will tell you. Because those in power do not wish it. While we are at war everything they do, the laws against liberty, the executions, the Terror, everything is in the interests of national security. If you oppose it, you are a traitor. That is the problem."

"Then you must change those who are in power," said Nathan, greatly daring.

But he had gone too far.

"Fine words," said Danton, "from one who does not have to answer for them. But to risk one's neck, one needs more than words."

He heaved himself up out of his chair.

"And now I must go home," he said. "I have to kiss my little girl before she goes to bed."

Nathan wondered if he meant his daughter or his wife.

"I fear," said Nathan as they walked up the road to Sara's house, "that I may have offended him."

"It is impossible to offend Danton," said Imlay. "But he is right about one thing: 'to risk one's neck, one needs more than words.'"

Nathan showed his empty hands. "What else could I give him?"

Imlay glanced warningly at Mary and Sara who were walking ahead of them, but not so far that they could not be heard.

"Have you ever been to the waxworks?" he said.

"The waxworks?" Nathan looked at him in astonishment.

"There is a very good one in Paris," said Imlay. "I often go there. It is a good place to meet with one's friends, or even one's enemies. The replica figures are most lifelike and they have this advantage over the genuine object: they cannot hear what you are saying about them, or anyone else."

CHAPTER 20

the House of Wax

ATHAN ARRIVED AT THE HOUSE OF WAX at six in the evening, as Imlay had proposed, and found it closed. He lingered a little at the door, peering at the exhibition in the window that depicted a man being tortured by the Inquisition. Finally he decided to ring the bell in the hope that Imlay was already there.

After a moment or two his summons was answered by a tall man with pale, gaunt features wearing a sombre black suit who would have looked very much like an undertaker or an apparition had it not been for the large flamboyant tricolour fixed prominently to the bosom. But perhaps even undertakers and apparitions had to advertise their allegiances these days.

"You would be Mr. Turner?" he suggested before Nathan could embark on an explanation.

"I would," agreed Nathan with relief.

"I am Curtius," said the man. "The proprietor of the Salon de Cire. Citizen Imlay has not yet arrived but you are welcome to wait for him in the studio."

Nathan followed him up several flights of stairs to a large room at the top of the building with a plenitude of tall windows and skylights that admitted what light remained in the sky. There were a number

of wax figures standing in various poses or reclining upon the floor:
some clothed, some not. A small woman, dressed like the proprietor
all in black, was working at a long bench with her back to them.

"My niece is working on a head," said Curtius. "I hope you are not
at all squeamish."

"Not at all," began Nathan. Then he saw the severed arteries trail-
ing from what was left of the neck.

"My God," he said faintly, putting a hand out to the wall for
support.

The woman turned and Nathan saw that she wore a white apron,
liberally spattered with blood. Her sleeves were rolled up and her
hands and arms red to the elbow. She held an open razor in one
hand. In the light of the setting sun she looked like some Hindu
goddess in the midst of some gruesome act of sacrifice.

"Really Uncle Philippe," she complained, "you might have told him
it was a real one."

Nathan stared in horror at the object on the workbench. It was
the head of a youngish man who might once have been considered
handsome.

"But what are you doing with it?" he managed to inquire, though
his voice sounded oddly constrained.

"Making a copy in wax. It is a private commission. Something for
the family to remember him by."

"And who is . . . who was he?"

"Oh some vicomte or other," said Curtius. "The name is on the tag."
He nodded towards a pile of brown paper beside it which, judging
from the stains, had been used to wrap it in.

"What are you doing with the razor?" Nathan asked the sculptor,
moved, despite himself, by a macabre curiosity.

"I have to get rid of the bristles," said she. "You'd think they'd shave
before they went, would you not?"

Nathan stared at her in astonishment.

"Why?" he croaked.

"Well, you'd think they'd want to look their best."

Nathan felt like laughing hysterically but she did not appear to be joking. She was a tiny, almost doll-like woman, possibly in her early thirties, with a long, sharp nose and round spectacles that made her eyes look enormous. She reminded Nathan of an odd little witch or some creature of the forest out of one of Perrault's fairy tales.

"I must get on," she said. "They want the head back in the morning."

She turned back to the bench. Nathan looked at Curtius inquiringly.

"To bury it," he explained, "with the body."

Nathan watched with a mixture of horror and fascination as the woman finished shaving the face, dried it carefully with a towel, and then took a scoop of pomade from a jar to flatten down the hair. She used the same towel to wipe her bloody hands and then anointed them liberally with oil from a bottle and began to massage it into the face, taking particular care with the indents around the nose and eyes. Then she applied plaster of Paris with a small brush to form a white, sepulchral mask.

"When it is set," Curtius explained, "it is removed to make a clay mould for the wax. Marie will then work on the clay to reflect the character the face wore in life. It is her particular skill."

They heard the sound of the doorbell.

"That will be Imlay," Curtius murmured. "If you will excuse me . . ."

It *was* Imlay but he was not alone. With him was Camille Desmoulins.

"So you met little Marie Grosholtz," said Imlay with a smile. "Extraordinary is she not? I do not think she is quite human. Almost demonic, do you not think, though an excellent sculptor of the human form."

They were in a small room off the studio which was clearly used as an office. It was comfortably furnished if a little untidy. But at least it was free of human heads.

"Her mother is Philippe's housekeeper and she calls him 'uncle' though it is rumoured she is his natural daughter. She certainly has

his talent for working in wax. Now—to business." He sat behind
the desk with an assurance that suggested he had been here before.
"Danton is ready to act but he needs support."

"Support?"

"Not to p-p-p-put too fine a p-p-point on it," Camille attempted to
elaborate, "M-m-m-money."

"If Danton is to act he needs to bribe people," Imlay explained pa-
tiently, "both in the Convention and on the street. You saw yourself
what happens when the Jacobins pack the galleries. And they also
control the mob . . ."

"When you say 'act' . . . ?"

"If he is to secure peace, he must first secure power."

"I have had no instruction about helping him to secure power."

Imlay shrugged. "I fear you cannot have the one without the other."

"I understood Danton could always count on the support of the
people, that he could bring twenty thousand on to the street with the
power of his voice alone."

"The people love Danton," Camille took a run at it, "but they fear
the Terror more. In a fight between Danton and Robespierre I am no
longer sure who would w-w-w . . ."

He stumbled and fell.

Imlay came to his rescue. "Loyalties are divided," he said. "And as
usual in such matters, what may tip the balance is money. There
are those whose loyalties can be bought, like any other commodity,
with gold."

"Gold?" Nathan repeated, to be sure he had it right.

"Yes. Not paper money. It is becoming worthless. To make something really happen one needs gold. In coin. Louis d'or to be precise."

"And where does one find this gold?"

"In the same place one finds one's tobacco," Imlay assured him with
a wry smile.

"You think . . ."

"I think it must be put to your masters that there are certain people we must have on our side. People in key places. In the National

Guard and in the Commune and in the Sections. And that they expect a reward."

"Are you seriously telling me they cannot be brought to act without being paid for it? Were they paid to storm the Bastille?"

"As a matter of fact they were, if what I have been told is correct. At least some of them. They were paid by Philippe Duke of Orleans, the cousin of the King, who had aspirations to wear the crown himself. You have perhaps heard of him as Philippe Égalité which was the name he chose to call himself subsequently, though it did not save him from losing his head. You will find him upstairs. Made of wax."

Nathan shook his head as if it was all too much for him; the perfidy of human nature.

"One does not wish to see Danton here," Imlay continued regardless. "Or rather, one does not wish this to be the *only* place one might see him. So you must go back to where you came from and tell the people who sent you that to be in a position to help them, he must have gold."

"How much gold, precisely?"

"Fifty thousand louis d'or," said Camille, with not the faintest hint of a stammer.

"Fifty thousand ..."

"A little over one hundred thousand English pounds. Or five hundred thousand American dollars," Imlay translated.

"The cost of building and fitting out two 74-gun ships of the line." Imlay stared at him blankly. "Is that supposed to mean something?"

"It means, is Danton as important as all that?"

Camille shook his head in apparent disgust and made to get up. Imlay put out a hand to restrain him.

"Let me make something clear," he began. "Danton will end the war, which will save a great deal more than two ships of the line, no matter how many guns they have. He will also stop the Terror, which is no small item in the accounts."

"And yet he is a Revolutionist."

"Yes. But he is not a fanatic. In fact, I would say he is probably a little corrupt. Or rather let us say, he is human. And he is not Robespierre. He will save the French from their excesses, he will save Europe from many years of devastation and he will save England a great deal of blood and treasure. So I think we may say Danton is important."

"But still," now Nathan shook his head, "fifty thousand gold Louis is a lot of money."

"It *is* a lot of money. But it is the price of buying a mob. Or, if you wish to be more idealistic, the price of peace."

CHAPTER 21

the Cook and his Wife

PEACE COULD NOT COME SOON ENOUGH for the embattled population of Le Havre—or Havre-Marat as it was now called. Until the war with the British the port had been the thriving centre of Atlantic trade and the headquarters of the French East India Company. Now, thanks to the British blockade it had become a ghost of the busy, bustling giant it once was—a silent witness to the death of commerce.

Ironically the harbour was still crowded with shipping—but ships that never sailed. Ships without a crew. Ships that stood rusting at the quayside or bobbing at their moorings, with masts and yards as skeletal as the trees of winter.

The *Speedwell*, by contrast, looked as if she was ready to put to sea upon the instant. Nathan had driven straight down to the docks in the chaise that had brought him from Paris and to his infinite relief the barky was exactly where he had left her when he departed for Paris and looking very much in the same condition. The decks freshly swabbed, the ropes neatly coiled, the shrouds newly tarred; everything shipshape and Bristol fashion . . . But he knew as soon as he stepped aboard that something was wrong. It was there in the looks he encountered from those members of her crew who were about the deck and even in the crooked smile with which Tully greeted his return.

Nathan congratulated him on the appearance of the vessel before inquiring whether he had encountered any difficulties in his absence.

"Only, I regret to report, sir, that the cook, Small, has been taken up by the authorities."

"The cook!" Nathan almost laughed aloud with relief but the tension about Tully's face suggested that his celebration was as premature as it was cruel. "On what charge?" he added with a slightly belated frown of concern.

He anticipated something in the nature of a drunken brawl or a slander upon the Republic—Small's stature being an inducement rather than an impediment to his aggressions—but it was something much more curious.

"Well, he has got himself a wife," said Tully.

This was startling news but it was not, as far as Nathan was aware, a criminal offence, even by the strict standards of the Committee of Public Safety.

"It is the fact that he was married in a church," Tully confided, "with a Popish priest who had not taken the oath."

This began to make some kind of sense. Catholic priests were permitted in Revolutionary France only if they had taken an oath of allegiance to the state: an oath that conflicted with their vows to the Church of Rome. Those who declined to break their vows were forced to practise in secret and if discovered subjected to the full penalty of the law. As were those faithful Catholics who continued to apply to them for the sacraments—whether they be for birth, death or in this case marriage.

"I did not know Small was a Roman Catholic," Nathan remarked. "Nor indeed of any religious persuasion."

"He isn't," said Tully. "'Tis his wife. Bonne-Jeanne."

The name struck some distant memory with Nathan which he was inclined to dismiss, it being a common enough appellation in France, until he recalled that it was the name of the prize he had taken in the *Nereus* in the first weeks of the war: the little hooker off Étaples.

He hoped this was not portentous.

Bonne-Jeanne was a good Catholic, explained Tully, and she had insisted upon being married in a Catholic church by a proper Catholic priest and not some "government tart," as Tully put it, presumably quoting Small.

But the happy couple had been informed against and were now in custody awaiting trial. The penalty, predictably, was death.

"But how . . ." began Nathan. He was going to say: how did he meet her? But this seemed to be the least of the obstacles he must have had to surmount. The woman's family, the fact that he spoke little or no French, that he was a Protestant and, not least in the list, his appearance. For Small was not a handsome man. In fact he was possibly the ugliest man Nathan had ever encountered who had not been disfigured by war or disease.

"The lady in question," said Tully, "is not a looker."

"No," Nathan acceded. "I did not think she would be."

"She is, however, an excellent cook."

Even less of a reason, Nathan considered, for her attachment to Small whose accomplishments in that line were far from impressive. Indeed, in other circumstances Nathan might have welcomed his enforced absence. The death penalty, however, appeared harsh.

And the crew apparently felt the same way. Small was, moreover, their fellow countryman and they were considerably angered by what they considered to be his unjust detention.

"In short, they have resolved not to sail without him," confided Tully with an apologetic grimace.

"I see," said Nathan thoughtfully.

Compared to the problems he had imagined in his darkest moments over the last few weeks—and indeed encountered—the problem of Small and his bride seemed of little account and yet it appeared it would prevent him from returning to England as effectively as a blockading fleet. More so, in fact, as his Admiralty protection was of no benefit on this occasion.

"Do we know when he is to be tried?" he inquired of Tully.

"It is not yet determined. I believe these things are somewhat arbitrary. It might be tomorrow or next year."

"And there is no such thing as bail?"

"Regrettably not; not in this case, at least."

"Does it not make a difference that Small is an American—and ignorant of the law? After all, one Catholic priest must appear to him very like another."

"I put that to the authorities," said Tully, "but they were unmoved."

"And the American consul in Le Havre?"

"Is indisposed. A mysterious malady I am informed."

He crossed to the larboard rail and leaned upon it with a dejected scowl. The wind was from the southwest and the tide on the ebb. All being well they might leave port within a matter of hours and be in England by tomorrow noon. He did not altogether like the look of the sky but it would not otherwise have deterred him.

"We could, I suppose, offer a bribe," he proposed.

"I doubt they would take it," said Tully. "They are become very stubborn on the issue. Small is their shipmate and their country-man, they say, and they will not abandon him to the guillotine."

"I meant the authorities," said Nathan, though the thought of bribing the crew had in fact occurred to him. "But I will need advice on the subject."

And right on cue came Imlay, walking briskly along the quay twirling his cane and looking more than usually pleased with himself.

"I have gotten us a cargo," he declared cheerily as he ran up the gangplank. "Wine and spirits only this time, it being very short no-tice, but at a very good rate. It will occasion only a short delay. I have arranged for it to be delivered by noon tomorrow."

He saw Nathan's expression.

"Is there a problem?"

Nathan told him.

"Dear God," he swore. "What was the man thinking on?"

"Love, I imagine. It tends to distract a man from more practical considerations."

"Oh bollocks, man. Besides we are not talking of love, we are talking of marriage."

Nathan declined to engage upon this issue, though Imlay's wife, he supposed, might have resented the distinction, had she been present.

"The point is, is there anything we can do about it?" he demanded.

"Well, short of breaking him out of jail, no," replied Imlay. He dropped his voice. "You must prevail upon the crew to sail without him. Tell them I will find him a lawyer—much good that will do. Tell them you won't pay them else, or offer them an additional bonus, whatever you think will impress them the most."

Nathan repeated Tully's remarks on the feelings of the crew. Indeed, he was beginning to share them, for he knew not what reason, save a natural predisposition to resent the arbitrary nature of authority, doubtless imbibed at his mother's breast.

"But this is monstrous!" Imlay exploded. "We cannot afford a moment's delay. The fate of France may depend upon it."

"And yet you were prepared to delay sufficiently for us to embark a quantity of wine and spirits."

"Oh, for God's sake, man, that is business. Without which, I do assure you, the activities of the *Speedwell* would be more closely inspected than has hitherto been the case. You have no idea of the favours that are involved, the money that is exchanged."

"I was wondering if such an approach might be helpful on this occasion," Nathan proposed.

Imlay stared at him. "You mean a bribe."

"Is that out of the question in the current political climate?"

"Good heavens, no. Just because they are Revolutionists does not mean they are honest. No, no. Business would be impossible else. It has to be put with a certain discretion, of course." He gave Nathan a penetrating look. "I take it you are prepared to bear the cost?"

"Well, within reason," said Nathan, who had not considered this aspect of the matter. "How much will it be?"

"I don't know. I will have to inquire," Imlay sighed.

While they waited upon Imlay, the wind changed, very much for the worse. A brisk westerly drove directly into the bay, whipping the sea into a froth of white horses and chasing them up the Seine to Harfleur and beyond, making it quite impossible to leave harbour. The sky, too, grew uglier by the minute, with black rain clouds massing on the horizon and their ragged outriders chasing overhead like the scouts of some advancing alien army.

"We are in for a night of it, I fear," remarked Nathan as he and Tully shared a scratch meal of bread and cheese in his cabin washed down with a jug of ale.

"It may be a long one." Tully appeared unconcerned. Having spent the best part of two months kicking his heels in Le Havre, he clearly considered a few more days of little account. But then he knew nothing of Nathan's involvement in the tortuous politics of Revolutionary France. He was too polite, or respectful, to ask Nathan what had kept him so long in Paris but he must have wondered. He was no fool. He must know the *Speedwell*'s mission had more to do with spying than smuggling. But the two had long been combined.

Nathan and Tully were still at their dinner when Imlay returned.

"Well, I have spoken with the public prosecutor," he said, "and he has agreed to release them on payment of what he is pleased to call a large fine."

"How large?"

"One thousand livres—in coin."

"Dear God, but it is a king's ransom!"

"Hardly. A little over one hundred and twenty pounds at the current rate of exchange. He will take louis d'or or English sovereigns."

"Is it not a crime in Republican France to deal in gold?" Nathan inquired indignantly, stirred to a sense of moral outrage at the prospect of paying such a sum.

"Indeed. And punishable by death. However, I doubt the public prosecutor will wish to raise a clamour in this instance."

Nathan counted out the coin in his cabin. Half of his profit from the prize he had taken off Étaples. One Bonne-Jeanne for another.

"I would not mind half as much," he complained to Tully, "if the man could cook. But it is a considerable outlay for one who has tried to poison me since I first came aboard."

He wondered if he might claim it from the Admiralty as a legitimate expense but they would probably laugh in his face.

"I will bring them back directly," Imlay promised as he prepared to depart with Nathan's savings.

"What, both of them?"

"But of course. They are man and wife. And it is a condition of their release that they both leave France without delay."

When he had gone Nathan gave vent to his feelings. "So now we are to have a woman aboard."

"I do not believe she will prove a distraction," Tully assured him, "as far as the crew are concerned."

Imlay brought the happy couple back in a carriage and they came aboard to loud huzzahs from the assembled crew: Small beaming and bowing as if he were an admiral and the blushing bride upon his arm.

"By God," Nathan marvelled in an aside to Tully, "she is his exact replica. In the female form."

Mrs. Small was indeed built to the same tonnage and dimensions as her spouse only with a mobcap and curls framing her plain features and a pink ribbon tied around her several chins. She made a very pretty curtsy to Nathan, however, and as pretty a speech of thanks, which made his face as bright as hers.

Imlay took the shine off it somewhat by requesting ten livres for the coach.

"What? Can you not deduct it from your profits for the cargo we are about to embark?" Nathan charged him with some fervour.

He was still smarting from the iniquity when Tully informed him that Small wished to thank him and the crew for his deliverance with what he was pleased to call a feast.

Nathan groaned. Small's idea of a feast doubtless comprised a larger portion than usual of boiled beef with an onion added.

"But it is a little late in the day for a feast," he objected.

"Well, we might compromise on a light supper," Tully proposed doubtfully, "but the couple are most anxious to show their gratitude—and it would very much please the crew."

"I suppose we have nothing better to do," observed Nathan with a scowl.

In the event he decided to make the best of it and invite his two officers, Tully and Keeble, to dine with him in his cabin. He even invited Imlay.

"Let us hope we might call it a leavetaking," he submitted without great expectation, for the breeze had freshened to a near gale and was blowing the rain in sheets across the bay.

The supper was a long time coming. "Madame" had been forced to go shopping, Gabriel replied to a somewhat testy inquiry on the subject, there being very little to her liking in store. She had clearly taken over in the galley, wisely relegating her spouse to a subsidiary role. Nathan, who had eaten a scrappy lunch and little better on his journey from Paris, would normally have stuffed himself with more bread and cheese, possibly toasted for a change, but when he proposed this solution to Gabriel as a stopgap the steward was firm in his rebuttal.

"No nibbles," he retorted sharply as if Nathan had not aged or advanced in status since Gabriel had first entered his father's service. "Supper will be served shortly. Madame is returned."

"Madame" had clearly established a measure of authority, no mean feat where Gabriel was concerned, and the smells emanating from the galley suggested that she might be as good a cook as Tully had intimated.

As it was a formal occasion and they were in port, Gabriel set the table with Nathan's Venetian glasses and his best blue Delftware and Imlay provided a quantity of wine from some nearby stash which helped to alleviate a certain tension, invariably present when dining at the captain's table. Nathan had of course entertained the officers on the *Nereus* from time to time but never with any great

success, largely on account of the brooding presence of the first lieutenant, Mr. Jordan, and he was not wildly optimistic on this occasion.
His own skills as a host were not impressive and he was thankful
to Imlay for keeping the wine flowing and the conversation at least
lurching gamely in its wake while they waited to be served.

The meal began, uniquely in Nathan's experience, with the presen-
tation of a menu. He raised his brows in pure astonishment at the
steward whose face remained as deadpan as if he were accustomed
to such embellishments at every meal. The document was written in
a bold but clear hand and announced that they were to commence
with a Tourte au Livarot et aux Pousses d'Epinards, followed by a
Mousseline de Sole Normande and a Canard de Rouen au Cidre
et aux Pommes; and for dessert, as a change from Small's plum duff
which had the consistency of a cannonball and was as lethal to the
teeth, a Terrine de Pommes Vallée d'Auge.

"So what are we having?" inquired Imlay rubbing his hands in
anticipation.

"Fish," replied Nathan, who was still somewhat stunned by the
menu, "and a duck. And some kind of tart."

The Tourte au Livarot turned out to be a form of cheese cooked
with spinach. It was received with some suspicion, by Keeble in particular, but it proved to be excellent, if a little less than filling to men
with a hearty appetite. This niggling objection was swiftly overcome
by the next two dishes, served together in the French style, and with
an assortment of vegetables, whose existence Small had not hitherto
acknowledged.

For a while there was a near silence, broken only by the conventional invitations to partake of this dish or that, and when they began to eat, it descended entirely. Finally Nathan, in his role of host,
looked up and remarked, "This is astonishing."

As a comment on the quality of the fare it lacked elegance but accurately reflected its effect on the company.

"The woman is a genius," exclaimed Imlay. "What on earth is she
doing in Le Havre?"

Out of common courtesy no one asked the more obvious question of what she was doing with Small.

The conversation remained stilted as they applied themselves to the serious business of eating but as their appetites were nourished and the wine continued to flow it assumed a satisfactory level of animation.

Imlay, of course, dominated, though Nathan was interested to observe that in the company of a fellow American, the bluff frontiersman was sublimated to the grand New England gentleman.

"My family own land in New Jersey and have extensive business interests in Philadelphia," he replied to Keeble's inquiry on the subject. "Indeed as a shipping man you may have heard of the firm of Imlay and Potts which was established by my brother and is much involved in trade with New Orleans and the West Indies."

Nathan was content to listen to the two Americans trading stories of their experiences in the Caribbean and more particularly New Orleans where they had both fallen foul of the Spanish authorities on more than one occasion. He was naturally anxious to avoid inquiry into his own antecedents and when Keeble did venture a dart in his direction he was relieved that Imlay was swift to divert the conversation onto safer ground.

"A glass with you, Mr. Tully," he proposed. "I fear our talk of the Americas can hold little interest for you."

"On the contrary," replied Tully, "for I have long desired a better acquaintance, my travels being largely confined to the seas off France and England."

Nathan was concerned that the wine might have loosened Tully's tongue rather more than he desired. He had no idea what he had disclosed to Keeble during their long stay in Le Havre but he did not wish for any public discussion of his connections with the Navy, particularly as their conversation had become somewhat loud. He need not have feared however for Tully proceeded to entertain them with an account of his smuggling activities in the English Channel, an entirely acceptable topic in the present company.

"And were you always a smuggler?" inquired Imlay with a lack of inhibition that Nathan was inclined to think of as characteristically American.

"No, as a babe I had little interest in the trade," replied Tully, "being more concerned with the supply of my mother's milk in which King George had not then expressed a financial interest. I did not lack for tutors, however, the Channel Islanders being much inclined to avoid sharing their profits with His Majesty—or indeed any other man."

"You are not then a loyal subject of the King?" Imlay persisted with a sly glance in Nathan's direction.

"Oh, loyal in every way, save the desire to pay taxes, like every honest Englishman."

"So you count yourself English, though a native of the Channel Isles?"

"I do indeed, as do most Channel Islanders, for what else could we be but French?"

"Hear him," called out Nathan hastily, lest the conversation become more personal. He was curious, however, as to Tully's background for he had better manners—and wit—than the wardroom of the *Nereus* and many other officers of his acquaintance. So he was not at all displeased when Imlay persisted in questioning him on the subject "for you are the first native of the Channel Isles I have ever met," he confessed.

"Well, there are those who believe we are the progeny of fishermen and mermaids," said Tully, "and are born with gills and webbed feet but though my father was a fisherman my mother was entirely human, being the daughter of Sir Charles du Maurier of Guernsey."

"A curious match nonetheless," remarked Imlay, raising his brow.

"Curious enough for Sir Charles to disown her," admitted Tully. "And I was brought up in a fisherman's cottage until, I regret, my father was drowned in a storm—the fate of many a Guernsey man. My mother, being impoverished by this event, felt compelled to apply to her family for relief. Which they were pleased to grant in my case but not, alas, in hers . . ."

His tone continued light but there was that in his eyes that betrayed a more serious view of this neglect.

"I was then but five years old and was not permitted to object to the arrangement, so I was removed to my grandfather's house and raised as a gentleman."

"And your mother," inquired Nathan, moved, despite himself, to ask so personal a question.

"I regret to say died within the year. My grandfather I remember was good enough to attend her funeral. He was not a particularly malicious man. I remained with him until I was sixteen when I ran away to sea and sought my own advancement—as a smuggler. Or, as we in the Channel Isles prefer to call it, a free trader, the which I have remained ever since."

"Well," said Imlay, "that is a story to surpass any of our own tales of the Americas, is it not, Mr. Keeble?"

"That it is," said Keeble, who had doubtless heard it before and whose eyes had begun to glaze over a little from drink. "To the free trade," he slurred, raising his glass.

And so they drank to the free trade and Nathan hoped that his red face might be mistook for the effects of alcohol rather than shame.

Upon the completion of dessert they summoned the Smalls to join them in a glass and to thank them for such a delightful feast, whereupon Imlay transferred his interrogation to Mrs. Small. She revealed that she had once been cook to the Comte de Bolbec until the Revolution took away her employment and her employer's head. She now had ambitions, she said, to open a restaurant in London.

They drank to her success.

"Though I hope you will not be in too much of a haste to leave us," Nathan implored her. "And we must discuss your remuneration—if you are to assist Mr. Small in the galley," he added tactfully.

When they had gone, he and Tully took a turn upon the deck. The wind had slackened somewhat and backed to the southwest and Nathan expressed a belief that if it remained there they might attempt to leave harbour upon the morrow.

"For we may keep it upon our larboard quarter until we are clear of Cap d'Antifer," he proposed. "Indeed, if it holds it may take us clear across the Channel."

Tully nodded but he seemed uncertain.

"Or is there something I have overlooked?" inquired Nathan politely.

"No, sir, it would work as neat as kiss my . . ." He forbore to complete the sentence but added with a frown, "If only the wind does not move once more to the west and we find ourselves with a freshening breeze upon a lee shore and the tide on the turn."

CHAPTER 22

Cap d'Antifer

IT WORKED AS NEATLY AS NATHAN had hoped until they were ten miles out to sea and a little to the east of the Meridian.

He had taken every precaution against the heavy weather. The hatches battened down, guns tethered cow fashion: swung round and lashed fore and aft across the ports. The anchors secured with double ring and shank painters. Reliever tackles hooked on to the tiller and hands detailed to man them. Tarpaulin placed in the weather rigging to give the watch a little shelter from the wind and lifelines rigged to give a handhold to the men working on deck.

But Nathan could not command the wind. And at a point some five miles off Cap d'Antifer, Tully's fears were realised.

The shift was announced by a sudden lull and then a violent gust from the west that took the mainsail aback and hurled the barky on to her beam ends, sending most of those on deck sprawling into the scuppers in several feet of rushing water. If the two helmsmen had not been lashed to the wheel, the same fate would have befallen them and the vessel would undoubtedly have foundered. But as the wave passed and the sea rushed out through her scuppers, she came back on a more or less even keel and they spun the wheel until her head came round three points to the northeast with the wind once more on her quarter. The danger was averted for the time being but they were now headed almost directly towards Cap d'Antifer and unless the wind backed or some helpful deity intervened they could not escape running upon the headland. To make matters worse the breeze was not constant. At times it would shift back a point or two so they were effectively scudding under their single reefed mainsail, barely keeping ahead of the following sea. At other times it would fall away entirely leaving the sail flapping against the mast with a very great danger of being pooped: the sea breaking over the stern and raking the deck, carrying all before it.

Nathan clung to the lifeline they had rigged across the deck, wondering what he could do to avoid disaster, with only himself to blame for the folly of putting to sea in a near gale. And all for Citizen Danton, the Bull of Arcis: a cut-throat Revolutionist whose idea of peace was doubtless to put all Europe under the power of France and install the guillotine in Whitehall to quell dissent. Nathan braced himself against the canting deck as the stern lifted, lifted at an impossible angle, plunging the flying witch at her bow deep into the sea and hurling the water back over her hoary locks so that he thought she would never rise. And then slowly, laboriously, almost groaning, up she came, streaming water, the long bowsprit pointing like an admonition towards the black sky he had not heeded. And the grey seas heaving all around them and the air filled with white foam and the incredible noise . . .

Now here came Tully, making a staggering run from the rail and clutching on to the lifeline next to him and shouting in his ear. Something about the sail.

"What? I cannot hear you. Say again!" Nathan volleyed back into the streaming face.

"The mainsail is losing wind in the troughs, sir."

So it was. It was not the wind that confounded them but the waves: casting them so low in the troughs the sail could not function. And so the sea was overtaking them and there was a constant threat of being pooped. But what could they do?

"If we were to hoist the main topsail . . ." he yelled back, working out the consequence in his head. Was there not a danger of carrying too much canvas—and carrying it away? "But we must first strike the course."

Could they do it with so small a crew—and six of them below deck working the pump?

Tully nodded his agreement. "And I respectfully submit, sir," the effort of this courtesy at full volume making the cords stand out in his neck, "we set the foresail—and the fore topmast staysail."

Nathan pictured it, trying to calculate the angles and the stresses. Why did this not come instinctively? Why was it always such a painful process? Was it different for Tully? Because he was a Channel Islander with webbed feet, born of a fisherman and a mermaid?

A part of Nathan urged him to leave it to Tully, to trust in his judgement, but the greater part would not let go. He could not give an order he did not understand. So he pulled him back along the lifeline, in the lee of the tarpaulin weather cloth they had spread in the mizzen shrouds to provide a little shelter from the wind. He still had to shout but at least he could hear himself think—and better expound his reservations.

"What is the point of rigging the staysail?"

If the vessel were dead before the weather, as it was most of the time, the staysail could hold no wind. He saw Tully thinking about this—or how to explain it—and possibly, who knows, resenting the necessity.

"It will prevent us being brought by the lee," he shouted back, "and help to pull the head off the wind in the event of a yaw."

Now Nathan understood. If the stern came across the wind, it would throw the mainsail back and bring them broadside on to the sea, sweeping the decks. Likewise if they yawed: the head swinging violently towards the wind.

Nathan felt as he had when he had taken his lieutenant's exam with three senior captains hurling hypothetical problems at him: "You are scudding under reefed mainsail off a lee shore and the wind two points on your quarter . . ." His head full of calculations and the clock ticking. But then he had not had Tully at his side.

"Very well," he shouted. "Carry on, Mr. Tully."

An excellent command. Carry on, Mr. Tully. Nathan watched through the water that streamed down his face as six topmen swarmed up the rigging to haul up the main course and six more lowered the fore course in its stead and then climbed even higher to let down the fore topsail while the masts described an arc of at least thirty degrees and the rain and the wind lashed at their frail bodies. Nathan could not contemplate joining them there though he longed to set an example. But he joined them to haul the sheets of the staysail aft, holding it amidships so it would exert more of a pull on the head.

He could feel the change at once. They could not outrun the waves but they had reduced their impact. They now passed comfortably under the stern instead of forever threatening to poop them.

And yet they were racing even faster to their doom on Cap d'Antifer.

Nathan stayed forward, clinging to the belfry and peering through the foam and the spray. How far? Two, three miles? His only hope was that on their present course they would just miss the rocks at the foot of the cliffs, that with the tide still on the ebb it would exert enough of a counter to the waves and they would be able to round the cape—if only by a whisker.

But then what?

The coast beyond curved away to the east but they would still be dangerously close to shore and from his memory of the chart it contained several sharp teeth that might snag them. And the tide must turn within the hour.

He fought his way aft to where Tully stood with Keeble, clinging to the lifeline by the helm, peering at the compass together with the water streaming off their sou'westers like a pair of gargoyles.

"We must go below," he shouted in Tully's ear, "and consult the chart."

They darted to the hatch, pulled aside the cover, and slid down the companionway in a deluge of water.

And here, swaying towards them came Small, his rotund figure swathed in oilskin and with a sou'wester pulled low over his head for all that he was below deck.

"Ah, Small," Nathan called out with desperate amity. "And how is your good lady? I fear we have given her a sharp baptism."

Was it only last night that they were supping upon her Canard de Rouen, safe in harbour and merry with Imlay's wine?

He imagined the poor woman spewing her guts out in their wretched cabin but then the figure raised its head and to his astonishment he saw that it was she—apparently none the worse for wear. It was Small who was laid out in the cabin, having taken a tumble and sprained his wrist, she informed them, and she was fetching the medicine chest and some rum to comfort him.

They wished him well and continued to Nathan's cabin where he spread out the chart under the storm lantern that Gabriel had hung from the beam.

"If we are to round the cape," said Nathan, "we are still in peril. Unless we can claw away."

They both knew that with the wind in its present quarter this was an impossibility, for even if they came a mere point into the wind they would be broached and driven helpless upon the shore. And yet if they did nothing it must happen anyway, sooner or later, for there was no hope of reaching Veulettes where the coast fell away even farther to the east.

Nathan stabbed his finger at a point some ten miles beyond Cap d'Antifer where the River Valmont came down to the sea at the little fishing port of Fécamp. On their present course, even if they managed to miss the headland, they were bound to run upon Pointe Fagnet at the far side of the port. But what if they were to bring the head round and run directly up river?

Tully shook his head. He indicated the note at the side of the Admiralty chart:

The channels in the estuaries of the Somme, L'Authie, La

Canche and Valmont are constantly changing. Passage through them should not be attempted without some local knowledge and never in unsettled weather.

"But what else are we to do?" Nathan demanded impatiently. "I think we must take the risk or run upon the point."

Tully nodded but his face remained troubled.

They had just emerged on deck when the vessel yawed. A great sea broke over the side and they were hurled off their feet by an enormous rush of water. Nathan was swept up against one of the 4-pounders on the lee side, giving his head a great crack that blacked him out. He came to spewing water and clutching at the gun lashings; saw the two helmsmen, still miraculously holding on to the wheel; looked round for Tully and saw him a few feet away swept up against the hatch for the main hold with blood pouring from a gash on his forehead.

Then the dread shout of "Man overboard!"

Nathan dragged himself to his feet, clinging to the barrel of the gun and peering over the rail, saw the head as it rose on the back of a wave, an arm raised in desperate appeal. But it was impossible to lower a boat or to come about. Nothing they could do in that terrible sea. Nothing but throw a line which Keeble did—and the line fell short and the head was gone.

"Who was it?" Nathan yelled. He looked about the deck. Four, five men, their faces bewildered, clinging to the lifeline or the rail.

"I think it was young Frankie," said one, "young Frankie Coyle."

He might have known. And he was entirely to blame for it. They should never have left port . . .

Then he saw him. Not in the sea but trapped under the launch that was lashed in the waist, between foremast and main, swept there like a bundle of rags, a piece of flotsam, more dead than alive. They ran to him and dragged him out and banged him on the back until he spewed out above a pint of green water. But he was as white as a corpse, coughing and clutching at his side; his face screwed up in agony. Tully thought he had broken a rib. They carried him below and laid him in Nathan's cot and when they came on deck Keeble shouted that it was Carter who had gone, one of their best topmen who had been safer on the yard than on the deck . . . And then he pointed over Nathan's shoulder, his eyes staring and his arm stretched out like some biblical prophet, and Nathan looked and saw no land of milk and honey but the great gaunt prow of Cap d'Antifer, an enormous wall of white cliff and white water, the breakers dashing against the rock and hurling their spray forty, fifty feet high in the air before they fell back into the seething hell below. Cap d'Antifer, the Wrecker, barely half a mile off their starboard bow.

Nathan turned to the helmsmen, every instinct screaming for them to turn into the wind. But it was a command he could not give. They could not turn into the wind: the sea would broach them. And looking forward he saw their bowsprit pointing at the clear if turbulent water beyond the cape. If they could only hold to their present course they would clear it by a cable's length. If only they were not sucked into that maelstrom at its foot, if only they did not yaw . . .

He bit his knuckles, skinned by his fall against the cannon, his mind forming a prayer.

And then it happened.

Some freakish devilry brought the wind across their stern and they were brought by the lee: the sails taken aback and the sea breaking over their stern, raking the deck and burying the bow deep into the trough, so deep it could never come up . . .

Nathan heard the crack, even above the roar of the breakers and the howl of the wind in the rigging and the rush of water across the deck. And when the bow came up, slowly, clawing its way up from that great weight of water, the bowsprit was broken in half, the jib boom gone and the staysail flapping helpless in the wind.

But the jib boom was not entirely gone. It was still there in a tangle of rigging under their bow, dragging them round, disastrously round towards the cape. Nathan pulled himself up and staggered forward and saw Tully running ahead of him with an axe in his hand. He ran straight up the bowsprit—or what was left of it—and over the side and when Nathan reached him he was hanging from the martingale, hacking at the twisted rigging below him—until the bow sank down into the trough and he plunged down with it into the surging sea.

Nathan ran back and seized another axe from the rack by the belfry and dropped over the side to join him. Hanging from the bobstay with one hand and hacking down at the hopeless tangle of spar and rigging. And the bow plunging and rising—but not so high now with the jib boom dragging it down—and the waves breaking over their heads, hacking into spar and rope, until the sea took it away and they went up over the bow and the hands dragged them aboard more dead than alive.

Nathan clung to the rail, coughing up water and staring through rain and spray at the great white wall of chalk and water as they passed it by, a half a cable's length, no more, off their starboard bow. But they were round it, by God, and still coming round, for Keeble had seen what he had not: that it had been no devilry but the answer to his prayer. No freakish eddy off the cliff but the wind backing to the southwest. And it held, freshened but held, and it took them off that foul shore and that murderous cape and with any luck it would take them clear across the Channel to England.

CHAPTER 23

the Conspiracy of Gold

NATHAN CONSIDERED WHETHER to help himself to another rasher or two of the excellent bacon that lay beneath the lid of the silver dish on his mother's sideboard
but he had already consumed several along with two fried eggs,
three sausages and a black pudding and he knew his mother would
be counting. There had already been some harsh remarks about the
amount he ate during the five days he had been back in London
and he was become quite defensive on the subject. He was, as he informed her, still growing—though he had no medical evidence of this
condition—and was besides striving to make up for the weight loss
he had suffered while feverish from his wound.

Lady Catherine was notably abstemious in her diet, her normal
breakfast consisting of two cups of coffee and a small roll with a delicate smearing of butter; it was a great concession that she permitted
anything more substantial and doubtless owed much to Nathan's
supporters in the kitchen, although they had rather overdone themselves this morning. The dishes on the heaped sideboard contained,
besides those he had already sampled, oatmeal with cream, smoked
herrings, sardines with mustard sauce, grilled kidneys, a cold veal pie,
beef tongue with horseradish sauce, three kinds of fresh-baked roll,
butter, honey and three different kinds of jam made from raspberries,

cherries and apples. It seemed a pity to spurn such thoughtfulness, and his mother was engrossed in her newspaper. He heaved himself from his chair and crossed to the sideboard, selected two slices of bacon and a roll, and added a spoonful of jam from each of the jars.

He returned to the table to find the newspaper lowered and a critical eye raised over the top of the elegant pince-nez.

"It were a pity," he said, "to let it go to waste."

"I doubt the kitchen would permit such a tragedy," observed Lady Kitty, "and there are those who have more need of sustenance than others." She lowered her gaze impolitely to his waist and concluded, "You will soon be as fat as one of your father's pigs."

"My father does not keep pigs," Nathan informed her coldly. "He breeds sheep. And I have as much spare flesh upon me as one of his greyhounds."

"Sheep or pigs, it does not signify; they are all lambs to the slaughter," she remarked obscurely. "And as to greyhounds, I have only a passing acquaintance with the breed but I confess I do not see an obvious resemblance."

"Has something upset you, Mother?" he inquired politely. "Or are you being gratuitously offensive?"

"Offensive? You consider I am offensive? Pah. I will tell you what is offensive." She brandished the paper at him. "That people should have their civil liberties taken from them on the ludicrous pretext that the government is engaged in a war against the *Terror*, as they call it, and if we do not cast innocent men in prison without trial merely for expressing their opinions we will have bloodshed upon the streets of London."

"You would not be so dismissive if you saw what was happening on the streets of Paris," replied Nathan briskly, though his personal experience of the French capital was not something he cared to share with her.

"You should not believe what you read in the newspapers, Nathaniel," she admonished him, "especially those you read at your father's house."

She raised her own like a barrier between them. He considered the bacon still reposing on his fork but he had lost his appetite.

"What happened to your Frenchman?" he said eventually.

"Which Frenchman?" she responded provocatively.

He sighed. "The one with the limp and a face like a corpse."

"Talleyrand?" She lowered the paper for a moment and frowned as if she was trying to remember. "I thought he looked pale and interesting. He's gone to America. He said England was getting worse than France before the Revolution."

"There's an indictment. And from a man of God."

"'Those who would give up essential liberty to purchase a little temporary safety deserve neither liberty nor safety.' Do you know who said that?"

"No, but I fail to see—"

"Benjamin Franklin," she informed him firmly as if this ended all possibility of dissent on the subject, or any other. "But do they heed him? Ha! You would think that the loss of the American colonies would have taught them that you cannot stifle people's liberties without risk of an explosion but no, they think they can bully and browbeat us into submission. I tell you we will have the King's German Legion camping out there in St. James's Park"—a wild hand thrown towards the window—"and Hessians riding us down on the streets of London just as they did in Boston. Not that he needs mercenaries," she added darkly, "when he can call on loyal British subjects such as yourself to make the world safe for tyrants and their minions."

And back she went behind her impenetrable barrier of print. He marshalled his arguments for he was not a little troubled by hers.

"There is no comparison, madam," he began, "between the present state of France and England. We still, thank God, have freedom of speech, the right to a fair trial, to the judgement of our peers. It is these that I am fighting for, not—"

"I will tell you what you are fighting for." She brought the paper down on the table with a force that rocked the cups in their saucers and spilled a quantity of coffee upon the cloth. "You are fighting for the banks."

"The banks?" Nathan repeated in some bemusement and a vague notion of the Dogger or the Bullock or possibly the cod banks off Newfoundland.

"Aye, the banks. As we were, in America, though many did not know it at the time."

"I am sorry, Mother, you have lost me."

"I am speaking of the conspiracy of gold which is behind most wars, including our own, which we mistakenly call the War for Independence. Did you ever visit the George Tavern in Wall Street?"

Nathan was familiar with his mother's scattergun method of debate but this appeared random even by her standards. He shook his head in bemusement.

"Well, throughout the war—as the British Army was in occupation of the city—the portrait of King George remained conspicuous outside the inn but the day the British left, a portrait of George Washington was hung in its place. Conveniently, the landlord did not have to change the name."

"I am sorry I do not think I have quite grasped the point."

"The point is that we beat the British Army and we won our so-called independence but *nothing changed.* Nothing fundamental. *We did not beat the gold.*"

Nathan slid his eyes about the room as if in search of it. "Whose gold?"

"Well, I have forgot exactly who owns it—and so have they—but it is the bankers who are the guardians of it, and lend it back to us at such and such a per cent. And everyone seems quite happy with this arrangement for they will lend it to anyone who has the means to pay the interest—even Americans. It was gold that fuelled our revolution and when we had 'won,' the bankers came to us and said: 'Now would you like some more to build the new nation, to build roads and bridges, and ships and shops and *banks?* And while we are about it, is there anything else you would like? Let us lend you a bundle to fight the Indians on the frontier or the pirates in the Caribbean or the Quakers in Rhode Island, for Quakers are a troublesome crew . . .'

And with the profits they made on these transactions they bought up all the properties that were going cheap and all the farms and all the land that was going to waste and by the time they had finished it did not matter whose picture was hanging outside the George Tavern in Wall Street for it is gold that rules, my love, and the banks that possess it and those that have access to it—not King George or President George or Farmer George who gets to sell his vote every five years to the highest bidder—just like his pigs."

She raised her newspaper again as if that was the end of the debate and she did not have to wait for the votes to be counted to know who had won it.

"Well, thank you, Mother," said Nathan after a moment, "for giving me a better knowledge of the world."

Nathan was not disposed to take his mother's views on politics too seriously, unlike the government of Mr. Pitt who still kept her house and its guests under strict surveillance and appeared careless of concealing the fact. Indeed Nathan strongly suspected that they used their agents as a form of intimidation. Few guests dropped by these days to partake of the hospitality and the spirited conversation available to them at Chez Kitty. Even Nathan had considered staying elsewhere whilst in London but it would have upset his mother grievously had she found out and, besides, he shared some of her indignation that political dissent was now equated with treason, though he would never have let her know it. Still, it was probably not tactful to have used her address on the confidential report he had sent to the First Lord and might explain why he had been waiting five days for the reply. It was now above a fortnight since he had left Paris and Imlay had stressed that there was not a moment to be lost. The political situation was as volatile as he had ever known it and if Danton did not act swiftly he would not only miss the tide but risk his neck upon the guillotine and all his friends with him.

While Nathan shared this concern, his greater anxiety was for Sara. The longer the Terror continued, the more likely it was that her true identity would be discovered and she would undoubtedly suffer the fate of every other aristocrat who had friends or relatives fighting with the enemies of the Republic. It seemed strange to be here in London eating a large breakfast—or as large as his mother would allow—while Sara lived off scraps and might at any time be taken up by the authorities. He was thinking about this when he stepped out of the house for his morning walk and did not notice the gentleman in his path until he had almost walked into him.

"Commander Peake," said the fellow, touching his hat.

Nathan was instantly transported to Paris for the man had the look of a policeman or at least a government official. But as his mother would doubtless have informed him, London was not immune from either.

"I do not think I have had the honour—" he began, stepping back a pace.

"I am sent to give you this, sir"—thrusting an envelope at Nathan's breast—"and to beg that you will attend upon the gentlemen at your earliest convenience."

"Well," began Brother William, easing back in his chair and inviting Nathan to sit in the one going spare, "I think you have once more exceeded your duty, sir."

He flapped a paper at Nathan much as Lady Catherine had save that this was the paper Nathan had written for the Admiralty, containing details of Imlay's proposal.

"I am sorry you should think so, sir," replied Nathan coolly. "But when Mr. Paine was arrested I was at a loss to know how to proceed and being reluctant to return empty-handed—"

"You thought you would come back to us with this preposterous request."

"If you consider it preposterous, sir, then I must apologise for wasting your time but given the importance you attached to the gentleman's goodwill . . ."

Pitt made a dismissive noise through his nose which nonetheless betrayed a certain ambiguity of decision. He glared down at the document in question. "You say it is to purchase the support of the mob."

"That was how it was put to me. The mob and the Garde Parisienne."

"Dear God, what a country! What a people!"

He shared his contempt with his brother who shook his head briefly and returned to his contemplation of the rug, though it appeared to be no more or less interesting in Nathan's view than when he had last given it his attention.

"And can Danton be trusted to deliver, do you think?"

"I am not a diplomat, sir, nor an oracle, but that appeared to be your own opinion when last we met."

"Whisht, sir, I did not then know the fee. One hundred thousand pounds—in gold!"

"It was put to me that it is a small price to pay for peace."

"Was it indeed? And if I was to put it to the House of Commons, do you think they would agree? Or do you think I should ask the King to provide it from his Privy Purse, explaining that it is for the man who provoked the attack on the royal palace and voted for the death of the King and Queen of France?"

Nathan said nothing.

"Or perhaps you thought I might provide it myself, or borrow it from some obliging banker?"

Recalling what his mother had just said, Nathan was inclined to suppose the latter but he maintained his silence, merely inclining his head and waiting for the conversation to move on.

"Well, and what did Imlay make of it?"

"He appeared to find the amount reasonable, sir, given the risk involved and the number of people who would share it."

Pitt looked at his brother again but receiving no advice from this quarter other than another despairing shake of the head, he merely shook his own and repeated, "One hundred thousand pounds— in gold."

All three sat in silence for some moments.

It was Nathan who, rather to his own surprise, broke it.

"With respect, sir, you appeared to have some expectations of Monsieur Danton when you sent me to Paris in December. Has his importance diminished in your view?"

Pitt sighed. "Perhaps I am become more cautious," he confessed. "I always become cautious when I am asked for money."

The First Lord made a noise very like a laugh. Pitt glared at him. Clearly it had not been meant humorously.

"Besides," he continued. "Danton is a French patriot. He has a reputation as a man of action. He rallied the French against the Prussians and the Austrians when they were at the very gates of Paris. He might well rally them against us if the need arose."

This thought had also occurred to Nathan but he kept his counsel.

"If we are to exchange the Tiger-cat for the Bull," continued Pitt in the voice he used for addressing the Commons, "we must ensure he does not gore us."

Nathan bowed in acknowledgement of the prose as much as the sentiment behind it.

"So. I will tell you what we will do . . ." Pitt selected another document from the small stack on the table beside him. "I have here a letter—I should say a copy of a letter. It is, as you perceive, sealed. However, I will tell you something of its content."

A secret exchange of glances between the two brothers.

"In the year '89—the year of the Bastille, as you will doubtless recall—the British government paid a certain sum of money to foster the disturbances in Paris." He acknowledged Nathan's surprise with a small inclination of his head. "It was thought then that they might be in Britain's long-term interests and that at the very least they would embarrass the French government, just as the French government had thought to embarrass us in America. The sum was distributed by our agents in Paris to certain individuals thought to have influence with the Paris mob. This document"—he lifted it to his face—"contains the copy of a dispatch from the French Minister in London—which we intercepted—naming Danton as one of the recipients."

He watched Nathan's expression carefully.

"You do not appear surprised."

Nathan recalled Imlay's remarks about Danton. It did not astonish him that Danton had taken a bribe from the British government. It would have astonished him more if there was evidence that he ever did anything to earn it.

"Well," Pitt resumed, tapping the envelope, "this also contains the copy of a letter written the following year by Count Mirabeau—who was then, you will recall, the King's chief minister—referring to a sum of thirty thousand livres that had been paid to Danton to support the monarchy."

He brandished the document at Nathan and fixed him with his pop-eyed stare. "You will present this to Monsieur Danton and require him to sign a letter, also enclosed, acknowledging receipt of the correspondence and the consignment that accompanies it. In this way we may be reasonably sure that both items reach their intended beneficiary and not some other. We may also be reasonably sure that Monsieur Danton is aware of the consequences should he disappoint us in the future."

"And I take it you consider Imlay is to be trusted?"

Pitt raised a brow and looked down his nose. "I do not believe we need to discuss Mr. Imlay," he began, but then, after a slight pause, "All I will say is that while American and British interests are identical—and while he may profit from the venture—you may trust him implicitly. Otherwise . . ." He shrugged.

"And am I to take instruction from him?"

Another exchange of glances between the brothers.

"You are to be advised by him. But remember that strictly speaking Mr. Imlay is not answerable to us. Whereas you are." He glanced at the clock above the fireplace. "Is that all?"

"There is the practical issue," Chatham spoke for the first time, "of how are we to deliver fifty thousand gold Louis at a time of war."

"We still have the vessel, do we not?"

"Yes, but several chests of gold . . ."

"Imlay proposed it should be concealed in soap," offered Nathan.

"Soap?" they said together. They stared at him with their pop eyes as if he were making game of them.

"On the grounds that it will effectively disguise the coin and can easily be melted. Also, I believe that soap commands a high price on the Paris market."

"Dear God," said Chatham wiping his brow. "What are we become?"

As no one seemed prepared to answer him he added, "And where are we to find this soap?"

"A chandler's store would appear the most obvious location," Pitt informed him, "but perhaps you might consult a purser on the subject."

He looked at Nathan and frowned as if there was something he had forgotten. Then his brow cleared.

"I take it," he said, "that you are willing to return to Paris?"

CHAPTER 24

the Artist's Model

PARIS WAS HAVING A SPRING CLEAN. Gangs of labourers had begun scraping the filth off the streets and shovelling it into carts to use as fertilizer and in the gardens of the Tuileries the first buds were showing through the dead leaves of winter. In the new revolutionary calendar it was Ventose, the month of winds, but in defiance of the prevailing order the air remained stubbornly calm and was in danger of prosecution under the Law of Suspects.

Sara had almost reached the Rue Honoré when she heard the drum. She knew at once what it meant and quickened her pace but she was too late. There were guards lining both sides of the street and already she could see the start of the procession winding its way towards her. She hesitated, wondering whether to turn back and linger in the gardens until it passed—she had no desire to watch the latest batch of human misery on its way to the guillotine—but then she heard a voice she recognised.

"Good day, Citoyenne. Anyone you know today?"

Eleanor Duplay. One of her fellow students. And though her eyes were mocking there was the suggestion of a threat there, too—or a warning.

"No. Why should I?" Cursing her lack of wit as soon as the words were out. Overhasty, defensive . . . Why could she not make a joke of it? Laugh in her face. Except that you did not laugh at Eleanor Duplay. And if you made a joke you had better make sure it could not be misconstrued as unpatriotic.

One such joke—incautiously told in Paris—was that wherever two people were gathered together, one would be an informer. But it was surely the curse of the Setons to have as your own personal sneak the daughter of Robespierre's landlord. Further incautious rumour suggested that she was also Robespierre's lover but Sara could not believe it of so cold a fish. But perhaps this was what they had in common.

"We all seem to know someone these days who has betrayed the Revolution," observed Eleanor reprovingly.

"What, even you, Eleanor?"

Eleanor looked at her searchingly a moment, to see if she was being ridiculed. Then, apparently satisfied that no one would dare, least of all none as inconsequential as Sara Seton, she added: "We have trusted too many who have proved false in the past. And doubtless will in the future. They all wear masks to hide their corruption."

One of the other students had whispered to Sara that when Eleanor said "we" she meant Robespierre and that she spoke as a kind of priestess or oracle, echoing the voice of the god.

"But at least some have been found out," she added with satisfaction, gazing past Sara towards the approaching convoy.

It was led by the drummer, beating the step. Next came a file of National Guardsmen with fixed bayonets and behind them, flanked by more guards, the death carts and those that were to die.

Sara was gripped by a fascinated horror that would have kept her rooted to the spot, even without Eleanor Duplay at her side.

What would it be like to be one of them?

It was more than a ghoulish curiosity. It could happen at any time. It was like living in a city ravaged by the plague except that you usually knew if you were likely to become one of the victims. She had nightmares about it. Going through this macabre ritual. The death march of the beasts, marked for slaughter. Through that door, along that corridor, into that yard ... Bowing your head so they could cut your hair, placing your hands behind your back so they could bind your wrists. Climbing into the waiting cart ... The frightful inevitability of it; nerves screaming against acceptance but your feet moving obediently along the destined route, closer and closer to the waiting blade.

How could they do it? Only because they had no choice. It was too late for choices. You had made the wrong choices a long time ago. Too late to change them now. Now you were in the death cart and the drum was beating and the wheels were trundling over the cobbles. She could hear them, beyond the sound of the drum, louder and louder. And now they were level with her. Five in the first one—three men, two women—all young, gazing stoically ahead. No imagined fate for them; this was their reality. Sara began to pray for them, silently, keeping her eyes open, the prayers she had been taught by the nuns at her convent school in Provence. Pray for us sinners now and at the hour of our death ...

She had seen it all before, of course. It had become a daily ritual. Sometimes just one victim—someone special like a king or queen. Other days there would be a whole batch of them, thirty or forty, even more. And they always took the same route—out of the Conciergerie, across the river and along the Rue Honoré past the art school. The students would crowd at the windows looking down and it was unsafe to be the only one to stay away, carrying on with your work as if disinterested or disapproving. But there was a sense of being distanced from it all when you were in a room, up above. Here at street level it was more tangible, more terrible.

Three carts today. She stopped counting the people in them, no longer speculating on who they were or what they could possibly have done to merit such a fate. Aristocrats or peasants, priests or prostitutes ... they were all beasts to the slaughter. And now, increasingly, more and more were revolutionaries themselves. The Indulgents or the Enragées, moderates or extremists, any who deviated from the strict path laid down by those in power, were sent down this other road—to the dread Machine in the Place de la Révolution.

"Shall we go—or do you want to stand here praying for them?"

The procession had passed and they were letting people cross the street and Sara was still there, staring into space.

"I wasn't praying," Sara said. "What makes you think I was praying?"

But Eleanor just smirked and shrugged and picked up her skirts and stepped into the street and Sara followed, hating herself for being so frightened, and wishing she could slap her.

The painter, Jean-Baptist Regnault, was one of the few acknowledged rivals of the great Jacques-Louis David who had his own studio in the Louvre. Sara was surprised Eleanor Duplay wasn't one of David's students because apart from his fame as an artist he was a Jacobin and a friend of Robespierre. But perhaps she was. Perhaps she studied at both schools. She was keen enough, you had to give her that: a dedicated student, she wasn't playing at it. There were some who considered Regnault a better painter than David; certainly he was a better teacher. Even at this time of the year he made use of what little light there was, posing the model close to the fire to show them how the light from the flames fought with the light from the window.

"Two sources of light," he told them, "one warm, one cold. One red, one blue, but of course far more subtle than that. See how they coil around the body like serpents."

The model was a young man, pale and undernourished. You could see the bone beneath the skin like a fledgling fallen from the nest. Perhaps that was why Regnault had chosen him so they could see how his body was made. More likely, though, he was just cheap. Poor enough to pose near naked for a meal and a small fee. He shivered, even close to the fire. Sara did not know where Regnault found his models and did not like to ask. It was said that some of the men—the healthier, more muscular ones—were Savoyards who ran messages round the city and that the women, old and young, were mostly prostitutes. They did not have many women lately in the life classes. Most of the prostitutes had been rounded up by the police. It was considered "uncivil" to be a prostitute, a betrayal of the principles of the Revolution. Regnault said that he would soon have to call for volunteers from among the students. This was taken as a joke. But why not? Sara knew there were rumours that she had posed nude for the artist—even for some of his students—but they were untrue. She had been almost nude but with a sheet artfully draped across her private parts and there had been no impropriety. It had been a foolish thing to do though. But even as she regretted it she wondered how she would feel about posing nude in front of the class. It would be shameful of course but the thought excited her all the same. One of her fantasies was to imagine the American, Nathan Turner, among the students painting her. She had thought of him a great deal since he had left Paris. Much of the time, in fact. In some ways the model reminded her of him. They did not look at all alike except that they were both young with long, dark hair but there was something similar in their eyes—a kind of . . . vulnerability. No—a wariness, like a feral cat, distrustful, always looking out for itself and the possibility of danger or betrayal . . . Like the folk tale they told in Tourrettes of the cat that walks alone. But she was being fanciful.

Regnault made them draw the figure first in charcoal, using their fingers to shade in the warm light from the fire and leaving pale, bare patches for the light from the window. Only when he was satisfied that they had captured the difference in charcoal did he let them start mixing up the paints they would use. They had to work very fast, because the light was always changing. That was part of the test, Regnault said.

But long before they had finished the firelight was winning, the daylight retreating fast, even from the window. The boy huddled close to the fire, the flames licking his meagre flesh.

Sara was hurrying to clean up her palette at the sink when Eleanor Duplay came up to her.

"Where are you off to, in such a hurry?" she said. She made it sound like an accusation, and Sara felt like a suspect, hurrying off to an assignation, up to no good.

"I have to be home," she said. "Before it is dark."

"And where is home?"

My God, this was serious. In her nervousness she dragged her sleeve across the palette. "I have an apartment," she said, "in the Rue Jacob."

Was that a crime? It was not a good address from a revolutionary point of view. She dipped a corner of cloth in terpentine and rubbed at her sleeve. The smear was like blood.

"You must come back one day for coffee," said Eleanor. "I live just up the road. Perhaps when the days are longer."

She drifted off, leaving Sara staring after her, astonished.

She was still thinking about it when she emerged from the studio and saw Nathan on the opposite side of the road.

They stared at each other for a moment and then she walked across the road towards him, her legs a little unsteady. As she reached him she stumbled and he reached out for her and it became an embrace. Later when she thought about it she was shocked at how easily it had happened but at the time it appeared natural. They walked into the gardens of the Tuileries hand in hand. They spoke a little. They made polite conversation. She thought she asked him what he was doing in Paris and that he told her that he had brought a cargo of soap and she said she could use some soap. And all the time they were holding hands and looking for a cab. Normally she walked home but today a cab seemed appropriate.

They found one and got in and began to kiss.

"I am become a strumpet," she said, breathless, in a tangle of limbs.

He put his hand under her skirt but she moved it back.

"No," she said. "Wait."

They sat side by side holding hands until they reached her house in the Rue Jacob. She was shivering but she felt as if her clothes might melt from her body.

In the event they came off less easily. There was even some tearing. She remembered thinking she would have to sew them herself; she could not possibly give them to Hélène. There seemed to be some level of detachment, of rational observation. She observed his body—not at all like that of the model she had been sketching but weightier, more solid, especially at the shoulder and chest. But you could see his ribs, feel them with your hand. She loved the line of dark hair that ran down his stomach, lower.

It was . . . an impossible delight. To be making love in the afternoon. Three hours since she had seen the death carts rolling down the Rue Honoré. The detached, rational, thinking part of her wondered at it and her own insensibility. Her recklessness. With Alex in the schoolroom and the cook in the kitchen and Hélène at whatever she was doing at this time of the afternoon. And she with a young man in her bedroom and lately widowed. She should be whipped . . .

But the greater part of her was lost, wild, wanton . . .

They lay across the bed, spent and heedless, soaked in sweat. After a while she moved over to him and stared down, brushing his face with her hair.

"You are beautiful," she said.

"No, *you* are beautiful," he said. "In England, we do not say that a man is beautiful."

"We do in France," she said. "Though I have never said it before, not to a man." Then she remembered and swung her body astride him, looking down with a fierce expression. "But what was it you said to me? In English. I think it was harlot."

"I am sorry," he said, "It was in the height of my passion and I did not mean it critically."

"You are not then critical of harlots?"

"Not at all. I expect they are driven to it."

She slapped his face though lightly and then bent to kiss him.

"I think I *am* a harlot—at heart," she mused thoughtfully.

He looked at her a little warily. She kissed him again, laughing.

"But only for you."

"I will have to marry you," he said. "I cannot possibly have you behaving like that and still a maid."

"Good, I'll fetch a priest," she said, moving to get off and then squealing as he threw her down. He reversed their positions, pinning her down and regarding her pensively in the pale light. He plucked at the thin red ribbon around her waist with its silken pouch, now empty.

"What is this?"

She wondered whether to tell him. It was for her sponge that she soaked in vinegar. Somehow she had found the sense to leave him for a moment and run to the screen to put it in.

But perhaps not. Perhaps some other time.

"It is for luck," she said. "Do they not wear them in England?"

"I would not know," he said. "I was a virgin before I met you."

"Liar," she said.

"Well, almost a virgin."

"You cannot be almost a virgin," she informed him.

He kissed her again.

"I love you," he said. *Je t'aime.* Easier in French.

He rolled off her.

"*J'ai faim.*"

"I love you and I am hungry," she said. "Well, I suppose you got the order right. Shall I ring for Hélène to bring us some scraps from the kitchen?"

"Would she not be shocked?"

"Oh my God!" she laughed. "You think I am serious. My God, what do you think we are, we Frenchwomen?"

She rolled off the bed and stood up, looking down at him.

He hooked his finger through the ribbon again and pulled her to him gently.

"I like this," he said. "It is very useful."

"Very useful indeed," she said. "I could not do without it."

"When you came out from behind the screen, naked except for that thin piece of ribbon, I thought I would die."

Love and death. Why did people so often speak of them together? She shivered. It was unlucky. She gently freed herself and walked to the screen and dressed in a robe. When she came back he was looking at the book next to her bed.

Phaedra by Racine.

She had a taste for the tragedies of Racine. He seemed especially appropriate to the times. She sat beside her lover on the bed and looked to see what page he was reading.

"Great crimes grow out of small ones," he read, slowly translating:

If today
A man first oversteps the bounds, he may
Abuse in time all laws and sanctities:
For crime, like virtue, ripens by degrees . . .

"I will go to the kitchen," she said, "and see what we have."

"I could eat a toad," he said.

She returned with a loaded tray and an expression of the utmost satisfaction.

"No toad," she said. "But better than I anticipated. The good Marie has been foraging in the black market."

There was bread and cheese, some cold sausage, half an onion tart and a flask of red wine.

"Amazing," he said, reaching out the moment she set it on the bed-side table, "and what favours did she give for this?"

"Watch your mouth," she warned him primly. "I'll have none of your salty humour, here, thank you."

He looked abashed and apologised with humility and she let him have some sausage.

"Still," he said when he had taken a bite, "it is wonderful what a little money can provide, even at a time of want."

She looked at him, wondering. Did he have any idea of the price of things in Paris on the black market? Some of her remaining jewellery would have gone to pay for this little feast.

When they had finished they lay side by side again more content than she could ever have imagined but melancholy too.

"What has been happening in Paris," he said, "while I have been away?"

"Oh nothing much," she said. "A few hundred more have had their heads chopped off. But nothing unusual that I can recall."

"Can you not get away?" he said. She looked at him. He had the look she had seen on the face of the model.

"It is too dangerous," she said, "without the right papers. Besides . . ."

But she did not want to discuss her family affairs with him, not now.

"Danton went to see Robespierre," she said.

A sharp look—and furtive. The cat that senses a threat, betrayal . . .

"Lucille Desmoulins told me. It did not go well."

Danton had gone to see if the two men could be reconciled and stand together against the "Terrorists." He was unusually humble. He begged for the liberty of the seventy-three deputies who had been arrested but Robespierre said they were all criminals and the only way to obtain liberty was to cut off their heads. Danton had burst into tears.

"Robespierre would hate that," said Sara as she repeated the story. "He dislikes any display of emotion. Then Danton tried to hug him and made it worse."

He frowned. "You know Robespierre?"

"No. I was repeating what Lucille told me who had it from Camille. But everybody knows what these men are like. Robespierre is cold and Danton is too warm."

He was still looking thoughtful. She knew he was not what he appeared to be; but then nor was she.

She walked to the window and looked down into the street. Empty at this time of the afternoon. Shadows falling. Soon she would have to go and find Alex or he would come to find her.

"It is all pretence," she said, as if to herself. "A masquerade."

"I beg your pardon?"

"Do you know the meaning of *sans-culottes*?"

"I think so."

"That it does not mean running around with their lower parts exposed like Cannibals in the South Seas, though they may at times behave like them?"

"I believe it means without breeches, such as a gentleman wears."

"So they wear baggy striped pants and red shirts and the Phrygian cap with the tricolour and wooden *sabots* on their feet and they carry a pike, often with a head on it?"

"Well . . ."

"Except that they do not. Anyone dressed like that, you may count on it he will be a student at the university or a man of letters, a journalist or an actor or some such impostor. The workers and the poor are to be found in the cast-off finery of their betters: tall hats and tricorns and frock coats and waistcoats picked up for a few sous in the flea markets or took from a corpse strung up from a lamppost. Nobody in Paris is who you think they are. It is all make-believe. Theatre. A masquerade."

She felt his arms around her waist.

"You are sad," he murmured in her ear.

She squirmed round and buried her face in his chest for a moment and let him hug her.

"There is a little town called Tourrettes," she said. "Near where we lived in Provence. I used to go there as a child. To the market with my father. Tourrettes-les-Vence. A walled town on top of a hill. It is very beautiful. I used to love going to Tourrettes. There is a café in the square where I drank lemonade and ate the little cakes—made of oranges—and watched the people coming to market."

He stroked her hair gently. She felt the tears in her eyes. She looked up at him: "If I leave Paris," she said, "that is where I would go. To Tourrettes-les-Vence. That is where you would find me. With Alex. In Tourrettes drinking lemonade and eating little cakes made of oranges . . ." And then she added after a moment: "and waiting for you there."

CHAPTER 25

the Pavilion of Flowers

WRAPPED IN HIS CLOAK WITH HIS hat pulled low over his brow, Gilbert Imlay hurried through the gardens of the Tuileries towards the west wing—once called the Pavillon des Flores but now the Pavillon de l'Égalité. In the days when the Tuileries was a royal palace, these had been the private rooms of the King and Queen—Marie Antoinette had the ground floor, Louis the floor above—with a staircase between that was still called the Queen's Stairs. But now they were the offices of the Committee of Public Safety: the twelve men who ruled revolutionary France. Clearly they were working late. Though it was close to midnight lights blazed in several of the windows on the upper floor and the guards at the main entrance had lit the flambeaus for the two 6-pounder cannons that stood there night and day, loaded with grape.

Imlay showed his pass and hurried across the marble lobby and up the stairs. Directly ahead of him was a double door with two sentries on duty. Imlay paused for a moment on the landing. He had only once entered the room behind the closed doors but he had committed every detail to memory in case it should prove of use: the magnificent Gobelin tapestries, the elegant furniture, the green baize table and the men who had been sitting round it at the time: Robespierre,

Saint-Just, Lindet, Carnot, Barrere and the crippled Couthon in his wheelchair ... They would be there now with the other six, recently returned from the provinces where they had been dispensing revolutionary justice. Marseilles, Toulon, Lyons, Nantes, Bordeaux, the whole of Brittany, all had felt the cleansing virtues of the Terror.

Meetings of the Committee were often routine but not tonight. Tonight Robespierre was back after an absence of several weeks with some mysterious malady—and if rumour could be believed, the leading members of the Committee of General Security had been summoned to join the debate. A joint meeting of the Robespierre Committee and the Vadier Committee. What great crisis in the nation's affairs had brought about such an alarming assembly? An uprising in the provinces? A new declaration of war? But who else was there to fight? Russia? America?

No. Imlay had a feeling that he knew what this was about and it was of far greater moment than insurrection or foreign war: to him, at least.

The guards were staring at him and he turned to his right and walked briskly along the corridor and into the rooms reserved for Citizen Robert Lindet, the member of the Committee with special responsibility for food supplies.

There were two clerks sitting at their desks, copying documents by the light of several candles. They looked up when Imlay entered but he was a familiar figure and they did not stop their work. There was a good fire with a murmuring kettle on the hob and he went to warm himself for a moment, rubbing his hands over the blaze before moving to the window. From here, if he pressed his face to the glass, he had a view across the gardens to the Louvre and a small strip of riverbank with the lanterns bobbing in the wind. He stayed there for some minutes watching the reflection of the room behind him. Eventually the door opened and a man entered. Without looking to right or left he walked straight over to Imlay and handed him a file. Imlay glanced at the cover. It was headed "Estimated Food Reserves, Paris Saint-Antoine, Germinal X, Year II." Imlay nodded briefly, tucked the file under his arm and left the room.

At the bottom of the stair he paused again and opened it. It contained ten pages. Nine were filled with columns of figures and scribbled notes in a hand he recognised as that of Citizen Lindet. The last page contained a list of names in the same hand. At sight of them Imlay felt the blood drain from his face. He looked around to see if anyone had noticed but he was alone in the lobby. He put on his hat and left the building.

Louise answered the door. She was in her nightdress, carrying a candle, and she looked like a frightened child, which was what she was. He saw from her face that she already knew or suspected.

"Where is he?" Imlay asked her.

He was kneeling in front of the fire in his dressing gown poking the embers into life.

"The servants have retired," he said to Imlay, like an aristocrat—or a lawyer with pretensions—caught doing the work of a menial.

"I've come from the Committee," Imlay said.

"I know," said Danton. "I've just heard." He turned but did not get up. "I've just seen Paris."

Imlay stared at him, uncomprehendingly, thinking he meant the city. Had he been looking out of the window, was this some poetic sentiment of his, some vision of the future? Then he remembered. Fabricius Paris was the name of his old law clerk, now Clerk of the Revolutionary Tribunal.

"They mean to accuse me before the Convention," Danton said calmly. "Tomorrow morning. Saint-Just has prepared the charges. Well, I will look forward to it. It is what I have been waiting for."

But Imlay was shaking his head. "They won't let you anywhere near the Convention. They're not that stupid."

Danton shrugged. "Saint-Just is. He wants to accuse me publicly. He has his speech all prepared. There was an argument about it. They know I'd tear him to pieces. Paris said he stamped his feet and threw his hat in the fire—"

"He did what?"

"He threw his hat in the fire and his notes, too . . ." Danton's smile was infectious, a genuine merriment that bubbled over into his eyes and into Imlay, too. God knows, there was little enough to laugh at, but what there was, you could be sure Danton would find it and have you laughing with him. "Only someone snatched them out," he managed to say, "in case they needed them."

He wiped his eyes.

"I expect they will give the job to Robespierre," he said. "And we will see if he does any better."

Imlay shook his head. "Georges, please, listen to me. They are still meeting but Lindet managed to send me a message. He is at the meeting."

He pulled the papers from his pocket, dropping some on the floor in his nervousness and haste and stooping to pick them up.

"An emergency joint meeting of the two Committees. They've ordered your arrest." He found the page and began to read out the names: "Danton, Lacroix, Desmoulins, Philippaux—"

"Camille?"

Danton stood up, the poker gripped in his fist like a sword. For a moment, looking at him, massive in the light of the fire, Imlay felt hope. This was Danton. They had sprung their little mousetrap and caught a lion.

"Was Robespierre there?"

"Of course Robespierre was there. Do you think they would dare without Robespierre?"

"And he let them arrest Camille?" He fell back in a chair as if deflated, all the fight knocked out of him.

"His name is on the warrant," said Imlay.

"I saw him with Camille this afternoon. He had his arm around him." He began to pull himself up from the chair. "I have to warn him."

"I've already sent to warn him. I've a cab waiting." Imlay turned to Louise who was watching from the shadows. "You should grab some things," he said. If he could just get Danton and Camille away tonight, Louise and Lucille could follow later, with the children.

"But we have immunity," Danton was saying. "They cannot arrest a delegate without a full vote of the Convention."

"They'll do that later," said Imlay. "When they have you under lock and key. They have sent the warrant to the mayor with the order for your arrest." He recalled the phrase in Lindet's hasty scrawl: "'To execute immediately.'" An unfortunate choice of words. "Georges, you don't have much time. They may be on their way already."

Danton had been staring at the dying embers of the fire, still with the poker in his hand but it no longer looked like a sword.

"Where would I go?" he said.

Imlay shrugged. He did not think it mattered where they went, as long as they went.

"England," he proposed, "Or—"

"I went to England before. But we were not at war then."

"America, then. England and then America."

But Danton was shaking his head.

"You cannot take your country on the soles of your feet," he said.

This sounded like something he had said before or prepared for an eventuality such as this, but he seemed to take heart from it. He straightened his shoulders.

"Where is your friend, the American?" he asked. "The one with the money."

Imlay felt a small surge of hope. Perhaps it was not too late. They could be at the border by morning.

"Why?" he said.

"Only, I would like him to hear my speech. To tell Thomas Jefferson."

Imlay stared at him in amazement. "Georges, they won't let you speak. They are going to arrest you and then they are going to cut off your head."

"If they arrest me they must put me on trial," Danton insisted. "And if they will not hear me at the Convention, they will hear me at the Revolutionary Tribunal. And then—we will see if the people love me more than they fear Robespierre."

CHAPTER 26

the Bull at Bay

NATHAN STEPPED OUT INTO THE LITTLE garden at the back of the house in the Rue Jacob. It was barely dawn. He had been woken more pleasantly than was normal by Sara's lips tickling his ear and the gentle but resolute suggestion that he might find another berth before the house awoke.

"You are turning me into the street," he complained.

She assured him that he need go no further than the room at the end of the landing where he had slept the night of his arrival in Paris.

"Very well," he agreed, struggling to rise. At once she threw a naked leg over him, trapping him on the bed and covering his face with kisses, causing more of a rise than he had contemplated but as he began to respond with some enthusiasm she pushed him firmly in the chest.

"Go," she said. "Go. Before you run into Hélène at the door."

His new bed was perfectly comfortable and the circumstances more pleasant than his last visit after the incident of the mob and the rope but mind and body were considerably agitated from more recent adventures and he found himself unable to sleep. His more erotic imaginings were neutralised by considerations of his precarious situation in Paris and the certain prospect of an abrupt ending to his bliss.

After he had delivered his precious cargo to Danton he would have no good reason to remain in the city. This might not have troubled him—reasons might be invented as readily as excuses—were it not for the presence of the *Speedwell* in Le Havre. For once Imlay had been waiting to greet them at the quayside with a lighter to take their precious cargo on to Rouen and a pair of barges waiting there to bring it up the Seine to Paris. He had not been pleased to discover that Nathan intended to accompany it and obtain a receipt for its delivery.

"Have I given you any reason not to trust me?" he admonished him severely.

"I am under orders," Nathan replied with a shrug.

"Then they do not trust me, which I must say I take very ill."

"Possibly they do not trust Danton," Nathan countered, "or what intercourse we may encounter on the way."

"And you seriously expect Danton to sign a receipt that would cost him his head were it to be discovered?"

"It is not quite a receipt, more a letter confirming delivery of an unnamed consignment. But the signature is to be compared with one already in their possession. Besides," he pointed out, "when the gold is in his possession he need have no fear for his head—or anyone else's—if he is as resolute as you have suggested."

This had thrown Imlay into some confusion. Danton, it appeared, was not as resolute as his supporters might have wished. He vacillated wildly. One day he wished for an accommodation with Robespierre; the next he was for marching on the Pavilion of Flowers and throwing him out of the window.

This was not the news Nathan wished to hear but Imlay had cheered up considerably on the journey to Paris, drinking and carousing with the crew of the barges and telling long stories of his adventures in Kentucky and other wastelands while Nathan sketched by day and watched the stars by night and felt morally superior without deriving as much satisfaction from that condition as he might have hoped.

It occurred to him now that he might justifiably insist on remaining in the city to observe whether the gold was used for the purpose for which it was intended but he had no such instruction from his superiors and he would have to send word to Tully. Besides it would secure only temporary relief. His feelings for Sara were more than merely erotic, or so he assured himself. He loved her. He did not wish to leave her. Not today nor next week.

Then would he marry her? A small but insistent voice in his ear.

Yes, he sternly replied; if she would have him. He would marry her and take her back to England with little Alex.

But would she be prepared to leave Paris?

The sun peeped between rooftops and flooded the garden with a soft golden light. The trees were a mass of pink blossom and he remembered the apple blossom in Rye almost exactly a year ago. And yet it was strange to recall a world in which he had not known the woman now lying in the bed upstairs; a world in which it was possible for him to feel inexplicable, heedless joy . . . or to contemplate a liaison with another woman. His brief passion for Tully's fiancée now seemed to him impossibly childish and trite.

So he was to return to England with a wife and child? A Frenchwoman some ten years older than himself with no property or income?

He found himself gazing into the importunate eyes of the carp. They were quite small carp which was presumably how they had survived the pot. He showed them his empty hands.

He had to be honest with himself. He was not burning to marry. But the alternative was unthinkable . . . *Unless the romance be prolonged.*

If Danton succeeded in his bid for power there would be peace. And if there was peace he could leave the Navy or at least take a long leave of absence. He would be able to stay in France as long as he wished. His relationship with Sara could be nurtured without undue pressure to make a decision before he was entirely ready for it.

The carp were still watching him and he detected a hint of suspicion in their fishy regard.

"What?" he said.

But he knew what. A mistress in Paris was a more attractive proposition than a wife in London. It was no use pretending otherwise.

But if it came to it, he vowed, he would marry her tomorrow.

It was the only honourable course and he was an honourable man.

Or at least he was not a complete satyr.

And you think she would have you?

It was entirely possible, he supposed, that she wished only to be pleasured by him and would be amused if he offered to make an honest woman of her. She was after all a widow, a woman of some experience. He recalled the stories Imlay had told him on their journey to Le Havre in the summer. What if they were true? What if one half, or one quarter of them were true?

The thought agitated him considerably—and for a variety of reasons. There was jealousy, sure, but also excitement. More than that. He looked up towards her bedroom window. He was not sure exactly which one it was but it was there somewhere and she was lying there naked. Warm and naked and ... perhaps thinking of him as erotically as he was thinking of her.

He could not give her up; not now, to resume her life before they met, whether Imlay's stories were true or not. For if the prospect of continuing their liaison was enticing, the thought of sacrificing her to another was entirely insupportable.

His deliberations were interrupted by the appearance of the maid, Hélène, at the kitchen door.

"Citizen," she called out to him, "Citizen Imlay is here ..."

And there he was behind her, with such a black look on his face that Nathan's troubles lurched into immediate perspective ...

The treasure, he thought, as he advanced to meet him.

But it was not the treasure.

Imlay flung himself down on the seat by the pool. The carp gathered hopefully again. But it was not their day.

"Danton has been arrested," he said.

Nathan stared at him. He looked exhausted. There were dark

shadows under his eyes and he had several days' growth of beard.

"They came for him this morning," he said, "with a warrant signed by Robespierre and Vadier."

"But this is Danton." Nathan still could not believe it. The man had seemed untouchable. "The Convention will—"

"The Convention," Imlay made a face as if he tasted something sour, "will do nothing. They met at seven this morning. I was there, in the public gallery. There was some anger when they heard—but then Robespierre came in. He went straight to the tribune and of course everyone made way for him as if he owned it and the rest were only allowed to use it on sufferance; preferably when he was not present. He said Danton was no better than any other citizen. 'We will have no more privileges here and no more idols,' he said. He looked at them through his glasses in that way he has. Of course no one had the guts to speak against him. They're all terrified. Scared stiff they'll be in the same tumbrel as Danton."

"Robespierre cannot send them all to the guillotine."

"No. But no one wants to be the next—or the last, before sanity prevails and they rise up against him."

"So what now?"

"The bull is at bay—and they have set the dogs upon him. Robespierre has been briefing Herman and Fouquier to make sure it all goes according to plan."

This meant nothing to Nathan. Herman was the President of the Revolutionary Tribunal, Imlay explained, and Fouquier the Public Prosecutor.

"They are putting them on trial with the bankers," he added.

"The bankers?"

"They have a number of men held on corruption charges. They are hoping it will confuse the issue to charge Danton with them—and that the people will think he has been lining his pockets. They've got it all worked out. Robespierre must have been planning it for weeks. All the time he has been 'indisposed.' Camille warned us. He said that whenever Max had to make a decision he went to bed with a cold.

Well now he has made his decision and they are to die."

"They?"

"Camille has been arrested, too. And Herault de Seychelles and Fabre d'Eglantine and other of their friends—"

"And they are in the Luxembourg?"

"With Tom Paine. He was waiting for them in the prison courtyard with others who had once been representatives of the people. Danton made a speech. Naturally. Wherever two or three people are gathered together, Danton makes a speech."

"How do you know this?"

"I have my sources. One of the guards is an admirer of Danton, a member of the Cordeliers Club. He said Danton seemed to think it was all up with him. He told them: 'I tried to get you out of here and now I'm in here with you.' He said he had tried to do for France what Paine had done for his own country—by which I presume he meant America and not England—but that it had been all in vain and now they would send him to the scaffold. Not one of his more inspiring speeches. I think I preferred 'Dare, dare and dare again . . .'"

"So Danton said it was all in vain."

They turned sharply. Sara stood behind them in her robe.

Even now, with this disaster upon them, her beauty took Nathan's breath away. He felt a ridiculous exultation.

"Sara . . ." Imlay moved towards her as if to embrace her and Nathan felt a different emotion.

Sara pushed him away. She looked like a Fury. Her gown opened a little and he glimpsed her leg. She is naked, Nathan thought, under the gown.

"He has led them to the point of battle," she said, "and they have followed like goats and now he has surrendered, without a fight. Damn all men. Oh, poor Lucille. I must go to her."

She turned away.

"Sara," Imlay called after her. "You know Danton. Sometimes he says the first thing that comes into his head, because he likes the sound of it. I expect he'll put up a fight. He usually does."

CHAPTER 27

the Trial

MY NAME IS DANTON. IT IS a name tolerably well known in the Revolution. I am a lawyer by profession and I was born at Arcis in the Aube country. In a few days time my abode will be oblivion. My place of residence will be History."

Danton, at the Revolutionary Tribunal, when they asked him for his name and address.

Nathan rolled his eyes at Sara who was sitting next to him in the public gallery with Lucille Desmoulins. Not Imlay. Nathan had not seen him since the previous morning when he had brought news of Danton's arrest. There were people he had to see, he said mysteriously, but he had promised to be there for the trial. The gallery was packed with Danton's supporters. Many more were behind the barriers at the back of the court all the way to the doors and beyond: the crowd outside ran to several thousand. Many were peering in at the windows, or pressing in as close as they could to the walls to hear what they could of the proceedings. Danton pitched his voice so it would carry to the farthest extremities of this vast audience.

He was the only one standing in the crowded dock. Some of the accused Nathan recognised or knew by repute: Camille, of course; Lacroix and Phillipaux; Herault de Seychelles who had been on the Committee of Public Safety; Fabre d'Eglantine, the playwright who had drawn up the revolutionary calendar . . . all friends of Danton. But the others were unfamiliar to him—and to most of the court. These were the bankers, the swindlers and forgers that Imlay said had been thrown in to confuse the issue. They were charged with fraud or hoarding, currency speculation, conspiring with foreign powers . . . The idea was that people would think Danton and his friends were somehow implicated in their alleged crimes: that they would be tainted by association even if they had only met them for the first time in the dock.

The charges against the Dantonists had not been made public yet. Doubtless they would be read out in due course, when the President managed to make himself heard. He kept ringing his bell furiously to bring the court to order but it was inaudible above the din. People were chanting Danton's name, stamping their feet, singing the Marseillaise . . . It was something between a carnival and a riot. It seemed that at any moment the mob would storm the courtroom and free the prisoners by force and carry them shoulder high through the streets.

Lucille was looking hopeful for the first time since the arrest. Danton's voice rolled out, overriding every attempt at interruption, rising above the whistles and the cheers.

"Who are my accusers? Bring them forward. Who dares accuse me, Danton?"

Nathan felt for Sara's hand and pressed it encouragingly. But privately he was not optimistic. He felt that it was all scripted—a performance—and that this was the noisy part, the prologue before it properly began. Now Danton had the stage but soon others would. Nathan saw the vulture face of Fouquier, the prosecutor, with his black hat and its patriotic plumage watching Danton carefully, his face impassive, waiting for the corpse to stop moving and waving its arms and shouting so the feast could begin—the real purpose of his life. And he saw the faces of the jury: the hand-picked jury who could be relied upon to do their patriotic duty. And a voice inside his head kept repeating: *theatre, pure theatre.* Or a bull fight, like one he had seen in the Argentine. There was music and noise and flags and ceremony, and the matadors in their garish costumes and the bull rushing into the ring, its head lowered for the charge. And then the shouting would stop and everyone would go quiet and they would get on with the serious business of killing.

When the court adjourned for the day, with nothing decided, they took the prisoners back to the prison and Sara went off with Lucille to stand in the Luxembourg Gardens in the hope of catching a glimpse of Camille while Nathan walked back to his hotel alone.

He was no longer staying at the Philadelphia. Most of the Americans had left—with neither idealism nor profit to keep them—and it had begun to have a run-down, end of season look. Besides, it seemed unlucky after what had happened to Thomas Paine and Nathan suspected it was still under surveillance. He had found a different place in the narrow cobbled streets behind Notre-Dame: the Hotel Providence, which, according to the proprietor, was where the great Peter Abelard had lived when he was courting the beautiful Heloise. Nathan wondered if he had been here on the night the girl's guardian sent his hired thugs to cut off his balls.

He was sitting in the taproom with a glass of red wine when Imlay slipped into the seat opposite.

"Drink up your wine," he said. "There is someone I want you to meet."

CHAPTER 28

the King of the Catacombs

"H IS NAME IS LE MULET," IMLAY announced as they headed
south out of the city. "Jacques Le Mulet."

"Jackass," reflected Nathan drily.

"In fact the English translation of Le Mulet would be the Mule,"
Imlay corrected him coldly. "The French for an ass, or donkey, is âne."

"I am aware of that. It was a poor play upon words."

"Well, I pray that you will not play upon them in Le Mulet's hearing," Imlay instructed him, "as he may take offence."

"And who exactly is he—this Mule?"

"Among other things, he is the owner of a limestone quarry on the
edge of the city which he uses to bury the dead."

Nathan looked to see if he was serious but the interior of the cab
was too dark to read his expression. It was a cold night with a hint of
mist in the air and a frost forming on the rooftops.

"He buries the dead?"

"Yes. Or it would be more correct to say reburies them. He digs
them up from the old graveyards in the city and dumps them in the
quarry."

"Is this a pastime of his—or does it serve some greater purpose?"

"It is a business, like any other. The graveyards were becoming
overcrowded, like the rest of Paris. So they are moving the corpses

to a new location. Le Mulet has the contract. However, his true vocation, one might say, is as Worshipful Master of the Grand Trouanderie."

This meant nothing to Nathan though it sounded impressive.

"A literal translation would be the Great Villainy," Imlay explained. "It is a criminal fraternity. It regulates most of the crime—the organised crime—in the city. Allocates territories, punishes trespass, arbitrates quarrels, settles feuds ... It is very much like a Chamber of Commerce for criminals."

"And why are we going to meet him?" inquired Nathan.

"Did I not say? Because he is a great admirer of Danton."

Nathan pondered this in silence for a while. They pulled into the side of the road to let a convoy of drays go past, the horses steaming in the lanterns, lumbering late into Paris with casks of wine. Whatever else Paris went short of, it was not wine.

"Le Mulet has a finger in a great many pies," Imlay resumed. "There is scarcely an underhand deal in the city that does not involve him in some way or another."

"I assume that is how you became acquainted."

"Correct." Imlay did not appear to be at all offended by this sally. "He has an affinity with Americans. He claims to have fought in the War of Independence, though I cannot see him as a soldier. His true talent is for smuggling."

"I appear to have an affinity with smugglers," Nathan remarked thoughtfully, "though I have not known many on land."

"His natural element is under the ground. He is the King of the Catacombs."

Worshipful Master of the Grand Trouanderie, Undertaker, Smuggler and now King of the Catacombs.

"And who are his subjects?"

"You will see," said Imlay mysteriously.

They were silent for a while; the only sounds the jingling of the harness and the crunch of hooves and wheels on the freezing ruts and the occasional oath from the cabby on his box. Briefly, Nathan glimpsed the dark towers of the Luxembourg but they skirted the prison and its gardens, heading farther south into a less populous area. Here were market gardens, windmills and slaughterhouses and even the occasional field, the frost sparkling in the moonlight. Beyond, Nathan glimpsed the imposing edifice of the Porte d'Enfer—Hell's Gate—one of the customs posts in the great barrière that had been erected around Paris by the tax farmers to extract duty on all freight passing in and out of the city. The wall itself was long gone, destroyed in the first flush of Revolution and the tax farmers with it but some of the gatehouses remained, manned by citizen soldiers checking passes.

They drove through a suburb, almost a village with a pretty church and a graveyard and a few farm buildings among newer, uglier tenements and workshops. There were larger industries too across the fields with tall chimneys belching smoke. A sudden eruption hurled flame and sparks into the air like a small volcano.

"Cannon foundries," explained Imlay, "built in the last few months. And there is Hanriot's works for the manufacture of saltpetre. Paris is become an armoury."

But Nathan was not interested in Hanriot's saltpetre works or any other. He was interested in Le Mulet and his catacombs.

"These catacombs," he ventured, "are they extensive?"

"They undermine most of Paris, I am told. The Romans started them for the limestone to build the city and people have been adding to them ever since. But there was a problem of subsidence. A few years ago several streets collapsed and the authorities put a ban on any future extensions."

"So they run under the streets? And the public buildings?"

"So I understand from Le Mulet. In fact he claims that one of them runs under the Luxembourg."

Nathan looked at him sharply.

"Am I to understand that he plans to use it to rescue Danton from prison?"

"No. The plan is mine. Le Mulet does not yet know of it."

Nathan still could not read his expression but he saw that he was smiling.

"And you think he will oblige—because he is an admirer of Danton?"

"No," Imlay said again, in the same patient tones. "I think he will oblige because we will pay him a great deal of money. In gold."

"Gold?" Nathan repeated. There was no answer. "Danton's gold?"

"It is not much use to Danton in prison."

"So you intend to give it to this criminal to get him out."

"No. You do. It is your gold. Or at least it is in your charge. That is why I am taking you to see him."

"So the plan—your plan—is to get Danton out of prison through the catacombs."

"It is. Along with Camille. And Tom Paine. And a great many others. It is to be a mass escape. We have contacts inside the prison who will assist us."

Nathan did not at all like the use of the word "us." But there was plenty to worry him aside from that.

"And then what?"

"And then the people will rise up against the present regime and Danton will assume power. Which is also the plan."

"I was instructed to ensure that this money reached Danton," Nathan pointed out, "and to obtain a receipt. That is all."

He sounded like a tally man. Perhaps he was.

"Then we had better get him out of prison," said Imlay smoothly, "and ensure he gives you one."

They turned off the road and into what appeared to be a vast builder's yard with ramshackle huts and lean-tos, piles of rock and timber discarded on the frosty ground. Gaunt limestone crags rose up in a semicircle around them to form a natural amphitheatre and amid a circle of smoking flambeaus a gang of labourers unloaded what Nathan took to be stones from a cart.

Why bring stones to a quarry? Then he saw with a shock that they were not stones but skulls. So at least this much of Imlay's narrative was true.

They climbed stiffly down from the cab and Imlay asked one of the workmen if he knew where the patron was. The man shook his head without interrupting his labour but another answered for him. He might be in the forge, he said, jerking his head in the direction of a large shed across the bleak expanse of yard. They saw the glow of a fire through a half-open door and heard the distant assault of iron upon iron.

It was the biggest building on the site, about the size of a small barn, the walls and floor stacked with wounded metal. Pots, pans, cartwheels, a pair of gates, even a coach that had clearly been in some accident. The blacksmith was hammering a glowing horseshoe on the anvil while his assistant held the horse at some distance from the sparks. Imlay raised his voice.

"I was told the boss was here."

The blacksmith gave him a look but didn't stop. In the confined space the hammer blows exploded in their ears and splintered, like case shot through their heads.

"You were told right."

The reply seemed to come from the coach, parked up among the debris on the far side of the forge. The windows and the wheels had been removed and the axles propped up on timber but the door was open and in the gloom of the interior they could just make out the figure of a man stretched comfortably across one of the plush leather seats with his feet up, smoking a pipe.

"Come into my office," he called over to them. And to the black-smith: "Jean-Baptiste, why don't you take a little break so we can hear ourselves think?"

No introductions were made but this, Nathan gathered, was Le Mulet.

He was a short, stocky fellow of middling years with narrow eyes and a large nose, which gave him a slight resemblance to his name-sake, though his ears were no bigger than normal. He wore a multi-layered cape, like a coachman's, and a good pair of knee-length boots and a tall beaver hat lay on the seat next to him with the ubiquitous

revolutionary cockade. He seemed genial enough, nodding and beaming at them over his pipe but the eyes measured them as if for coffins.

"So, Citizens, what can I do for you?"

"We have some friends in the Luxembourg," said Imlay, "and we
would like to get them out."

The expression did not change.

"And what friends would they be?"

"Danton, Desmoulins, Thomas Paine and a few others. But
Danton is the important one."

Le Mulet nodded complacently over his pipe.

"I like Citizen Danton," he said. "He is a man after my own heart.
Desmoulins I am not so sure of. He looks like a catamite. And Paine,
he is the American, yes?"

"Yes."

"And your friend here?" He gestured with his pipe at Nathan. "Is
he an American?"

"He is," said Imlay.

"I like the Americans," said Le Mulet. "I fought with them against
the British, did he tell you?" With a jerk of his head at Imlay.

"He did," Nathan acknowledged.

"But I am a man of business; did he also tell you that?"

"He did."

"Good." He stood up. "So you will want to see the catacombs."

CHAPTER 29

the Empire of the Dead

L E MULET LED THEM ACROSS THE yard to where the men were still unloading the skulls from the cart in a circle of smoke and flame. Beside them was a structure very like the guillotine but with an iron pulley at the top instead of a steel blade and a length of cable dropping down a shaft. The other end of the cable was wound round a wooden drum or windlass with long handles on each side operated by four men. As they heaved, a large metal cage emerged slowly from the shaft.

"Your carriage," said Le Mulet, stopping the men from loading it with skulls. He opened a door in the side and invited them to step in.

"We can only take two at a time," he said. "When you reach the bottom pull on the cord for us to raise it. I will join you there."

He handed Nathan a lantern and signalled to the men at the windlass. They began to lower them slowly into the pit.

It was impossible to look down. The cage fitted the shaft almost as tightly as a cork, bumping with an unpleasant grating noise against the limestone rock. Nathan reflected that he was taking a great deal on trust and it was not a natural inclination. If they were stepping into a trap it was with wilful negligence.

Down, down for about fifty or sixty feet, then suddenly the walls fell away and they were dropping through a wide vault to land with a final jolt on solid ground. They opened the gate and stepped out. The cavern was about the size of a small chapel, dimly lit by a few lanterns and almost entirely lined by skulls.

"Dear God," breathed Nathan, "what is this?"

"It is the Empire of the Dead," said Imlay. "I have heard tell of it but I never imagined it was like this."

Nathan remembered what Le Mulet had said about the signal rope and gave it a jerk. After a moment the cage began to ascend.

"We would look mighty foolish if he don't join us," he remarked. His voice sounded overloud and it echoed back mockingly in the great vault.

But after a minute or two they heard the grating of metal on rock and the cage reappeared with Le Mulet and a companion. At first Nathan thought he was a child, for he was no more than about four feet in height but as he stepped out of the cage they saw that he was a dwarf, or more correctly a midget, for he was perfectly proportioned. His face—which was not at all childlike—was distinguished by a small pointed beard and an oversized moustache extending several inches to either side of his cheeks, twisted and waxed at the ends, giving him something of the appearance of a cat with a handsome set of whiskers. He wore a red liberty bonnet, a quilted jacket and a pair of thigh-length boots like a cavalier—or, indeed, Puss in Boots. He carried a lantern in one hand, a coil of rope over his shoulder and—to complete the picture of roguish charm—a bandolier across his chest with three or four knives thrust through it, possibly of the kind designed for throwing.

"Bulbeau," said Le Mulet by way of an introduction and the midget made them a bow that might have been ironic.

"We must go in single file," said Le Mulet, "and watch your heads, it is low in parts."

He led them off through a narrow tunnel in the side of the vault with Bulbeau bringing up the rear. This, too, was lined with skulls on both sides to a height of about five feet, the roof dripping water and the ground sloping down a little. After a few minutes they reached a fork but their guide strode confidently ahead without a pause and they struggled to keep up, their step unsure on the slippery path. They entered another cavern like the first and with the same circle of ghastly faces, like spectators in some demonic theatre. Nathan felt like an actor on a stage, the macabre audience grinning down at him as if they knew something he did not—his ending, perhaps; the drip of water was like a slow mocking clap. They carried on past nooks and crannies, galleries running off to left and right and once a pit. Nathan stooped, lowering his lantern, but could not see the bottom. He had no stone to hand but formed a ball of spittle in his mouth and let it drop, watching the silver bubble drifting through the beam of light into a universe of darkness. Le Mulet called and he moved on, Imlay stumbling behind, muttering, and sometimes cursing. Fewer skulls now and not so neatly stacked, some had rolled in the path. Le Mulet kicked them aside.

"Why are there no bones?" Nathan asked.

"There are bones," Le Mulet replied. "We throw them down the pits. Be the devil's own job to put them back together again on Resurrection Day." His laughter did a drum roll off the walls.

So why stack the skulls, Nathan wondered. Not for God's convenience. Perhaps it was part of the contract with the Commune, in case the relatives should ever want to see them. He almost laughed aloud at the absurdity of it. How to find father, mother, sister, brother; husband, wife . . . or lover . . . in this faceless multitude? Who was count or commoner, saint or sinner in the Empire of the Dead?

The floor was sloping up and they were sloshing through running water, deep enough to flow over their boots. No more skulls. Strangely Nathan missed them, fearing they were venturing where even the dead would not. The walls narrowed and the ceiling dipped in parts. Nathan crouched, shambling forward like an ape or a cave bear, one hand raised with the lantern but more blinded than aided by the light. He hit his head hard on the roof; put up a hand and felt blood. But Le Mulet did not pause and he had to hurry to catch up.

They stumbled out into another cavern larger than the others they had seen, the walls receding into darkness. The floor was uneven and littered with rocks, some as large as boulders and looking very like trolls in the lantern light. Nathan veered a little off track and peered up to what appeared to be a glimpse of sky far above. It was night but nothing like as dark as in the caves.

"It's just a shaft," said Le Mulet. "Come."

But then as Nathan turned away he saw something else, draped across one of the boulders. He thought at first it was a bundle of rags but he raised the lantern again and saw that it was a body.

He took a few steps closer, regardless of the Mule's muttered oath. No ancient cadaver this. Death had filed a much more recent claim and violently too. It lay on its back across its chosen tombstone, limbs grotesquely contorted, the head thrown back so that from Nathan's perspective it was upside down and ghastly in the lantern light; one eye staring, the other a blackened pulp, mouth gaping as if in one final scream for life. A man, probably quite young when he was alive. Had he fallen down the shaft? Then Imlay was beside him with his lantern, doubling the light, and Nathan saw the gash in the dead man's throat and the black blood matted on his chest.

Le Mulet came back to see what they were staring at. He made a tutting noise. "They keep doing this," he said.

Nathan stared at him and felt hysterical laughter bubbling in his throat.

"They throw them down the quarries. We have complained about it to the Convention. They chuck so many down there it gets choked up with them."

"They?" Nathan queried. "Them?"

"The mob. Anyone they take a mind to."

This could have been him, Nathan thought, if he had not been saved by Imlay the first day he came to Paris. He looked up and saw the gleam of moonlight on cloud.

"Come," said Le Mulet again, with a firm hand on his shoulder this time. "Someone may look down and see the lights."

They entered another tunnel, wider now and certainly man made, the stones chipped and scoured by tools, the floor level. Small niches, even grottoes had been cut just above head height. In one there was the stump of a candle, in another a religious statue. They reached a crossroad. Le Mulet turned right; then left. They would never find their way back without him. The ground was running water again, the air fouler than it had been. Nathan sniffed to draw attention to the fact.

"Sewer," said Le Mulet shortly.

Nathan thought of his *égoutier* Philippe—the failed footpad—and thought how extraordinary it would be if he met him down here. But the *égoutiers* were not the only denizens of the Paris sewers.

Nathan heard the rats before he saw them, the squeaking alarums in the dark. Then they were scurrying at his feet, running at him along the walls, even upside down on the roof. A brief glimpse of sleek, wet fur, black eyes in the lantern light and a frightened, vicious squealing. He kicked, nearly lost his footing and they were behind them, vanishing into the black hole.

Le Mulet had not paused. Nathan plunged after the dark, squat figure which almost filled the passage ahead . . . and then suddenly they were in another cavern—but very different from the others.

"Christ!" He heard Imlay exclaim behind him with more fear in his voice than wonder.

It was a chapel—but what a chapel. Nathan raised the lantern high and felt the hairs lift on the nape of his neck. There the altar and the pews, there the candles and christening font. But no Christian had worshipped here. The Christ hung inverted on his cross, suspended in an eternity of pain, the eyes that should have been raised to heaven gazing down on the empty pews. And at the altar a darker figure presided. Nathan arced the light to expose the face of the Beast, horned and hairy, teeth bared in a welcoming grin. Nathan stepped back with a muttered oath, almost dropping the lamp, darting a glance to left and right, thinking to see shapes rushing at him from the gloom, of demons or of men. His hand grasped the hilt of his sword.

And the Mule slapping his thigh and filling the chamber with his barking laugh.

"What, *sabreur*, would you use a blade to prick the Devil?"

"What in God's name is it?" demanded Imlay. He seemed badly shaken.

"Nothing in God's name. Satan holds dominion here." Le Mulet held the lamp to expose the date carved into the beam above the dangling crucifix. 1348. "The year of the Great Plague. God could not save them, or would not, so they turned to Satan."

"It was so long ago?" Nathan looked around, marvelling.

"Well, others might have used it since. The candles are not so old, even if the Devil is."

He set his lantern upon the edge of the stone font and sat down in a pew, putting his feet up—as much at home as he had been in the forge.

"The Black Mass," said Imlay, in a hushed voice. Almost worshipful. He looked mesmerised: half repulsed, half drawn towards the figure of the Beast.

Now Le Mulet was opening a cupboard in the wall, taking out a black bottle and four silver chalices. He pulled the cork, poured wine into each. Offered one to Imlay who shook his head, fear in his eyes.

"What? 'tis not Communion wine, imbecile. Think I'd drink that piss? Me, to worship the Devil? Bollocks! I worship no one." He waved his hand at the altar, spilling wine. "'Tis all one to me. Plaster saints or demons."

"Then why bring us here?"

"Oh it is one of my little hideaways; where I keep my wine—and other things. Come, 'tis good burgundy." Reluctantly Imlay took the chalice and passed another to Nathan. Le Mulet raised his to the ceiling, looking up above the dangling Christ. "And above us—the Luxembourg."

They looked up at the ceiling.

"What part of the Luxembourg?" demanded Imlay.

"At one time it was a chapel. To a different god."

"At one time?"

"When this was built." He indicated the room they were in. "It was the chapel crypt."

"But the palace was not built then," Imlay corrected him, "at the time of the Black Death."

"No. But a chateau stood on the same site. The Chateau de Vauvert. You cannot fault me on the history of Paris, my friend. Above or below the ground."

"So what is up there now?"

Le Mulet heaved himself to his feet. "Come. I will show you."

They stood uncertainly, exchanging wary glances, as he crossed to the altar and ducked behind the effigy of the Beast. But now they saw that what they had taken for a dark recess was in fact a black velvet curtain. With a mocking bow he held it aside and invited them to enter.

Nathan went first. A row of stone steps leading upwards, bending to the right. He advanced cautiously holding the lantern before him, his hand on the hilt of his sword, vaguely aware that Le Mulet was playing him for a fool but not sure quite how or why. But when he negotiated the bend in the stair he confronted a wall of rock. Or rather a wall of rocks, for the individual stones were fitted together in the manner of a dry stone wall in England.

He retraced his steps to where Le Mulet waited, smiling.

"My men built it," he said. "I did not wish for anyone to wander into my den. Come, let us talk."

They followed him back around the altar and sat again among the pews. Bulbeau still had his feet up drinking his wine, directly under his dangling Saviour. Le Mulet proceeded to give them a history lesson.

"When they were building the Luxembourg for Marie de Medici they must have discovered what lay in the crypt. But for some reason they did not destroy it. Perhaps someone wished to continue the tradition of Devil worship. The Medici herself, perhaps; I have heard she was something of a she-devil. Or perhaps she thought it an amusing diversion, something to show her guests after dinner. But for whatever reason, it was left as it is now—and the entrance concealed."

"So what is up there now?" asked Nathan.

"A theatre," said Le Mulet.

Of course, thought Nathan. It would be. This was Paris.

"How do you know that?"

"Because we went up to have a look. Two years ago, when it was still a royal palace. Disused. We came up under the stage—in the room where they used to keep the costumes. They were still there, hanging from the rails, covered in dust."

"But you don't know what it is being used for now?" Nathan pressed him.

By way of a reply, Le Mulet dug in his pocket and produced a notebook and a pencil. He licked the lead. "So, what do we require? One: to discover what is on the other side of the door."

Neither of them responded but he wrote it down.

"Two: removal of rocks. Yes?" He looked at Nathan.

Nathan nodded carefully. They might have been discussing a building contract.

"Three: access to the prisoners."

"How can that be arranged?"

"Well, one could go up and find them." Le Mulet jerked his head at the ceiling. "But it is probably better that we have someone already in the prison. Someone who can lead them to the tunnel. So," he wrote it down, "accomplice in prison."

"I may be able to help with that," said Imlay quietly.

Nathan looked sharply at him. But it would keep for later.

"Very well," said the Mule. "I leave that to you." He closed the notebook. "So, all that remains is the price."

CHAPTER 30

Betrayed

IT WAS LATE ON THE NIGHT of the fourteenth day of Germinal but smoke rose from the chimneys of the new workshops in the gardens of the Tuileries and lights still burned in the upstairs rooms of the Pavillon d'Égalité. The twin cannon at the entrance were loaded with grape and the guard had been doubled. Messengers came and went. The atmosphere in the streets was tense. Tomorrow would be the fourth day of the trial and Danton was still challenging the authority of the court.

A little before midnight the trial judge, Fouquier, was observed crossing the gardens and entering the West Wing of the palace between the two cannon and their flaming torches. He mounted the Queen's Stair and was admitted into the room at the top where the Committee of Public Safety met. Only three members were present. Robespierre, Saint-Just and Couthon in his wheelchair. The Triumvirate. Nothing like a quorum, though, and no minutes were kept. While the four men talked a faint breeze arose from the northeast. It rustled the dead leaves in the gardens and stirred the new growth they had until lately concealed. As Fouquier left—a little after midnight—it began to rain.

It rained throughout the night. It was still raining at break of day as Imlay, Nathan and Le Mulet huddled in the shelter of the forge and gazed bleakly out across the deserted floor of the quarry to where the pulley stood draped in tarpaulin, reminding Nathan uncomfortably of the guillotine when he had first seen it on Christmas Eve.

Le Mulet expressed the hope that the rain would not be a problem.

"Why should it be?" Imlay demanded tensely. "We shall be under the ground."

"The catacombs connect with the sewers at several points," Le Mulet informed him, wearily, as if it was something he should have known, "and in heavy rain there is sometimes a flood. Especially if the river is high."

Nathan looked up from loading his pistols. If there was a flood he wondered if he would get his money back. He rather doubted it.

He was still suspicious that the whole affair was a put-up job to cheat him—or rather the British government—of their treasure. Even the rain might be a part of it.

Imlay consulted his watch by the light of the lantern hanging from the beam above his head.

"Flood or not," he said, "it is surely time we made a move."

Imlay had explained the plan.

Le Mulet's men had cleared the rocks from the stair above the Black Chapel and ensured that the door to the old theatre—now the prison store—was not locked. Imlay, Nathan, Le Mulet and several of his men would wait there until a few minutes before seven o'clock. At that hour the prisoners were due to be escorted into the inner courtyard, directly outside the store, to board the coaches procured for their journey to the Palais de Justice. At which point, Le Mulet's gang would emerge from the store, overcome the guards and lead the prisoners back the way they had come.

Danton would be escorted directly to the Cordeliers Club where he would declare an insurrection. The people of the old Cordeliers and Saint-Antoine districts had been prepared. All they waited upon was the sound of the tocsin and the news that Danton was free.

That simple. The best plans, in Nathan's experience, usually were. If they had any basis in reality.

There was no way of knowing if the arrangements Imlay claimed to have made were a piece of theatre and that Le Mulet was playing a leading part. No way of knowing, for that matter if the Black Chapel lay beneath the Luxembourg palace or the Comédie-Française.

This was the main reason Nathan had insisted on accompanying Imlay on the enterprise, though a certain spirit of adventure also played its part. He had never before assisted in a jailbreak and this, if successful, would make history.

"Very well," said Le Mulet, "let us be on our way."

He pulled an oilskin over his head and lurched out into the rain. At once a number of other figures emerged from the various sheds and workshops scattered around the sides of the quarry, among them a diminutive figure that must be Bulbeau. They congregated in a sodden group around the shaft, water streaming from their water-proofs: seven men, Nathan counted, besides himself and Imlay. They tugged off the tarpaulin cover to reveal the tripod and its iron wheel, the bucket dangling above the black hole. Four of them inserted the wooden spokes into the windlass and prepared to take the strain when the brake was released.

"After you," said Le Mulet to Imlay with a nod towards the cage.

Then the first shot rang out.

For a moment no one reacted. It might have been thunder, especially as there was an impression of lightning.

Then came the volley.

At least two shots struck the iron bucket with a ringing double clang like the opening chords of a demon drummer. Others splashed into the mud at their feet. Two found their targets in the huddled knot of men.

They scattered right and left but not before Nathan glimpsed the snarling face of Bulbeau thrust towards him in the rain and heard his angry cry: "Betrayed!"

Nathan and Imlay reached the door of the forge together and

hurled themselves over the threshold. Flashes and bangs. A long splinter of wood torn away from the door lintel and something whining away across the interior of the forge. Nathan pressed his eye against a hole in the wall, saw two prone figures in the mud beside the deserted scaffold and the rain lashing down. Another crash of musketry and he flinched away and then put his eye once more to the crack and saw the long line of figures on top of the limestone cliff. There must have been over a hundred of them. He checked his pistols. Too long a shot for the soldiers but they might save him from Bulbeau. Where was he? He squinted around the site just as two figures broke cover: one squat, the other short—Le Mulet and Bulbeau. Others behind and from other buildings, firing as they ran at the men on the cliff. One went down, writhing in the mud.

Men at the windlass and Le Mulet waving his arms, shouting instructions. He and Bulbeau jumped into the cage and the others began to lower it down the shaft. Another volley from the ridge and sparks flew from the wheel. A man fell at the windlass and another leapt to take his place. You could not fault their loyalty for they were sitting targets in the bottom of the quarry. But the shooting was wild, very wild—or else the rain had soaked the powder and the guns were misfiring. But then two more men were down and the rest began to run for the cover of the buildings.

"The shaft," yelled Imlay and darted forward into the rain.

It was a moment before Nathan understood, another before he decided to follow.

He was halfway there when he heard the trumpet. The trumpet and something like the thunder of hooves. He twisted round as he ran, stumbled and fell and looked up to see a sight to remember the rest of his life, long or short: a cavalry charge viewed from a position directly in its path. Then he was up and running. Another volley from the ridge, kicking up the mud at his feet and the wind of a shot past his ear. Imlay leapt and grabbed the cable, whirling round with his coat-tails flying, like a boy on a swing, and then he was gone. Nathan heard the horses bearing down on him; turned and fired his pistol. A trooper came straight at him slashing down with his sabre and Nathan leapt directly into the path of the horse and went flying backwards, all the wind knocked out of him, a sharp brutal pain in his chest and then a crack on the head that plunged him into a world of darkness as deep and as black as the Empire of the Dead.

CHAPTER 31

the Children of the Revolution

WITH A RISING SENSE OF PANIC Sara scanned the crowded courtroom for the faces of her friends. Nathan had gone off with Imlay the night before on some mysterious errand he clearly did not wish to discuss with her. All being well I will see you in the morning, he had said. But he had not come back to the house and he was not here in the courtroom. Nor was Imlay. She could not even see Lucille.

They fetched up the prisoners. Danton was on his feet almost at once but he looked terrible. His massive form was swaying in the dock; his great voice a harsh croak. For three days he had fought them but now he was finished and everyone knew it.

And Fouquier stood to deliver the coup de grâce.

"I have urgent information to lay before the court," he began.

Astonished, Sara heard the name of Lucille Desmoulins . . . Why was he naming Lucille? She strained to hear what he was saying for though the court was silent for once, his voice seemed to be filtered through some thick distorting mask.

"Agents of a foreign power in concert with Lucille Desmoulins and others . . . plotting to free the prisoners from the Luxembourg . . . to raise an armed riot inside the Convention and assassinate members of the Committee of Public Safety . . ."

It took a moment to sink in. Even the judge and jury appeared amazed. Then a single anguished cry from Camille: "They are trying to murder my wife!"

And then uproar.

Most of the defendants were on their feet shouting to be heard, Danton's harsh croak rising above them, pointing at the bench: "Murderers. See them. They have hounded us to our deaths."

Camille was trying to climb out of the dock and Danton and Lacroix holding him back until he collapsed between them, a sobbing bundle of rage and despair. And Herman ringing his bell and Fouquier waiting for the din to subside and then reading out in his dry, deathly tones the emergency decree of the Convention:

"In response to the threat to national security the President shall use every means that the law allows to make his authority and the authority of the Revolutionary Tribunal respected . . . All persons accused of conspiracy who shall resist or insult the national justice shall be outlawed and shall receive judgement without any further proceedings."

Danton was still on his feet, still demanding witnesses for the defence, but he had almost lost his voice and he was tugging at the stock around his throat as if it was a rope strangling him.

And Sara caught sight of two faces she knew: Vadier and the artist David, both members of the Police Committee, leaning on the back of the bench where the jury sat and looking towards Danton and laughing.

"Your rights, Danton, are in abeyance." She heard the voice of the President, Herman, exultant in victory. He turned to the jury: "Have you heard enough?"

One of them stood. "Yes, we have heard enough."

"Then the trial is closed."

The mob was surging towards the doors, trying to get out and Sara thought there must be some hope of a rescue. The prisoners would have to be taken back to the Conciergerie and from there to the Place de la Révolution. Half the number that had crowded into the court to voice their support would be enough to free them.

Camille was on his feet waving a bunch of papers. She heard his voice with no trace of a stammer for once.

"I have not yet read my statement. I have been here three days and you have not heard my defence. I demand to be permitted to read my statement to the court. You cannot condemn people without hearing their defence . . ."

Herman said something Sara did not catch and then Camille threw the papers at him. They sailed like a dart across the courtroom and with surprising accuracy. The judge ducked so violently his hat fell off and the bunch of papers fell apart in the space behind him, floating separately to the courtroom floor. Before they had landed Fouquier was on his feet shouting, no longer calm or impassive, but the flecks of spit plainly to be seen in the light from the windows: "The prisoners have insulted national justice. Under the terms of the decree they may now be removed from the court."

Herman putting his hat back on and ringing his bell more in a bid to recover his lost dignity than in any hope of imposing order.

"The jury will retire to consider its verdict. Remove the prisoners."

There was a fight going on in the dock. The guards were trying to get the prisoners out and Camille was trying to stay. One of them was pulling at his long hair and then they knocked him down. The last Sara saw before she was borne back by the tide of bodies was his limp form being carried down to the cells.

She did not hear the verdict. By then it was impossible to get back into the court and she was carried in the surge of spectators across Pont Neuf to line the route along the Rue Honoré. She heard later that Fouquier had already told the executioner, Sanson, to bring three *charrettes* to the Conciergerie. She also heard that they did not bother to bring the prisoners back into the court and that the sentence of death was read out to them in the prison while Sanson's men were cutting their hair. It was four o'clock in the afternoon and she was still looking for Nathan's face in the crowd.

She joined the great tide of people flowing across the bridges from the Île de la Cite. She was still convinced they would storm the convoy. That was why she stayed with them; that was how she saw what she saw. It was inconceivable to her that the *sans-culottes* who had cheered Danton's every word in court would just stand idly by and watch him die, much less cheer his executioners. But when they reached the Rue Honoré she found the National Guard lining the route forcing the crowd into the sides of the road. When the death carts came, hundreds tried to follow them, pushing and shoving their way along the narrow gap between the guards and the walls. It was impossible to stay in one place even if you wanted to. Sara went with the flow.

For at least part of the time she was in that section of the crowd moving in line with the *charrettes* and she would rise herself up to catch a glimpse of the prisoners, then lose them in the froth of heads and bodies. Later, she was not sure what she had seen for herself or what she had imagined seeing from the descriptions of others or read about in the press. She was sure she had seen Danton standing in the front of the cart like a primitive god: a giant figurehead with his arms tied behind his back and his shirt open to his chest, his great head unbowed, his expression defiant, the lips curled in what could have been a mocking smile or a sneer—you never knew with that mouth. But it was the same image as that captured by David who had once been his friend and who now managed to make a sketch of him in that immense crush of bodies; a last sketch: to record the death of Danton for history.

She definitely saw Camille, his shirt ripped from his back in the fight with the guards and wrapped like a ragged shawl around his shoulders exposing his thin, pale body, his face bruised and bleeding.

"I am thirty-three," he had told the court, "the same age as the *sans-culotte* Jesus Christ when they nailed him to the cross."

He was trying to exhort the crowd, to use the same desperate magic that had moved the crowd to storm the Bastille five years before.

"People, they have lied to you, they are sacrificing your servants!

My only crime is to have shed tears."

But then he gave up and slumped against the rock that was Danton. And later she read that Danton, ever the realist, had told him: "Be quiet. Leave that vile rabble alone."

So Danton must finally have realised that the crowds were there simply for the spectacle and that no one would try to save them. Or perhaps he had known it all along. That the Revolution would devour its own children.

Towards the end of the Rue Honoré they passed the house of the Duplays and the prisoners began to shout up at the shuttered windows and she heard the voice of Danton again, restored for one last roar, the great voice that had dominated the Convention:

"Vile Robespierre, you will follow me! Your house will be levelled and the ground it stands upon will be sown with salt."

Then they were in the great square and there was the Machine rising above the ranks of soldiers, black against the sky and the blade gleaming blood red in the last rays of the setting sun.

Sara did not watch the executions. She looked up only once, towards the end, when it was Danton's turn to die. She saw him mounting the scaffold unaided, his hands still tied behind him, turning for one last moment to face the sun. He said something to Sanson, the executioner, whom he must have known well when he was Minister for Justice. Then Sanson's assistants took hold of him by the hands and feet, and big as he was threw him down on the wooden plank. Sara turned her head away then and put her hands to her face but the crowd had gone very quiet of a sudden and she heard three distinct thuds: one as the plank was run forward under the blade; one as the brace was clamped around his neck; and the last when the blade hit the block.

She heard later that he had told Sanson: "Show my head to the crowd; it's worth a look."

She was running. Back along the far side of the river. She must have crossed by the Pont de la Révolution but she had no memory of it.

There were no crowds. In fact she did not remember any people at all though there must have been some. She ran until she could run no more and then she walked, hobbling in her wooden clogs, pressing her hand against the stitch in her side. She had started with some idea of going to the Rue Marat, to see if she could find Lucille, but instead she found herself in her own street outside her own front door.

It was open and the police were there. They were carrying things out in boxes. She was frightened but not entirely surprised. She thanked God she had sent Alex away with Hélène to Mary's house in Neuilly. She had thought it would be safer for him out of Paris.

"What are you doing?" she cried. "Those are my things. What right have you to take my things?"

Then she saw the sketches of Nathan with his penny whistle: the charcoals she had made after they had saved him from the mob.

"What do you want with those?" she demanded, snatching at them. Then a hand seized her violently by the hair and pulled her back, so violently she felt a snap in her neck.

He had a knot of hair in his hand and he pulled her close to him and shoved something in her face: a paper with some writing on it, too close for her to read.

"You are Sara Marie de la Tour d'Auvergne, *ci-devant* Countess of Turenne and you are under arrest."

She glared up into his face.

"Who are you?" She tried to keep the fear out of her voice: to stay calm and in command.

"My name is Commissioner Gillet," he said. "Of the Bureau of General Security."

"And what is the charge?"

"Conspiracy. Correspondence with the enemy. Congress with foreign powers." He smiled as if it did not matter. They had plenty to choose from, after all, or they could make do with nothing at all.

III—THERMIDOR

the Time of the Heat

CHAPTER 32

the Grand Châtelet

IGHT, BUT NO STARS THROUGH THE narrow slit of a window and no light, not so much as a candle. Not that he
needed one. He had nothing to read and he knew his present quarters as intimately as he wished, having paced them out some
several hundred times over the past month or so. Two paces one way,
not quite four the other. Bare stone walls. The ceiling a little over two
feet above his head. The floor covered with straw, changed every few
days. The only furniture a plain wooden pallet and a bucket.

He sat on the pallet and ran his fingers through his beard. He was
shivering though he had known colder nights. It was, he thought, a
form of panic. He had to fight it but it was difficult at times, especially at night when he felt himself losing all sense of time and space
and self. He had to maintain a very tight discipline or he feared he
would go mad. In the daylight he did physical exercises. He would
leap up to the tiny window above his head and grasp the solitary
iron bar and heave himself up until his chin was level with the
ledge. There was nothing to see—just the blank wall of the building opposite—but it was something to do and it strengthened the
muscles in his arms. He tried to maintain a routine. He even cleaned
the walls using a little of the water they gave him for washing and a
piece of rag given him by one of the guards. Or he would sketch on

the walls using a straw with a sharp point and an ink made from a mixture of water and dirt and a little of the gruel they brought him.

But at night he had only his thoughts and they were not good ones. He had seen no one for five weeks except his jailers—and once a surgeon who told him he had two cracked ribs and a crack on the skull which he knew already and to get plenty of rest of which there was no shortage. He knew he was in the prison of the Grand Châtelet, the ancient fortress on the river guarding the Port au Change, but he knew nothing of the world outside his cell. Nothing of Danton or Imlay. Nothing of Sara. He maintained the pretence of being a citizen of the United States, repeatedly demanding to see the American Minister—but to no avail. He was fed twice a day, once in the morning, once in the afternoon.

He tried to occupy himself with astronomy though in the absence of books and a sky this was no easy feat. He tried to remember the positions of the planets and the major nebulae in relation to the Earth. He drew them on the walls of his cell and wiped them off every evening so he could start again in the morning. And he devised a mental exercise that involved the imaginary exploration of the universe in a conveyance of his own invention which he called a Star Ship.

This craft was conical in shape and made from thin copper plates hammered on to a large wooden frame, much strengthened by interlocking struts and braces, and containing a number of compartments. To wit: a steerage and navigation room, living quarters and galley, a chamber with an inventive device for the disposal of waste, a storeroom and a detachable section at the rear for the accommodation of a large hot air balloon and the necessary equipment to inflate it.

The craft was assisted into the heavens by a series of giant rockets strapped to its side, each of which fell away when it reached the limit of its trajectory after first igniting its successor. In Nathan's scheme of things, by the time the last of these was exhausted the craft would have risen far above the gravitational pull of the earth and would continue to move—consistent with the principles discovered by the late Sir Isaac Newton—at the same speed and in the same direction until some other force diverted it. Accordingly, Nathan had designed an ingenious system of magnets which could be raised and lowered and otherwise manipulated by means of several wheels or windlasses whose purpose was to lock on to the diverse magnetic fields emanating from the planets: not unlike the practice of mariners in following the trade winds. When the time came to return and the gravitational pull of their own planet caused the craft to drop more rapidly than was desirable, the crew would remove themselves to the detachable chamber at the rear of the craft, inflate the balloon by means of a small furnace, and float safely back to Planet Earth.

Nathan named this craft the SS *Isaac Newton* in honour of its main inspiration.

To further entertain himself he populated the universe it was designed to explore with various species of being, each with a social, political and religious system that enabled him to indulge his satirical views on their earthly equivalents. Thus he travelled his imaginary universe rather in the style of a Gulliver and to much the same purpose.

But it took an enormous effort of will to keep himself occupied and there were times when he would be reduced to shivering uncontrollably or rocking silently from side to side like a madman in an asylum.

At such times a terrible panic would come upon him and he would imagine staying here forever, forgotten, until finally he even began to forget himself and became something animal, inhuman. Insane.

He stood up and began to walk, or rather stumble, from one wall to another, at first in a crouching shuffle under his blanket but then gradually straightening his shoulders, until finally he was pacing as he had paced his imaginary quarterdeck on the *Nereus* until he had command of himself, as he had once commanded a sloop of war . . . I am Nathaniel Peake, he reminded himself sternly, master and commander of the sloop *Nereus*, of 16 guns. My father is Admiral Sir Michael Peake, of Windover House, Sussex. My mother is Lady Catherine Ann Peake of St. James's, London.

He also said Sara's name a lot. And conjured up an image of her. He thought of the last time he had been with her . . .

But that made him too sad, too desolate. And so he stretched himself out on the hard wooden pallet and pulled the blanket around him again and thought of the sea. He thought particularly of Cuckmere Haven where he had played as a child and the tide sucking at the shingle and the sun on the white cliffs of the Seven Sisters ...

He had slipped into a meagre doze flavoured by dreams of travelling through an immensity of space when his own small universe was filled with light. He raised an arm against the glare and was addressed by a single rude command: "Come."

He was alarmed. This had not happened before—and after so many weeks he found himself strangely loath to leave the confines of his cell. But it seemed he had no choice in the matter. He slid his feet down from the pallet and stumbled through the door into a dimly lit corridor. There were two men. One with a lantern, the other with a short pike or halberd. Nothing more was said but the Lantern set off down the corridor and the Pike gave Nathan a shove to indicate that he should follow. In this manner they proceeded through the bowels of the Châtelet opening and closing doors, mounting a flight of stairs and finally arriving at another door which they did not open but upon which the Lantern rapped politely with his knuckles. A voice bid them enter.

A room that seemed vast compared to Nathan's cell with a desk at the far end and a lamp upon it. Behind the desk two men, their faces in shadow. The only other furniture a chair about halfway between desk and door. Two windows, shuttered. And hanging down from the ceiling, a double length of chain.

You shall first show him the instruments of persuasion, then apply them, beginning with the least and proceeding by degrees to the worst.

Where had he read that?

"Set down the light and let the prisoner advance."

A History of the Gunpowder Plot. The instructions of King James for the interrogation of Guido Fawkes ...

"Sit."

Nathan sat, squinting into the glare of the lamp. He was conscious of his beard and his filthy matted hair. He felt like an old man. He straightened his shoulders.

"Nathaniel Benedict Turner. Merchant and ship's captain. Citizen of the United States of America."

A not unpromising start.

One of the men was reading from a document which Nathan recognised as the American passport provided for him by the Second Secretary at the Admiralty. A little light spilled over on to a face that seemed vaguely familiar, though he could only see a part of it. The other man was entirely in shadow.

There was silence, as if they were waiting for him to confirm this information. Nathan licked cracked lips, swallowed . . .

"That is correct," he confirmed. His voice sounded hoarse and strange. He had hardly used it in over a month. He swallowed again. "And as such I believe I have the right to know why I have been arrested and to communicate with the American Minister in Paris."

"You have not been arrested."

The voice almost echoing in the vast room.

"Then I will take my leave." He made to rise.

"Sit down."

The firm hand of one of the guards forced him back into the chair. The figure leaned forward and with a shock Nathan recognised the features. Commissioner Gillet, the man who had arrested Thomas Paine; the man he could have sworn he saw beneath the trees in the gardens of the Tuileries.

"Travel permit issued by Henri Santerre, Mayor of Le Havre, 2nd Germinal, valid for ten days." His voice reflected the bored indifference of officialdom forced to inflict necessary but tiresome formalities but as he read on, it gradually rose in volume and became expressive of some emotion. "Certificate de Civisme issued by the Surveillance Committee of the Saint-Jacques Section permitting the said Turner to remain in Paris for up to six months for the study of astronomy." He raised the offending document to the light so that his companion might share his incredulity.

"So you are a student of the black arts?" with a sneer. "And what is your particular interest? Sorcery or divination?"

"I believe you are confusing it with astrology," Nathan replied. "Astronomy is more in the nature of a science and my own particular interest is in the exploration of the universe."

"And this is what brought you to France." The sneer permeated the voice.

"No. Not entirely. I sailed to France with a cargo of soap, running the British blockade at great risk to my ship and crew." He was gaining in confidence, his voice in power. "However, when I reached Port Marat I availed myself of the opportunity to travel to Paris to study the works of Tycho Brahe which, as I am sure you know, are maintained in the Observatoire."

"And is this why you were in the quarry near Porte d'Enfer? To study the works of some astronomer?"

What did they know? Who else had they caught? What had been said?

"I had . . ." His voice cracked. He coughed and tried again. "I had an appointment with the owner of the quarry to discuss the import of certain equipment which is not readily available in France."

"You expect us to believe that?"

"I do not expect you to believe it but it is the truth."

"What was the name of this man?"

"Le Mulet. Jacques Le Mulet."

"And how did you come to meet him?"

It was probably best to tell the truth—in this instance at least— and it could surely do no harm.

"We were . . ." Another fit of coughing. This time he asked for water. "It is difficult for me to talk without—"

"Oh we can make it easier for you to talk."

But the other man poured water from a jug on the desk and the guard brought it to him.

"Thank you," he said. "We were introduced by an American shipping agent called Imlay."

Silence. Was that an exchange of glances?

A different voice. Gillet's companion, still in the shadows.

"And what were your dealings with Thomas Paine?"

Nathan raised his arm against the light but could not make out the features. The voice, however, seemed familiar. Where had he heard it before?

"I am sorry. I don't know what you mean. I have had no dealings with Thomas Paine."

"But you know who I mean?"

"Of course I know who you mean. He is a father of American independence and a friend of President Washington but I have had no particular dealings with him—except as a fellow guest of the Hotel Philadelphia."

"You did not come to Paris specifically to meet with Citizen Paine?"

"No. Why should I?"

"That is what we would like to know, Citizen."

Nathan spread his hands in a gesture of bewilderment. "I supported the petition for the release of Citizen Paine from prison. As would any American, I believe. But I assure you I have had no 'dealings' with him. I cannot imagine what dealings they could be."

"No? Well, perhaps we should allow you a little more time for you to think about it."

Nathan allowed himself to become indignant. It was not hard.

"Citizens, I have been held without charge for over a month. I am a United States citizen. I demand, at the very least, the right to communicate with the representative of my government . . ."

"The American Minister has been informed of your arrest—on suspicion of smuggling."

"Smuggling?" Nathan showed them his empty palms again. "What have I been smuggling?"

Had they found the gold?

"Again, we wait for you to inform us."

"But this is nonsense. What would I be smuggling into France?

I have made sufficient profit running the British blockade with supplies—essential supplies—for the Republic, why should I stoop to smuggling?"

"Then why did you wish to meet the man known as Jacques Le Mulet—a notorious criminal and smuggler?"

"A criminal? Is he a criminal? I had no idea. You have evidence of that?"

"You are not a lawyer, Citizen, nor are you here to question us. It is we who question you, is that understood?"

He waited for Nathan to acknowledge the rebuke before resuming: "The man known as Le Mulet has long been under suspicion. I ask you again, why did you wish to meet with him?"

"As I informed you, he wanted me to bring him some equipment from America."

"What equipment?"

"We did not have a chance to discuss it. We had barely met when the quarry came under attack."

Another silence. They know nothing, Nathan thought, or very little. They could not have found the gold or the letters to Danton.

Gillet spoke again. "I think you are lying. I think you were involved in the plot to free certain prisoners from the Luxembourg prison including Thomas Paine, Georges Danton and Camille Desmoulins."

Nathan contrived to look shocked.

"However," Nathan detected a sigh and the voice when it resumed sounded disappointed, almost sulky, "it has been decided that, in view of the lack of 'evidence,' you are to be permitted to return to the United States."

Nathan stared into the light. Was this a trick? Despite the water his mouth felt too dry to speak but he managed a dry croak.

"Then I am free to go."

"You will be taken under escort to Havre-Marat where you will rejoin your ship. You will meet with no one on the way, you will communicate with no one—"

There was an interruption from his companion: a muttered

consultation behind the lamp. Then Gillet's voice again, even sulkier:

"Apparently there is one who wishes to meet with you before you leave Paris. You will be escorted directly to his apartment and from there to the coast—"

Another muttered aside from Gillet's companion.

Gillet addressed the guards.

"See that the citizen is made presentable. Take him away."

"Who is it I am to see?" Nathan rose to his feet.

"You will find out when you get there."

He was escorted to the door. It occurred to him that to be held for five weeks in solitary confinement and then released without charge merited at the very least a spirited protest—and that such might be expected of an American citizen. He turned at the door—but the protest died on his lips. Gillet's companion was leaning forward bringing his face out of the shadows. It was the face of an old man with a long nose, thin lips and sunken cheeks, almost cadaverous in the yellow light of the oil lamp. And it was a face Nathan knew. The face of the man he had last seen presiding over the National Convention: Marc-Guillaume Vadier, chairman of the Committee of General Security. The man they called the Grand Inquisitor.

CHAPTER 33

The Carpenter's Lodger

THE COACH HEADED WEST OUT OF the city along the route taken by the death carts on their way to the Place de la Révolution. Nathan had to presume from the care they had taken with his appearance that this was not their destination. They had permitted him to wash and shave and equipped him with a new suit—almost certainly donated by one of their previous guests—which was not the usual preparation for a trip to the guillotine, though it could be Gillet's idea of a joke. The commissioner sat opposite him with two gendarmes, presumably to ensure that Nathan did not take it into his head to leap from the carriage: a course of action which did in fact occur briefly to him as they passed Regnault's studio in the Rue Honoré where Sara took her lessons in fine art. He peered eagerly out in the wild hope that he might see her on the street or in one of the windows but the shutters were up and the door closed. He saw Gillet looking at him with a smirk and wondered if there was some significance in this.

A short distance from the church where the Jacobins held their meetings they turned down a narrow alleyway, just about wide enough for the carriage, and into what appeared to be a builder's yard, stacked with timber. Here the coach stopped and Gillet curtly invited Nathan to get out.

"We will wait for you here," he said. He took a small pistol from his pocket and laid it on his lap. "And do exactly as instructed. I will have no compunction in shooting you should you attempt to escape—in fact it would give me a great deal of satisfaction."

Nathan stepped down into the yard and looked about him. It was more of a carpenter's than a builder's with a not unattractive smell of sawn timber and varnish and glue. To his right was a workshop, more in the nature of a lean-to, where he could see several men and boys, presumably apprentices, sawing and hammering away. And directly in front of him was a house or cottage with a middle-aged woman sitting on the front doorstep washing vegetables in a pail of water and a younger woman hanging washing on a line. Nathan was mystified. Do exactly as instructed, Gillet had told him, but who was to instruct him if it was not Gillet himself?

He was not long in doubt.

"Citizen!"

He looked up and saw another woman on the balcony that ran along the front of the house at the level of the first floor. She summoned him with a wave.

Nathan negotiated the washing and the woman on the step who smiled at him and nodded without apparent curiosity as he entered the house. It was modestly furnished but clean and there was a smell of baking. The other woman was waiting for him at the top of the stairs.

"My name is Citoyenne Duplay," she said. A young woman with a curt manner, almost stoically plain as if she worked hard at it, with much scrubbing of skin and severe brushing of hair. "You will be Citizen Turner."

Nathan removed his hat and bowed but she had already turned away. He followed her, as he assumed he was meant to, along the landing and into a small but elegantly furnished drawing room at the rear of the house with the blinds drawn against the sun. Two men were sitting there.

"Citizen Marshal Brune," said the woman, "and Citizen General Danican."

Nathan tried to hide his surprise. These must be the men he had been brought to meet—but why? As they were military men he must assume it was something to do with the war. They rose and bowed to him but appeared uncomfortable. Nothing further was said. The woman left. They all sat down. The silence stretched a little. Then, while Nathan was wondering if he should open the conversation, in came the two women he had seen in the yard, smiling self-consciously and no longer wearing their aprons.

More standing and bowing and sitting and saying nothing.

Back came Citoyenne Duplay with a tray of refreshments. Cups and saucers and little plates were distributed and balanced precariously on knees. Coffee was poured and cake allocated in equal proportions. The usual pleasantries were exchanged. The weather was discussed. It had, Nathan discovered, been very windy of late but now the wind had dropped and the sun was very pleasant. A bee buzzed against the window pane in a desperate struggle to escape and Nathan did not blame it in the least. But then presumably Commissioner Gillet was not waiting for it outside with a pistol. He was desperate to know what he was doing here and why.

"And you are an American, I believe," Citoyenne Duplay suddenly prompted him with a glare, as if he had somehow failed in his function.

"I am," he confirmed smiling, braced for further interrogation. But it was far less of an ordeal than that which had preceded it at the Grand Châtelet. He was able to gratify their curiosity about Savages and Grizzly Bears and other exotica on the peripheries of New York society and from there the conversation flowed naturally to General Washington. Had he ever met the great man? Nathan regretted not. More silence during which he noted his hostess glancing rather anxiously towards the door, presumably calculating her own chances of escape, but then one of the officers—field marshal, general?—inquired of the older woman—"And how is your esteemed lodger, Madame, I had heard he was unwell?" Such was Nathan's evaluation of the conversation thus far he was fully prepared to learn that the "esteemed lodger" had died overnight or was at that very moment having a limb amputated but after glancing nervously at the younger woman—her daughter?—she replied: "He did have a slight indisposition but is now quite well, thank you, Citizen and anxious to resume his public duties."

And it suddenly hit Nathan with some considerable force who they were talking about.

Imlay had told him the story: a famous story in Paris. In July, 1791, a great crowd had gathered in the Champs de Mars to celebrate the second anniversary of the storming of the Bastille. It was more in the nature of a festival than a demonstration—people were there with their children and there were stalls and a carousel—but tensions were running high and the National Guard had been sent to keep order under General Lafayette. Some small incident flared into violence and suddenly the troops began to fire into the crowd. When it was over the ground was strewn with bodies. The number of deaths varied from fifty to five hundred—men, women and children—and the event was known ever after as the Massacre on the Field of Mars. Robespierre had been caught up in the crowd fleeing back into Paris along the Rue Honoré and some of them turned on him. He was not as well known then as he subsequently became and it was possible that in their anger they took exception to his aristocratic mode of dress. Another, more popular, version of the story had him being attacked by soldiers. But either way, the event occurred quite close to the premises of a master carpenter called Maurice Duplay who was a member of the Jacobin Club and one of Robespierre's greatest admirers. So Duplay shouted for his sons and apprentices and led them in a rescue which probably saved Robespierre's life. They took him back to their home in a state of shock and he had lived there ever since.

So this was the esteemed lodger; and almost certainly the man Nathan had been summoned to meet.

There was a small knock on the door and everyone sat up as if it was a gunshot. The young woman—who must be Robespierre's reputed mistress, Eleanor Duplay—opened it a crack and bent her head. Nathan glimpsed the figure of a child. A low-voiced exchange that none of them heard. Then the woman turned and summoned Nathan by the simple expedient of crooking a finger. Feeling very much like a schoolboy anticipating a caning from the headmaster, Nathan followed her from the room.

She led him out of the house and across the yard past the waiting coach to what might have been taken for a storeroom except that it had drapes on the windows of the upper floor and a small wooden staircase leading to a door with a large mailbox attached to the front. The woman knocked gently and a voice bid them enter: the same high-pitched voice Nathan had last heard in the Convention extolling the virtues of the Terror. Eleanor Duplay held open the door for Nathan to step through and then shut it firmly behind him.

Citizen Robespierre was standing by the little fireplace, as if he had struck a pose in expectation of visitors, wearing a kind of dressing gown, or chemise-peignoir, but with a quantity of immaculate linen at the throat so as not to appear too informal. His thick, brown hair was un-powdered and looked the better for it, Nathan thought. In fact, he looked much younger than he had in the Convention and of less consequence.

The room was sparsely furnished with a wooden bedstead and a cupboard, a small table with a bowl of oranges, and two cane chairs. A single book lay open on the mantelpiece. Also some papers . . . and the infamous green spectacles.

He greeted Nathan amicably enough and invited him to sit. Nathan sat but his host remained standing, one arm thrown casually across the mantelpiece, almost as if he needed the advantage of height; or perhaps it reminded him of being at the people's tribune and the authority that went with it. Almost immediately he launched into a speech—though at least he did not read it from notes and it had the merit of being short and to the point.

"I am sorry you have been inconvenienced on your visit to Paris," he began. "I wanted to take the opportunity of assuring you that it has not been with any hostile intent and I trust you will take back no harsh opinions to your countrymen."

As if five weeks on bread and gruel in the Grand Châtelet was no more than a minor irritant; the kind of thing most tourists took in their stride.

"And we are very sorry to disoblige a friend of Thomas Jefferson."

With a great effort Nathan forestalled an expression of incredulity. To be taken for an American was one thing, but a friend of Thomas Jefferson . . . Who could possibly have given him such an impression? Morris? Imlay? But Imlay had last been seen disappearing through a hole in the ground and was now presumably a fugitive from revolutionary justice.

Whoever it was he had clearly done Nathan an enormous favour. Jefferson's was a great name in Paris, almost as great as Ben Franklin's, at least among Frenchmen of a certain class and political persuasion.

"But I hope," continued Robespierre, "that you will assure him we had the most compelling reasons of national security."

Nathan spread his hands—what could he say?

But Robespierre was reaching for the dreaded green spectacles.

"As a member of the Committee of Public Safety, I receive a multitude of reports. They are a regrettable consequence of the current emergency."

The papers on the mantelpiece appeared to be a small sample of this multitude. He adjusted the spectacles on his nose the better to inspect them, though Nathan suspected he knew very well what they contained.

"One of the more recent details your contacts with Citizen Danton . . ."

A pregnant pause.

"I have had but the briefest contact with Citizen Danton," Nathan protested. "On a social occasion."

Robespierre regarded him coldly. The eyes were no longer childlike.

Or indeed, even blue. They glittered like two cold emeralds, polished
with malice.

"That may well be," he murmured, "that may well be. However
Citizen Danton who, as you are doubtless aware, has been executed by order of the Revolutionary Tribunal on charges of gross
corruption—"

Nathan was aware of no such thing. He felt the blood drain from
his face. The man had seemed indestructible, even in the courtroom
with his back to the wall and the wolves at his throat—but this little
man with the green glasses had destroyed him. And if he could destroy Danton he could destroy anyone.

"Citizen Danton was no more a friend to America than he was to
France. Indeed, I have evidence that he was in the pay of the English
who are enemies to us both."

The letter! The document Pitt had given him to remind Danton of
his obligations to the British taxpayer—it had been on the barge with
the gold; well concealed but not so well that a thorough search would
not detect it. But if Robespierre had seen the letter he must know
that Nathan was not an American . . . It made no sense. He must be
guessing or have evidence from some other source.

Robespierre said nothing for the moment but he pushed the spectacles to the top of his head and contemplated Nathan thoughtfully,
as if he was trying to make up his mind about something. Then he
came down from his extempory tribune and sat in the chair opposite. His manner when he spoke again was less formal. Yet it was a
modified version of the speech Nathan had heard him make to the
Convention.

"Citizen, we are engaged in a War against Tyranny. A degree of suffering is perhaps inevitable in the interests of democracy—even to
those who may be innocent of any crime. It became necessary to hold
you under the Law of Suspects while certain investigations were carried out. Certain of our law enforcers wished to hold you for a great
deal longer but I prevailed upon them to release you and permit you
to return to America."

He appeared to be waiting for Nathan to thank him.

Nathan did.

The Tiger-cat inclined his head in polite acknowledgement.

"I am aware," he said, "that certain of your countrymen have been critical of our recent policies. Even General Washington himself. Perhaps they are not aware of the grave danger that we face—a danger, I might say, to both our great Republics."

He stood up again and returned to the mantelpiece. The green spectacles came down once more. He held a note in his hands, which he studied thoughtfully before passing to Nathan.

"Do you know what this is?"

There was no mystery about it. Nathan had seen a great many during his visits to France.

"It is an *assignat*," he said, "to the value of twenty livres."

"That is certainly what it looks like. Doubtless it would surprise you to know it was made in England?"

It took a moment for Nathan to register the significance of this.

"A counterfeit," Robespierre continued, "made in England, smuggled into France and distributed by criminals. We have reason to believe that many millions of such forgeries are being circulated in the Republic. As a result the value of the *assignat* is rapidly declining. If this continues it will result in a complete loss of confidence and a collapse of the economy. The Republic has little or no reserves of gold. We should not have the means of paying our armies or of purchasing their ordnance or food supplies; not to speak of the general misery and confusion it is already causing among the civilian population. It is a most effective weapon, Citizen, more effective than any number of foreign armies. And you, as one of our American allies, must surely deplore it."

"Indeed," began Nathan, "but—"

"Then I hope that you will inform your friends in America of our concern in this matter and the necessity of adopting extreme measures to counter it. It is no exaggeration to say that this note"— he reached over and took it back—"this note is responsible to a large degree for what our enemies are calling the Terror."

Robespierre accompanied Nathan to the door and out on to the staircase. Eleanor Duplay was waiting at the bottom. The coach was waiting in the yard.

"I am sorry that you are leaving France," Robespierre simpered almost coyly as they parted. "Perhaps if circumstances allow you will return and visit us again. We occasionally have a few friends round for some entertainment in the evenings: to read a little poetry or play a little light music. I think you would enjoy it."

CHAPTER 34

the Pilot's Mate

THE COACH STOPPED ONCE MORE ON its way out of Paris, this time at the Porte de Neuilly where it appeared that Gillet was to leave them.

"I am to be deprived of your company to the coast?" Nathan expressed polite concern.

"You are. However, these gentlemen will ensure you arrive safely." Gillet indicated the two gendarmes. "And if I see you again," he added coldly, "you will regret it."

Nathan touched his hat and smiled with an assurance he did not feel. "For once," he said, "we are in agreement."

They travelled through the night. Nathan remained in the coach at every poste. When it became necessary for him to relieve himself they pulled up at the roadside and he was obliged to step behind a bush, with his personal escort watching over him.

They reached Le Havre late in the afternoon and drove straight to the docks. The *Speedwell* was at the berth where he had left her two months earlier, with two militiamen at the foot of the gangplank. Tully awaited him at the top, with Keeble at his side grinning and winking as if he had pulled another rabbit out of the hat. There was a cheer from the crew as he stepped aboard.

"I am very glad to see you," Nathan told them, "but I thought I said if I was not back within the month you were to return without me."

Tully nodded towards the guards presently conferring with Nathan's escort at the foot of the steps. "Several days after your departure for Paris an officer arrived with a squad of soldiers and informed us we were impounded. Since when I regret we have been under constant guard."

Nathan gazed around the crowded deck.

"Are all the crew aboard?"

"All present and correct, sir, saving Joseph Gurney who I regret to say has skipped ship."

"Which he run off with a whore, sir," added Keeble.

And now here was Gabriel, as unmoved as if Nathan had been gone two hours instead of two months but with a disapproving frown at the clothes he had been given in the Châtelet. "I hope you had a comfortable journey, sir. I expect you will be wanting to change."

"I believe these once belonged to a duke," Nathan informed him, glancing down at his attire, "before he was sent to the guillotine."

"I trust a similar fate befell his tailor," Gabriel replied smoothly. "You will find hot water and a clean suit of clothes laid out for you, sir, in your cabin."

"What are our orders, sir?" requested Tully with a glance toward the gendarmes down on the quay.

"We are to sail at once." Nathan looked up at the pennant hanging limp from the mizzen. "Or as soon as we are able."

"The pilot is come aboard already." Tully indicated the gentleman at the stern: the same gentleman who had guided them into the Baie de Seine on their last visit when they had taken the *Vestale*. "And his mate."

"His *mate?*"

"He is waiting below—in your cabin."

Tully's expression was wooden but his eyes spoke volumes, if only Nathan could read them. Wondering, he proceeded below deck.

"Well, well," said Imlay, looking up from the letter he was writing at Nathan's desk, "look what the cat's brought in."

Nathan stared at him in astonishment.

"I hope you do not object to my making free of your quarters," Imlay waved an arm airily. "It is more private than the deck."

He was wearing a sailcloth shirt and trousers with a red scarf tied round his neck like a common *matelot* but had apparently lost none of his easy authority.

"So," Nathan recovered his powers of speech. He sat down on the only other chair. "You are back from the dead."

"To be honest I found their company a little tedious—though I had little choice in the matter. I am sorry you were left behind. I thought you were following me."

"The dragoons had other ideas."

"What can I say?" He spread his arms. There was a bottle of brandy on the desk and a brimming tumbler. "What could I do? It was an unfortunate business. It appears they were after contraband."

"I wonder why."

Imlay ignored the sarcasm or failed to notice it. "Brandy?"

Nathan nodded and Imlay poured and raised his glass.

"Well, to your return. I hope the Châtelet was not too grim."

"I have known better accommodation. How did you know I was in the Châtelet?"

"One hears. If it is any consolation you were safer there than outside. Le Mulet thinks he was betrayed and his immediate suspicions fell on you."

"I trust you managed to allay them."

"I did my best but he is an awkward fellow. However, I also spoke to Robespierre on your behalf. Yes, you may well raise your eyes; it was not easy. I told him you were a very good friend of Thomas Jefferson."

"So it was you. I did wonder what put that idea into his head. Well, I must thank you, then; it appears to have worked wonders. And how did you know to find me here?"

"I confess your presence comes as a pleasant surprise. I came with Citizen Bouchard. The pilot. He was kind enough to inform me when he received the summons from the National Guard that his services were required. I was going to give this to Tully"—he indicated the letter he had been writing—"but you will save me the effort. Now you must listen to me very carefully, my friend, for what I am about to tell you is of the very greatest consequence. Are you acquainted with the commander of the English fleet, Lord Howe?"

Nathan raised a brow. "I would not say acquainted, though we have met once or twice. And my father served with him in America."

"Then he would know you—and trust you."

"Trust me—for what?"

"There is a great convoy sailing from America to France. Over one hundred ships laden with grain and other supplies vital to the war effort. It is said that French agents have purchased the entire surplus of the American harvest—a billion bushels of wheat. It will save the French from starvation. It will save the Revolution. It will save Robespierre. And it is on its way across the Atlantic."

"But . . . surely this is known. It cannot have sailed in secret."

"The British must certainly know that the convoy has left the Chesapeake. But they will not know where it is headed. And the Atlantic is a very big place. This is why you must find Lord Howe and tell him the French plan. The convoy is headed for Brest."

"For Brest? Then it will sail straight into his lap. Brest is under blockade. Howe's entire fleet—"

"Listen to me. Lord Howe wishes the French fleet to come out and fight. He has a few frigates keeping watch on Brest but he keeps the main battle fleet off Ushant or across the English Channel in Torbay."

This was true. Nathan had read critical reports in sections of the English press. They had taken to calling him Lord Torbay because of his readiness to seek shelter there.

"This is what the French are counting on," insisted Imlay. "Two days ago Robespierre sent orders to Admiral Villaret-Joyeuse in Brest. He is to sail out with his entire fleet—twenty-five ships of the line—and lure the English fleet after him into the Atlantic while the convoy slips past into Brest."

"How do you know this?"

"My dear friend, it is my business to know these things. Why do you think I am in France?"

"But you are an American."

"So?"

"America and France are allies, or at least friends."

"Believe me the present regime in France is not composed of men the President would count as friends. As I have told you before they are an embarrassment to him. He would very much like to see them replaced by men who do not use terror as an instrument of policy."

"Then why throw them a lifeline—and sell them a billion bushels of wheat?"

"How can he prevent it? He cannot prevent men from making a profit. But now that the money is jingling in their pockets . . ."

"So you want Howe to wait outside Brest?" Nathan shook his head. "He will not do it. As soon as he hears the French fleet is at sea he will follow them—to the ends of the earth if need be."

"That is what I am afraid of. Lord Howe must be made to understand that the destruction of this convoy is far more important than taking a few ships of war—even the whole fleet. *You* know that. You have seen the bread queues outside the bakeries in Paris. You have heard the anger. Every change of government since '89 has been started by bread riots. This is what Robespierre fears more than anything else. That is why he has fixed a maximum price. Ten sous for a four pound loaf. As if! When the same loaf can fetch sixty on the black market? The man is an innocent. But a billion bushels of American wheat will bring the price crashing down."

Nathan had a sudden suspicion that Imlay had more than a political interest in the price of bread—but whatever his motives he was undoubtedly sincere.

"You must find Howe and tell him the French plan. If he insists on chasing the French fleet he must leave a sizeable force off Brest."

He broke off. There were shouted commands from the quayside. They crossed to the starboard window. A file of National Guardsmen had arrived at the quayside led by an official in a Republican sash with red, white and blue ostrich plumes in his hat.

"That is Citizen Thierry," said Imlay. "The local commissioner. With your escort to Le Havre." He pulled a Breton sailor's hat out of his pocket and crammed it on his head. "You must go on deck. If you see me, do not under any circumstances reveal that you know me. I will leave you at Petite-Rade."

But Nathan had another question and it did not concern the movement of fleets.

"What of our friends in Paris?"

Imlay looked at him in surprise.

"You mean Danton? My God, you don't know?" He put his hand on Nathan's shoulder. "Oh my friend, Danton is dead. I thought him indestructible but they took off his head. And poor Camille . . ." His distress seemed genuine. "Robespierre has triumphed—for the moment. But it is not yet over. There will be others and—"

"I heard about Danton," Nathan interrupted him. "Robespierre himself told me. I meant Mary—and Sara."

A blank look came over Imlay's face. Did Nathan have to remind him? But then he nodded. "Mary is in Le Havre. Her confinement is due any day now. Sara, I suppose, is still in Paris."

There was a clump of boots on the gangplank. Imlay gripped his arm. "You must go. Find Howe—and that convoy. The outcome of the war may depend upon it."

CHAPTER 35

Close Action

S UNDAY, THE FIRST OF JUNE: MORNING. The first clear morning in days with not a trace of the persistent fog that had hounded and haunted the British fleet for the best part of a week now, hiding their ships from one another as effectively as it had shielded the enemy. But at six bells in the morning watch Nathan came up on to the quarterdeck of the admiral's flagship the *Queen Charlotte* to find clear skies and a fresh breeze from the south-southwest and the entire French fleet strung out across several miles of ocean on the northern horizon. He was even able to count them. Twenty-six sail of the line and in fairly good order as far as he could tell.

"Sorry you came?" said a voice at his elbow and he turned to find the *Charlotte's* master, James Bowen, at his side, nursing a cup of coffee and gazing out at the distant sails.

"I will let you know," said Nathan, "at the end of the day."

The master gave a grim chuckle. "Well, I hope you are satisfied," he said, "for it is you who have brought us to this."

"I?" Nathan protested indignantly. "It was not my idea to chase halfway across the Atlantic so you can all cover yourselves with glory."

Nathan had found the British fleet off Ushant with the benefit of a brisk southwesterly the second day after leaving Le Havre and delivered his report to Lord Howe who had bent his black brow and sent a sloop to look into Brest. She had returned with the news that the roads were empty. The French fleet had put to sea just as Imlay had said it would. And just as he had feared the English admiral went charging after it into the wide wastes of the Atlantic Ocean.

"Thankee for the advice," he had told Nathan briskly, when he ventured to repeat Imlay's warning about the convoy, "but my duty is clear. I must seek out the French fleet and bring 'em to battle."

His one concession to Imlay's concerns was to detach Rear Admiral Montagu with six ships of the line to find the grain ships—but even Montagu would not wait outside Brest for them.

"For even if your information is correct and that is where they are bound, what is to stop them changing their minds," the admiral argued, "especially if they learn of our intent? They have the entire French Atlantic seaboard at their disposal."

This was true. And besides, a mere commander did not challenge the decision of an admiral of the fleet.

"At least permit me to accompany you, my lord," Nathan petitioned him, "for I could not bear to return to England and not know the outcome."

And so Nathan was a supernumerary aboard the admiral's flagship while the *Speedwell* tagged along with the support vessels in the rear.

They had found the French five days ago and been playing hide and seek with them ever since in a dense mid-Atlantic fog. But now the two fleets were sailing in clear view of each other in two parallel lines about five miles apart and it seemed inevitable that there would be a general action before the end of the day. The only question was whether it would come sooner or later.

Nathan looked up to the poop deck where they could see the admiral conferring with the captain of the fleet, Sir Roger Curtis, and his flag captain, Sir Andrew Douglas. Near seventy, Howe was one of the oldest officers in the service—known throughout the fleet as "Black Dick" as much from his morose and taciturn nature as his dark complexion. He had little time for the Earl of Chatham whom he considered an ignorant upstart and he had never forgiven his brother William for cutting the naval estimates on the grounds of economy. He could be a fierce enemy, yet he and Nathan's father had served together in Rodney's fleet during the American wars and been good friends.

"He is shy with strangers," Nathan's father had told him once, "but a kindly man at heart, when you get to know him."

He did not look kindly now, Nathan thought as he watched him talking with the two captains. He looked exhausted after the long chase across the Atlantic and four days of constant manoeuvring to win the weather gage, mostly in conditions where he did not know whether he was among his own fleet or the enemy.

"So what will he do, do you think?" Nathan inquired of the master. "Bring us in close or pound them at a distance?"

If the wind stayed in the present quarter the British fleet could slowly converge on the enemy until they were within firing range. Then every ship would engage her opposite number until they struck or were dismasted. That would be the conventional approach and with the British advantage in gunnery it might be the most effective. For the eighteen months or so they had been locked up in Brest, the French had been unable to practise with their big guns—at least not with live ammunition—and in single ship encounters they had been far inferior to the British gunners. But it could take several hours to bring the two lines together, particularly if the French veered away. The alternative was to bear down on them in line abreast and bring them to action at once and at close quarters. But that would mean sailing directly into the enemy broadside for anything up to half an hour without being able to fire back with anything but their bow chasers.

"He will bring us in close if they do not talk him out of it," growled Bowen, a bluff Devonian who had been in the merchant marine before he joined the service and was known to have little time for some of Howe's captains. Though he was only a warrant officer he was rated Master of the Fleet and had a reputation for plain speaking. He treated most men, whatever their rank, as equals and some did not love him for it. But he appeared to have taken a shine to Nathan and was often indiscreet in his conversation.

"He wanted to attack last night but thought better on it." He leaned close to Nathan's ear and dropped his voice, for the quarter-deck was crowded with officers including a detachment from the Queen's Regiment of Foot serving aboard the flagship. "'I cannot rely on them, Bowen,' he says to me, 'I require daylight to see how they conduct themselves.'"

Nathan frowned. "Meaning?"

Bowen lowered his voice even further, for this was plainer speaking than even he considered prudent.

"Meaning he thinks they might hold back in the dark."

"He thinks them shy?"

Nathan was aware that the admiral had misgivings about some of his captains but he had assumed it was on account of their low intelligence and high opinion of themselves rather than their lack of courage.

But Bowen merely sniffed by way of reply and continued to gaze at the distant fleet.

"His lordship's compliments, sir, and would you report to him at your earliest convenience?"

With a significant glance at Nathan, Bowen tossed the dregs of his coffee over the rail and followed the midshipman aft. Nathan watched him join the huddle of senior officers and then crossed to the weather rail and sought out the *Speedwell* among the dozen or so frigates and sloops and support vessels. He wondered, not for the first time, whether he should have stayed with her but he had been compelled by a primitive need to put himself to the test: the ultimate test of a sea battle between two powerful fleets. To discover if he had the nerve to stand unflinching in the face of a thousand heavy guns; to go about his duties in a lethal hail of shot and not curl himself into a shaking ball upon the deck.

I will let you know at the end of the day.

He might live to regret that glib response. Or not.

He picked out the barque easily enough but she was too distant for him to make out any of the figures on her deck even through the glass. They should be safe enough, though: well out of the line of fire with their only task that of repeating the signals from the flagship so other ships could see them in the smoke of battle. The admiral set great store by signals and was constantly testing his junior officers in their knowledge. He had devised and written the *Signal Book for Ships of War* currently in use throughout the fleet—a system of numbered flags that could be used in different combinations to deliver a range of complex orders—but they were too complex for some of his captains in Bowen's view—and possibly the admiral's for he had sent many of his brighter officers from the flagship to help their understanding.

There was a string of flags going up now at the mizzen. Nathan approached the midshipman who had summoned Bowen—Codrington, a man of his own age almost, which was to say old for a midshipman, who appeared to serve the admiral as aide-de-camp. He was standing at the rail gazing through his glass towards the French fleet.

"What is the signal?" Nathan asked him.

"Number thirty-four," said he, without taking his eye from the glass.

"Which is to say?"

"'Having the wind of the enemy, the admiral means to pass between the ships in the line and engage them to leeward.'" Still without bothering to look at Nathan and in a bored voice that hovered on the edge of contempt.

"Thank you," said Nathan, wishing he could kick him, but then he caught the admiral's eye upon him. He had sunk into an armchair on the quarterdeck next to the wheel with his greatcoat buttoned up to the chin and a cheap woollen hat upon his head.

"Well, sir," he called out to Nathan. "You see what you have brought us to?"

This could become history. Nathan wondered how he could

respectfully point out that it was the convoy he had wished to bring them to, not the fleet.

"I trust they are to your liking, my lord," he said, touching his hat.

Howe looked up at the flags fluttering above his head.

"What think you of the signal?"

Nathan thanked his stars he had taken the trouble of asking the snotty for the meaning.

"A bold move, my lord, and I wish you joy of it but what do you desire the rest of us to do?"

This might have passed for wit in his mother's salon but not on the quarterdeck of the *Queen Charlotte*. The admiral's face grew blacker.

"I desire you to hold your tongue, sir, if all you can do with it is play the fool."

But then he saw that Bowen was chuckling to himself and several of his officers had turned away to hide their grins. His own lips began to twitch.

"Well, well, what do you think of that then, Sir Roger? Impudent young pup. But let us have number thirty-six so there can be no misunderstanding." He turned back to Nathan and frowned fiercely: "'Each ship independently to steer for and engage her opponent in the enemy line.' Is that good enough for you, sir?"

"Very good, my lord. Thank you." Nathan bowed low, infinitely relieved.

There were cheers from the crew as the heavy three-decker came ponderously round until its bow was pointing directly towards the enemy line. Climbing a little way up the shrouds Nathan saw a sight that would stay with him, he knew, for the rest of his days, or the few hours he had to live, as the entire fleet turned to face the enemy in line abreast. The great beasts of the fleet: mighty three-deckers of 100 guns like the *Royal Sovereign* and the *Royal George*; the 80-gun *Caesar* leading the distant van with the *Bellerophon* close behind her: the *Billy Ruffian* that had saved the *Speedwell* from the French privateer almost a year ago with her captain, Pasley, now a rear-admiral in command of the flying squadron. More 74s: the *Leviathan* and the

Invincible and the *Thunderer*, the *Brunswick* and the *Culloden*, the gilded figureheads lining up like giant chess pieces for the charge. Twenty-five ships of the line. The black hulls and the chequered bands of white or buff or red. Over two thousand heavy guns and fifteen thousand men charging across five miles of ocean towards their ancient enemy. And now the bands and the fiddles were starting up. The strains of "Rule, Britannia!" drifting across the water from the *Gibraltar*, "The Roast Beef of Old England" from the *Brunswick* and from their own decks, "Heart of Oak":

> *Heart of oak are our ships,*
> *Jolly tars are our men,*
> *We always are ready;*
> *Steady, boys, steady!*

Nathan looked to his own guns for he had been given command of the eight pieces on the quarterdeck: six 12-pounders and two 32-pounder carronades. He had never fired the latter even in practice for they were a relatively new weapon developed by the Carron Company in the eighties and none had been fitted to any of the ships on which he had served. They were peculiarly short in the barrel but with a large bore rather like a mortar. Their main advantage seemed to be that they were extremely light and manoeuvrable but fired a very heavy shot. Their disadvantage was they didn't fire it very far—two hundred yards was about the maximum, the gunner informed him, a young Cornishman called Dowling, though "they are regular smashers at short range, sir." They appeared to be loaded and fired in much the same way as regular cannon, the only puzzling feature to Nathan being a large screw which pierced the ring at the end of the breech and was used for elevating and depressing the barrel instead of wedges or quoins. Nathan decided to leave the carronades to Dowling while he concentrated on the 12-pounders, though it seemed likely, if they were to pass through the enemy line, that he would have to fire both sides simultaneously, which meant spreading his crews more thinly than he would have liked. His instructions were to load up with round shot at least for the first broadside and change to grape when they were at close quarters but thus far he had not heard if they were to aim high or low. Doubtless someone would tell him in plenty of time to make the adjustments.

He looked about him and saw that the admiral appeared to have taken the con though he kept to his armchair, with Bowen standing beside him to direct the sails. He had hauled up the courses and they were constantly backing the mizzen topsail to keep station but other ships were forging ahead of the line and Howe was become extremely agitated about it. Then a dull rolling roar like distant thunder announced that the French had opened fire. Nathan leapt on to the starboard carronade so he could peer over the rail and saw the whole enemy line engulfed in smoke penetrated by flashes of orange flame. Hundreds of individual water spouts rose up in front of the advancing British ships and kept on rising as if the sea was boiling: a vast pan of spitting and seething water. A sound in the air above and a hole appeared as if by magic in the foretopsail. Another and another. The French ships lying to leeward and a decent swell running, they were heeling hard over and firing high; though at such extreme range most of their shot was still dropping short. The smoke billowed back on them obscuring the hulls so that the sails seemed to be moving through a dense low fog. A halliard parted with a loud twang, the broken end snaking across the deck and two more holes appeared in the foretopsail.

Nathan looked astern and saw the *Speedwell* about half a mile behind and lifted his arm to wave in case Tully or Keeble were watching through their glasses. Beside her was the strange two-decker the *Charon* that had been converted into a hospital ship. An unfortunate name for such a vessel, Nathan reflected: Charon being the name of the ferryman who rowed the newly dead across the River Acheron to Hades. It was to be hoped they did not become better acquainted in the next few hours.

He became aware that people were yelling at him.

"Lie down, sir," thundered Douglas. "Did you not hear the order?"

Nathan saw that everyone was either sitting or lying on the deck, saving the two helmsmen and Bowen—and the admiral himself in his armchair at the con. He jumped down off the gun and sat with his back to it facing forward. After a moment he realised he would have been safer sitting behind it but he did not like to draw attention to himself by moving. In any case the main danger, he thought, would come from above, from falling spars and rigging. He pulled out his watch. Twenty past nine. The firing was now like a continuous roll of thunder and there were more crashes from up forward. Nathan wondered how long they must endure this without returning fire. Still they kept backing and filling the mizzen topsail to slow the ship down. They could not have been moving at more than two knots, Nathan calculated. At which rate they would be twenty minutes or more under fire before they reached the enemy line.

He became aware that the admiral and the captain of the fleet were engaged in another argument. Howe had told Curtis to prepare the signal for "close action" but Curtis maintained there was no such signal.

"No, sir, but there is a signal for closer action," maintained Howe. "And I should know for I devised it."

He had the signal book open—*his* signal book—and began reading it out aloud with Curtis sitting at his feet looking up at him like an overgrown schoolboy with a sulky frown.

"Number five, sir. Number five: 'To engage. If closer, a red pennant over the flag.' So, sir, if you fly number five with a red pennant the meaning is clear: 'Engage more closely.'"

"Very well," Curtis agreed petulantly, "but I doubt more than a few will understand it, my lord."

Howe looked up from his book and saw the whole quarterdeck watching them.

"Oh very well," he said, closing the book and throwing it down to the deck. "No more book, no signals. I look to you to do your duty of engaging the French admiral. I do not wish the ships to be bilge and bilge but if you can lock the yardarms so much the better, the battle will be the sooner decided."

The thunder louder, closer, the shot thudding against the hull like the beating of a giant drum or flying the full length of the ship in a lethal hail, though mostly above their heads. Nathan caught the eye of one of his gun crew who was not much older than Francis Coyle and was muttering some incantation to himself that sounded like the chorus of "Heart of Oak." He smiled encouragingly.

"It will not be long now and we will be able to give it back to them with a vengeance," he assured him.

"Yes, sir," said the boy with a shaky grin. "The gunner says I am so small, sir, that the shot will pass over me, even when I am standing up."

"Very good. I am sure he is right. What is your name?"

"Jameson, sir, if you please."

Nathan pulled out his watch again. Just after nine-thirty. Surely they must be almost there. He was tempted to stand up and look but then came the roll of the drum beating to quarters, though technically speaking they were already at them and the ship had been cleared for action these past few days. They scrambled to their feet and Nathan raised one of the gun ports so he could look out. A huge three-decker loomed through the smoke, startlingly close, so close he thought they must run down on her. Her massive hull was painted black and yellow with three broad black-and-red chequered stripes and he knew her at once as the French flagship, the *Montagne*, of 120 guns. Even as he looked the lower deck guns blossomed flame through the black smoke and he jerked his head back so fast he almost fell over, losing his hat. He stooped to pick it up and saw the admiral on his feet shouting that there was no room to pass between the *Montagne* and the *Jacobin*.

"That's right, my lord," shouted Bowen, apparently having misheard him. "The *Charlotte* will make room for herself!"

But Howe still appeared agitated. "Starboard your helm!" he shouted. "Starboard your helm!"

Bowen turned on him, his face red: "If we do we will run aboard the *Jacobin*, my lord."

"What is that to you, sir," snapped Howe. Nathan saw Bowen turn away again: "Damn my eyes if I care if *you* don't," he said, clear enough for Nathan to hear him if not the admiral. "I'll go near enough to singe your whiskers, you old bugger."

Another crashing roar and Nathan felt the wind of the shot. The noise was deafening. He pulled out his handkerchief to tie round his ears as the gunners already had.

"Why do we not fire?" he asked Dowling who looked at him wildly as if to say "Why are you asking *me*?" then fell back with his hands to his face and blood spurting through his fingers. The lad, Jameson, took a step towards him and a cannonball took off his head.

Nathan stared at him in astonishment. It had taken off the top of his head as cleanly as an axe leaving his ears still sticking out on each side. His body remained upright for a minute and then fell to the deck with the blood gushing out of the gap where his scalp should have been. Even as Nathan stared in shock two of the boy's mates picked him up and threw him through the open gun port.

Nathan looked wildly about the quarterdeck. Christ, who was supposed to order them to fire? He had never served on a first rate. He looked to the admiral but he was arguing with Curtis again, pounding his fist against the chair in his agitation. Douglas, the flag captain, was leaning against the first lieutenant, blood pouring from a head wound. One of the other lieutenants was lying on the deck clutching his knee with nothing left of his leg below it. An officer of the Queen's Regiment drew his sword with a flourish only to have it shattered in his hand by a shot. He staggered back, staring in dismay at the hilt sticking out of his stomach and the red stain spreading across his white waistcoat.

Nathan thrust his head back through the port. Another ship, a two-decker, heading straight at them; she must be the *Jacobin* that Bowen had been shouting about. They were crossing her bow and could fire down the length of her if only someone would give the order.

"Oh for God's sake." He pulled his head back in and ran to the starboard carronade and crouched down beside the gun captain to peer along the stocky barrel. The *Jacobin's* bow filled the port.

"Fire!" he yelled, remembering just in time to leap back from the recoil. He rushed forward into the smoke and thrust his head through the port again just as the *Charlotte's* lower decks erupted in a rippling broadside. He could see nothing for smoke.

"Take command here," he shouted in the ear of the gun captain and raced across the quarterdeck, stooped down by the larboard carronade and glimpsed the huge stern of the *Montagne* through the open port.

"Fire!" he yelled again. As he leapt back he felt the *Charlotte* shudder as her larboard guns fired from one end of the ship to the other. Through the smoke he saw the *Montagne* sailing serenely on apparently unharmed. Then it cleared a little and he saw the shambles of her gilded stern and the bodies hurled out from her gun ports and the blood running down the yellow paint work. But if the *Jacobin* crossed the *Charlotte's* stern she would serve them the same way. He saw Bowen at the quarterdeck rail shouting through his speaking trumpet and the men hauling on the braces to bring the flagship ponderously round in the lee of the enemy line. Nathan could see the *Jacobin* coming up beside them at a distance of no more than a few yards. Why did she not fire? Then he realised: the French had not manned the guns on their lee side. Once she was round *Charlotte* could run down the length of the enemy line, pouring broadside after broadside into them. Nathan turned to pull his men off the starboard guns but in that instant he saw the foretopmast lurch at an impossible angle, then come crashing down on to the deck in an avalanche of falling sails and rigging. The ship began to fall away, the stern swinging back towards the *Jacobin*.

Nathan shouted at his gunners to traverse. He grabbed a handspike himself and thrust it under the truck of the carronade. It moved surprisingly easily, much easier than the 6-pounders on the *Nereus* or perhaps panic gave him manic strength. He peered along the barrel and glimpsed the figurehead of the *Jacobin*: an ancient goddess with a red Phrygian cap on her head.

"Fire!" he roared as he jerked the lanyard, arching his body as the carriage shot back beneath him. He ran forward and thrust his head through the port. The figurehead was still there but the bow was falling off to larboard and still she was not firing. His men were cheering as if they had won some great victory, wild-eyed and exultant. They were stripped to the waist with their handkerchiefs round their heads, their faces black with smoke, more like demons than men.

"Silence!" he roared. "Remove the charge."

The long worm was thrust down the bore and came wriggling out with the smoking rag at the end of it.

"Sponge your gun." The sponger splashed his sheepskin swab into the fire bucket and crammed the flexible sponge down the bore of the carronade, bringing it out blackened and steaming.

"Load with cartridge."

The powder boy had the cloth bag ready and the rammer rammed it down the bore. Nathan glanced along his small line of guns and saw the crews working at the 12-pounders but it would be the carronade that did the most damage at this range.

He thrust his head once more through the port. The *Jacobin* was no longer there but here was another ship bearing down on them through the smoke. French or British? Flames blossomed along her side and he jerked his head back in like a startled rabbit. Shot ploughed into the hammocks above his head and a great splinter of wood pierced the deck at his feet.

"Load with canister," he roared running down the line of guns and repeating the order so they would all hear him. The noise was deafening. Impossible. He lowered his head to peer along the barrel of one of the 12-pounders and something struck the breech in front of him and flew into his head. He fell down with a cry, a terrible pain above his left eye. He clapped his hand to it thinking half his head was gone but then to his utter astonishment he saw the thing come flying back at him: a ball of red and black fury, striking again and again as he lashed out at it with his fist. And then it went flying up to perch on the yard, flapping its wings and crowing. He felt the warm blood flowing down his neck.

"What?" he said looking round at the crew who were looking as astonished as he and then they were laughing.

"Which it is a cock, sir," called one. "Got free when the coop was smashed by a shot and the waist is full of dead hens."

Nathan scrambled up and bent his head to the gun again, the blood from his wound boiling and spitting on the hot breech. He saw the yellow and black hull filling the port and stepped back.

"Fire!" he roared again. "Remove the wad . . . sponge out your gun . . ."

And so it went on. It was pointless to give orders. No one could hear him. And besides, every man knew what he had to do. Every gun fired and loaded at its own speed. All he could do was run along the line encouraging them. At times he would catch a clear glimpse of the battle, or at least part of it, as the wind tore a hole through the smoke to reveal the kind of tableau an artist might have attempted— a detail rather than a bird's eye view. Only a handful of British ships appeared to have penetrated the French line. The only two Nathan recognised with any certainty were the *Brunswick* and the *Queen*, flying the flag of Admiral Gardner, another of his father's old shipmates. She was way down to leeward with her mizzenmast gone and no fewer than three French ships pouring their broadsides into her. Nathan saw Lord Howe gazing anxiously towards her over the taffrail. The *Charlotte* seemed to be on her own now, her guns quiet, and Nathan heard him call out to Curtis, "Go down to the *Queen*, sir, go down to the *Queen*."

"My lord, we can't," came the frantic reply. "We are a mere wreck, the ship won't steer and there are three sail of fresh ships coming down upon us." The captain was practically wringing his hands. "What can we do when the ship won't steer?"

"She *will* steer, my lord." Bowen's angry voice as he came striding aft. "We have the spritsail up and we can get her before the wind."

Then there was a shout from the tops that the French were running. Nathan leapt up to the shroud. The firing had fallen off and the smoke was clearing. He saw a cluster of French ships closing on the

Montagne far to windward but the sea between them appeared to be full of shattered and dismasted hulks and he could not tell if they were French or British. The only two ships still firing at each other were the *Brunswick* and the *Vengeur du Peuple* way over on their lee. The *Charlotte* had come up into the wind now and was moving towards the *Queen* but the three French ships had broken off the contest and were closing on their distant flagship. Nathan felt a desolate sense of loss akin to despair. Surely they could not have gone through all of this only for it to end without a clear-cut victory. He found himself next to Bowen who was shaking his head and muttering under his breath.

"What is it?" He was conscious that he was shouting. But he could barely hear his own voice. "What's the matter with you, man?"

"The captain of the fleet will not permit us to pursue the enemy," said Bowen through gritted teeth. "He has persuaded his lordship to make the signal to close round the admiral."

"But why? Surely we can still catch them?"

Bowen turned away. "Try telling him that," he said.

"By God, I will," said Nathan.

He looked round but could see neither of the two men on the quarterdeck. The door of the poop was open, though, and he made his way towards it, tugging his handkerchief off his head. The deck had been cleared for action and he saw the two men at the far end framed against the light from the stern windows and heard the captain's frantic voice: "If you renew the action, my lord, who knows what may be the result? Many of our ships are dismasted or can no longer steer. Make sure of what you have got, for I am persuaded that if you do not assemble the fleet they will turn the tables on us."

Howe said something Nathan did not hear and Curtis continued in a calmer voice: "Your lordship is tired. You had better take some rest. I will manage the other matters for you."

They came forward towards Nathan, still standing in the doorway. Curtis glared at him. "What do you want, sir? Go about your duties."

But then the admiral stumbled and almost pitched forward on to the deck. Nathan caught him and supported him with an arm round his waist.

"Let me help you to your chair, my lord," he said.

"If you want to be of any assistance," sneered Curtis, "help his lordship to his bed."

"You hold me as if I were a child," said Howe with a weary grin. "Better do as the captain says."

When Nathan came back on deck he saw many of the crew standing on the rail or clinging to the shrouds staring out to their lee. He leapt up on the carronade and put his hand on the rail to steady himself and saw the French 74, the *Vengeur*, that had been fighting the *Brunswick*, laid on her beam ends with hundreds of her crew clinging to her sides. The *Brunswick* had ceased firing and many of her boats were in the water picking up survivors. Nathan took out his glass and saw men clinging to a floating spar and a cutter with an English lieutenant in the stern directing his men to fish them out of the water with boathooks. Then there was a great shout and he lowered his glass and saw the French ship roll over in a cloud of smoke and steam and spray. When it cleared she was gone.

"Dear God," said Bowen, clinging to the shroud at Nathan's side. "Did you ever think to see such a sight?"

Nathan shook his head. Ships sometimes blew up but he had never heard of an incident where a ship that size was sunk by gunfire.

He pulled out his watch. It was almost a half after twelve and firing had now ceased all along the line.

"I don't know about you," he said, "but I am about ready for my dinner."

Later, the midshipman Codrington came up to him and told him the admiral wished to see him in his cabin. He found Howe lying in his cot. He looked as if he had aged ten years.

"I give you joy of your victory, my lord," he said, for this seemed to be the considered opinion now that the smoke of battle had cleared and the tally took. One French ship sunk and six taken: the *Sans Pareil*, the *Juste*, the *America*, the *Impétueux*, the *Northumberland* and the *Achille*. More than in any naval battle since the Dutch wars of the last century, according to Curtis who was talking up the victory as loudly as he could.

"I am sorry so many got away," said Howe, "but it cannot be helped. The Captain of the Fleet says we are in no condition to pursue."

And Howe was in no condition to argue, Nathan thought. Then the admiral raised himself on one elbow and regarded him with something of his old fire.

"Well, you will be able to tell your father what it is like to take part in a real battle," he said, "for the Saints was just a skirmish by comparison and the French running from the start."

"Yes, my lord," Nathan agreed. He took a chance: "And the convoy, my lord?"

"The convoy?"

"The grain convoy—from America." It seemed churlish to harp on it but the victory would be meaningless, he thought, if the convoy was allowed to escape.

"Ah, the convoy." He frowned. "We must leave the convoy to Admiral Montagu, for the fleet must away to Spithead for repairs."

But half our ships barely saw action, Nathan longed to inform him. Can you not send them to join Montagu in the hunt? But he held his tongue—more out of respect for the admiral's years and his present vulnerability than for his rank.

"I want you to go ahead," said Howe, "in the . . . what is she called, your barky?"

"The *Speedwell*, my lord." Nathan's heart was in his mouth.

"The *Speedwell*. A good name for the task. Speed well, my boy, and take the news of our victory to England. I doubt but they will be glad of it, even the Earl of Chatham." He signalled to his clerk who came forward with a sealed letter. "Give him this and tell him I will write a longer report when I am able, but this will give him the bare bones of the story to share with his miserable brother." He fell back on his pillow. "And I hope they choke on it," he added with a weary smile.

CHAPTER 36

Spoils of Victory

N O NEWS OF THE CONVOY, I suppose?" inquired the First Lord with a frown as he looked up from the report.

"I regret not, my Lord," replied Nathan. "At least, not when I left the fleet."

"Well, I suppose we may still call it a victory." He regarded Nathan doubtfully as if for confirmation.

"Of course, my lord. A great victory. We took six ships," he reminded him, "and sank another."

"Quite, quite. Yes, if it were not for the convoy . . ."

Nathan watched Chatham thinking about it, the strategist in him bewailing the loss of the convoy while the politician weighed what he might make of the "victory." They were in his room at the Admiralty with the blinds partly drawn against the sun and Howe's report open on his desk.

"Well, I must send to the King and let him know." Chatham brightened. "In fact, we could take the news ourselves. But first I must inform brother William. We had better go there on the way."

"As you wish, my lord." He was exhausted after the *Speedwell's* four-day sprint for the English Channel and two days and a night in the chaise from Falmouth.

"I must say a victory is most opportune. The news from the

continent has been universally bad and people are complaining about the security measures we have had to take. The country is not happy, not happy at all. In fact there is talk of turning us out. This will put a stop to that. In fact it will dish the liberals well and truly. Mr. Fox will be most put out."

The politician having clearly risen above the strategist.

"I am glad to be the bearer of good tidings, my lord," said Nathan coolly.

"Yes. We can put quite a good complexion on it if we play our cards right. No one need know about the convoy. It is smashing their fleet that counts. And as you say, seven ships and none lost." He rubbed his hands like a miser counting his coin. "Not a bad score at all when you think on it. How was Lord Howe when you left him?"

"A little tired, my Lord, but otherwise in good spirits."

"Well, perhaps he will want to retire after this. Did he have any special message for me?"

"Only that he hoped you would be pleased, my Lord."

"Yes." He sniffed. "Well, and I suppose we must give him his due." He looked at Nathan thoughtfully. "And I suppose you must have your promotion."

Nathan tried to look as if the thought had never occurred to him.

"Oh, we have to reward the messenger," Chatham assured him. "It is expected. If he be blamed for defeat it is only right that he be rewarded for victory." He seemed to be disappointed at Nathan's response. "Would you not like to be made post captain?"

"Of course, my lord, if it is deserved."

"Oh, as to that," he gave a barking laugh, "if we were only to promote men who deserved it we would have none to command our ships. Besides, your activities in France are more than deserving of promotion, except that we cannot publish them. This gives us the excuse."

"Well, my lord . . ."

"We cannot give you much of a plum at the moment, mind. Too many senior men waiting. We can probably find one of the older frigates for you if someone dies."

"That would be most welcome, my lord. But . . ." He hesitated a moment as Chatham raised his brows. "I am more than willing to resume command of the *Speedwell*, my lord, if you need her to return to France."

"What?" Chatham's astonishment appeared genuine. "Good God. What, you would go back to France?"

"Willingly, my lord, if you require it."

"Well, I will not disguise the fact that it would be convenient. In fact there is a cargo waiting at Newhaven as we speak. We were debating how best to dispatch it but as the *Speedwell* is known to the French authorities as an American vessel and a blockade runner . . . Yes, it would serve very well indeed." But then a thought occurred to him and he frowned again. "And while you are about it, you might ask Mr. Imlay what has happened to our gold. Mr. Pitt never ceases to remind me of it."

"I will, my lord," Nathan assured him, though the gold was the last thing on his mind.

"I must say, I am surprised at your eagerness to return to the land of Terror. Have you formed an attachment to the Revolutionists—or do you have some trollop stowed away there?"

Nathan was still struggling for a reply when Chatham rose from his desk and rang the bell for his servant.

"Well, whoever she is, I am obliged to her. Now let us to our masters. Ah, Danvers, my coat if you would—I am going out."

"You seriously mean us to visit the palace, my lord?"

"Why, yes. His Majesty is always eager to hear first-hand accounts of a battle. If we have won it, of course. Do not mention the convoy, by the by."

"No, my lord. But I fear I am not dressed for a formal occasion."

He still wore the uniform he had borrowed on the *Charlotte*. Gabriel had done his best with it but it still bore the stains of battle and it had been none too smart to begin with.

"You'll do. The more you look like you've been through the mill the better. What is that on your head?"

"Nought but a scratch, my lord."

"I can see that, but how d'you get it?"

"I was attacked by a cock, my lord, in the heat of battle."

Chatham frowned as if he was being made game of but merely remarked, "A pity. A wound is always useful."

"I am sorry, my lord, I will try to do better next time."

"He might want to knight you, of course. He sometimes takes it into his head to knight people if he is particularly pleased with them—or himself—or has lost his wits entirely. If he does, don't let it go to your head. It is to reward the fleet, not you. We can send you back to Paris with a ribbon on your chest. I expect she'd like that, your little French madam."

CHAPTER 37

the Supreme Being

NATHAN ARRIVED IN PARIS—BY THE DILIGENCE from Le Havre—to find the city decked with flowers and the streets filled with people in their Sunday best. A pretty girl in a white frock handed him a leaflet to tell him what it was all about. God had returned to France. It was officially proclaimed by the Convention, announced in the press and sanctioned by the Committee of Public Safety. Indeed, Citizen Robespierre himself had proposed it. Atheism, he had declared, was an aristocratic conceit. There *was* a God, he was probably French—by inclination if not birth—and he was unquestionably a Revolutionist. Being a Revolutionist himself, of course, Robespierre had been compelled to change God's name. He was now the Supreme Being. And to celebrate His return, Paris was having a party.

The programme notes informed Nathan that the famous painter and Revolutionist, Citizen David, had devised a vast public spectacle stretching from the Tuileries Gardens to the Champs de Mars. It involved thousands of people, dozens of effigies and set pieces, hymns, speeches and an artificial mountain.

This made it extremely difficult for Nathan to get to the Rue Jacob. He tried to push a way through the crowd but many of the streets had been closed off and he kept running up against barriers and lines

of National Guardsmen so in the end he resigned himself to his predicament and went with the flow, slinging his bag over his shoulder.

The weather had been regulated for the occasion. The sun shone,
the sky was blue and many of the women and children carried
bunches of wild flowers to symbolise Prairial, the month of the
meadow. In the gardens of the Tuileries three monstrous effigies
had been built to represent Atheism, Egotism and Insincerity, according to the programme notes, though not a few among the crowd
seemed to think they were the new gods of the Revolution. Even
more, judging from the comments Nathan heard, thought that the
Supreme Being was Robespierre himself and that this was the title
he now wished to be known by—instead of the Incorruptible, or
the Tribune of the People—though it was quite all right to refer to
him as all three and did not risk prosecution. There was a band playing and a choir of boys and girls dressed in the uniform white, the
girls with wreaths of wild flowers in their hair and the boys carrying
wands of oak, singing a hymn to Nature.

When it ended there was a fanfare of trumpets, the doors of the
palace were thrown open and a long procession of representatives
wound down the steps of the assembly hall and into the gardens.
They all wore suits and carried sheaths of corn—which might be
considered tactless with the price of bread still standing at fifty sous a
loaf on the black market. There was no news in the press of the battle
in mid-Atlantic or of the fate of the grain convoy from America.

The procession was led by Robespierre, whose turn it was—almost
certainly not coincidentally—to be President of the Convention.
This was his day, his triumph, and he was dressed for the occasion.
He wore a magnificent blue silk coat and yellow trousers (robin's-egg
blue and jonquil, according to the programme notes), he carried his
hat in his hand and his powdered hair reflected the light of the sun—
rather like a halo, Nathan thought. He was presented with a flaming
torch and advanced alone on the figure of Atheism, like a little boy in
a fairy tale confronting the ogre.

A roar from the crowd as he applied the torch and Atheism went up in flames. Oohs and aahs as a similar fate befell Egotism and Insincerity. Was there a note of irony, even of ridicule? Or was it simple pleasure, the relief of watching a spectacle that did not involve bloodshed and the guillotine; a break from the endless drudgery of work and finding something to eat?

Another collective gasp from the crowd. Atheism had collapsed in a shower of sparks to reveal another figure within, a little scorched but miraculously intact.

"What is it?" asked a woman on Nathan's right standing on tiptoe to see above the heads of the crowd.

"Wisdom," Nathan read from his notes, "emerging from the ashes of Atheism and Ignorance."

The procession flowed on along the river to the Place de la Révolution and across the bridge to the Champs de Mars. Here Citizen David had built his "Mountain"—a towering structure of grey cardboard decorated with rocks and trees and shrubs and wild flowers and with a hidden staircase winding to the summit.

Another fanfare of trumpets and Robespierre led the representatives of the people up the Mountain. Cries of *"Vive la République!"* and *"Vive Robespierre!"* from the vast crowd that had followed the procession.

But there seemed to be a hitch. The representatives of the people were hanging back. They did not seem anxious to follow their leader to the summit. Were they fearful of encroaching on his territory— or was it for some other reason? Nathan noted expressions of scorn, even hatred, on some of the faces. Then he saw Vadier—his interrogator of the Châtelet. He was standing with a small huddle of the most reluctant deputies with a face even more cadaverous and scowling than ever.

"Look at them," Nathan heard a male voice in the crowd just behind him. "They hate him. One false step and they'll tear him apart."

"But why?" A woman's voice.

"Because they fear him. He's the Incorruptible and they've had their hands in too many pockets."

Robespierre had reached the summit. He turned to face the crowd—quite alone. He seemed to be unconscious of this—or perhaps he did not mind: perhaps he thought it was his right. He raised his arms and there was a roar from the crowd. "*Vive la République, Vive Robespierre!*"

He was still the People's Tribune, thought Nathan, still commanding the adulation of the crowd.

"Listen to them cheering," said the woman's voice again.

"They cheered Danton, too," said the man's, "and would not raise a finger to save him."

Nathan had to stop himself from turning round to see what manner of man this was but he knew better than to do such a thing in Paris, especially when he heard the woman say, "Hush, or you'll find yourself in the House of Arrest."

Another hymn to Nature, another dance, and the celebration was over. And Nathan made his way northward through the thinning crowds towards the Rue Jacob.

He approached the house with some trepidation. After an absence of three months he was not sure how he would be received. He was braced for anger, recrimination or, worse, indifference, embarrassment, a new lover . . . Or of not finding her at all. She might have left Paris, returned to her native Provence or fled France altogether. But if she was there and she still wanted him, he would ask her to marry him. He had made up his mind to it. He could not offer her much—the King had unhappily neglected to make him a baronet—but he was reasonably confident that Chatham would keep his promise to make him post captain on his return and at the very least he could ensure her safety.

He stared for a moment, uncomprehendingly, at the sealed lock on the door.

There was a handwritten sign above it, peeling from rain and heat: Property of the Republic. Sealed by order of the Committee of General Security. Perhaps it was the wrong house. But no there was her name among the obligatory list of residents.

He stepped back and pressed his knuckles against his teeth. He might have known this would happen. Indeed he had feared it but pushed it to the back of his mind as too fearful to even think about. But it must be a recent occurrence or surely Imlay would have told him when he had last seen him aboard the *Speedwell*. Had she been arrested or had she fled? He looked up at the shuttered windows. Who could he ask? He tried the houses on each side. No reply. The house opposite. An old woman, the concierge, sharp with suspicion. She knew nothing of a Madame Seton or her maid Hélène. He should try the *violin*— which, after a moment's confusion Nathan identified as Paris slang for the local police station. He thanked her and walked away. There was a hotel at the end of the road where he ordered a carafe of wine and some bread and cheese and sat down to think it over. A plaque above the fireplace informed him that this was, or had once been, the Hotel York where Benjamin Franklin and John Adams and John Jay had signed the Treaty of Paris to end the war with Britain in 1783.

Imlay, he thought. Imlay would know. And so would Mary. Both were in Paris according to Imlay's clerk in Le Havre. Or at least Mary was: in Neuilly-sur-Seine where Nathan had met them at Christmas after Tom Paine's arrest . . . He left the rest of his wine, paid the bill and headed back into the baking streets.

She was sitting on a bench in the garden with a babe at her breast and the maid Hélène pushing little Alex on a swing. There were flowers, trellises with climbers, a rambling rose . . . As pretty a picture as even David might have contrived for one of his set pieces. Until Nathan appeared at the garden gate.

"Oh my God," she cried when she saw him, her hand leaping to her throat as if she felt the blade of the guillotine upon it. The babe, shaken from the nipple, let out a terrible howl and Hélène scooped Alex off the swing and ran for the house.

"I'm sorry, I didn't mean to startle you," Nathan called from the gate. "I will come back later."

"Don't be ridiculous." Mary shut the babe up by the simple expedient of shoving her nipple back in its mouth. "Come in off the road before someone sees you."

Nathan did as he was told and stood with his hat in his hands looking at his feet.

"Have you not seen a woman breast-feeding before?" she demanded. "So . . ." She surveyed him with suspicion and a measure of hostility. "Here you are again. I thought we had seen the last of you."

"I was hoping to find Imlay," he began but his eyes roamed towards the house looking for Sara.

"You are not the only one," she responded tartly. "I have not seen him since the child was born. Her name is Fanny by the by, in case you are interested. Is she not beautiful?"

"Beautiful," Nathan agreed. Indeed she was a pretty babe, as babes went. He could not see Imlay in her. "My sincere congratulations. I heard . . . in Le Havre . . . that you had had it. Her."

"Why do you wish to find Imlay or should I not ask?"

"I have another cargo for him. And besides, I thought he—or you—might have news of Sara."

She watched him carefully, saying nothing.

"I went to the house in Rue Jacob," he said, "but it was locked up and—"

"You did not know?"

"Know what?" But he felt as if he had been thumped violently in the stomach, the wind knocked out of him.

"She is in prison."

It was almost a relief. He had feared worse.

"When?"

"It must be two months now. Just after the trial of Danton and Camille. Did you really not know?"

"How could I have known? I was in prison myself. And then I had to leave the country."

But Imlay must have known. He must have known when they met in Le Havre.

"You were in prison?" She was staring at him, shaking her head. "I do not know what game you are playing Nathaniel Peake. Your mother always said you were more complicated than you looked. But for her sake you should leave. Go back where you came from. Now."

"I came back to find her," he said, "and I will not leave without her."

"Well . . ." Her expression was less severe. Nathan wondered if Sara had told her about them. "She is in the Luxembourg."

"You have seen her?"

"No. They have stopped the visits—since the business of Danton. But we have had news of her and she is well. At least as well as can be expected in such a place. I came to take Alex back with me to Le Havre. You are lucky to find us here. We leave tomorrow."

"And Imlay?"

"I told you—he left a day after Fanny was born. He feared he might be under surveillance. In 'dire need'—as he put it—I may contact him through the American Minister, though quite what is more dire than having a baby I cannot imagine. Oh, but of course, another cargo waiting for him in Le Havre. I suppose that will flush him out."

Clearly her passion for Imlay had cooled somewhat.

"So you have come from Paris? I suppose you saw the festival?" And when Nathan indicated he had, "Ridiculous! Now Robespierre thinks he is the Christ come to save France from its sins. But then he was taught by Jesuits. At least I think they were Jesuits. They certainly taught him the bit about coming with a sword."

"And yet I did not see the guillotine—in the Place de la Révolution."

"That is because it is removed to the Place du Trône. People had begun to complain about the stench of blood. But the Machine is busier than ever. Before they killed Danton they rarely got through more than a dozen a day. Now it is thirty or forty. As fast as the tribunal can convict them. Which is fast, I can assure you, now they have stopped people from putting up any kind of a defence. There, there my little one, am I upsetting you with my talk of blood and Robespierre? Or has it dried? Here, sup upon the other and I will try to think tranquil thoughts."

"I am sorry." Nathan stood, looking away. "I will leave now. I came only to hear if you had news of Imlay. And Sara."

"Well, and now that you have heard, what will you do?"

How much did she know? And how much could he risk telling her?

"There is a quarry," he began, cautiously, "near the Porte d'Enfer ..."

"I know. Another of Imlay's business concerns." She shook her head sadly. "It is closed by order of the Committee. And guarded by the police."

"He told you that?"

"I learned of it." She lowered her head over the baby at her breast. It was asleep, making little puttering noises with its mouth, a milky dribble on its chin. She wiped it gently with a piece of cloth. "So many fingers," she said, "in so many pies. And I thought he was such a simple man when we met. He was saving for a farm, he said, on the American frontier where we would live together. The dream of Rousseau. Well, clearly he has imbibed his views on parenthood."

"Mary," he prompted her gently, "if you have any idea where he is ..."

Her eyes flashed angrily. "I have told you. He could be anywhere. He could be skulking in the catacombs. Or in the sewers, more like, with the rats."

The sewers. He remembered the smell where the two sets of tunnels met—and the rush of rats ...

And then he remembered Philippe.

Philippe, the failed footpad, the *égoutier* from the sewers ...

If I can ever be of service, ask for me at the Café de Carthage in the Rue Saint-Antoine ...

CHAPTER 38

the Cloaca

THEY WENT IN FROM THE RIVER after dark through a grim black maw that opened on to the Seine just below the Palais de Justice, breathing its noxious fumes into the night air like Cerberus, the canine guardian of the Underworld.

Classical references batted at Nathan's memory and distracted him from more troubling thoughts of disease. He recalled the five rivers that surrounded Hell: the Acheron, river of woe; the Styx, river of hate; the Lethe, river of forgetfulness and . . . He had forgotten the other two. You had to put a coin on the mouth of a corpse to pay the ferryman. If a god gave his oath upon the River Styx and failed to keep his word, Zeus forced him to drink from the waters, which were said to be so foul the god would lose his voice for nine years.

Nathan peered down at the filth beneath his feet. A mouthful of that and you would lose more than your voice, he imagined.

"Have you ever fallen in?" he inquired of his guide.

His voice echoed down the dark shaft like a challenge. An irreverence. What gods might he offend, or what demons? All might enter but none might leave the world of the dead.

"No," said Philippe, which was one word more than he had spoken since they had left the river. It had taken more than one coin to secure the services of this particular ferryman who had been less eager to be of service than when they last met. And he would not venture into the catacombs, he insisted, for he had a great fear of ghosts.

It was Nathan's first direct experience of a sewer and saving the stench it was by no means as bad as he had anticipated. The construction was of brick and possessed a narrow ledge above the stream of effluent which allowed one to stand almost upright without being immersed in the stuff. The entire system, Philippe had revealed in one of his rare confidences, was between twenty and thirty kilometres in length and went back to Roman times. In fact the *égoutiers* continued to call it by its Latin name: the Cloaca. There was no official map and though Philippe had made a rough sketch map at Nathan's request he had no concept of scale, or indeed, of the points of the compass. He navigated entirely by memory and the homing instincts, Nathan suspected, of a sewer rat, which creature he somewhat resembled with his sharp features and spiky unwashed whiskers.

And there, a few yards in from the entrance, was his boat.

At least that was what Philippe called it. Nathan would have called it a plank with sides. More generously it might have been described as a punt, and like a punt it was propelled with a pole thrust from the stern. There was just sufficient headroom for Philippe to stand while Nathan crouched in the prow, with their two lanterns at his feet. Their gleam projected no more than a few yards ahead and cast huge shadows on the walls and roof as they glided by. And at first it *was* a glide. There was enough water within several hundred yards of the mouth of the sewer to allow them to float but viscous enough for their passage to cause little more than a ripple. After that it became more difficult. They moved through a thick, black ooze, like treacle, that soon made punting impractical so that they were forced to push the craft along with their hands against the wall. They both wore gloves and hooded oilskins and Nathan had covered his mouth and nose with a scarf steeped in oregano and vinegar as a disinfectant.

It was increasingly difficult to move the craft across the sludge and the tunnel itself had deteriorated rapidly. The walls and roof were

no longer of brick but bare rock with only the crumbling concrete
ledge on each side and the rotting timber supports to indicate that it
was something more than a fissure in the limestone. Finally they became embedded in a glue of stagnant mud and excrement which only
shifted, from what Nathan could gather, when it rained, generating
a sufficient flow of water down the drains to move at least some of
this sludge in the direction of the Seine. Philippe indicated that they
must continue on foot.

Reluctantly Nathan climbed out of the boat and crouched uneasily on the concrete ledge constricted by the slope of the walls while
the *égoutier* set off down the tunnel with a confidence that Nathan
could not hope to emulate, dragging his boat behind him on the end
of a rope. After about fifty yards he found an iron ring set into the
side of the wall where he tied it up. Nathan found it hard to breathe,
much less walk, in his contorted position, especially through the scarf
round his face but he had no intention of removing it. It was his only
protection against the wide range of infectious diseases that doctors
attributed to the foetid miasma of sewer or swamp. The squealing of
the rats increased his fears. He could see more of them now, the dark
furry shapes scuttling out of the light. Where there were rats there
was always disease. Cholera, typhoid, yellow fever. Even the plague.

What on earth had possessed him to come anywhere near this foul,
stinking place? And with no certainty of finding what he was looking for.

Well, he knew the answer to that.

Philippe had stopped a few yards ahead at some kind of intersection. The tunnel that led off to right and left was clearly not a sewer.
Was this where Le Mulet had brought them? Philippe clearly believed so, and would, in any case, go no further. He was crossing
himself already.

How anyone could fear the catacombs more than the sewers was
beyond Nathan's comprehension but he knew there was no reason-
ing with the man. From now on he must go alone. Philippe would
wait for him for one hour. After that, he must find his way out alone.

At least he could walk more or less upright again. He could breathe without a pain in his chest and there was no fear of slipping into that unspeakable filth. But surely it was too easy. He seemed to remember having to crouch more. He walked on. Then he reached another crossroads. Which way? Impossible to tell. He took the opening to the right and continued with an increasing sense of futility. Then he saw a light.

A light in the tunnel ahead—and advancing towards him dancing on the walls . . .

Whether its bearer was human or supernatural, Nathan had no desire to make its acquaintance. He began to walk rapidly back the way he had come. But looking back he saw that the light was gaining on him. And it was not just one. There were several. He began to run, stumbling on the uneven ground. He reached the crossroad and paused for a moment, wondering what to do next. He did not wish to lead them back to Philippe in the sewer. Besides, they would probably catch him before he got there. He slid up the glass of his lantern and blew out the candle; then turned to the right, groping his way forward in the dark until his probing hands encountered an opening in the wall, some kind of fissure in the rock. He pressed himself into the crack, peering back towards the intersection . . . and there they were. Three of them. At least they were human. He could see them clearly in the light of their lanterns. Two men . . . and a smaller figure that could be a child or . . .

The figure turned its head. In the second before Nathan darted his own head back into the rock he recognised the unmistakable features of the dwarf Bulbeau.

So he had survived his drop into the Empire of the Dead. And so presumably had Le Mulet. Nathan held his breath and groped for the knife in his boot, bracing himself for a fight. But there was no sound of approaching footsteps—and no advancing light. He inched his head around the rock. They were no longer there. They must have moved straight across the junction. Nathan waited a moment, wracked by doubt. If he waited long enough they would be out of sight and he could return safely to Philippe. But what if they were going to the chapel?

He had to stay with them. He darted out from his hiding place, moving as rapidly as he could in the dark and trying to make as little noise as possible. When he reached the crossroads the lights were bobbing away from him in the distance.

He followed, feeling his way with his hands on the sides of the wall, trying to keep the lights in view but after a few minutes they vanished and he was forced to go much slower in the darkness. Eventually he reached a turning and saw them again, a long way ahead. He proceeded in this manner for some time, mostly keeping the lights in view, sometimes losing them when they turned a corner. He had lost all sense of time and direction. He knew he would never find his way back to Philippe.

Then he turned another corner and they were stopped about thirty yards ahead of him. They appeared to have reached a dead end. Nathan was prepared for them to turn round and start back towards him when an oblong of light appeared in the rock wall directly in front of them. A door. He watched as they filed through. Then the door closed with a loud definitive slam that echoed down the passage towards him like a gunshot and he was plunged into darkness.

It felt as if someone had slammed down the lid of his own coffin.

CHAPTER 39

the Counterfeiters

NATHAN HAD NOT FEARED THE DARK as a child, or in the cramped cabin of a ship at sea—but this was something more than the darkness of night: this was the darkness of the pit, the eternal abyss. Darkness so complete it pierced his eyes and filled his brain. Striking a light required the utmost concentration for to lose any of his materials in the dark would spell disaster. He squatted down and felt the ground. It was cold but surprisingly dry which made things a little easier. He sat down with his back to the wall and his legs stretched out before him. Then he laid out his materials very carefully in the space between them. Lantern, candle, tinder box, flint and steel. He prised open the lid of the metal tinder box and pulled out a bunch of tinder, making a small bird's nest on the ground between his legs. He placed a wad of char-cloth in the centre, took the steel in his left hand and the flint in his right and struck down as sharply as he dared in the dark. At first he was too cautious for fear of gashing his finger but it was a fine piece of quartz and at about the sixth or seventh stroke he succeeded in knocking a good spark down from the steel. A small red glow started in the char-cloth and he quickly dropped flint and steel between his legs and blew at the widening ember until the tinder caught. The smoke made his eyes water but he lit the candle from the flame and set it firmly in the lantern. Then he stood up to inspect the door.

It was a substantial affair of oak reinforced with iron studs and struts fitting into a stout timber frame that had been cemented into the rock. There was an iron ring-pull and a large keyhole—but no key. Nor was there a knocker or bell rope. Clearly visitors were neither expected nor encouraged. Nathan knelt down and peered through the keyhole but either it was dark on the other side or there was something blocking it. He could feel no draught. He put his ear to it and listened. Not a sound.

He examined the hinges. The door clearly opened towards him. He tried twisting the ring-pull both ways and pulling hard but the door was firmly secured. He took out his knife and forced it into the slit between door and frame just above the lock and eased it down, not without difficulty, until it encountered an obstacle, presumably the bolt. He was not sure if that helped him much, except to assure him that the door *was* locked. He wondered if he could chip away with the knife at the doorframe until he exposed the bolt. He tried an experimental jab but was not encouraged. A midshipman's dirk is excellent for some things but not for cutting wood. What he really needed was a chisel. Or a carronade. Failing which . . .

He sat down on the floor again and considered the alternatives. He could stay here until the door was opened, *if* it was opened, and take his chances with whoever opened it. Or he could go back the way he had come. He took out his pocket watch and held it to the light. Ten past twelve. Twenty minutes before Philippe would give up waiting for him. Probably too late to get back to him in time, even if he could find the way.

It now seemed the most sublime act of folly to have followed the men so far. But he had been so convinced that they had been going to the Black Chapel. There were probably other exits but he did not care to start wandering around trying to find them. It was probably wiser to abide here a while to see if the door was opened from the other side—and to abide in darkness. Accordingly he settled himself as comfortably as possible with his back to the wall, opened the lantern and blew out the candle.

Darkness complete. The darkness of the eternal abyss. A black void so absolute the eye and the mind could not comprehend it. He applied himself to the mental exercises that had sustained him in prison and when he had satisfactorily fixed the stars and their planets in their correct spheres, as clearly as he could remember them, he placed himself in his universal conveyance and considered which of the constellations he might favour with a visit. He was not entirely satisfied with the seating arrangement and made some small adjustments to the design. Then he turned his mind to the problem of music. He would have his flute of course but while he had often defended its qualities against the derision of acquaintances (and considered Mozart's remarks upon its inadequacies to be harsh) he felt it was a little insubstantial to capture the epic nature of the universe. He had reluctantly abandoned the idea of taking an orchestra with him, or even a single musical companion, on considerations of weight and space but he did not think it beyond his powers of invention to contrive some mechanical means of expression. Bells—of a size that would fit into his small craft—were too tinkling. It needed something that boomed, something like a drum, or the sound made when the tide rushed into a cave.

Then he heard a different sound. The sound of a key turning in a lock.

Before he could make a move the door had opened and a shaft of light penetrated the darkness. But he remained hidden, huddled between the open door and the side of the cave. He congratulated himself on blowing out the candle.

A squeaking noise and through the shaft of light came a large handcart with a lantern hooked on the front and a man pushing it from behind. He trundled it off down the tunnel without a backward glance and after a moment a second man appeared with another cart. It appeared to be loaded with brown paper parcels. Nathan watched the bobbing lights proceed down the tunnel. But he had seen three men go in; it was reasonable to assume that three men would come out—and that the third would close the door behind him, thus revealing Nathan.

The third man was of course Bulbeau.

Was it better to wait for him here—or to go through the door and tackle him on the other side? This largely depended on who, if anyone, was on the other side with him. The fact that the men had left the door open indicated that either they were expecting someone to follow them or they planned to return the same way. Nathan made up his mind and moved quickly round the edge of the door with his dirk at the ready, fully expecting to run full tilt into the midget.

But no one was there.

He was confronted by a large vaulted room, like a cellar or a crypt, filled with casks and barrels, numerous wooden crates and large earthenware jars. Like a smuggler's den. Which was almost certainly what it was. A shaft of light pierced the gloom at the far end of the room, apparently coming down from the roof. Nathan advanced cautiously into the room and saw that it came from an open trapdoor with a ladder descending from it. And he could hear voices in the room above. He stepped behind one of the brick columns supporting the roof and peered carefully round the edge. A figure appeared at the top of the ladder. Bulbeau. Nathan drew back his head and tried to stop himself from breathing. Moments later Bulbeau passed within a few feet of where he was hiding and entered the tunnel, closing the door behind him.

Nathan was left once more to consider his options.

And once more, they appeared somewhat limited.

After a moment's reflection he moved cautiously through the vaults towards the ladder. He had heard voices so there had been at least one other person in the room above with Bulbeau—but was he there now? Nathan was almost at the foot of the ladder when he heard footsteps and before he could move the trapdoor was slammed shut and he was plunged once more into darkness.

He waited for some minutes, then groped his way forward until his hands encountered the wooden ladder. He climbed to the top and pressed his ear against the trapdoor but he could hear nothing. With infinite care he raised both hands to the door and began to push. Slowly, an inch at a time, he eased it open until he could see through the narrow gap.

He was looking into what appeared to be another storeroom. And in a pool of light at the far end were three men seated at a table.

One he recognised instantly. Le Mulet. He was sitting facing Nathan but the light was poor and there were so many objects on the floor it would have been remarkable if he could have seen the very small amount the trapdoor had been opened. The men were drinking from what looked like a bottle of brandy and appeared to be engaged in animated discussion, though they were too far away for Nathan to understand any of it. The Mule was doing most of the talking. He had his pipe in one hand and was making emphatic gestures with it as he leaned forward over the table, his bald head gleaming in the light of the lantern hanging from the roof above.

The other two men were sitting with their backs partly turned to Nathan so that he could not see their faces. One was heavily built and wore a powdered wig and there was something about the shape of his head and shoulders, or perhaps in the way he sat that seemed oddly familiar. He could almost have been Danton. But the memory of Danton obscured another. He was trying to think who it was when Le Mulet stood up and raised his glass in a toast. As the others rose with him Nathan saw their faces in the light. One was the American Minister Gouverneur Morris and the other was Gilbert Imlay.

Perhaps he should not have been so surprised but he was. He stared foolishly as Le Mulet reached up for the lantern and took it down from the beam. If they had come towards him now they could not have failed to see him but they didn't. They left through a door at the far end of the room, the American Minister taking Imlay by the arm and leaning heavily on his crutch.

Long after they had gone Nathan remained staring into the darkness, occupied with his thoughts. Then he pulled himself together. There were so many questions in his mind but clearly the most important was to find out where he was.

He raised the trapdoor more fully and climbed into the room. There were no windows and it was as dark as it had been in the catacombs but he retrieved his lantern from where he had hooked it on the top of the ladder and applied himself once more to the business of striking a light. When he had succeeded he raised the lantern above his head and surveyed his new surroundings. The walls here were of brick, the floor of wood, and the ceiling supported by stout timber beams instead of vaults. He began a closer inspection of the stores stacked against the walls or arranged in irregular piles on the floor. Casks of brandy, crates of wine, large terracotta pots of olive oil and other produce, boxes containing jars of preserves . . . sugar, coffee, tobacco . . . Perhaps this was where Morris came to do his shopping on the black market though it might be supposed he would send one of the servants. Then Nathan's wandering eye fell on a neat pile of packages, wrapped in brown paper, just like the packages on the handcarts. On closer inspection he saw that each package was tied in a neat parcel, sealed with a blob of wax and numbered. He took his knife and slit one of them open to reveal four stacks of paper *assignats*. The top ones were to the value of ten *sous*: the kind of note that might be used by families in a working class area like Saint-Antoine to buy bread, if they could get it. He pulled one out and held it close to the lantern. The background image showed two goddesses or nymphs, carrying sheaves of corn with the wording: *Domaines Nationaux. Assignat de dix sous, payable au porteur. Loi du 23 Mai, 1793*. Signed by one Guyon, presumably the Finance Minister at the time. A government bond secured against the value of national assets. Or as others might have it, land seized from the Church and the aristocracy.

He ripped open another package. It contained notes to the value of five livres. A hundred in each stack, worth about twelve English pounds. He was about to put them back when a thought occurred to him, or perhaps he detected a lingering smell. He picked up the package and held it to his nose.

The unmistakable scent of tobacco.

He stood there a moment as if stunned. He held one of the notes to the light so he could see the watermark. It appeared to be genuine. The note even bore the inscription: *Le Loi Punit de Mort de Contrefacteur. The Law Punishes the Counterfeiter with Death.*

But there was no doubt in Nathan's mind that it was a forgery, made in England and conveyed to France in the ample hold of the *Speedwell.*

He stuffed one of the bundles into his jacket and made his way to the door by which the three men had left the room. To his relief it was unlocked and he eased it open a crack so he could peer through. He was looking down a long, dark corridor. Apparently empty. He opened the door fully and stepped through. At the far end was another door and to the right a flight of stairs leading up. He listened carefully for a voice or any sound of movement but there was none. The door was locked. He bent down and applied himself to the keyhole. Nothing. And no telltale draught against his eye. He did not think he was looking at the outside world. This was either another dark room or another tunnel. He was more puzzled than ever. Were all these chambers carved out of the rock, deep underground? Was he in some vast subterranean warehouse, or a building with a great many cellars? The brick walls suggested the latter but if it was a building, what kind of building?

He went up the stairs. Another door at the top. This, too, was locked but there was a key hanging from a hook on the wall beside it. It seemed to open onto another corridor but when he raised the lantern he saw that it was formed of bookshelves. They rose high above him on both sides and above *them*—a long way above—was an ornate panelled ceiling. He was in a vast library. No, not a library, for there was nowhere for anyone to read. An archive. He walked through the rows of books, inspecting the titles. Books and manuscripts, all on one subject.

Astronomy.

Nathan felt as if he had entered a fantasy world composed of his own personal dreams and nightmares. He walked between the tall shelves of books and arrived at another flight of stairs. Metal stairs in a spiral with yet another door at the top. Which opened, just as he knew it would, into the main library of the Paris Observatoire.

Moonlight poured in through the long, narrow windows. Through them he could see the trees of the observatory gardens and the night sky. There were the bookshelves in alphabetical order where they kept the works of Cassini and Copernicus, Franklin and Galileo, Halley and Herschel and Huygens, Kepler and Lagrange and Newton and Pascal . . . There was the table where he had sat day after day to study the unpublished works of Tycho Brahe.

And there was the door that led to the lobby and the way out.

Locked of course and this time there was no key.

He went over to the nearest bookshelf, selected one of the thickest tomes that he could see—an edition of *De Revolutionibus Orbium Coelstium* by Copernicus—lay down on the floor, took off his muddy boots, put the book under his head and went to sleep.

He slept remarkably well in the circumstances—he had slept in worse conditions at sea—but dawn came very early at that time of the year and he was roused by the sunlight pouring through the windows. He sat at one of the tables and ate the food he had brought with him in his pack while he pondered the events of the night before. It was clear to him now why the Brothers Pitt had emphasised the importance of his mission and been so opposed to petty diversions like the capture of a mere frigate. He had not been carrying tobacco as the perquisite for a spy but a substantial quantity of forged *assignats*. He took the bundle from his pocket. It measured about four inches by three and was about half an inch deep. He calculated that even allowing for a good layer of tobacco leaf there could have been around seven thousand bundles in each crate. Over eighty thousand pounds. And each cargo had consisted of five hundred crates.

Forty million pounds.

An astronomical sum. Presumably many of the crates had

contained notes of a much lower denomination—like the ten *sous* notes he had seen—but even so it would explain why Robespierre was so concerned about the level of inflation.

But what did Morris and Imlay have to do with it? Were they agents of the British government or had they gone into business on their own account—with Le Mulet as a partner?

A sound at the door alerted him to the arrival of the librarians. Nathan cleared up his breakfast and his notes and replaced *De Revolutionibus Orbium Coelstium* on the bookshelves. He recognised the two men at the front desk from his previous visits and greeted them with a confident *"Bonjour"* as he headed for the front door. He heard one of them shout after him but he was already halfway down the steps to the gardens and no one chased after him.

The sun was already warm and he found a public pump and stripped to wash off the residue of the Cloaca. By the time he had finished he had formed a plan, of sorts. But first he must find Imlay.

It took him less than an hour to walk to the American Minister's house in the Rue de la Planche. A servant answered the door. The Minister was not yet up, he said. Nathan left a message to say that Captain Turner had called with an urgent message and would return in an hour. Then he went for a walk in the Luxembourg Gardens. He stood for a while at the corner of the west wing staring up at the windows of the first floor hoping against hope that he might see Sara staring back. In fact he saw no one, not in the prison. Only a pair of gendarmes in the gardens who insisted on checking his papers. They were in order but they instructed him to move on.

He arrived back at the Rue de la Planche just before ten and was approaching the Minister's house at number 488 when a black cab drew up in front of him and two burly men leaped out and set about him with staves. This was unusual even in Paris and he was indignant enough to knock one of them down and seize the other by the throat only to have his efforts nullified by the press of cold steel against the back of his neck and a voice that was becoming wearily familiar informing him that it was a loaded pistol and that the very slightest movement on his part would set it off and make a quite unnecessary mess in the street embarrassingly close to the American Minister's front door.

"And we would not wish him to step in it," said Citizen Gillet, "in the course of his official duties or, as is far more likely, on his way to the theatre with Madame Flahaut or another of his paramours."

CHAPTER 40

the House of Arrest

THERE WERE CURTAINS ON THE COACH windows so Nathan could not see where they were taking him and Gillet's response to his inquiries on the subject was a curt instruction to shut his mouth. But they did not travel far: no more than a couple of miles, Nathan guessed, before the coach drew to a halt and he was told to get out. He stepped down into a small court-yard from which rose the walls of a tall building with narrow barred windows. Another prison, though several religious statues—defaced or beheaded—suggested that it had once been a convent. Nathan supposed it to be one of the *Maisons d'Arrêt* set up by the authorities to house the growing prison population. The door was opened from within and he was propelled along a corridor and down a flight of stone steps into a large stone-flagged room in the basement.

Two items caught his immediate attention. One was the chain hanging from the ceiling; the other a metal grid on the floor.

He threw himself back against his escort, lashing out with fists and feet, but they clubbed him to the ground and he took several kicks be-fore Gillet called them off and told them to hoist him up to the ceiling.

A pair of manacles were clamped around his wrists and they pulled on the chain until he was standing on his toes with his hands high above his head.

"I was under the impression," he said, "that torture is forbidden since the Revolution."

"You call this torture? We have not yet begun."

"I am an American citizen—"

Gillet struck him in the mouth.

"Pig. You are an English spy and will be treated accordingly. Strip him."

They slit his clothes with their knives and yanked off his boots and left him hanging naked from the chains, alone with Gillet. The police officer walked around him slowly and stopped in front of him, his face expressionless. Nathan's lip was cut on the inside and he could taste blood.

"Now, we will begin," Gillet informed him coldly. "What are you doing in Paris? And do not tell me that you are studying astronomy or I will cut out your eyes."

"I am an American seaman," Nathan insisted. "I have business with several American merchants in the city."

"And what was your business with the *ci-devant* Countess of Turenne?"

Nathan felt sick.

"I don't know what you're talking about."

His voice no longer sounded like his own.

"No. Have you forgotten the lady already? We shall have to remind you."

But he did not hit him. Instead he left the room, shutting the door behind him. Nathan took a deep shuddering breath but there was a tightening band around his chest. He recalled hearing that victims of crucifixion, who were similarly restrained, died of suffocation. He looked up at the chain above his head. It ran through a pulley on the ceiling and the far end was attached to a ring in the wall. Impossible to reach either. He lifted his feet from the ground, taking the entire strain on his wrists. The pain was excruciating and the chain did not give an inch. He lowered his legs so he was standing on his toes again.

The door opened and Gillet came back carrying something at his side.

With a horror that swamped all pain, all other feeling, Nathan saw that it was a human head.

Gillet held it by the hair and tossed it into the room so that it rolled at Nathan's feet, the eyes glaring, the mouth opened in a final soundless scream. He felt as if he would lose his senses, was barely conscious of the convulsion that emptied his stomach and spewed vomit down his chest.

"I thought you would like some company," said Gillet. "To your taste. Fresh from the butcher's in the Place du Trône."

Nathan forced himself to look down at the terrible thing at his feet.

It was the head of a woman. A woman who had once, not very long ago, been young and perhaps pretty.

But it was not Sara.

He sobbed with relief. Then came the rage. An animal rage beyond reason. He released a stream of obscenity, straining at his chains, his mouth flecked with spit and vomit, until Gillet, smiling, left the room.

Nathan was shivering, his whole body in spasm, fighting for control. He looked once more at the pulley on the ceiling. The pulley was the weakest link. All those weeks in the Châtelet he had strengthened his arms with exercise, hauling himself up to the little square of window, but did he have the strength to haul himself up to the pulley? It was about five or six feet above his head and his arms already felt as if they were being wrenched out of his shoulder sockets. The longer he waited, the harder it would be. But he was stretched to the limit; he could not reach up any further, not even to grip the chain above the manacles.

He looked down at the head, inches from his feet. He stretched out his right leg as far as he could and trapped a clump of hair between his toe and the floor. He tried to edge it towards him but he did not have enough leverage. The more he stretched the more the gyves dug into his wrists. Blood was trickling down his arms. He managed to hook a strand of hair between two toes. It moved an inch or so towards him. The eyes stared directly at him now in what might have been a mute appeal, or silent reproach. He tried again. Slowly, inch by inch, he dragged it towards him until it was at his feet, the glazed eyes staring directly up at him.

"I'm sorry," he told the thing that had once been a woman. "God, forgive me."

Then he stood on her face.

He balanced precariously as if he was standing on a football, except that he could feel her teeth through the ball of his foot. He felt like a clown in some macabre circus act but now he could reach the chain above the manacles. Slowly, hand over hand, he began to haul himself up. The pain in his arms was beyond belief but he had the strength. All those weeks in the Châtelet had not, after all, been entirely wasted. His face was up against the pulley. One final effort and he had grabbed the long metal bolt that fixed it to the ceiling. If he could hang on for long enough with one hand he could use the other to lift the chain off the wheel and drop it down over the axle. That would give him three or four inches of slack. Enough to put his feet on the ground. And he might even be able to use the chain as a wrench to split the casing round the pulley. He gripped the bolt with one hand and let go of the chain.

But it was impossible. He did not have the strength to hold on that long with one arm. With a cry he let go and fell awkwardly to the floor, wrenching his shoulder so badly he blacked out for a moment. When he came to, the first thing he saw was the head, lying beyond his reach now with one eye closed in what appeared to be a macabre wink.

The door opened and Gillet came back. This time he carried a cane. A long thin cane tapering slightly towards the end. He stood in front of Nathan, flexing it in both hands.

"Despite our several meetings," he began, "and the level of intimacy we have attained, I do not believe I know your name."

"Turner," said Nathan through his split and swollen lips. "Nathan Turner."

Gillet stepped behind him. The swish of the cane and a fiery pain across his buttocks. Again and again. Then Gillet began to walk around him, slashing and cutting, taking his time, picking his targets. Nathan had seen men flogged at the grating with a hundred strokes of the cat but nothing like this, the man contemptuously circling him and slashing the cane at his exposed body. Chest, shoulders, back, buttocks, thighs. The swish and sting, swish and sting, with scarcely a second between. Nathan hung with teeth bared, staring at the wall through a haze of tears, sustained by a rage that burned as hot as the cane on his naked flesh.

A pause.

"Why did you come to Paris?"

"Business. With . . . an American . . . merchant."

"Called?"

"Imlay."

Knowing he must know already.

"And Thomas Paine?"

"I have told you . . . I had no . . . dealings . . . with Thomas Paine."

Gillet drew back the cane.

"No!" It was not quite a scream, not yet. "I was sent . . . to find him . . . in Paris."

"By whom?"

"The President. Washington."

"You are an intimate of the American President?" Gillet bent the cane as if he was testing it for flexibility.

"He is a friend of Thomas Paine. He wished me . . . to bring him back to America."

"And when he was imprisoned, you were to rescue him."

"No. There was no . . . no plan to rescue him."

"So why were you in the quarry at Porte d'Enfer?"

"I have told you . . . I had business with the owner, Le Mulet."

"Yes, yes. But it is the nature of that business that interests me. When I asked you before, I had not the means of eliciting a true answer. Now, as you perceive, I have."

The punishment resumed. The swish and the cut. On and on. Nathan tried to count the strokes thinking they might stop at twenty, then thirty . . . His whole body was on fire but incredibly he could still feel each individual stroke, like a hot coal suddenly bursting into flame.

Even more incredibly, his mind was working on a plan. A story. One that Gillet might find convincing. Not yet, though, not yet. Or he would not be believed. It had to seem as if it was forced from him by the extremities of pain. And so much depended on who had informed upon him. Imlay? Morris or his servants? Philippe the *égoutier*? Le Mulet, or one of Le Mulet's men?

Another pause.

Nathan hung limply from the chain, his head drooping to his chest. His skin was striped like a tiger's except that it was red on white. He could see the blood running in rivulets down his body, down his legs, down the drain at his feet. The woman's head lolled on its side, a single eye gazing in blank indifference.

He mumbled something incoherent.

Gillet raised his chin with the point of the cane.

"I cannot hear you. Repeat."

"He wanted me . . . to take . . . a cargo. To England."

"What cargo?"

"Silver . . ."

Slowly, with shuddering sobs, he told his story. Le Mulet had a cache of silver plate from confiscated aristocratic households that he wished to get out of the country. Worth around a million livres. He wanted Nathan to take it to England to sell through contacts he had there.

"You were aware that this was illegal?"

"Yes."

"Punishable by death."

"Yes."

"But you agreed?"

"No. I refused."

A single cut of the cane across his cheek.

"I agreed. I agreed. But then . . . we were . . . the police, the Guard came." The cane was raised. "Please. No more. I . . . You know . . . I was taken . . . to the Châtelet. I came back to Paris to find it . . . for myself."

"And where is it now, this silver?"

"He did not say."

Gillet slashed the other cheek.

"Please. I beg you. He would not say. You must . . . believe me. But I guessed. It was close to . . . the bottom . . . of the shaft. In the Empire of the Dead."

Silence.

Save for the drip, drip of sweat or blood. He closed his eyes and hung limply from the chains. He could no longer feel the pain in his arms or wrists for the pains elsewhere.

"It should be easy enough to check. And if it is not there, well, we will resume the interrogation."

The guards came back and took him down from the chain and dragged him from the room. A corridor, another door and they were in a small yard. Walls rose up all around but high above he could see the sky. In the middle of the yard stood an iron pump and a trough. They dumped him on the ground and pumped water over him. It was cold and wonderful. When they had finished they dragged him back into the building and into another room and gave him some clothes, not his own, which were in shreds. But they did give him his boots.

And with them a grain of hope.

Once he had put them on they marched him back into the courtyard where there was a black vehicle waiting with a pair of horses, not the same vehicle that had brought him here, but a prison wagon with a door at the back and bars on the window. They threw him in and chained him to a rail.

He wondered where they were going to take him. To the Châtelet? Or for more coffee and cake with the Duplays and a second interview with their lodger? But it was neither of these places.

They took him to the Luxembourg.

CHAPTER 41

the Palace of the Medici

NATHAN WAS IN A CELL WITH nine others, one of them a doctor: an Englishman called Brand who examined his wounds and treated them with a salve.

"You will not believe me," he said, "but you are lucky it was not a whip."

Nathan did not believe him.

"A whip would have cut you to the bone. These are mostly welts and will heal without a mark. There are a few cuts here and there but they are not deep."

But Nathan carried scars that could not be seen and they went very deep indeed. He had not thought of himself as a vengeful person but revenge now seemed to be all he could think of. Feverish on his thin mattress, his whole body a burning torment of flayed skin, he kept himself sane with a vow: he would get out of here and he would find Gillet and he would kill him. It was his only reason for staying alive.

But then, as the pain ebbed and the wounds healed, at least on the surface, he began to think of other reasons.

Sara was here. In the Luxembourg. And he had the means of getting them both out.

It had of course occurred to him that he had been brought here, rather than to any other prison, because Gillet must suspect the existence of an escape route and hoped that Nathan would lead them to it. He knew there had been searches just after the death of Danton because Brand and several other prisoners had told him about them. One even said they had been looking for a tunnel and began to speculate as to its location but this merely confirmed Nathan in his suspicion that the man was an agent provocateur sent to draw him out.

All of this convinced Nathan that they had been unable to find the secret door behind the stage in the old prison theatre, now the prison store. So it must still be there.

The problem was, how to find it?

But first he had to find Sara.

Male and female prisoners were kept apart. The men in the west wing, the women in the east, with a courtyard between. Both sexes were allowed into the courtyard for an hour each day but at separate times: the men in the mornings, the women in the afternoons. There was a metal pump and a trough where they could wash themselves or their clothes and naturally when the women were at the pump many of the men crowded at the windows to gaze at them and sometimes to communicate with women they knew or wished to know.

As soon as he could leave his bed, Nathan joined this admiring throng.

He saw her at once. She had some soap—a much sought after commodity in the prison—and she was standing by the pump and washing her hair. For a while Nathan just stood, clutching the bars of his window, and watched her. She seemed little changed, still stood out from the crowd: statuesque, her figure emphasised by the thin muslin dress she wore, a cotton smock around her shoulders, wooden clogs on her feet. She looked like a peasant woman—or rather Rousseau's ideal of the peasant—doing her washing at the village trough. She was absorbed in her toilette, working her hair up into a lather and then lowering her head for one of her companions to pour water over it from a jug. But after a while she walked away a little, rubbing at her hair with a towel. And then she looked up and saw him.

She made no sign of recognition and nor did he. He had some

notion that it might be dangerous. But one of the other men noted her stare and nudged him and said, "Hey, it is your lucky day, *monsieur*. She is the belle of the Luxembourg."

"Much good it does me," grumbled Nathan, "as there is no way of contriving an introduction."

"Oh, but there is," said the fellow, "and more than that."

And that was how Nathan discovered that the prison store had another, unofficial function besides the sale of supplies.

Although the two sexes were not allowed there at the same time, for a small consideration the staff permitted notes to be left and, for a much larger sum, assignations to be arranged. The male party would be invited to step through a drape into a room at the back and his lover would join him there when it was the women's turn to use the store. It was a lengthy process to arrange such a liaison but it could be done.

Nathan went back to his cell to think about it.

He was still afraid that the authorities had set a trap for him. He had to take his time, to make sure he was not watched.

But how much time did he have? How long before Gillet gave up trying to find the non-existent silver in the Empire of the Dead and came back for him? To resume where they had left off. And for Sara, too, time was not something that could be relied upon. Sooner or later her name would appear on the List—and they would take her on her final journey.

The List came round between eight and ten every evening, with the names of the prisoners who had been selected for trial the following morning. The cell doors were left open during the day but at night they were shut and locked and the turnkey would chalk a number on the outside, according to how many prisoners from that particular cell were on the List. There were up to a dozen people in each cell and of course none of them knew the number or what the names were so they would lie awake, wondering. Then later that night, usually around midnight, the Death Squad came round. And then they knew. That was when the screaming started, though sometimes it began earlier.

Like everyone else in the prison Nathan expected the next twenty-four hours to be his last and every night he listened for the sound of the turnkeys doing their rounds and for the scratch of the chalk on the door and the clump of boots on the stairs. After midnight when they had been and gone he was usually able to get some sleep. But sometimes there was an inexplicable delay and the Death Squad didn't come round until the early hours or even after the first streaks of dawn had appeared in the sky and those nights were the worst. The prisoners had their own rule to stop people singing after ten but no one could stop the screaming.

By day it was not so bad. There were things to do; they had their routine.

The prison was divided into blocks known as chambers and every chamber formed a society with an elected president to enforce the rules. Each prisoner was given a task such as lighting the fires, sweeping the room, doing the laundry, making the beds—everyone in Nathan's room had a trestle bed and a straw mattress, some with a cupboard or a little table next to it and sometimes a candle bought from the prison store. The rooms varied in size but most were high-ceilinged and quite large and each was named after a republican hero from the classics, such as Brutus or Cassius, Cato or Cincinattus, Socrates or Plato. Nathan was in Cato. His cellmates were typical of the diverse society of the prison: a cross-section of the bohemian Faubourg of Saint-Germain where wealth and want were close neighbours. There was a viscount and a marquis, a lawyer, a priest, a couple of medical students, a theatrical scene-maker, a valet who was much put upon by the two aristocrats, and of course, the English doctor, Brand. Nathan maintained the fiction that he was American, fearing an informer: there were plenty of those, according to Brand.

They even had news, of sorts, from the government newspaper the *Moniteur*. It was from this that Nathan learned of the safe arrival of the grain fleet from America. The French fleet, he read, had won a great victory over the British. But bread was still in short supply according to Brand who had his own informers. The bread on sale in the prison store at the legal maximum of ten *sous* was mostly sawdust and oatmeal, though you could buy good white bread at ten times the price under the counter.

There was plenty of freedom to move about within the prison, at least during the day, when the cell doors were not locked. In the afternoons they tended to congregate in the large antechambers or common rooms where they walked, talked, played games such as cards or chess, or simply stared out of the windows into the gardens below, hoping to see a relative or a friend looking out for them.

It was here that Nathan met Thomas Paine. He was talking animatedly to a circle of acquaintances but he stopped in mid-sentence when he saw Nathan and stared at him in some astonishment and not a little alarm.

"Mr. Paine," said Nathan quickly, doffing his hat. "It is good to see a fellow American—though I had rather it were in New York."

Paine still said nothing but Nathan could almost read the thoughts that must be running through his head.

"Perhaps you do not remember me," he continued, aware of the curious glances he was getting. "Captain Turner. Nathan Turner. Of the barque *Speedwell*. Of Salem. We met at the Philadelphia Hotel on the night of your arrest."

"Aye," said Paine, his expression a little more relaxed. "Captain Turner. What . . . how . . . ?" He spread his arms to indicate their present surroundings.

"I am suspected of smuggling," Nathan told him, "or at least of associating with smugglers."

Paine nodded as if he understood. He looked older and thinner than when Nathan had seen him last, which was not surprising after several months in prison. He had been held in solitary confinement since his famous meeting with Danton but now he was back in his communal cell. He'd had no word from the American Minister or any of his friends in the city and was anxious for whatever news Nathan could impart, which was not much. Later they talked more privately and Nathan told him that as far as he was aware the prison authorities still considered him to be an American seaman.

"I believe my masters thought it would give me some protection," he said, "if I was caught."

"Or throw the blame upon the Americans for your misdemeanours," replied Paine thoughtfully.

Nathan was not sure what he meant.

"Well think on it, man. If your mission succeeds all well and good. Danton is the new Messiah. He makes peace. We all go home. If it fails . . ." He shrugged . . . "Well, you are an American citizen acting on instruction from the United States government. It would not please the French I can tell you. They do not like people interfering in their affairs. It certainly would not please Robespierre."

Especially if he discovered the true nature of his business in France, Nathan reflected, and that he was wrecking the French economy with forged currency.

But he kept this thought to himself. Paine was still a Revolutionist. He might be supposed to raise some objection if the Revolution collapsed in an avalanche of useless paper, manufactured in Britain.

They met frequently after this first encounter, usually in Paine's cell when he was not writing. He was completing an essay on the character of Robespierre, a subject that obsessed him more than most; just as Robespierre, he claimed, was obsessed with him. He thought that Robespierre was jealous of his reputation as a philosopher and a writer and that this was the real reason he had ordered his arrest.

"He has long had pretensions to the literary life," he argued. "But unhappily for the rest of humankind he failed to impress his talent upon his contemporaries and like many a mediocrity before him took to politics—by way of the law. Mark my words, the most dangerous men in the world are those who fancy themselves as artists or writers—or even actors—and who, in frustration at their lack of success, become politicians: a profession for which their poor artistic endeavours appears to make them remarkably well suited. Possibly because of the element of duplicity involved."

What made Robespierre particularly dangerous, in Paine's eyes, was his utter conviction that he was right. About everything.

"And therefore any who disagree with his judgement must be wilfully blind or motivated by evil intent and destroyed without compunction. Though interestingly, he is not by nature inclined to violence. He cannot bear the thought of bloodshed, though he forces himself to order it for the sake of society. But he would faint at the sight of a cut finger."

"If he was aware of a plot to destroy the Revolution," Nathan ventured, "would he not be justified in employing extreme measures to counter it?"

The discovery of the forged notes in the catacombs had been preying on his mind. Could it be that the British government's attempt to undermine the Revolution had only succeeded in undermining the moderates and driving the French people into the hands of the extremists? That in some ways the British government had itself brought about the Terror?

"Robespierre sees plots where they do not exist," Paine insisted. "He uses them to justify every attack on liberty, justice and human rights. It is he who has destroyed the Revolution, and any who have a different opinion to his own."

Nathan conceded that he was probably right. In truth, he was more concerned in escaping the Terror than explaining it.

Slowly, forever looking over his shoulder, he had worked out a plan.

Sewn into the hem of his boots—the boots he had recovered at the last minute in the House of Arrest—were twenty gold pieces. This gave him a means of shopping in the prison store—and of bribing the guards. But he had to be careful. The possession of gold was a criminal offence in the Republic, punishable by death. You could not simply go to the store, slap your gold coin on the counter and wait for the change.

What you did was slip it *under* the counter.

The guards at the prison store were in the money-changing business. Those prisoners in possession of gold coin—and Nathan was not the only one—could exchange it secretly for *assignats*. At the rate of 100 livres to one louis d'or.

It took Nathan a few days to discover this but once he had he became a regular visitor to the store. Prisoners were permitted to enter in
batches of ten at a time to what had once been the theatre lobby and to
stand in line at the old box office where a list of stores and prices were
displayed. The stores themselves were kept where the theatre stalls
used to be. And for private conversations—and transactions—there
was the old manager's office.

This was where Nathan changed his money and where—a few
days later—he explored the possibility of meeting one of the women
prisoners.

"Name?" inquired the guard, taking out a tattered notebook and
licking the lead of his pencil.

Nathan hesitated.

"You have to give me her name," the fellow sighed, "if I am to give
her the message."

"You will give her a message?"

"Well how else are you going to meet her?" The fellow shook his
head.

"Sara," said Nathan. "Sara Seton."

But she might no longer be known as that. What was he to do? He
did not wish to get her into trouble. But she was in trouble enough
already. He had to take the risk.

"Or she might be known as Sara de la Tour d'Auvergne," he added.

The fellow wrote it down.

"When?"

"When?"

"When do you want to meet?" Rolling his eyes.

"Tomorrow? Tomorrow night?"

Nathan anticipated some objection but the fellow merely said,
"Two hundred livres. Payable in advance."

Nathan returned to his cell to find Brand rooting through his bag
of medicines and looking worried.

"Thomas Paine is ill," he said. "He has a fever."

"What kind of fever?"

Brand looked at him in exasperation. "I don't know the precise nature and even if I did I would not have the medicines to treat it. And he certainly does not have the strength to fight it."

Nathan went with him to see the patient. He looked terrible. He lay on his bed covered in a thin blanket, shivering and covered in sweat. He could not eat and could barely speak.

The weather had turned warm after a period of rain and the cell was stifling. Brand asked the turnkey if they could leave the cell door open at night to allow the air to circulate a little.

"I cannot do that," he protested. He was a great, slow ox of a man called Bastien, not one of nature's brightest but amiable enough and willing to oblige if there was profit in it, at no trouble or inconvenience to himself.

"Why not?" inquired Nathan.

Bastien frowned as he gave this some thought. One possible reason occurred to him.

"They might escape?" he proposed.

"How can they escape?" Nathan demanded. "The outer door is always locked. Even were they to leave the cell they could not leave the block, much less the prison itself."

"This is true," said Bastien, nodding thoughtfully. "What's it worth?"

They settled on fifty livres.

But it did little to alleviate Paine's distress and Dr. Brand was not hopeful.

"It is as much a mental affliction as anything physical," he told Nathan. "He has suffered months of anxiety under the shadow of the guillotine. The discomfort and the indignities have contributed to his condition but I believe the primary cause is disappointment. He grieves at the course the Revolution has taken. And now he must face the possibility that he has been wrong and men like Edmund Burke were right. In short, he has lost the will to live."

"It were a pity to die from losing an argument with Edmund Burke," Nathan remarked, but he acknowledged that philosophers were more sensitive than mortal men.

But then Paine's will to live ceased to be of any relevance.

After dinner Nathan went back to Paine's cell to see if there was anything he could do for him. He sat beside him for a while reading to him and mopping his brow from a bowl of lukewarm water. Then Bastien came round jangling his keys. Nathan took this as the signal for him to be locked up in his own cell for the night but as he left he saw to his surprise that Bastien was closing the door behind him and preparing to turn the key in the lock.

"I thought we had agreed to leave it open," he said.

Bastien looked troubled.

"I regret," he said, "that it cannot stay open tonight. I will have to give you back your money."

"Why not?"

But even as he asked the answer came to him.

"They are on the List," he exclaimed.

Bastien said nothing but continued searching among the keys on his ring.

"How many?" Nathan demanded.

Bastien still would not answer.

"Is Paine one of them?"

Bastien looked at him directly, his big round eye almost tearful, and nodded. "The only one," he confirmed.

"But that's inhuman," Nathan rebuked him. He recognised the absurdity of this observation. "They'll have to carry him out of here. He'll be dead long before they fetch him to the tribunal, let alone the guillotine."

"It won't be the first time," said Bastien. This was true. They had executed corpses before, in the interests of revolutionary justice.

Nathan thought quickly.

"Leave the door," he said. "Leave him in ignorance until they come."

"I can't do that."

"I will give you another fifty livres to leave the door open."

The turnkey looked at him. Greed battled with the fear of exposure.

"I must still put the number upon the door," he insisted.

"Then do so," said Nathan, "while the door is open."

He could see the ox brain struggling to weigh up the implications of this.

"After all, they cannot escape if the outer door is locked," Nathan assured him before Bastien could think of another way the prisoners might turn it to their advantage.

He went to fetch the money from where he had concealed it in his cell. When he returned Bastien was locking up one of the other cells and Nathan took the opportunity to take one of Paine's cellmates aside and tell him what was happening.

"What are we to do?" the man agonised, pulling at his whiskers. He was a Belgian, one of three in Paine's cell: army officers who had been on leave in Paris when the French had marched into their country.

"Why, when he has gone you must rub the number off the door," Nathan told him, marvelling that he appeared as dull-witted as the jailer. But then he had a better idea. When the door was open it lay flat against the wall and the jailer had chalked the number on the side that was facing him. "No. Simply close the door. Then the mark will still be there, but on the inside, do you see?"

Bastien never accompanied the Death Squad on their rounds. If the Belgian opened the door again after they had been and gone the turnkey might not realise how the error had occurred and with any luck it would serve for another night.

Nathan returned to his cell and lay awake listening for the familiar sounds of the Death Squad. They came a little after midnight. The boots on the stairs. The jangle of keys. The names called out loud. And then the screams. But he had no way of knowing if they had stopped at Paine's cell. Not until morning when he saw Bastien again.

"They did not take him," he said. "I cannot understand it. The number is clearly marked on the door."

"Well, I won't tell anyone," said Nathan, "if you don't."

Bastien gave him a reproachful look.

"They are bound to find out," he said. "They'll be back for him tonight."

This was true. And this time, Bastien said, he was going to make sure the door was locked and then there could be no mistake.

Nathan agonised all through the long hot day. That evening he was due to meet Sara in the prison store. But could he go through with it, knowing that he was leaving Thomas Paine to certain death?

He decided he could not. He would have to take Paine with him.

He worked out another plan. It was desperate but so were the circumstances. He would have to involve others. Brand, certainly. And the three Belgian officers. Between them they would get Paine down to the prison store. And then . . . Well, there were never more than two or three prison staff there. They would overcome them and reach the secret passage before they managed to alert the guards.

But first he had to ensure that the passage was still there.

When the prison store opened at four Nathan was the first in line. They knew what he had come for.

"Round the back," said the guard, jerking his head towards the curtain at the back of the lobby.

The guard he had paid was waiting for him on the other side with a lamp. "You'll need this," he said. And then with a smirk, "And there is a mattress on the stage area. For the use of our clients."

"How long?"

"It will be an hour before I can let the women in."

"But—she knows?"

"She has had the message. If she doesn't come, that's up to her."

So he had an hour. Not long for all he had to do.

He walked through what had once been the theatre stalls, now with the seats removed and the area stacked with provisions. A regular black market. A short flight of wooden steps took him up on to the stage and what had presumably once been the backstage area; nothing now dividing them. There was no sign of a door or any other means of exit or entrance. Le Mulet must have got it wrong—or made the whole thing up.

Then his eye fell on the mattress. He kicked it aside with his boot. And there it was. A trapdoor set into the floor of the stage.

Nathan worked back the bolt, not without effort, and heaved it open. A flight of steps descended into darkness. He picked up the lantern and climbed down into what was clearly a props room. His light exposed various weird and wonderful objects that had obviously been used in past productions: a dragon and the face of an ogre, suits of armour, wood and plaster trees and parts of a castle. And there were the costumes Le Mulet had mentioned. Hundreds of them. On wheeled racks stacked against the back wall. In a fever of impatience now Nathan pulled and pushed them aside, setting up clouds of dust and moths ...

And right in the middle he found the door.

He seized the brass doorknob and twisted it both ways. But the door was locked and there was no key. He searched the walls, the floor, even rooted among the racks of costumes. He could not possibly have come so far only to be cheated by a locked door.

He lifted the lamp to examine the lock. A mortise lock screwed into the wood. He looked around for something he might use as a wrench but there was nothing. He considered piling some of the props against it and starting a fire but the staff would smell the smoke.

In despair and anger he kicked the door with his boot ... and the lock moved. He kicked again and the entire lock fell out leaving a hole big enough for him to put his hand through.

He almost laughed aloud. Le Mulet's men must have chipped the back off the lock and stuck something there to hold it in place. He turned the handle again and the door swung obligingly open ... And there were the steps where the stones had been piled.

Nathan grabbed the lamp and descended into the Black Chapel. Just as it had been when he had first seen it: the Beast on its altar, the upside down Christ ... And the tunnel leading back into the Empire of the Dead.

He was so exhilarated he could have shouted out loud. But he still had much to do. He had to wait for Sara and leave her here. Then make some excuse to the guards and return to Paine's cell and persuade the Belgians to co-operate . . .

He turned to go back to the theatre but then something made him pause. A smell.

Of candle wax.

His candle? But then he lifted the lamp and saw the others on the altar with the wisps of smoke curling from the wicks.

He had started to turn when the blow came, catching him high on the head and pitching him senseless at the foot of the altar.

CHAPTER 42

the Death List

A THROBBING PAIN IN HIS HEAD CENTRED at a point just above his right ear and a red glow in his eyes like a fireball; then sunlight, flickering through a moving window, hurting his eyes. A jolting sensation as if he was in a coach.

Sudden shadow, the light taking shape and form. He *was* in a coach. And there was a figure seated opposite him, a child ... No ... He tried to focus on it raising his hand against the glare. Bulbeau. Tugging at his whiskers and smiling to himself as if at some private joke.

And he was not alone. There was another man sitting next to him, of normal stature. Someone Nathan had not seen before.

Nathan put a hand up to his head where it hurt and felt a lump there and dried blood crusted in his hair.

"Sorry about the head," said Bulbeau, still grinning. "It was Pierrepoint. He gets excited."

Nathan looked at the man sitting next to him. Was he Pierrepoint? Judging from his expression he probably was.

"Sorry," he said. "He told me to do it."

The coach emerged from the shadow of the buildings and the sunlight lanced through the window once more. And yet it was the dying of the light, the last before sunset, and Nathan saw that they were crossing a vast square with a fountain in the centre and a tall statue of a goddess, black against the sun. And he knew where they were—for this was where the Bastille had once stood; before they tore it down and built the fountain in its place. And the goddess was Isis, the Egyptian goddess of rebirth whose ample breasts gushed the "milk of liberty" on ceremonial occasions.

Then the coach swung to the right and they were in shadow again, heading north through the Porte Saint-Antoine in the direction of the Temple.

"Where are we going?" he asked Bulbeau but the midget shook his head and said, "You will see."

It had been just after four when he went into the theatre and now it was sunset. Across the rooftops he could see the dark mass of Butte-Montmartre rising against the sky. A beautiful evening sky. But the smell was worse even than usual as if the wheels of the carriage had splashed through a pool of excrement. He wrinkled his nose against it and Bulbeau caught his eye and said "Monfaucon," as people did when they wished to explain a sudden, disgusting smell and feared that others would think it was them.

Monfaucon. My falcon, my hawk. The great dump to the north of the city, where the slaughterhouses were and where they took the rubbish and the filth they scraped from the streets. It had been a place of execution in the days of the kings.

And was still, Nathan had heard, though less formal, unsanctioned by the law: where the Trouanderie made an end to informers and others who had offended against their criminal code, leaving the bodies to rot among the garbage and the filth.

So was this where they were taking him?

But why bother, when they could have left him to rot with all the other bones in the Empire of the Dead?

And then they stopped and Bulbeau invited him to get out and he saw they were in the Rue du Temple, outside the House of Wax.

They took him up the stairs to the studio where he had met little Marie Grosholtz. No Marie, not this time, but there *was* a head—presumably awaiting her attentions on the workbench—and he saw with a shock that it was the head of Danton.

Then he looked again and saw that it was made of wax. In the poor light it looked remarkably real, even to the scars from his fight with the bull and the light of battle in his eye. Various other portions of anatomy were spread about the room and at the far end stood a group of headless figures dressed in the costumes of the ancient regime, their hands arranged in elegant gestures as if in the middle of some polite discourse. The absence of their heads seemed of little consequence.

Nathan's escort led him through into the office—and there were the three men he had last seen in the Paris Observatoire, sharing a bottle.

"Here he is," said Le Mulet. "Our friend of the catacombs."

"By God, sir," said the American Minister, raising his glass. "Back from the dead."

"And looking more dead than alive," said Imlay. "If you'll forgive me for saying so."

Clearly Nathan was expected.

They sat him down and poured him a glass of wine.

Wine was probably not a good idea with his pounding headache but he drank it anyway. He was having difficulty coming to terms with the reality of his situation and he doubted if a glass of wine would make it any less real; it might even help.

"Sorry about your little accident," said Le Mulet. "They didn't know it was you." Clearly he no longer felt betrayed—or if he did was prepared to let bygones be bygones.

"You are to be congratulated on your escape," said Imlay. "You must tell me about it some time. Your timing is perfect. You will be in at the kill, as I believe they say in England."

Nathan shook his head and was sorry for it.

"What kill?"

"The fox. Or I should say, the Tiger-cat."

"The next twenty-four hours," said Morris, "will decide the fate of France."

This was not greatly helpful.

"Well, Tom Paine's fate is already decided upon," Nathan informed him pithily. "He is to be tried tomorrow—and likely to be executed unless we can help him." He turned to Le Mulet. "I need to go back for him tonight, through the catacombs."

It was not Tom Paine's fate that most concerned him but they need not know that. He might still have time. And if Le Mulet could let him have some men . . .

"You do not understand," said Imlay. "They are ready to act—to end the Terror. Then no one will be executed. Your gold has been put to good use while you have been in prison."

"My gold?"

"Danton's gold. Danton is their inspiration but it is the gold that will achieve the business."

They had been speaking French, presumably out of courtesy to Le Mulet, and Nathan did not quite grasp his meaning.

"I am sorry," he said, raising his hand to the back of his head. "I am not sure . . ."

"The Convention is ready to act against Robespierre," explained Imlay.

He saw from Nathan's expression that he was not entirely convinced.

"It's true. Believe me. Robespierre has gone too far, even for them. He says there are traitors in their midst, a league of scoundrels, enemies of Virtue. They called on him to name them. When he stepped down from the tribune hundreds were on their feet demanding he name the names but he would not."

"A fatal error!" Morris exulted. "If he had named ten he would have reassured the rest. But now . . ."

"They all think they are on his death list," Imlay finished for him. "And they know they must strike before he strikes them."

"So . . ." Nathan looked from one to the other. He was beginning to get his mind round this. A small hope began to form. "Where is Robespierre now?"

"At the Jacobins, rallying his supporters."

Were they mad or was it him? Was it no great matter that Robespierre was rallying his troops?

"And what of the National Guard?"

"That is where your gold comes in," said Imlay.

"Pitt's gold," Nathan reminded him. "And by the way, he wants it back."

"But it will achieve the fall of Robespierre. Which is what it was intended for."

It was intended for Danton—and to achieve peace. Should he mention that? But this constant reference to his gold intrigued him. Clearly Imlay was anxious to account for it—or to have Nathan account for it to Pitt if he ever got back to England.

"Certain key figures have been bribed," Imlay continued. "Among the Guard and in the Sections. Men who can bring people out on the streets—or keep them at home. Believe me, your gold—Pitt's gold—has found its way into a lot of pockets."

Including your own no doubt, thought Nathan.

"What of Hanriot?" he said.

Hanriot was commander of the Garde Parisienne. Nathan had seen him at the Luxembourg on his notorious tours of inspection. He was a madman and a drunk and everyone feared him. He had been one of the main organisers of the September massacres and during the last insurrection he had ringed the Tuileries with cannon, demanding the surrender of every delegate on the Jacobin blacklist. When the President of the Convention rejected the demand he told the messenger, "Go back to your fucking President and tell him he's fucked and if he doesn't hand the bastards over in ten minutes we'll blast the place to shit."

As speeches went it was not up to Danton's standards but they sent out the men he wanted and all of them were executed. Hanriot was a joke but he had power and he was dangerous. And he supported Robespierre.

"We haven't approached Hanriot," said Imlay. "He is too unpredictable."

This was not encouraging.

The door opened and Bulbeau came in with a note for the *patron*.

"News from the Jacobins," Le Mulet announced. "Robespierre was loudly cheered. They set on two of his critics and beat them to a pulp. He said, 'We must deliver the Convention from these scoundrels. If we fail, you will see me drink the hemlock with calm.'"

This seemed to amuse him.

"So now he thinks he is Socrates," said Imlay. "And they all shouted they would drink it with him. My God, the French."

He shook his head but then frowned, possibly recalling that Le Mulet was French.

"So—this is good news? Or bad?" Nathan thought he had better get this straight.

"Vadier is confident," Morris insisted.

"Vadier? Where does Vadier . . . ?"

But Imlay was glaring at the Minister warningly.

"Vadier is but one of them," he said. "There are many others. It is them or Robespierre. They know this now."

Nathan remembered the Festival of the Supreme Being when Robespierre climbed to the top of the Mountain—and Vadier and the other malcontents stood at the bottom, waiting to sink their daggers in his back.

"Let us hope so." Nathan pressed his fingers into his eyes. He was so tired he felt he was going to black out. He made an effort to stay awake, to concentrate. People's lives depended on it. Tom Paine's certainly, Sara's possibly. Did it always come down to the personal? Yes, unless you were a fanatic like Robespierre. That is what he must tell his mother if ever he saw her again. It was the right to a personal life, free from dogma. That was what he was fighting for.

But not now. His head was spinning but there were things he must do.

"One thing you must do"—he turned to Le Mulet—"you must pack the gallery."

He had seen how the gallery dominated the Convention. The

delegates were terrified of the mob. When they saw a sample of it— those howling faces in the gallery, screaming murder—their blood turned to water.

"Pack it with your own men. Men, women, children, if necessary. You must stop him filling it with his Jacobins. Or he'll have us all on his death list."

"Don't worry," said Le Mulet. "It is all arranged."

CHAPTER 43

the Palais de Justice

THEY CAME FOR SARA AT TWO in the morning. She knew it could happen at any time and it did not surprise her. Nothing surprised her any more. Not even seeing Nathan watching her in the prison courtyard or receiving the message to meet him in the prison store . . . or waiting there in vain for him to turn up.

It was fate. She could do nothing about it. Her name was on the List. They took her first to the Conciergerie for what was left of the night and then to the Palais de Justice to wait until it was her turn to be tried. She still did not know the charge and was allowed no lawyer.

They left her there for most of the day among the gradually thinning crowd in the cell, sweating in the terrible heat, mostly silent, some talking quietly, others writing their final letters or compiling a detailed defence but for the most part resigned to their slaughter. And like cattle they stood there, those that did not wish to lie down on the filthy straw, flapping sometimes at the flies that buzzed around their heads.

Then there was only Sara. And she began to think they had missed her and would have to bring her back the following day. This made her neither sorry nor glad. A kind of fatalism had settled on her. It was her only defence.

And then at last they called her name.

She was led up into the courtroom and placed in the dock. A surprisingly empty courtroom, very different from the last time she had seen it, when Danton was on trial. There were the same three judges, or ones very like them, but they seemed to be going through the motions, playing their allotted roles in an endless, pointless charade. The emergency decrees allowed no witnesses and no counsel for the defence. The Public Prosecutor put the case to the jury and the judges asked the jury to give a verdict of guilty or not guilty and that was it. Not guilty verdicts were not unheard of but they caused a great deal of trouble for all concerned. The Prosecutor would insist on an immediate retrial and on bringing in witnesses for the prosecution— who had to be dragged off the streets and paid—and everyone had to hang around for a great deal longer than was necessary including the prisoners who had already been condemned and the executioner's assistants who were waiting to cut their hair and the men who drove the *charrettes* and the horses who pulled them and the soldiers who escorted them to the scaffold and the executioner himself. And when they'd heard the witnesses for the prosecution the jury invariably changed their verdict to guilty and it was all for nothing and in all probability they'd be struck off the jury list and lose their attendance fee. So guilty verdicts were easier all round.

Sara searched the faces in the public gallery, looking for Nathan but not really expecting to see him. She had long since given up hope of that.

Someone began to speak. One of the clerks, spectacles on his nose, shuffling papers, and at last she heard the charges against her.

Item one: that she was the wife of the *ci-devant* Count of Turenne who had been condemned to death for various crimes against the Republic. She was therefore guilty of association with a convicted criminal. Punishable by death.

Item two: that she was an associate of the woman Lucille Desmoulins who had been convicted of conspiracy to free the prisoners from the Luxembourg. She was therefore guilty of association with a convicted criminal. Punishable by death.

Sara attempted to speak. True she had been the wife of the Count of Turenne, who had died of natural causes but—

But then the President rang his bell. The prisoner was not allowed to speak, he instructed her sharply, until all the charges had been read and all the evidence laid against her.

Then Fouquier stood up. The Public Prosecutor. In his black robes with his long nose stuck into a thin file of papers, he reminded Sara of a crow pecking at something dead on the ground, something that was scarcely worth the bother. She recalled another image in a book of nursery rhymes—one of the English books she'd had as a child— showing a raven dressed as a doctor visiting a family of rabbits, and the apprehensive looks on their faces. She recalled the lines of the rhyme that went with it:

> *I do not like thee, Doctor Fell*
> *The reason why I cannot tell,*
> *But I do not like thee, Doctor Fell*

It seemed strangely significant to her now that this was one of the very few English rhymes she had ever been able to remember.

Fouquier read out a statement from a police informer who could not be named, he said, for reasons of security. Citoyenne Seton was the daughter of an English officer.

Again Sara attempted to protest. Her father was Scottish, she said, and had been an officer in the French Army. Again the President rang his bell. If she continued to interrupt, he said, she would be removed from the court.

Fouquier resumed: she had smuggled messages into the Luxembourg to the convicted English spy, Thomas Paine. A clerk shuffled papers and muttered something in his ear. Fouquier looked taken aback for a moment. He shook his head as if in despair at the people he was forced to work with. It had come to his attention that the aforesaid Thomas Paine had not yet been convicted, due to an administrative error.

However—Fouquier had returned to his script—a number of letters had been found in the Citoyenne's apartment including some
that were clearly in code from contacts in England. Correspondence
with the enemy at time of war, he reminded the jury, was in itself a
crime of treason, punishable by death.

The word "death" seemed to hang in the air. Or perhaps only for
Sara. It must have been heard many times that day and every day by
most of those present. But it seemed to wake a few of them up as if
reminding people that the day was somewhat advanced and it must
soon be time for dinner. The judges conferred; the President asked if
there was much more.

There was more, Fouquier replied, but as it was late in the day, he
proposed to bring the evidence to a close. The President asked the
jury if they had heard enough to make a decision. It seemed to Sara
that no one was listening. Their minds were elsewhere. In fact, she
noticed a palpable air of tension as if they were in a hurry to get away.
Then the door at the back of the court was flung open and a drunk
lurched in shouting something about a plot. He was a large man
dressed in an exotic costume, like a general, red, white and blue feathers in his hat, a sash on his chest, a sabre at his waist, and a bottle in
his hand. The ushers hurried to remove him but then fell back in
confusion. For it turned out he was a general. General Hanriot, commander of the Garde Parisienne.

And behind him, running to catch up but in a semblance of military order, a squad of soldiers with fixed bayonets.

He had come to defend the Revolutionary Tribunal from attack,
Hanriot announced, swaying and slurring his words. There was a
plot by royalist and counter-revolutionaries to take over the Convention. He was posting his men at all public buildings.

The spectators started to edge towards the doors. One of the jury-
men tried to sneak out too but was turned back by the guards.

But Fouquier and his assistants managed to calm the general down
and finally he staggered out followed by his bemused squad. Turning

at the door he drew his sword with a flourish and shouted confusingly, "Kill all policemen!"

The trial was resumed. The President asked the jury if they had reached a verdict. There was a muttered consultation. Yes, they said. Guilty.

The sentence was, of course, death.

They marched her across to the Conciergerie. The *charrettes* were waiting in the Cour du Mai, clouds of flies buzzing round the horses' heads, the drivers dozing under wide-brimmed straw hats. Heat rose in waves from the cobbles and guards huddled in the shade leaning on their muskets. Sara looked up at the sky, shading her eyes against the glare. It was like burnished steel but with a hint of bronze in it as if it had been coated with several layers of varnish.

They should not keep the horses waiting, she thought, in such heat.

Then it dawned on her: they were waiting for her. This sentence of death was not something proposed for some distant future. Not even for next week or tomorrow. It was today.

"Alex," she said aloud, turning as if she had left him somewhere.

They turned her back and prodded her towards the carts.

"My little boy," she said. "I have to see my little boy."

And then she began to cry.

CHAPTER 44

the Theatre of the Tuileries

NATHAN JOINED THE CROWD OUTSIDE THE Convention waiting to take their place in the public gallery. It was already hot and the sun barely up. He watched the first of the delegates arriving. Perspiring faces, limp collars, frayed tempers. Make way, make way there, for the representatives of the people. A buzz of rumour. And a distant rumble of thunder. The tricolours drooping in the heat and a sky like molten lead, a burnished lid on the overcooked city. Paris playing up the drama, as usual.

He had asked Imlay to send someone to the Palais de Justice to take down the list of those coming before the Tribunal. But if Paine was on it there was precious little Nathan could do to save him. Le Mulet said it was useless to attempt a rescue on the way to the guillotine; there were too many guards.

The crowd started to shuffle forward and the guards checked their passes. Some were pulled aside and checked for weapons. Nathan had papers supplied by Le Mulet's men. He was now a stonemason called Antoine Pomme. Anthony Apple. He thought they could have done better.

He was a little more hopeful than he had been in the House of Wax—at least as far as the Convention was concerned. Robespierre appeared to have succeeded in uniting his enemies on the left: the

THE TIME OF TERROR

surviving Dantonists in hatred, the terrorists in fear that they would be next on his list. And if the Mountain moved against him, the men of the Marsh would join them, for they had always both hated and feared him.

But if the Marsh could be relied upon for once, the Street was a different matter. Even Le Mulet was not sure whose side the Street was on and he was closer to it than most.

"No one's side but its own," was his terse comment on the politics of the mob. But he was puzzled by its mood. Sullen and brooding like the weather, rumbling with discontent, ready to erupt but wonderfully indecisive, trying to make its mind up.

"It's Saint-Antoine that really counts," he told Nathan. "They can put twenty thousand men and women on the streets in a matter of minutes."

"I thought you'd bought them," Nathan said, "with Danton's gold."

Danton's gold. Even he was saying it now.

"We've bought the Section leaders," Le Mulet corrected him, "but will they do the business? It's tricky."

And then there was Hanriot and the National Guard.

There was a roar from the opposite gallery as the leading players made their entrance. Robespierre in his blue coat and yellow breeches: the clothes he had worn for the Festival of the Supreme Being; Saint-Just in grey and white, the Angel of Death, gold rings glinting in his ears; and Couthon in his wheelchair, furiously winding the twin handles that turned the wheels and glowering at the delegates on either side. The Triumvirate that ruled France.

The spectators surged forward, craning their necks for a view. Le Mulet seemed to have packed one gallery but there were plenty of Jacobins in the other and already a fight had broken out. The ushers were struggling to get through and break it up. The President ringing his bell for order. It was no longer Vadier but someone Nathan did not recognise.

Instead of heading for his usual seat high on the Mountain, Robespierre seemed to be making for the benches at the very front of the chamber. Was this deliberate? Some kind of a statement? But Saint-Just made straight for the people's tribune, clutching his speech.

The script is written; the play begun.

But at once an interruption.

"I demand to be heard!"

A man rushed up to the tribune, pushing Saint-Just aside.

A shout of "Tallien!" from Le Mulet's men in the gallery. They know their theatre, the crowd; they are familiar with all the principal players and some of them even seem to know the plot.

Tallien struck a dramatic pose. "The curtain must be thrown aside!"

Cheers, stamping of feet. Robespierre looked puzzled; this was not how it was meant to be. Saint-Just was frowning, searching through his papers as if he had lost his place in the script.

"I was at the Jacobins last night," roared the man at the tribune. "As I watched I shuddered for my country. I saw the army of the new Cromwell. I have armed myself with a dagger that will pierce the tyrant's breast if the Convention lacks the courage to order his arrest."

Sensation! He *has* armed himself with a dagger! Weapons are forbidden in the Convention. Why do the guards permit it? Is this a good sign?

And now all the delegates were on their feet. They brandished their fists: "Down with the tyrant!"

Robespierre made a dash for the tribune. Already he had begun to speak. But the President was ringing his bell, drowning out his words. And a thunderous voice rose from the crowd: "I demand the arrest of Robespierre!"

It sounded like Danton. But Danton was dead.

Pandemonium.

Nathan leant perilously over the edge of the gallery, the crowd pushing at his back. People fighting in the crush. Robespierre was screaming at the President but the only word that reached the gallery was "Assassins!"

Outrage.

"The monster has insulted the Convention!"

Robespierre fled up the slopes of the Mountain. But the Mountain hurled him back.

"Scoundrel! Get away from here. The ghosts of Danton and Camille reject you."

Again he tried to speak but his voice was too thin for such a heated atmosphere.

"The blood of Danton chokes you!"

He fled to the far side of the chamber and sank panting on a bench. The delegates of the Right withdrew from him in horror.

"Murderer—you sit in the chair of Condorcet!"

In despair he appealed to the gallery. But Le Mulet had triumphed, the Jacobins were in flight. Overwhelmingly the Convention voted for Robespierre's arrest and his friends with him. And Vadier's waiting policemen marched into the chamber.

"The brigands have triumphed," declared Robespierre as they led him away.

His last words to the Convention he has ruled so long.

It is over. And like the good Frenchmen they are, they go off for their dinner.

Nathan found Imlay in the Café Carazzo just off the Rue Honoré, much patronised by members of the Convention. The atmosphere was festive, the wine flowing, the noise deafening.

"It is over," Imlay shouted at him, his face flushed and beaming. "The tyrant is no more." He was at a table with a group of delegates. Nathan recognised one of them as Tallien—the man who had waved the dagger at the tribune. "Here is my friend, Turner, a fellow American," Imlay announced to the table at large. They cheered and someone poured Nathan a bumper of wine.

"What happened in court?" Nathan asked him.

"Don't worry. All executions are suspended by order of the President. Everyone will be released."

"So Paine . . ."

"Paine was not in court. I heard from my man." He fumbled in his pocket and produced a crumpled piece of paper. "Here is the List. See for yourself."

Nathan scanned the scrawled names. He was right. Paine was not on it. Perhaps they had decided he was too ill.

"I tell you, it is over," Imlay assured him again. "The order has been sent to the Tribunal. No one else will die."

"Besides Robespierre," said someone, "and a few hundred of his friends."

This amused everyone.

Nathan brought a stool over from the bar. He might as well join in the celebrations, he thought. Imlay clapped him on the shoulder and leaned close to his ear.

"You can tell your boss we did it," he said. "The Terror is over."

Nathan was not sure this was what his "boss" wanted to hear.

"So who are the new rulers of France?" he said.

But Imlay was not listening. He had bent his head to the man on his right. The Dagger Man. Youngish-looking and handsome. Was he one of them, the new rulers of France? Nathan drank his wine and looked around the room and was startled to see a man he knew. Vadier. The Grand Inquisitor. But of course. And was he another? Vadier looked up and met his eye. He looked startled for a moment and then winked, raising his glass.

A sudden commotion at the door. Messengers rushing into the café . . .

"Robespierre is released! The tyrant is freed!"

Panic. Everyone shouting at once. More men running in from the street. Some running out. Gradually Nathan made sense of what had happened. The mayor—an ally of Robespierre—had sent to the prisons instructing the governors to admit no new prisoners without an order from the Commune. When Robespierre arrived at the Luxembourg he was turned away—and his escort took him to the Hotel de Ville. The Commune was calling for an insurrection.

And right on cue they heard the distant sound of a bell.

They were ringing the tocsin at the Hotel de Ville: the call to arms.

Aux armes, Citoyens. And then an answering peal, louder and closer, from the Faubourg Saint-Honoré, the district of Robespierre and the Jacobin Club. And again, across the river, and to the east, in the Faubourg Saint-Antoine, the powder keg of Paris.

The call to the people—to rise up and defend the Revolution.

CHAPTER 45

the Place of Honour

S ARA WAS WAITING TO HAVE HER hair cut when she heard the tocsin.

All the condemned prisoners were gathered in the records office while one of the guards called out their names and ticked them off on a list. He was stumbling over the pronunciations and struggling to make himself heard above the din. One of his colleagues had a dog that kept barking and straining at its leash. Two of the other guards were drunk and were staggering from prisoner to prisoner taking anything of value—rings, necklaces, even handkerchiefs—and putting them in a sack, shouting and sometimes striking out at anyone who resisted. There were about forty prisoners, sitting in benches against the walls, some sobbing and praying, some in hysterics, others clinging to each other. Two men were lying on straw pallets, their eyes staring into space as if they were already dead. But others were singing and laughing and appeared to be as drunk as the guards. If prisoners had enough money they could have as much food and drink as they wished. Bits of bread and meat littered the floor—and empty bottles. Someone offered Sara a drink from his brandy flask but she shook her head. A song kept running through her mind: a song she remembered her father singing and that she had sung to Nathan after they had become lovers:

Last nicht the Queen had four Maries
This nicht she'll hae but three,
She'd Mary Beaton and Mary Seton,
An' Mary Carmichael an' me.

It was six o'clock and as hot as noon. The prison door was open and she could see into the courtyard to where the *charrettes* were waiting, the death carts. Three of the executioner's assistants were cutting people's hair and ripping back their collars to leave their necks exposed.

When they heard the tocsin everything came to a stop. No one seemed to know what was going on.

There were reports of disturbances in the Faubourg Saint-Antoine on the route to the guillotine. The executioner, Sanson, wanted to postpone things until tomorrow but the jailers wanted to get on with them; they were anxious to get rid of people. There was nowhere to put them, they said, the prison was overcrowded enough already.

Then Fouquier arrived from the court on his way home from work. He lived in one of the towers of the Conciergerie—the Caesar tower overlooking the river—and he had seen the *charrettes* still waiting in the yard. What was the delay he wanted to know, why were the prisoners still here? Sanson started to explain about the trouble on the streets but he was more diffident than he had been with the jailers and Fouquier overruled him.

"Get them out of here," he said, turning away. "Am I wasting my time? Justice must be done, do your duty."

There was a wild look in his eyes as if he too were drunk.

So Sara took her place on one of the stools and they began to cut her hair. She stared down at the dark locks lying on the dirty floor, frowning as if trying to make sense of it all. Did she want to save it for anyone, they asked her but she shook her head. Then she thought, was it something Alex might want to keep? But it was too awful, too ghoulish. She was trying not to think of Alex or she would not be able to bear it.

They tied her hands behind her back and led her out into the yard and helped her up the steps into one of the *charrettes*. It was full of women, half of them screaming, hysterical, the rest drunk and singing. There was one she recognised. They had spent several hours together in the same cell, waiting for their trial. She was a prostitute called Catherine Halbourg, nicknamed "Egle." She had been picked up the previous summer with one of her women friends in the Rue Fromenteau. Later she had found out that the Queen's trial was coming up and a man called Chaumette, an influential member of the Commune, had suggested putting a couple of prostitutes in the dock with her—presumably to make some kind of a point. The Austrian whore and the Paris whores. But the Committee of Public Safety thought it was a stupid idea and the Queen was tried—and executed—alone. But instead of being released Egle had been held in the prison of the Carmes ever since, without charge. She did not know why they had condemned her now. She seemed strangely exhilarated, like an actress about to go on stage.

"I am ready," she told Sara. "I have been rehearsing."

They had held mock executions in the Carmes, she told Sara, and they had practised with their hands tied behind their backs, laid out on a plank of wood. They had also held séances, when they conjured the Devil.

"He is not like the priests say he is," she told Sara earnestly. She spoke in the voice of a little girl—it was something that appealed to her clients, perhaps. "He is very handsome. I am to be his bride. He has many brides but I am the only one that is French. He told me. Believe in me and you will be saved."

Sara moved away from her. Faces swam in a haze of heat and flies. The sky was now the colour of a corpse. A terrible sky, a sky like a painting of the apocalypse. It was not real, it was too close to her nightmares to be real. Her brain was playing tricks with her. She could not breathe. A fly settled on her nose and it was all it took to upset her fragile composure and she shook her head wildly and cried out. And then suddenly the car jolted forward and her legs went from under her. She fell into the lap of one of the women seated on the bench that ran around the sides of the cart.

"Steady, my dear," said the woman calmly.

She was very beautiful, even with her hair shorn and she seemed entirely composed. Not drunk, not hysterical, not even sad. She made room for Sara beside her.

"What is your name?" Sara asked her, almost shyly.

The woman smiled.

"I am Princess Catherine of Monaco," she said.

Another lunatic. Another prostitute with delusions of grandeur. Was she too going to marry the Devil? The cart swayed round a corner and onto the bridge across the Seine and Sara began to cry; silently, the tears rolling down her face.

"Don't cry," said the woman next to her. "Don't give them the satisfaction."

"I'm sorry," she said. "It's my little boy."

She felt the woman's lips against her ear. "Move your back to me," she said. "I am going to try to undo your hands, and then you can undo mine. We should not die with our hands tied."

Sara drew apart from her and stared at her through her tears. But she did not seem mad.

They squirmed around so their backs were almost turned to each other, looking out over the side of the cart. There were cavalry riding along beside them but they were staring straight ahead. A few people lined the streets but not many, nothing like the crowds that had lined the Rue Honoré when the guillotine had been in the Place de la Révolution and Sara had been at her art classes. She felt the woman picking at the cord around her wrists. She had strong fingers and nails that dealt skilfully with the knots.

"Sing," the woman said. "Sing with me so the guards do not see what I am doing."

She began to sing a verse that Sara recognised, a troubadour song of Provence that she knew from her childhood:

> *Je vous aime tant, sans mentir*
> *Qu'on pourrait tarir*

La haute mer
Et ses ondes retenir
Avant qu'on puisse me prévenir
De vous aimer...

It was one of the songs Sara had sung in the *fiacre* on her way to Tourrettes-les-Vence with her father on their way to market. She must have been eleven or twelve, just about aware that she was singing a love song.

"Who are you?" she asked again, mystified.

"Sing," commanded the woman.

They were winding through the narrow streets behind the Hotel de Ville. There were a few people here but still not many. She looked at the faces, thinking she might see Nathan among them. Or even that he would come to her rescue. Defiantly, thinking only of the sunshine and the road to Tourrettes, Sara sang:

Vous parler, vous regarder
Votre mien tenir, font fuir et haïr et détester
Toute vice et tout ce qu'est chérir et desirer

The way you talk, the way you look,
Your whole being makes me detest
All vice and desire all that is good.

It could be a song to your lover, or your God. The God of Provence, the God of the Cathars.

Je veux rester fidèle, garder votre honneur
Chercher la paix, obéir
Craindre, servir, et vous honorer
Jusqu'à la morte

I would stay faithful, guard your honour
Seek peace, obey
Fear, serve and honour you
Unto death . . .

The knots were coming apart and the cords felt loose enough for Sara to wriggle one of her hands free. She kept them behind her back but started working at the ropes on her companion's wrists. Her nails were not as long—she had been biting them—and it was difficult to prize open the knots. They had entered the long Rue Saint-Antoine heading east, the convoy and its escort strung out over several hundred yards, the street almost empty. Just a few women and some little children watching from the windows of the houses.

Alex, she thought again. She saw him so vividly, even through her tears. There, standing in the windows with Hélène. But it could not be Alex. Hélène would not bring him here.

Suddenly they jerked to a halt. There was a great tide of people rolling down the street towards them, with banners and drums. Many of them armed with pikes and muskets. They swarmed around the tumbrels. Everyone was shouting, some singing the "Marseillaise." All the prisoners were standing up now and some of them were trying to climb out of the carts but the guards were beating them back with the flats of their swords.

Sara stood up and shouted down to the people.

"Help us, good Citizens, we are innocent."

The people seemed to be remonstrating with the guards and Sara strained to hear what they were saying. Then one of the other women began to shout almost hysterically.

"They are saying Robespierre is arrested and they must stop the executions!"

Sara finished untying her companion's hands, working openly now.

But suddenly there was another diversion. An officer was riding up the line of tumbrels, waving his sword, red-faced and shouting. Sara recognised him from the Tribunal. Hanriot, commander of the Garde Parisienne. More troops riding up behind him. And the people falling back, silent now and sullen.

"Move on," Hanriot was shouting, "move on. Robespierre is at the Commune. There is your duty, Citizens, to the Hotel de Ville to join the Commune."

The tumbrels began to move again, the cavalry pressing round them, gathering speed, heading across the great square where the Bastille had once stood and onwards towards the Place du Trône, the Place of the Throne where the guillotine now was.

Sara sat down again and the woman with her. She felt drained. The tears started to roll again.

"Don't cry," said the woman again. "The one thing that is left to us now is courage. Courage and contempt."

Contempt? Were they not supposed to show forgiveness to their enemies? But Sara did not feel like forgiving them. And who were her enemies, anyway? She did not even know that. Fouquier? Hanriot? Robespierre? They did not seem real. They all seemed to be playing a part.

"Contempt for who?" she asked her.

"For Death," the woman answered. "Hold my hand."

And they held hands, standing up in the cart, as they rode into the Place du Trône and she saw her enemy clearly at last: Death rising up against the terrible sky.

CHAPTER 46

the Place of Grief

I T WAS STRANGELY QUIET IN THE gardens of the Tuileries, ominously quiet. Black clouds were massing to the east and there was a distant rumble of thunder. The air was like warm soup. Nathan imagined they would be covering the guillotine in its shroud for the night. But with Robespierre on the loose it could be busier than ever in the morning.

He paused at the entrance to the Convention, undecided, wondering whether to walk across the Pont Neuf to the Palais de Justice. Just to make sure that Paine's name had not been on the list. But even if it was, they had suspended the executions. He would be back in the Luxembourg by now.

He decided to go on into the Convention, to see what they would decide to do.

He passed through the unguarded doorway and climbed the stairs to the gallery. The empty gallery. Below, in the auditorium, the delegates were straggling back from dinner, in far less sanguine a mood than when they had left. The news of Robespierre's release had clearly reached them by now. They started to pull themselves together and do what they did best—pass resolutions.

The first was to deprive Hanriot of his command of the National Guard. In his place they appointed one of their own—Paul Barras, a former officer in the Royalist Army; Nathan had seen him with Imlay in the Café Carazzo. Then they outlawed all who supported Robespierre and declared the Commune to be illegal.

No one seemed to have confronted the awful truth that their decrees meant nothing outside the theatre of the Tuileries. Perhaps the reality was too fearful to contemplate. Barras was a commander without an army. Of course they had half a million men on the borders of France, the scourge of Europe. But in Paris they looked what they were: two or three hundred frightened men: lawyers and actors and writers for the most part, guarded by a handful of policemen who wished they were somewhere else and in different company.

But now Barras was on his feet, proposing that the delegates arm themselves. There were weapons in the police armoury in the basement, he said. No one seemed very keen. We are not soldiers, said one. But about a dozen delegates followed him out of the hall. Nathan ran down the stairs to join them. He had no desire to go down fighting with the elected rulers of France but whatever happened in the next few hours it would clearly be advisable to have a sword or a pistol to hand, preferably both, and he had lost his own when he went to prison.

The armoury was a long, low room in the vaults, stocked mainly with pistols and swords. But only one keg of powder. Presumably they did not care to keep any more there for fear of an explosion—or a French version of the Gunpowder Plot. Nathan chose a brace of neat little flintlocks no more than about six or seven inches long and known as greatcoat pistols because they could conveniently be carried in the pocket of one.

But he did not return to the Convention. That was not where the battle would be fought. It would be fought in the streets. As he made his way along the river towards the Hotel de Ville he heard the noise. Then he turned the corner into the Place de Grève and saw them: a great mass of people filling the square, men and women, soldiers and civilians, bristling with muskets and pikes. His heart sank. Danton's gold had been too thinly spread, if it had been spread at all. But then on a more careful observation he saw that there were not as many as he had first thought and there was no spirit in them. The noise was more of the murmuring of bees than the roar of lions. They seemed to be standing in groups, waiting for something to happen.

Nathan threaded his way between them to the steps of the Hotel de Ville. There were a few soldiers standing around in the blue and white uniform of the Garde Parisienne but none of them challenged him and he sauntered into the lobby as if he owned the place. More men here, some in uniform, some not. A flight of stairs leading up to a kind of gallery. Nathan went up the stairs, two at a time. On his right there was a large room, the size of a ballroom, filled with people and in the centre a group of officials gathered around a table covered in papers and maps. Couthon was there, in his wheelchair, and Saint-Just, still looking immaculate in his white waistcoat. But not Robespierre.

Still, clearly, this was the centre of operations. Nathan kept to the sides in the shadows. It was almost dark now and there were only a few candles lit in the chandeliers. People were calling for more lights but no one seemed to be paying much attention. He spoke to a tall, grizzled guardsman leaning on his musket by the fireplace and asked him what was happening. The soldier shrugged and gestured towards the men around the table.

"Ask them," he said, with a curl of his lip, as if it would not do much good if he did.

Then Hanriot came in, with the usual bluster, trailed by his bodyguard. He was flushed with excitement or drink or both. He was greeted by one of the men at the table. Nathan gathered from his informant that this was the mayor, Fleuriot, a Robespierre loyalist. There was some conferring. Hanriot was waving his arms around a lot. Then two guards marched in with a man who looked as if he might be a prisoner. But he had a paper in his hand which he gave to the mayor so perhaps he was a messenger.

The mayor read it and passed it to Saint-Just who handed it back. And then the mayor tore it up and threw the pieces in the messenger's face.

"Tell the Convention we shall come soon," he said, in a voice loud enough to carry, "but that we shall bring the people with us."

There was a small cheer.

Hanriot climbed on a chair and waved his sword.

"The Convention has declared that we are outlaws," he announced. "I, Hanriot, declare that the Convention are outlaws."

Not the best speech he had ever made, certainly not what the troops were hoping for. And when he stepped down from the chair his spurs became locked and he had to be saved by Saint-Just from falling over. There were more cheers that could have been interpreted as ironic.

Nathan kept moving around the fringes of the room. There were about a dozen windows running from floor to ceiling, most of them open, and he stepped through one onto a narrow balcony overlooking the square: the Place of Grief where common criminals were executed during the time of the kings; broken on the wheel with iron bars. From this vantage it appeared much less crowded than at ground level. He guessed that there were probably no more than a couple of thousand people down there, less than half of them soldiers: far less than he might have expected after the call to arms. And significantly, no cannon. The sky was now black with thunder clouds as far as the eye could see and suddenly the entire city across the river was illuminated by a flash of lightning. The thunder came on the instant: a great shattering roll that shook all the windows.

Someone stepped out behind him and he turned swiftly with his hand on the butt of his pistol but it was just another soldier, packing tobacco into a short clay pipe.

"Where are they all?" he growled, looking down on the sparse crowd in the square below. "Where is our support?"

He looked at Nathan as if he might know but Nathan just shook his head as if at the folly and mystery of man and said, "More to the point, where is Robespierre?"

The soldier shrugged. "I heard he's in the Mayor's house. They've sent for him at least three times but he won't come—the last time they sent a squad of soldiers to drag him here—by the scruff of his neck if he won't come willing."

Why would Robespierre not come? Did he think he could hide from the storm and let it pass? He might as well run back to the Duplays' house and hide under the bed. But Robespierre had never been a man of action. His great talent was in persuading others to act.

Nathan took the opportunity to load his pistols. They were short, stubby affairs with Fabrique en Liège stamped on the barrel. Brand new and well greased, they looked and smelled as if they had never been fired but the butts were satisfyingly solid. They would make good clubs even if they did not shoot straight. He sighted along the barrel at one of the towers of Notre-Dame across the river and as he did so he felt the first drop of rain. He went back into the hall.

And at last here was Robespierre. Just arrived, still in his blue coat and yellow breeches. He was frowning, rather petulantly, as if he did not see why it was necessary for him to be disturbed. They pulled him over to the table with the map of the city spread upon it. He put on his spectacles to look at it but he seemed baffled as if it was a place he had never seen before.

And then Nathan saw Gillet.

He must have come in with Robespierre. He was shaking a few drops of rain from his hat. Otherwise, he looked as bored and contemptuous as ever but there was a sword and a couple of pistols at his waist so presumably he was ready for a fight.

Nathan drew back a little further into the shadows, the blood pounding in his ears. He put his hand in his pocket and slipped his fingers round the pistol. The rain was now pouring in at the open windows but no one made an attempt to close them.

"They're leaving," someone said. "They're running off."

Nathan tore his eyes away from Gillet and looked down upon the Place of Grief. The rain was dropping like lead shot into the emptying square. The crowd had scattered. A flash of lightning showed them scuttling down side streets and he thought of the rats in the

Cloaca. A few were left huddled in doorways or in the lee of the houses all around but they did not look many.

Back in the hall, Fleuriot was trying to get Robespierre to sign a piece of paper but he seemed reluctant. Nathan had the odd notion that they were trying to make him abdicate but he gathered from the onlookers that it was an appeal to the National Guard and the Sections to come to the aid of the Commune. It seemed a little late in the day for that.

Suddenly Nathan thought: this is the wrong place to be, this is a trap. And he would be caught in it, with the wrong people. He began to edge his way towards the stairs but now people were shouting and pointing down into the square. He joined the general rush to the windows. A column of armed men had entered the square, marching in some kind of order, with flaming torches, even in the rain. The flames caught the glint of pikes and bayonets.

"It's the Guard," someone shouted.

"It's the Sections," said another.

Whoever it was, the general opinion seemed to be that they were friends but Nathan saw the purposeful way they were marching on the building and he did not think it was to shelter from the rain. He made his way to the door again and out on to the landing, peering over the balustrade. The front ranks were coming in through the main entrance and he saw Barras at their head, shouting commands, his ostrich feathers sodden and drooping but a sword in one hand and a pistol in the other. Then they were coming up the stairs, the mob retreating before them, and Nathan found himself forced back into the hall.

It finally seemed to have dawned on the men round the table that the enemy was upon them. Hanriot started to climb on the chair again but then thought better of it and led a stampede for a small door in the far corner of the room with the mayor a step or two behind him. Couthon threw himself out of his wheelchair and started to crawl under the table. Only one man seemed to be prepared to fight. He was waving a brace of pistols in the air but then he put one of them to his head and blew his brains out. Robespierre still had the pen in his hand, poised above the document that Fleuriot had been trying to make him sign. He seemed to be in a state of shock. There was blood and brains all over his powder-blue jacket. Then Nathan saw Gillet again. He was standing just a few yards behind Robespierre and aiming a pistol at his head. There was a flash and a bang but either he missed, which was unlikely at that range, or it was a misfire. Robespierre flinched and turned and picked up one of the pistols the suicide had dropped. He looked at it in much the same way as he had looked at the map; as if he had never seen one before. Then Nathan's view was obscured and he heard another shot and when he saw Robespierre again he had both hands up to his face and blood was spurting through his fingers.

Now men were pouring in through the double doors. The room was filled with swords and pikes and bayonets. All was smoke and confusion. Nathan saw Gillet fighting his way through the doors towards the stairs. Nathan pushed through the crowd after him and emerged on to the landing just as Gillet reached the bottom step. He shouted, "Assassin!" As if it meant something in this company. But men scattered and Gillet looked back over his shoulder and raised his pistol.

It was not as Nathan had imagined. Pistols at dawn in a clearing. But it would do. He turned sideways as he took the pistol from his pocket, bringing his arm up and sighting down the barrel. He saw the flash from Gillet's gun and felt the wind of the shot past his ear. Then he fired. Gillet fell back, dropping his gun. But he was up almost immediately clutching his arm and moving in an awkward, crouching run for the door. Nathan bounded down the stairs after him but people were in the way and then he heard a great shout of *"Gardez vous"* from above and whirled to see a group of men at the top of the stairs swinging a screaming figure by the arms and legs. Couthon. Nathan stepped to one side as they launched him into space. He flew halfway down the stairs before he hit the step just below where Nathan was standing. They threw his wheelchair after him, bouncing from step to step and then taking off and smashing on the marble foyer just a few inches from the recumbent figure of its former occupant.

When Nathan reached the door to the square Gillet was gone. He stood in the rain as it streamed down his face, with the unfired pistol at his side.

They carried the torn and mangled bodies into the Pavillon des Fleurs and up to the room where the Committee of Public Safety had always met. Lebas, already dead, half his head shot away. Couthon paralysed from the neck down, his limbs horribly twisted. Robespierre's brother, Augustine, also crippled after jumping from a third-floor window. Hanriot, his face beaten almost to a pulp and one eye knocked out. And Robespierre himself with his shattered jaw tied in a bandage. They laid him on the table with its green baize cloth and sent a doctor to pull out his broken teeth. Some people took them as souvenirs. Nathan found a wet cloth and wiped the blood from his face.

"Thank you, monsieur," he whispered through his ruined mouth. Not Citizen, Nathan noted, as if it had been a passing fad. Nathan did not think he recognised him.

He was going down the stairs—the Queen's Stairs—when he ran into Imlay coming up. Imlay looked at him with a strange expression. He put his hand on Nathan's chest to stop him but he did not speak.

"What is it?" said Nathan. He thought the man was drunk. Most of Paris seemed to be drunk on something or other, even if it was only euphoria.

"Sara," Imlay said. Just the one word, *Sara*.

Nathan felt something like a knife twist inside him.

"What?" he said.

"She was on the List."

He didn't understand.

He clutched the rail and fumbled in his pocket. It was still there, the crumpled piece of paper he had taken from Imlay. He stared at it but the names were swimming before his eyes. He rubbed them and looked again.

And then he saw it.

Turenne, they had called her. Madame Raymond de Turenne.

He had been looking for Paine earlier and he had not seen it.

"What happened?"

"She was found guilty. They took her to the Conciergerie and from there to the ... She was in the last batch."

"But the executions were suspended. They sent an order—"

Imlay was shaking his head. "The Tribunal had already adjourned. And Fouquier said the executions must continue."

"No." Nathan whispered. The blood had drained from his face. "No, it's not true."

"I have just heard from Hélène. Her maid. She was there. She saw her ... in the ..."

"It's not true," said Nathan again.

But he sat down on the stair and put his face in his hands because he knew that it was.

CHAPTER 47

the Time of Terror

HE WALKED ALONE THROUGH THE GARDENS of the
Tuileries where he had met her after art class. The sun
was back, flitting between white clouds, but the air was
fresh as if newly laundered by the rain. He had been up all night and
walking most of the day, not noticing a great deal. Around him Paris
went about its ugly business. The guillotine had been moved back
to its original site on the Place de la Révolution so that Danton's
prophecy might be fulfilled and Robespierre would follow him to his
death. The tumbrels had paused for a while outside the home of the
Duplays on the Rue Honoré while people brought a bucket of pig's
blood from the market and threw it over the door. They pulled the
bandage from Robespierre's shattered jaw just before they slid him
under the guillotine and he screamed like an animal.

"It's over," people kept shouting, "it's over."

It was the tenth day of Thermidor, the Time of the Heat.

CHAPTER 48

the Homecoming

A NIGHT RUN ACROSS THE CHANNEL AND a misty dawn that shredded visibly in the rising sun to reveal the untidy scrawl of coastline on the *Speedwell*'s starboard bow. A raucous gallimaufry of gulls come out to greet them and the Seven Sisters rising from the fleeing wraiths of mist like the sails of a distant battle fleet.

"Is that England?" said the boy.

"That is England," said Nathan lifting him up beside the belfry at the bow, with the spritsail bobbing in courtly homage and the salt spray stinging his cheeks like tears.

He sought the break in the cliffs where the Cuckmere came down to the sea, remembering the fight between the dragoons and the smugglers on the shore and the black lugger against the white sisters in the moonlight.

"Will we see your house?"

"No. Not from here. It is farther back, up the little river you can see there coming down to the sea. But you will see it later today."

"Will we see the horses?"

"Yes. You will see the horses. I might even let you ride one if you are not too tired."

"I won't be tired."

He had told Alex about Windover House and his father and some of the servants he would meet there and the animals. He had told him about his own childhood in Sussex, about fishing in the Cuckmere and hunting rabbits on Hope Point and sailing his boat in the haven, and he had told him he would be able to do all these things and more. He sat him on the bow rail with his arm round him, and the boy looked at him gravely.

"Will they want to fight me because I am French?"

"No, they will not want to fight you. Will you want to fight them because they are English?"

"No. Because it would not be polite. *Maman* said I must not fight people when I am a guest in their house."

"Did she? Well, it will be your house, too, you know."

He was glad Alex talked about Sara, though it turned a knife in his heart. Mary had told the child what had happened to his mother. She said it was better that he knew now than that they lied to him or told him some fairy tale. But Nathan was not sure that he had understood it. Sometimes he thought that Alex did not believe his mother was dead; or that he expected her to turn up suddenly and say it was all a mistake. Perhaps that was no bad thing. Sometimes he thought it himself.

It was Mary, too, who had suggested he take the boy to England.

"He will be safer there, at least for a while," she insisted. "Until things settle down. If they ever do."

Besides, she said, he had no one now except for Hélène and herself and she thought she would soon be joining them there for she did not see much future for herself in France.

Nathan wondered if she meant much future with Imlay.

"I will take him to my father's," he said, expecting an argument about it for Mary was his mother's friend, but she had been surprisingly docile, simply nodding and saying it would be good for him in the country.

But he wondered now why it had seemed such an obvious choice. Did he expect the boy to have exactly the same childhood as he had? To have the same sense of security, the same careless adventures?

"I think I will like it here," said the boy, nodding solemnly to him-self as if he had come to a carefully considered conclusion. "But I would like it better if *maman* was with us."

"So would I," said Nathan. He held him a little tighter.

"And will you stay with me?"

"I will stay for a while," said Nathan, "but then I must go back to sea."

He knew it was the only life he could bear and there would prob-ably be no other. And if he still had only a vague idea of what he was fighting for he had a much clearer notion of what he was fighting against.

The boy leant forward and tugged swiftly at the bow tying Nathan's hair and it flew about his face in the wind.

"You look like a girl," he said, laughing.

"Thank you," said Nathan. "There is nothing wrong with being a girl."

"Do you think *she* is happy, my *maman*, where *she* is now?"

"Where do you think she is now?"

"In Heaven," said the boy, looking at him in slight surprise. "That is what Hélène says. Where do you think she is?"

"I think she is in a place called Tourrettes," said Nathan, stroking the boy's hair gently back from his eyes, "sitting in the market square drinking lemonade and eating little cakes made of oranges and wait-ing for us there."

HISTORY

On the subject of research . . . while many of the events and characters of *The Time of Terror* are fictitious others are rooted in history
and it might interest readers to know where the lines are drawn.

The arrest, trial and death of Georges Danton and the events of
9th Thermidor are all based on recorded history. Robespierre is
widely believed to have shot himself but I have seen the document he
was signing at the time with the first three letters of his signature—
Rob—and then bloodstains. It is possible, of course, that a man will
pause in the middle of signing his own name to blow his brains out
but I think it is more likely that someone else saved him the trouble.

The counterfeiting operation is part of the secret history of these
times but enough is known about it for me to feel confident that it
happened much as described in the novel. I first came across the story
while making a film about a similar operation during World War
II and I was lucky enough to meet John Keyworth, curator of the
Bank of England museum, and the paper historian Peter Bower, who
both know a great deal about it. The *assignats* were forged at several
English mills including Haughton Castle in Northumberland and
smuggled to France by Pitt's secret agents where they had a significant effect in wrecking the French economy.

Whether or not Gilbert Imlay was one of these agents is pure
conjecture. He and Mary Wollstonecraft are real enough and so
was their relationship; much of their circumstances at the time are
taken from her letters to him and others. Imlay was a shipping agent

in Paris and Le Havre during the time of the Terror and made his money from running goods past the British blockade. But he was also suspected of being a secret agent, working for either the Americans or the British or both.

There is no evidence that the American Minister, Gouverneur Morris, was involved in the counterfeiting operation. However, his activities in Paris are so cloaked in mystery and intrigue I felt this conferred a degree of license. He helped to fund the attempted escape of King Louis and Marie Antoinette in 1792 and after he left Paris in the summer of 1794 he was exposed as a British agent.

The account of the bombardment of the sloop *Nereus* in the mouth of the Somme is based on a similar incident involving the sloop *Childers* at the entrance to Brest harbour in January 1793 while the account of the Glorious First of June is taken from various personal recollections of the battle.

The story of Tom Paine's arrest at White's Philadelphia Hotel, his internment in the Luxembourg and his extraordinary escape from death are based on his own account of these incidents while the details of prison life are corroborated by the writer Helen Maria Williams who was there at the same time.

The Catacombs are real enough—and they are still full of skulls. You can visit the Empire of the Dead legally at certain times of the year through a black hut very like Dr. Who's Tardis near the Porte d'Enfer. But the entire system is far more extensive: an ancient labyrinth under modern Paris. The tunnels have been used by outlaws and dissidents throughout history, notably by the French Resistance during World War II, and they continue to have some curious uses today.

The Trouanderie, or the Grand Villainy, was a secret organization of thieves, beggars and smugglers similar to the medieval Cours des Miracles. It has since made way for grander villainies.

And Marie Grosholtz was the maiden name of the woman who later became known to the world as Madame Tussaud.

ACKNOWLEDGMENTS

Thank you to Pat Kavanagh and to Martin Fletcher at Headline for getting this into print; to Michael Ann and Martin Tullet for their knowledge of the English Channel and the boat to test it; to Square Sail at Charlestown and the captain and crew of the *Earl of Pembroke*; to Bill Cran, Brian Lavery and Colin White for the pleasure of working with them on Nelson's Trafalgar and the knowledge I gained from it; to Cate and Nash Olsen of Much Ado Books in Alfriston for digging out such a wealth of publications, especially the details on smuggling in Sussex, the journals of Helen Maria Williams in the Luxembourg Prison and the love letters of Mary Wollstonecraft to Gilbert Imlay; to my daughter Elesa for helping me with the research into Paris during the Terror; to my father for inspiring me with a lifetime of novels, films and his own stories of the sea; and to the English Arts Council for awarding me one of their literary grants so I could do the job properly.